Praise for Jerzy Pilch

"A very gifted writer. . . . The hope of young Polish prose."
—Czesław Miłosz

"Pilch's antic sensibility confirms that he is the compatriot of Witold Gombrowicz, the Polish maestro of absurdist pranks. But readers with a taste for the fermented Irish blarney of Flann O'Brien, Samuel Beckett, and John Kennedy Toole might also savor Pilch."
—Steven Kellman, *Barnes & Noble Review*

"If laughter actually is the best medicine, fortunate readers of *A Thousand Peaceful Cities* will surely enjoy perfect health for the rest of their days."
—*Kirkus Reviews*

"Jerzy Pilch's *Thousand Peaceful Cities* are . . . the unruly, wonderfully erudite, and hilariously surreal product of a boisterous imagination set loose."
—Valentina Zanca, *Words Without Borders*

"Fans of Gombrowicz will find this a much gentler, yet almost equally rich, examination of what it means to be an individual in a bygone world."
—Jennifer Croft, *World Literature Today*

Also by Jerzy Pilch in English Translation

His Current Woman
The Mighty Angel
A Thousand Peaceful Cities

JERZY PILCH
MY FIRST
SUICIDE

TRANSLATED FROM THE POLISH BY DAVID FRICK

OPEN LETTER
LITERARY TRANSLATIONS FROM THE UNIVERSITY OF ROCHESTER

Copyright © by Jerzy Pilch, 2006
Translation © by David Frick, 2012
Published with the permission of ŚWIAT KSIĄŻKI Sp. z o.o., Warsaw, 2010

First edition, 2012

Library of Congress Cataloging-in-Publication Data:

Pilch, Jerzy, 1952–
    [Moje pierwsze samobójstwo. English]
    My first suicide / Jerzy Pilch ; translated from the Polish by David Frick. — 1st ed.
    p. cm.
    ISBN-13: 978-1-934824-40-5 (pbk. : acid-free paper)
    ISBN-10: 1-934824-40-2 (pbk. : acid-free paper)
    I. Frick, David A. II. Title.
    PG7175.I49M6513 2012
    891.8'538—dc23
                        2011043996

This publication has been funded by
the Book Institute - the ©POLAND Translation Program

INSTYTUT KSIĄŻKI

©POLAND

Printed on acid-free paper in the United States of America.

Text set in Caslon, a family of serif typefaces based on the designs of
William Caslon (1692–1766).

Design by N. J. Furl

Open Letter is the University of Rochester's nonprofit, literary translation press:
Lattimore Hall 411, Box 270082, Rochester, NY 14627

www.openletterbooks.org

Contents

MY FIRST SUICIDE

The Most Beautiful
Woman in the World

I

WHEN GREAT LOVE COMES ALONG, A PERSON ALWAYS THINKS HE HAS fallen in love with the most beautiful woman in the world. But when a person *has* fallen in love with the most beautiful woman in the world, he can have problems.

If she wasn't The Most Beautiful Woman in the World in the strict sense, she was in the top ten, and if it wasn't the top ten, then the top one hundred—the details are unimportant. She was dazzling in a planetary sense.

I saw her, and I committed a rookie's mistake. Instead of being satisfied with admiring, I resolved to conquer her.

I saw her at a certain reception—that is, I saw her for the first time and in person at a certain reception. Before then I had seen her likeness hundreds of times on various photographs, advertisements, posters, and billboards. The famous visage of the depraved madonna—which so excited photographers, cameramen, and directors—was universally known. The reception took place in the gardens of a Western embassy. It was a very significant, very ritual, and very annual reception. On the societal bond market, an invitation to that reception was considered an unusually valuable security.

The uniqueness of the garden reception at the embassy was also made clear by that fact that, in addition to the habitués—virtuosos at the art of the reception—lost intellectuals were wandering around, intellectuals who never attended receptions, but who had to their credit works devoted to the culture of the Western country whose ambassador was hosting the reception. They were distinguished by their archaic suits, immoderate gluttony, and great enthusiasm. When the jaded habitués confessed to them that they hated receptions, the intellectuals tried to comfort them somehow and urged them on to eat, drink, and have fun. The jaded habitués—who, at all receptions, would drone on gloomily about hating receptions, and who found an equally gloomy hearing for their confessions among other jaded habitués of receptions, who likewise hate receptions—gazed stupefied at the hearty, smiling oldsters, who, flushed with champagne, grabbed them by the elbow with an unexpectedly iron grip, led them to the groaning table and, looking around, exclaimed in triumph:

"But why so sad, young man! You've got to appreciate the sunny side of life! Especially today! Especially here! What a wonderful reception! You simply must eat something! Here you are! Exquisite fish! Exquisite cold cuts! Exquisite salad!" and they shoved plates into jaded hands, and piled up heaping portions and shoved them before jaded faces. "You simply must eat something! And then the drinks await us. The libations are excellent! Please be so good as to help yourselves!"—and the intellectuals, seemingly lost, but in truth feeling like fish in water in the gardens of the embassy, winked roguishly and dove merrily into the undulating throng.

It was a steamy July day. Clouds dark as lead and light as electricity were scudding along toward Warsaw from the west. The Most Beautiful Woman in the World didn't budge from her spot for a good two hours. I circled.

At first I didn't notice that I was circling. Without a goal—so it seemed to me—I sauntered about the gardens of the embassy holding a glass of still water. I didn't particularly seek anyone out. Nor did anyone seek me. I instinctively attempted to avoid the bores who were lying in ambush for victims. After enough receptions, this ability becomes second nature. Bores lying in ambush for victims are like sharpshooters in war—they sow death. Somehow I managed to pull it off. True, one bore, a colorless columnist in civilian clothes, what might be called "Independence Style," managed to take my bearings. He approached and began to blather—for the thousandth time he told the story of how he was arrested during Martial Law. I was already beginning to think I was a goner, but once he got closer, it turned out that my assailant, in spite of the early hour, was already distinctly fuddled—I lost him without trouble. I, of course, didn't drink a drop myself; true, in the depths of my soul I wasn't excluding the possibility that yet that evening, having locked myself up tight and alone at home, I might uncork a bottle, but here—out of the question.

By the time I was passing The Most Beautiful Woman in the World for the third time, I realized that I was circling, and that I was circling in ever tighter orbits. She stood near one of the numerous wicker chairs set out on the grassy areas. She was smoking cigarettes, which was a rarity among the stars, who were so hysterically concerned with their health. She stood, and she didn't budge. Time and again some sort of jittery habitué would appear in her vicinity, tight like a bow string, but all of them flagged and quickly fell away.

I made ever smaller circles. I could already see quite well the legs that had paced the most prestigious catwalks of the world; the shoulders that, season after season, were wrapped in the most expensive creations of Dior, Versace, Lagerfeld, and Montana; the hair, fragrant with the most expensive shampoos of the globe; the décolletage boldly presenting the profile of the famous bust, which the floodlights of Hollywood film studios had briefly lit up. Briefly, since she hadn't had a big career as an actress. That is to say, it is true that fifteen years ago she played a stewardess who served Harrison Ford a drink—even that was the pipe dream of the majority of professional European actresses—but after this episode offers didn't come pouring out of the proverbial bag. It goes without saying: this did not diminish her in the least—at least not in my eyes. On the contrary. There was a logic in this. Her uncanny beauty decided her fate. Nothing else came into play. Putting it the other way around, which is to say point-blank: in everything she took up, with the exception of her own beauty, she was rather a clod. And, unfortunately, she took up various things. She recorded a CD with her own songs—the chief value of which was its almost complete lack of background hiss. She published a slender volume of verse—a rare sort of catastrophe, since it was bloody, and at the same time completely lacking in expression. She painted and organized an exhibition of her own work—oh, Jesus Christ! To tell the truth, even her one-second performance as an actress at the side of Harrison Ford—especially considering its minuscule time span— knew no bounds. It was sorry consolation that, at the side of such a virtuoso, everyone—and especially a fledgling artist—looks pale.

But her defeats had no bearing on the fact of her beauty. Who cared about the fact that she was no singer, a wretched poet, and a miserable painter, since—when they came into contact with her—the greatest singers lost their voices, the most distinguished poets didn't know what to say, and the most original painters peed their pants from sheer sensation?

I was already close to that beauty. I was close, but I wasn't tight like a bow-string—I was shaking like jelly.

"I'm happy to see you alive," I managed to stammer, absurdly. I had intended to say, of course: "I'm happy to see you live," which was supposed to have been the ritual and safe phrase of the admirer who knows his idol from the movie theater, from television, as well as from the thousands of photographs, and now gives expression to his ecstasy at seeing her in real life. Instead of this, my nerves made me blurt out some sort of, I don't know—some sort of post-traumatic or post-heart-attack line. "I'm happy to see you alive" sounded, after all, as if she had just escaped from some sort of life-threatening danger, but no one had heard anything of the sort. There isn't anything bad, however, that can't come out to the good. She looked at me and burst out laughing unexpectedly loudly. Quite clearly—to use literary Polish—my unfortunate *lapsus* had amused her.

"I, too, am happy to see *you* alive," she said with a light touch, but that lightness immediately weighed like lead upon my brain.

It's impossible—I feverishly began to mull over the facts—it's impossible for her to know that, two weeks ago, I was at death's door, in the strict sense of the phrase. How could she have known? I had locked myself up at home, I had pulled the Venetian blinds, I had turned off the telephones, I talked with no one, I didn't go out anywhere, except to the twenty-four-hour delicatessen *William* . . . Someone must have noticed me when I was crawling to the store, and the news had immediately made its way around town. It was possible. I tried my hardest, but in the end you always had to go out to the store . . . Yes, someone saw me as I was crawling to the twenty-four-hour delicatessen *William*. There was no other possible explanation.

Except, it was also possible that she had answered without any ulterior motive; that she had answered mechanically; that, for the sake of reinforcing the joke, she had repeated my clumsy opening as an echo. Such a possibility existed, and it was even highly probable, but, in order to accept it with equanimity, I would have to have been cured of my complex. And I had a gigantic complex about this. Every time someone asked me in completely neutral tones: "How are you doing? How've you been feeling? How's life? Everything OK?"; every time I received similar SMSes; every time I heard such questions posed on the phone, or face-to-face—each time I was unable to answer normally and make light of it. Instead, I always shrank with fear, and I always groaned before I answered under the weight of the one-ton question: How does he know? How does that louse know that I am hitting the bottle again? And this time it was the same, or even worse, since, after all, in the assertion "I'm happy to see you alive" lurks not speculation *about*, but the certainty *of* my downfall. Nothing to be done about it, I thought. On the whole, it's even better that she knows about my afflictions. At least then it won't be an unpleasant surprise if I go on a bender right after the wedding.

"It's true. I'm barely alive," I said carefully. "To tell the truth, I'm completely exhausted."

"That's not good," she replied with an inordinately subtle motherly tone. "Not good at all. Even bad. Very bad."

"I had a Russian teacher who spoke the same way. Exactly the same."

"I beg your pardon?" Not that she immediately stiffened, but she was unquestionably startled, and she was well on the way to absolute stiffening. Besides, there's nothing strange about it. There hadn't been any teachers of Russian in Polish schools for more than ten years now, and yet the summoning of even the specter of a teacher of the Russian language continued to give rise to problematic associations. Evidently The Most Beautiful Woman in the World was, like many Poles, painfully sensitive when it came to Moscow. No doubt she had this from her parents.

"I once had a Russian teacher"—hoping to soothe her trauma, I began to tell her the story, feverishly and in haste—"he was a fantastic guy, we liked him a lot. Also because he was not only intelligent, but also understanding. He didn't go overboard in the enforcement of knowledge. Not that he allowed us to walk all over him, but, all the same, he allowed us quite a lot. Nonetheless, every now and then, more or less once every two months, a frenzy of inordinate severity would seize him. He would enter the room with a boundlessly severe facial expression, summon us to the blackboard with boundless severity, and, inordinately severely, in absolute silence, listen to our answers. He wouldn't interrupt, he wouldn't correct, he wouldn't speak up. Without a word, he would listen to the delinquent as he writhed like an eel, and when he had finally finished, he would say: 'Very bad.'"

She laughed, she laughed the entire time I was telling my story, she laughed, and that was good, but also a bit irritating, since when the punch line came she went on laughing in just the same fashion, and, strictly speaking, it wasn't clear whether she had noticed and appreciated the end of the story at all. But I didn't delve deeper into this. Distant, still golden and leisurely threads of lightning intersected the dark horizon. Three, maybe four storms were approaching the city.

"Very good," she said (she had noticed and appreciated after all!). "Very good. You get high marks from me for that answer. But it is very bad that you are barely alive, and that must change."

"What must change?"

"Life. Life must change."

"You know, it is difficult to change life. Life isn't likely to change. Unless it's for the worse. And from a certain point on, it is exclusively for the worse."

For a moment I considered whether to intensify the pessimistic tone, and even whether to push the pedal of pessimism to the floor, but I eased off. Pessimism and bitterness were means of arousing comforting reflexes in women, which are as certain as they are standard; her all-embracing beauty, however, cautioned against playing this one from memory.

"If you go on to tell me that you don't have anyone for whom to change your life for the better, and if you gaze meaningfully into my eyes as you say this, the situation will admittedly be clear, but also quite finished."

She had passed me a difficult, a very difficult ball—one that would be downright impossible for a rookie to handle—but as bad as I am, out of boredom, at handling weak balls, difficult balls lend me wings, and I climb the heights.

"Of course I don't have anyone for whom to change my life. It's just that I couldn't care less about that. God forbid I should change my life, or anything *in* my life for anyone. I am too accustomed to myself and to my own solitude, and I value it too much to change it. If you tell me that, when true love appears in my life, I will certainly and enthusiastically change my life for the better; if you tell me this, and if you gaze knowingly into my eyes as you say this, then the situation will also be clear, but also quite finished."

I knew that she wouldn't be able to field a riposte let loose with that sort of spin, but I also didn't foresee that she would go for a feint.

"The situation is clear," she said with irritating infallibility. "The situation is clear. You've got no idea about life. You don't know what life is."

"So what is it?" I feigned irritation, and even fury, in my voice. There was no retreat. The game was heating up. If she should conclude that I was a madman—game over. If, in an access of vanity, she should be filled with pride, thinking that she had destroyed my equilibrium, I will have won. "So, I humbly beg your pardon, what is life? Please be so kind as to enlighten me, because I truly don't know."

"Of course you don't know. He pretends to be a connoisseur of souls, a man of letters, a theoretician of everything—and he hasn't a clue."

I had succumbed, at that moment I had succumbed definitively and—I would say—far-reachingly. I had succumbed, because I had thought, with a rookie's haughtiness, that I had the victory in my pocket. When a woman proceeds to a seemingly sharp, but in fact tender, attack, the victory is usually in your pocket.

"But of course I haven't a clue about anything. And when it comes to life, not the least, not even a hint. Just what is life? I don't know. I say this in dead earnest: I don't know."

"Oh God, man, don't go to pieces on me. Don't you see that I am full of nothing but good intentions, even eagerness? Don't you see that either, you dope? What year were you born?"

"Fifty-three," I responded mechanically, and not without distaste; after all, the date of my birth usually stood plain as day on the covers of my books, and *she* has to ask? Hasn't she ever picked one up, or what? For a moment I even considered taking offense and giving up, but after brief consideration I came to the conclusion that the operation would succeed, that I would punish her for ignorance of my work with attacks of eccentric brutality in bed.

"That's just beautiful. Born in fifty-three, and he has to ask about the meaning of life! Hasn't anyone informed you by now, you poor thing, about the meaning of life. Really no one?"

"No one. And I sense that if you don't tell me, I will never learn and I will die in ignorance."

"Listen. Life depends on finding the right proportion between work and relaxation. Do you understand? Understand? Or is it too difficult for you?"

"As far as work is concerned, I know more or less what *that* is . . . But as far as *relaxation* is concerned . . ."

My gaze must have betrayed me. I must have gazed at her for a moment with excessively ostentatious greed, since she shook her head with pity.

"Forgive me, but that is an excessively one-sided conception of relaxation, too exhaustive and, basically, embarrassing. And as for work," she adopted, after a second of ominous silence, a conciliatory tone, even *very* conciliatory, "and as for *work*, what—if I may allow myself the banal question of the enchanted female reader—what is the master working on at the moment?"

"God bless you for that 'enchantment.' No writer can resist a friendly load of crap. Especially in such a . . . especially in your performance. I am composing short stories now. A collection of short stories of a different sort."

"A novel is less than a novel, but a volume of short stories is more than a volume of stories?" she suddenly blurted out.

"What gibberish," I thought at the first, "what gibberish are you spouting, you miraculous bitch?" But the first moment had passed; after it a second, a third, and perhaps even a fourth, and in the next one, I don't know which one, slowly, very slowly—*langsam und trübe*—it began to dawn on me that, who knows? . . . Who knows how this blind hen had stumbled upon the secret of my literary workbench.

II

As I now recreate and record our first conversation, I see clearly that literature can never keep pace with life. Even a faithfully recorded exchange of sentences—word for word—says nothing about the heart of the matter. In this instance, the heart of the matter was my terrible paralysis over the fact that The Most Beautiful Woman in the world was chatting with me at all. That's in the first place. And in the second place, I was paralyzed by the fact that I myself was chatting. After all, greater wizards than I were struck dumb in her presence. And yet, a conversation had occurred: she spoke to me, and I spoke to her; but that's not all—she gave the impression of listening intently to what I was telling her; then she would answer, then I would answer, then she, then I . . . Everything, seemingly, was going along just as normally as could be. Seemingly. Very seemingly. For at bottom, our conversation was very much feigned and very fragmentary, and I—a very illusory and very partial I—was taking part in it. With every word spoken, I was immediately panicked by the fact that a word had been spoken. Already when I was approaching her, I was in panic—in amazement and fear—that I was approaching. Oh, f . . . , I'm approaching her! Oh, f . . . , I'm close! Oh, f . . . , I said something! Oh, f . . . , she glanced at me! Oh, f . . . , she sees me! Oh, f . . . , she's talking to me! I raised such shouts the whole time in my heart of hearts, and they dominated. They were the essence of the thing. In them also lurked the harbinger of tragedy. Instead of concentrating on the operation, I was in permanent triumph over the fact that there even was an operation. That was to be my undoing.

Three of four storms came crashing down on the garden; lightning bolts made it white like winter, thunder claps made it hushed like a silent film. Salads diluted by streams of water began to withdraw from their platters; cold cuts, cheeses, fruits swam the length of table cloths in a torrential stream; waiters soaked to the marrow tried to rescue what they could; the lawn was transformed in the twinkling of an eye into a quagmire; the army of reception-goers, decimated by the gale, tried to storm the buildings of the embassy. The chaos was spreading.

The Most Beautiful Woman in the World disappeared between my one glance at her and the next. When the heavens abruptly darkened, and the rains came down in sheets, I lifted my face; then, with the instinctive thought that one ought somehow to shield the Venus of the Third Republic—perhaps take off my jacket and throw it over her shoulders; by some miracle, produce an umbrella from somewhere; conjure up a cape out of a handkerchief—all this lasted a second, my protective visions didn't even have time to take on concrete shape; I glanced again in her direction, and she was gone. I think I even glanced instinctively in the direction of the swaying crowns of the trees, but this was a childish instinct.

Apart from everything else—granted, she *was* The Most Beautiful Woman in the World, she belonged to the top ten, or to the top hundred, of the most beautiful women in the world—but some sort of slender and ethereal beauty she was *not*. A healthy broad, to tell the truth: six feet tall, a glorious bust, not pumped up with any element lighter than air, massive thighs, and a wrestler's frame. Just a few years ago, all sorts of abundance had been heaped high on this frame. The story of the trademark diet she had worked out to perfection, and of her shockingly effective loss of weight, was known to the nation just as well as the story of the resurrection of Lord Jesus, and perhaps even better. Now, of course, she was slender and slim like a poplar, but still there wasn't a chance that the wind would carry her off like a feather to the height of the genuine poplars growing next to the fence.

I searched for her like a madman. I crossed all the rooms of the embassy from the cellars to the attic. I set the entire guard on its feet; they followed me, but at a distance; I was supposedly pale as a corpse, wild gaze, disheveled hair. Water poured from my shoes and pants, since I rushed, time and again, out into the garden, to that place where she had stood motionless for two hours next to a wicker chair. I kept feeling delusional impulses that she was still standing there, and, like a fool, time and again I ran there. The guards followed me, but, as I said, at a distance, since they were operating under the reasonable assumption that they were dealing not with a calculating terrorist, but with an unpredictable madman.

Time and again someone would ask me who I was looking for—I didn't answer, I didn't say, I didn't speak up at all. How could I confess to such boundless stupidity? What was I supposed to say? That I was looking for The Most Beautiful Woman in the World? Let's say that you were looking into various rooms in deadly panic, searching, let's say, for Sharon Stone, and let's say someone were to ask you who you were looking for. What would you answer? I'm looking for Sharon, because she vanished somewhere. An impossible dialogue! A situation that's beyond all categories! You can't ask about the whereabouts of beautiful women: vile intentions, even if they don't betray you, will be ascribed to you. Even if you were I don't know what sort of famous ascetic. And I wasn't. I was, however, unprecedentedly desperate, and the circumstances seemed—in spite of everything—propitious.

On account of the collective and instant evacuation of the banquet, which was now drowned by the downpour and bombarded by lightning bolts, the atmosphere became—as it happens when the commoners suddenly take control of the salons—more and more unrestrained. Under the pretext of drinking to get warm, everyone ignored the extraterritoriality of the embassy and drank as is drunk throughout our entire land: one bottle per person. And so it was no wonder that in short order almost everybody was in the same state as the colorless columnist of the so-called "Independence Style" had been from the very beginning. I wasn't very fond of him, but I couldn't think about his predatory swilling with anything other than respect. If a person has to be fuddled in the end, it is better that he be more generously fuddled. And so in a pinch, very much in a pinch, I could put together a thin disguise. I could attempt—pretending to be fuddled—to ask someone who was equally plastered (except that they really were), as if for a joke, about the whereabouts of The Most Beautiful Woman in the world.

But then, I didn't know this company very well. That is, I knew more or less, who could have her cell phone number. It was clear that the designer who was living in New York most probably had it, and the former minister most certainly had it; that the famous illustrator most likely had it, and that the right-wing journalist probably didn't; that the film director, known for his conquests, might have it, but the composer, who boasted of his monogamy, did not; that the scandalous female painter almost certainly did, but the philosophy professor from Oxford almost certainly not.* This much I knew, but I didn't know what, in this particular case, would be the reaction to my request. I hesitated a good while, I looked around carefully, I feverishly attempted to find some friendly soul, but, in the end, fear prevailed—the fear that the person I should finally ask wouldn't manage sufficient discretion, might even, in his cups and for a joke, make a fuss throughout the entire embassy.

As a sort of farewell, I ventured into the private apartments of the ambassador and his wife. Now I was acting in cold blood and as if for my own amusement; I knew that I wouldn't find her there, but suddenly the power I still had over the guards began to excite me. Calmly, and even phlegmatically, I roamed through personal offices, closets, bathrooms, bedrooms; I went into the toilet for a moment; upon exiting, with an eloquent gesture to the unit that was following me, I made it clear that it was now unoccupied, and—quietly writhing with rage, sorrow, and a feeling of irreversible loss—I went home.

III

IN THE TAXI, WHILE STILL ON THE WAY, I WAS ABSOLUTELY CERTAIN that I would suddenly be washed away. I was tired, soaking wet, hungry. (Because of nerves, I almost never eat at receptions and here, to boot, before I was able to make up my mind about some slice of cheese, the flood swept all the food in its wake.) I was alone, since, in

---

*Actually, it was precisely the professor who could have had it—and even, as I think about it now—most certainly did.

my desperate search for the irrevocably lost star, it didn't even occur to me to look around for some sort of substitute for the evening. I was furious at myself over this, too. After all, a couple of very impressive body doubles—you could even say, a couple of very daring and dexterous stuntwomen—were strolling consentingly, very consentingly, about the gardens.

But now the gardens and the city were plunged in rain and darkness. The temperature had fallen at least twenty degrees. I didn't have a single reason not to have a drink. On the contrary, I had fourteen reasons *to* have a drink. Fourteen 50 ml bottles of stomach bitters awaited me in the refrigerator. For some time now, I had preferred coin divided up precisely in this fashion, convenient for parcelling out among my pockets. Each of the fourteen named reasons was individually good for a beginning, and all of them together were good for an end.

I paid the taxi driver, ran into my apartment, and, as is my custom when it is bad (and this time, it was very bad), without taking off my shoes I ran straight to the refrigerator in order, as quickly as possible, to open up, unscrew, drink down; in other words, to perform three ritual ceremonies, after which it would stop being bad. But before I plunged myself into the rites, and even before I had made it to the refrigerator, I remembered about the air rifle. That's right. There was indeed something worth remembering. I had something to recall. And I'll put it even more forcefully: there is something to tell a story about.

A week earlier I had fulfilled the eternal dream of my childhood, of my youth, and of my maturity—I had bought myself a gun. I had bought myself a pneumatic rifle, commonly known as an air rifle. For a week now, I have been the owner of a dazzling Spanish flintlock from the firm Norica. For a week now, I have been placing the smooth cherry wood butt to my cheek. I raise up the black oxidized barrel, and my dithering hands are calmed, and my weakening eyes once again see every detail. I release the safety, I pull the trigger, and all the artificial flowers, sticky suckers, and black-and-white photographs of film stars, which I shot to bits at Wisła church fairs, fly circles around my head. All the matches, threads, and glass tubes that I was able to shoot up in the shooting galleries I have happened upon in the course of my life (and I haven't let a single one pass by) spin under the ceiling. All the targets I have managed to hit come flying like squadrons of paper swallows. I don't like vulgar sentimentalism, but when I load my rifle (I bought—it goes without saying—a significant stock of ammunition), take aim, and hear the metallic clang, I am as happy as I was as a child.

And so, before I rushed to the refrigerator, I remembered about my weapon, and I decided, after all, to take a look at it first, to make sure it was really there. I still had a feeling of unreality. For my whole life, I had been certain (and I still have this fear) that an air rifle belongs to the realm of things that will never be accessible to normal mortals. The place for such collectors' items was in some sort of closely guarded arsenal. Only the most privileged, and those of the highest standing, had access to them, and even they couldn't always take them home with them. The owners of church fair shooting galleries—athletic men with insolent eyes—always made an incredible impression upon me. It was clear that they belonged to some sort of dark Areopagus, with no one knew what sort of powers. And it seemed that it would always be so, that the world of dark Areopaguses, inaccessible air rifles, church fair shooting galleries, and mysterious store rooms—full of weapons stands, heaps of artificial flowers, and pyramids of shot—would last forever. And now, when my own, my endlessly beautiful Spanish lady stands there, leaning against the wall, when I look at her—it is with the greatest difficulty that I realize that *that* world has come tumbling down.

I turned on the light in the room—there she was. She is.* Without taking off my shoes, without changing clothes (and without looking

---

*"He is!"—the ecstatic text on a license plate of a certain American automobile noted in an essay by Stanisław Barańczak. I like this phrase, and I use it rather frequently in various forms and with various intents.

into the refrigerator), I approached, grasped, broke, loaded, and began to shoot.

When a person becomes the owner of a weapon (even one—as some would claim—so childish as an air rifle), the image of the world changes. The world is transformed into a collection of targets. If you have a gun, you automatically begin to examine the world from the point of view of its usefulness for shooting at. In the infinite number of objects that create the surface of reality, only those that are good for shooting count. In this sense, the light bulb hanging from the ceiling ceases to be a light bulb and becomes a perfect and very tempting target. The pigeon on the windowsill is no longer only a pigeon, a tree stump ceases to be exclusively a tree stump, an empty cigarette pack only an empty cigarette pack, etc. In my case, the Coca-Cola bottle caps ceased, in an exceptionally radical manner, to be bottle caps *per se* and became dazzling and narcotic targets. I placed a cardboard box on my balcony sill, I pounded a pencil into the box, I hung a bottle cap from the pencil, and out of the depths of my living room—Aim! Fire! Aim! Fire! Aim! Fire! Since—I should add—I am addicted to Coca-Cola, I have a considerable reserve of bottle caps.

Now, after the irrevocable loss—so it seemed—of The Most Beautiful Woman in the World, after the irrevocable loss of a chance at The Most Beautiful Woman in the World, I was as if in a trance. I was in a fever of despair. I was blasting away mercilessly, and not only could I not stop shooting, I also could not stop hitting the target. Between my eye, the rear sight, the muzzle sight, and the target hanging from the pencil ran an icy, steely, and inexorable line. The successive bottle caps—hit each time in the very heart—flew to pieces in hundreds of tiny, yellow, lightning flashes. When I ran out of bottle caps, I increased the distance twofold, and I scattered my entire stock of empty cigarette packages and matchboxes. Then came the time to set cigarettes on end. I had four unopened packages of Gauloises, which—like it or not—offer eighty hits in a row. Then I mowed down all my pencils. Then six empty lighters. Then I began to look for what might come next. I found three sticks left over from "Magnum" ice cream pops, five cartridges for a Parker ballpoint pen. I broke an old glasses frame into a series of tiny targets. I shot through a one-grosz coin that I had glued for good luck to a miniature calendar. I hit an antique mask that was prominently displayed on the cover of *Literary Notebooks*. I reduced to pulp the dried up lemon that had been wandering about the kitchen since time immemorial. Finally, I found a pack of playing cards from a *Playboy* jubilee issue, which soothed me for a moment, but only apparently. I was convinced that shooting at the playing-card likenesses of naked beauties would occupy me for the rest of the evening.

I hung the card with the first naked beauty that came to hand on the pencil, took aim—and my hand shook. The first that came to hand—or if not the first one that came to hand, then one of ten, one of a hundred, one of a thousand of the first naked beauties that came to hand—looked a bit like The Most Beautiful Woman in the World. That same ideal outline of the shoulders, that same self-satisfied smile, that same motionless gaze.

My hand shook. I lowered my weapon. I was near tears from helplessness and sorrow. I became keenly aware that even the most accurate shot at the effigy of the first naked beauty that came to hand would be a complete embarrassment. Some trashy, *per procura*, symbolic execution was about to take place in my head. There was no point in shooting. Neither at the substitute likenesses, nor at seemingly neutral targets. There was absolutely no point in shooting. I would have to bear the defeat like a man. Not surrender. To fight, to search, to obtain her coordinates at any cost—even at the cost of humiliation. To try to identify a trustworthy soul, and, in spite of everything, to ask heroically, paying no heed to adversity, for her cellphone number . . . Heroically, since, after all, even if I would be successful, there is no guarantee what would come next . . . Jesus Christ! So greatly did the recurrence of a recent nightmare batter me and make me white-hot with rage that I did it. Not in a trance, but in cold calculation. All of my trances—once the trance itself has already basically been strained away—have an icy finish (recall my stroll through the private apartments of the ambassador and his wife), and that's how it was now, too. I did this in cold calculation, with complete calm, and, toward the end, not without amusement. I brought fourteen 50 ml bottles of stomach bitters from the refrigerator, placed them methodically at decent intervals on the edge of the balcony, and—this will come as no surprise to you—I used fourteen shots on them. It goes without saying that there were no delaying tactics of the sort: empty the fourteen bottles, pour the hooch out into a jug, shoot away at the empties, and then engage in a little private revelry on top of that. No question of any of that. First, whoever has shot at a full bottle and at an empty bottle knows the difference this makes. It is a fundamental difference. It is like the difference between I won't say which one thing and that other one. Second, I finally needed the smell of blood. And the subtle cloud of stomach bitters coming from the balcony, from the fourteen shattered 50 ml bottles, was like the smell of wolf entrails, like the vapor of tropical swamps, like poison gas. I fell asleep intoxicated and unconscious.

And when I woke up, and when, as usual, before getting out of bed I checked to see whether anyone had left some desperate message in the night, on the screen of my phone I found letters tapped out with the thumb of an angel: "I'm sorry that I disappeared so quickly, but I had to. In any case, I say yes. I say yes. Yes to the next installment of our conversation about life." I got up, put on Vivaldi's *First Violin Concerto* full blast and wrote back: "I say yes to our life." "To our life together?" she replied three seconds later. "Yes," I replied. "Do you think we will be happy?" she replied. "Yes," I replied.

IV

I AM WRITING THE FIRST BEDROOM SCENE OF MY LIFE, AND HERE I commit the classic debutant's error: instead of getting right down to business, instead of beginning right off the bat and describing the body of The Most Beautiful Woman in the World as it evaporates like a cloud, I enter upon intricate preambles and digressions. But once you have The Most Beautiful Woman in the World in your bed, you feel so intellectually energized that you think you have the right to formulate fundamental theses. You have the right to pose and to settle key questions. And so, I pose (and also immediately settle) the following key question: What, namely, is the key question in sex? I answer: The key question in sex is the opening position. Oh, of course, it isn't a matter of any opening position in bed. I'm not providing pitiful technical counseling here—where to place the feet, under what to place the pillow, etc. I'm concerned with the opening position in the fundamental sense, about the first—I use this term in the classical philosophical sense—position.*

To find the place to occupy the first position, and subsequently to occupy the first position—that is the fundamental question in sex. Fundamental, because it is the first. Without it, there are no further installments, and even if there are, they are chaotic and unharmonious. And chaos and lack of harmony are the extermination of sex. In short, it is a matter of sitting down in the proper place. The first position is always a sitting position. Schemes of the sort that would have us walk up to the window together, and at that window, or on the way back, have me embrace her; or the complete catastrophe that would have me lie in ambush for her on her return from the bathroom, and then romantically jump on her back—such schemes are disastrous because they are doomed to briefness. Just how long are you going to stand with her at that window? Just how long will the two of you rock back and forth in an amatory frenzy by the bathroom? Sooner or later you will have to loosen the passionate hold, and everything starts again from the beginning. Unless—God forbid!—seized by panic in such an ill-fated moment, you pick up the pace, thereby making matters worse. It is quite another matter that then at least you've gotten

---

*The first position is analogous to Aristotelian *prote philosophia*, first philosophy. Of course, it is possible to gain practice in the understanding and occupation of the first position *without* knowledge of Aristotle, but then the taste of corporal relations will be less substantial.

the thing over with. You've succumbed. You're dead. Don't try to tell me that death has only its bad sides.

It is my deepest conviction that the thing to do is to sit down next to the woman, to sit down properly next to the woman, to sit down next to the woman in the appropriate place—this is the essence of the art of love. He who has grasped the simplicity of this craft has learned much. He who has not grasped it will achieve little.

For various reasons, mankind has suffered amatory fiascos. It has suffered them because it was timid, because it didn't have the proper conditions, because the hour had gotten late, because it was too early, because she wasn't ready yet, because he was ashamed, because she became paralyzed with fear, because he got drunk, because she undressed too soon, because he said something stupid, because she suddenly remembered that she had to call her sister, because he didn't take off his socks, because she spent half the night in the bathroom, because he had such an attack of nerves that he was constantly running to the can, because she, out of habit, addressed him as she did her husband—shnooky-lumps, because he, while sitting on the edge of the bed, began to reply to an SMS, because she suddenly broke down in tears, because he suddenly broke out laughing, because she cleared her throat significantly the whole time, because when he asked with a muffled voice, "When did you last fall in love?" she replied with hasty frankness, "Yesterday," etc., etc. Mankind has suffered amatory disasters for a billion reasons. Mankind has suffered disaster a billion times, a billion times it came to nothing, because he didn't know how to move from the armchair to the couch. A billion disasters—or perhaps a billion billions—derived from the fact that he didn't know how to take up the first position. It's quite another matter that, if you have a small apartment, then this is a genuine tragedy. That's right—a small one. It's worse in a small one than in a large one. After all, you're not going to pile on next to her on the sofa bed, just as soon as she sits down, on account of the cramped quarters. Contrary to appearances, in a small apartment—stricter rules apply.

I had a small apartment. The Most Beautiful Woman in the World sat on the couch, I, on the other side of a small coffee table, on the arm chair. Seven mountains, seven rivers, seven seas, and seven infinities separated me from the first position. And that was terrible. But I already had scores of mountains, rivers, seas, infinities behind me. And that was good. Although incomprehensible. All the more incomprehensible in that, basically, it was not so much that I myself had overcome all those obstacles, as that The Most Beautiful Woman in the world had transported me across them. I didn't have to make my way across scores of rivers in order to ask her to go to a bar, because right away she said: OK. I didn't have to climb scores of mountains with the goal of taking her to the movies, because right away she said: OK. I didn't have to sail across scores of oceans in order to go with her for a walk, because right away she said: OK. Whatever I said, she said OK. To each and every of my propositions—OK. And I, instead of taking a moment to give it some thought—that something isn't OK here, because everything was too much OK—was in permanent euphoria over the fact that it's OK. Oh f . . . ! OK! Oh f . . . ! OK! Oh f . . . ! OK! Oh God! OK! She is eating dinner with me! Oh God! OK! She is with me in the Saxon Garden! Oh God! OK! She allows me to be with her when she walks the dog! Oh God! OK! She is holding my hand! Oh God! OK! She is kissing me at the gate! Oh f . . . ! OK! Oh God! OK!

It was the second half of July. The sky over a deserted Warsaw shimmered like a field of lime. We sat in *Yellow Dream* on Marszałkowska Street, in *Modulor* at the Square of the Three Crosses, in *Tam Tam* on Foksal Street, in *Antykwariat* on Żurawia Street. We went to the *Iluzjon* to see *Dolce Vita*, to the *Rejs* to see *Seven Seals*, to the *Kinoteka* to see *Other Torments*.

In the *Atlantic*, at *Girl with a Pearl Earring*, The Most Beautiful Woman in the World cried with delight. I skillfully pretended that I shared her emotion. It came easily to me, because in my euphoria I shared all her emotions and said OK to everything.

I said OK to her conception of life on earth; it was grounded—as you will recall—in finding the appropriate proportion between work and relaxation. I said OK to her conception of life beyond the grave: after death, the soul goes to Heaven, Hell, or Purgatory; but if it doesn't want to, it doesn't have to; it can enter into another body— whether human, animal, or vegetable depends upon the deceased's Zodiac sign when he was alive. I even said OK to her literary hier- archies: she adored Wharton and Coelho. It didn't come easy—but I said OK. My God! Deny a detail like literary taste for the sake of such a beauty? No problem. I said OK. We strolled around deserted Chmielna, Krucza, Wspólna, Hoża, and Wilcza Streets, and I con- stantly shared her emotions, and I constantly said OK. The empty city ennobled her gibberish. The burning-hot cement center of the city was dead, as if the world had ceased to exist. Even the few specters of dying drug addicts, drunken beggars, and municipal watch guards, all tormented by the sweltering heat, had disappeared somewhere. We were the last people on earth, and the last people on earth have the right to talk nonsense.

"Drop by my place," I said. We were standing in front of her building. Her dog, in whose evening pissing I had once again had the honor to participate, looked at me with hostility.

"OK," she said. "I'll be there at six."

Everything was clear. A pure love united us, but the time for get- ting dirty was drawing near. I had fears, premonitions. I foresaw a catastrophe. After all, at some point she would have to stop saying OK. And when she stops saying OK, she will say No. And most certainly she will say No at that point when they all say No.

I sat across from her as if on red-hot coals. I was a million light years away from the first position, and I knew that as soon as I should make even one move to approach her, as soon as, with even one reck- less gesture, I should signal my wish to move from the armchair to the couch, I would hear the word No. Basically, I couldn't move at all, because in my panic I became hysterical at the thought that, as soon as I make any move at all, I would hear No. And I couldn't let this happen. True, women often say No, and *sometimes*—as is well known—this doesn't mean very much. But if a woman who says OK all the time says No even once, this can have far-reaching—and catastrophic—significance. Still, one way or the other, sooner or later, I would have to make my move. And so I moved. I moved because the telephone rang. As soon as I heard the ring, I knew right away—by the very sound of the tone, so to speak, I recognized that it was the Lord God who was calling me. I was absolutely certain that when I lifted the receiver I would hear the voice of the Lord God. And I was not mistaken. I lifted the receiver, and I heard:

"Hey. Did you read what that cretin wrote?" the Lord God spoke in the voice of my friend Mariusz Z.

"Of course I read it. You bet I read it!" my voice shook with joy—I was saved, I was delivered. The Lord God Himself was leading me to the first position.

"Actually, it's odd that you've read it. It's basically unreadable. The typical class dunce's composition."

"Something bad has happened to him. He's lost control of his thought."

"What thought? There isn't a *trace* of thought there. That is a piece by a guy who has lost control—not of his thought, but of his urine."

"However you look at it, it's a downhill slide. There was a time when what he wrote still made sense."

"Rubbish. It never made sense. I always said he was a graphomaniac."

"At the beginning at least he was humble."

"Every graphomaniac is humble at the beginning. Him too. He used to be a humble graphomaniac, but now he is a brazen and impudent graphomaniac."

"It's quite another matter that they print this blather. This basically belongs in the editor's waste bin."

"Why are you surprised that they print the stuff? After all, they're all imbeciles."

•

I chatted eagerly with my friend, the well-known literary critic Mariusz Z. With expert knowledge and taste, we discussed in great detail an article (or perhaps a book, today I no longer remember) by one of our mutual friends. With the receiver on my ear I circled about the room. I took turns feigning this and that: first complete immersion in the deep substance of the conversation, then I would make conspiratorial glances and apologetic gestures in the direction of The Most Beautiful Woman in the World. I was in ecstasy. God was reaching out to me. I jabbered with absolute inspiration, I made my analysis, I interpreted, and I summed up. I circled—just as in the embassy gardens—in ever tighter orbits. And when, from behind the voice of my friend, I heard in the depths of the receiver the true voice of God, Who, in the language that today fulfills the function of Latin, called out to me—*Now! Man!* Boy! It's time!—I feigned total immersion in the conversation, together with total separation from reality, and in this immersion and separation I made yet another circle around the room, and I began the next, and half way through the next—in complete fervor, trance, and reverie—I sat down next to her on the couch. I didn't, however, pay the least attention to her, as if I didn't know where I had happened to sit down. I jabbered away, I jabbered a good two, three minutes more, and when I had finally finished, when I put the receiver down, and when God, seeing that I had occupied the first position for good, withdrew and grew silent, I looked around. And I saw not only that I was occupying the first position; I saw that slowly the first position was being occupied by . . . that toward the first position slowly glided the hand of The Most Beautiful Woman in the World.

V

EVERYTHING FELL INTO PLACE. MY FINGERS SKILLFULLY UNBUTtoned her blouse, and my fingers were pleasing to the buttons of her blouse. And her blouse was pleased that it was slipping from her shoulders, and her shoulders were pleased that slipping from them was her blouse. The clasp of her bra probably felt unsatisfied by the fact that my fingers were occupied with it so briefly, but my fingers were proud of themselves. Her jeans, which I grasped at the height of her hips, were pleased by the strength of my hands, and they were pleased by the fact that I compelled The Most Beautiful Woman in the World to stand for a moment. Her jeans knew that they look best on straightened legs, and they knew perfectly well that, if they were to slip from her hips, then it certainly wouldn't happen sitting down. And they slipped away like an ocean wave revealing the thighs of Aphrodite. And that was all. The Most Beautiful Woman in the World *as a general rule*—as she put it—*didn't wear panties, and not only during heat waves.*

You can't please everybody. We closed the Venetian blinds, which didn't please the light of day very much, for only its remnants passed through the slits, but the sweltering dusk eagerly embraced us. Not to cast aspersions, but The Most Beautiful Woman in the World was about to turn forty—and with this age, which is most correctly seen as the apogee of feminity, comes the unconscious reflex of turning down the lights. It was, however, a luminous July dusk, and it was, in spite of the Venetian blinds, sufficiently light that I could appreciate, not only by touch, the artistry of her depilation, the simplicity and modesty of the coiffure under her belly button—thin like a watch band; the full moon of the evenly tanned breasts; the sternum between them, unsymmetrically wide and bumpy; the back, endlessly perfect and—as is usual with backs—marked with endless sadness.

The sheet beneath us was intoxicated with our sweat. The light of day withdrew from between the Venetian blinds. Her skin was created for my hands. God had created her ribs and sides thinking about my arms. Her thighs were fantastic, but only once they were intertwined with mine did they form an absolute whole. We crooned a great love song in two-part harmony. We blurted out fiery filth in two whispers. The specters of my solitude left me once and for all. The superstition that you had to have intellectual communication with a woman fell to dust. I knew, I knew without a doubt that I had finally met someone ("someone," my God!), with whom I would spend the rest of my life, who would give me strength, who would watch over me, and over whom I would watch. I had finally met someone with whom I would live in a house eternally buried in snow, feed the dogs and cats, watch films on HBO in the evenings, and drink tea with raspberry juice. I knew this without a doubt, and I immediately decided to share my new knowledge with The Most Beautiful Woman in the World (by now also The Only Woman in the World): "I will spend the rest of my life with you," I whispered into her ear. "That's impossible," she replied with an unexpectedly strong voice. "Why?" I touched her wet hair with my lips. "Because I love my husband." I don't know whether she said this in a whisper or out loud. I don't remember. I *do* remember the catastrophic silence that set in over the bed sheet, over us, and over the whole deserted city. Somewhere you could hear the sound of a child crying on a balcony, the far-off siren of an ambulance, a radio playing in a window, the rumble of a train leaving Central Station, then a sudden and interrupted car alarm. "I love my husband," she repeated after some delay, or perhaps because of the sleepiness that slowly, after the amatory frenzy, had taken her in its grasp. "I love him. He just came back from Paris. That's why I could come to you. Because today was his day to walk the dog. That's how we arranged it."

VI

LIFE CONSISTS IN ESTABLISHING THE APPROPRIATE PROPORTION between work and relaxation. After three weeks of relaxation, and real relaxation at that, even—I would say—*extreme* relaxation, after three weeks of complete rest from the world, after three weeks of truancy and absence from the world, I came back and got down to work. I wrapped my Spanish rifle in black plastic, I put a box of

Diabolo Boxer sharp shot in my pocket, and an hour before the zero hour I set off in the obvious direction. The air rifle wrapped in black plastic looked, under my arm, like a curtain rod or some element of some piece of furniture. The dead expression on my face said nothing to anyone.

Across from the gate in which I had madly kissed the divine lips of The Most Beautiful Woman in the World—several times goodbye, and twice in greeting; across from this gate, on the other side of the street, rose the two-story building of an elementary school. It was already the end of August, and from all sides feverish repair work was underway. Even now plasterers were bustling about before the front wall. In the back, however, on the side of the school playground, there wasn't a soul. Emptiness and stillness, and heaping stacks of broken objects, up which I easily climbed onto the roof.

With a couple lightning fast bounds, worthy of the special forces, I reached the opposite edge and lay down on my belly in the classic position of the sharpshooter. I removed the air rifle from the plastic, loaded it, and waited. I had about thirty minutes to wait. The roof under me had heated up like a pond toward the end of summer. Three red Fiats drove by below. A Fiat Seicento, a Fiat Brava, and a Fiat Punto. Along the sidewalk went a woman with a yellow plastic shopping bag, a bald guy in black, two workers carried a mirror that was turned in my direction. I hid in fear that they would catch sight of the reflection of my head. After a moment I looked out again—now there went a redheaded girl in a jean-shirt, after her another, black-haired in a black T-shirt and red slacks, then a guy with a black plastic shopping bag, and just when it seemed that black was beginning to predominate, again there appeared three red Fiats. My head was spinning. I was on the roof of a two-story pavilion, but my fear of heights bordered on insanity. Three red Fiats drove around my skull. I turned over on my back and looked up at the sky. When was the last time I had lain on a heated surface, on warm grass or on hot sand, and looked at the sky? Into space that became, supposedly, ever colder and darker? Forty years ago? The sun was shining, clouds scudded by. I half-shut my eyes, and I guess I fell asleep, for when I again opened my eyes, the air was one degree darker, and The Most Beautiful Woman in the World—I knew it without looking—was already standing by the gate. I turned over on my belly. At least you, my intuition, hadn't let me down. There she was. In a white blouse, gray slacks, she stood in her full beauty and surrendered herself to thought. The dog, just like all living creatures, fawned at her feet. Calmly, I raised the weapon to my eye. I had one last minute, but a good full one. I knew quite well that The Most Beautiful Woman in the World would ponder for at least a minute whether to go left or go right. The dog sat motionless and frozen, as if in a canine presentiment of its final hour. I had him in my sights. From down below you could hear the even murmur of the engines of three red Fiats. In a moment the live round of Diabolo Boxer would pierce dog skin, dog muscles, and dog guts, and a terrible squeal would resound. I unlocked the safety, and I delicately touched the trigger, and I knew that I wouldn't pull it. Genuine life was insuperable and impenetrable. And I raised the oxidized barrel of my air rifle, beautiful as a dream, and I guided it carefully upward in the direction of an analogous beauty. I passed by the thighs, belly, heart, and when I was at the height of the neck, I took aim very precisely. I could shoot with a clean conscience and without any fear that blood would flow—I had before me Beauty, as perfect as geometry and as permeable as air.

My First
Suicide

THIS YEAR I AM CELEBRATING THE FORTIETH ANNIVERSARY OF MY
first suicide attempt. By my count, I have been attempting to kill
myself for exactly four hundred seventy-nine months, and, on account
of various bits of misfortune, I haven't been having any luck. I was
twelve years old when, for the first time, the black thoughts teeming
in me took shape, to the extent that I attempted to jump off the sixth
floor. It happened at night. My folks were sleeping in the other room,
and the main problem was not the jump itself, but getting out onto
the balcony so silently that they wouldn't wake up. Especially Mother,
since my old man always slept the unwaking sleep of the dead.

Mother slept incredibly lightly. Every slight vibration of air woke
her. I don't think she ever got used to the sounds of the city, even
though we lived on an unusually quiet street; in fact, in the period I
am talking about—in other words, during the sixties of the twentieth
century—it was downright dead. Compared with what we have now,
there wasn't any traffic to speak of. Especially in Krakow. Especially
on Syrokomla Street. Especially at night. Which was all the worse,

since it seemed to me that, in the absolute silence, you could even hear when I lifted my bed cover. The main acoustic obstacle to going out onto the balcony was the drapes, which were hanging from metal curtain rods. At the least touch, the tin hooks to which they were attached made a crunching noise, like the tracks of an accelerating tank.

The idea of killing myself always came at night. At two or three in the morning, someone would sit at the side of my couch and try to convince me. In the thickening air there were more and more insects. The indistinctly pronounced arguments were irrefutable. I knew that one of these times their amorphous but inexorable logic would shove me out onto the balcony, and then off the balcony. It excited me. I knew I could do it. I was suicidally gifted. I was crazy about jumping to the cement from the sixth floor. I had a talent for suicide. But you have to work on your talents. Reproofs of instruction are the way of life.

As King Solomon says: "Reproofs of instruction are the way of life!" As King Solomon says: "Reproofs of instruction are the way of life!" As King Solomon says: "Reproofs of instruction are the way of life!" My old man shouted these words of wisdom so many times a day, and with such solemn dignity, that finally, if he did not become King Solomon in the strict sense, he certainly traded places with him for a bit. Full of majesty and dread, the shadow of the biblical monarch would attack his accounts book, and the thunderous voice would roar upon the heights. Reproofs of instruction are the way of life! This time he didn't have to tell me twice. I was preparing myself intensely for the final match. Just like, if I may say so, a debutant preparing for the Olympics. Practically every day, when no one was at home, I doggedly practiced the silent opening of the drapes. And also the curtains, an otherwise easier matter. The hooks from which the curtains hung practically didn't grate at all. After numerous attempts, I had worked out the following technique: you had to place a chair at the balcony window, stand on it, reach out your hand, and, once you had grasped either the hook itself or the drape at the point closest to the hook, you carefully manipulated it and moved it aside, very slowly—this is how it could be done in absolute silence. I was rather tall, even as a teenager, and standing on a stool I could easily reach the ceiling. The drapes parted more quietly each time. Reproofs of instruction were the way of my suicide.

I regret that first attempt to this day. There was no point in wasting time training for the silent opening of the drapes. I should just have gone out, simply, normally—since they were open during the day, and since my folks weren't at home—onto the balcony and jumped. There was always plenty of free time between when I came home from school and when Mother returned from work. Even on Thursdays, when I had seven classes, there was always at least an hour. I was a contemplative child, and from my early days I knew that I wouldn't be able to do it in a sudden, lightning-fast impulse, that I would not be able to leap over the balustrade in one bound before someone managed to hold me back. Sure, I wanted to kill myself, and to do it with dispatch, but I also wanted to be present for the act.

I knew from the teachings of Pastor Kalinowski what the other world would be like. But I hadn't the faintest clue what the passage, what the *passage itself* from this world to that, might look like. When I asked Pastor Kalinowski about the path (and also about the time and speed) from earth to heaven, or to hell, he lied his way out with theological hermeticisms. I knew that I wouldn't get clear and simple answers, but there must have been minor approximations, or some sort of (even the most distant) analogies.

Is it indiscernible, like the moment of falling asleep? Incomprehensible, like the flight of Sputnik? Breathtaking, like downhill skiing? Painful, like an inner-ear infection? Could it be *that* painful? Impossible. I had a high pain threshold. Practically nothing ever hurt. Nothing ever—with the exception of my inner ear. When I was five or six years old, my (inner) ear hurt so horribly that, after that time, at least for a year, because of the trauma and fear of it, I never even uttered the word "ear." Even today, I remember Doctor Granada muttering over my head "inner ear, inner ear." Even today, whenever I hear "inner ear," I experience phantom pains, and even today I doubt that anything—even suicide—could cause more pain. Was that what I wanted to test back then? Was it because I had withstood every sort of pain, and I wanted to try out the pain of falling from the sixth floor? Very likely. At that time, I didn't yet know Kirillov's famous dictum about the pain that deters people from suicide. I read *Demons* for the first time in the *lyceum*, in other words at least three or four years after my first suicide. I was then, and I still am now, a great admirer of that book, but it had no influence whatsoever upon my various subsequent suicide attempts. Dostoevsky's hero, and perhaps all literary heros in general, make a great fuss over their suicides—I don't fuss. I just want to have peace and quiet.

Whatever the case, I wanted to examine everything precisely and calmly. Slowly. Very slowly. I'm phlegmatic by nature. Whatever I do, I do precisely, but slowly. I was one of the best competitors in playground pickup matches and on school teams, and at the same time one of the slowest. You can charge me with what you like, just not quickness. Even on the sports field. And so, as befitted a phlegmatic, I prepared myself phlegmatically for a phlegmatic suicide. I wanted to know at every minute, and even at every second, that I was just then in the process of killing myself.

The simplest move—going to sleep with the drapes opened—was out of the question. Mother guarded the opening of the drapes in the morning, and their closing in the evening, with Lutheran ferocity. In our parts, houses in which the drapes were closed during the day were the houses of the dead. And the houses in which the drapes were not closed at night were the houses of demons. At the break of dawn, in winter at six at the latest, five at the latest in summer, Grandma Pech would open the drapes, lest anyone should glance at our windows and get the idea that someone had died in the Pech household; or, what is worse, that the Pechs were still sleeping.

"Get up! Wake up! Don't bring on a funeral!" She would burst into the back room, in which Uncle Ableger still couldn't quite wake up after the previous night's excesses. She would shake him by the shoulder and tear the yellow drapes from the window and, with lightning-fast movements, fold them into perfect squares and place them on the windowsill. "Get up! Don't lie about! Don't tempt death!" Uncle would open his puffy eyes, glance in distress at the wall clock that was left over from the Germans, and stiffen in horror—it was already well after seven. He would jump out of bed and begin to look for his clothes in a panic. He, too, knew the sacred principle that windows that were left covered a bit longer, even if only until eight, augured death for the members of the household. And for the citizens of Wisła who were on their way to work, they signified death. One way or the other, you had to close and open the drapes at the appointed times, and with full orthodoxy.

Mother repeated that custom in Krakow, in a somewhat gentler version—in winter at seven at the latest, and in summer at six. This version was gentler as far as the times were concerned, but in its spirit it was infinitely more the deed of a hero, even that of a martyr. Everywhere around us, in the neighboring apartment blocks and townhouses on Ujejski, Włóczków, Smoleńsk Streets—everywhere, literally everywhere—there lived nothing but Catholics, who didn't pay the least attention to covered or uncovered windows. During the first mornings I spent in Krakow, I was certain that plague ruled the city. Every day at least half the windows remained covered all the time—a sure sign that the number of victims was growing.

In our parts, a different light surrounded the house in which someone had died. You could see the covered windows all the more distinctly—even at dusk, even late in the evening, even at a distance. The members of the household who remained among the living would hasten to Pastor Kalinowski, the death notice would be posted at the parish house, and news of the death would pass through the valleys at lightning speed. The deceased would lie in the darkened chamber on a door that had been removed from its hinges and placed on stools. The soul-snatchers from Cieszyn would arrive late with the coffin. In the winter it wasn't so bad. All you had to do was crack the covered window and make sure that no cat or weasel jumped in. In the summer you had to bring flowers, right away and all the time—as many as you could, whole buckets of them if possible. To this day I don't like flowers, nor do I keep them at home. To this day, when I smell peonies, lilies of the valley, phlox, dahlias, I catch the scent of deceased Lutherans.

Whoever, in turn, late in the evening or, God forbid, at night, neglected covering the windows and turning out the lights, did wrong, sinned, exposed himself—and, most certainly, succumbed—to Satan's temptation. He was reveling, drinking, God knows what he was doing that was even worse. Nothing good, in any event. Working at night? There was no such excuse. He who works at night does wrong, since during the day he is unable to do what is needed. Work done at night was bad work by virtue of its nocturnal, which is to say demonic, nature. When the news got around that Szłapka, the cobbler—even though he was an outstanding cobbler and sewed fancy footwear to measure as late as the fifties—had the lights burning in his workshop late at night, that it was then he cut leather for soles, he began to lose orders, and in no time he was bankrupt. Explanations that he suffered from insomnia, and that he was incapable of lying idly in bed, were of no use. Granted, illness gave one the right to keep the lights burning at night, but it had to be a serious illness—flu, or pneumonia, or an attack of asthma; then, OK, then you could turn on the lights, but even *then* not all night—just for a moment, in order to give medicine to the patient, or tea, and then lights out! But Szłapka had the lights on all the time. What is more, you could see with the naked eye that there was nothing the matter with him. What sort of sickness is *that*—insomnia? What sort of sickness is *that*, when an allegedly sick man goes to his workshop and sets to work? No, Szłapka wasn't sick;

he was in the grasp of demons; it was the demons who didn't allow him to sleep and drove him to nocturnal work. Who would want to wear shoes like that? Who would want to put on and take off shoes that had been sewn at night, at the instigation of demons? Nobody.

"In darkness Satan lays his snares; his are nocturnal lairs. / Into the light before him flee; there he'll let you be." This couplet of Angelus Silesius—I knew it in Mickiewicz's translation (about which, of course, I had no idea at the time)—was a favorite of Pastor Kalinowski, and we heard it remarkably often from the pulpit in our church. Night was Satan's time, and you had to cover the windows, turn out the lights, and go to sleep. To this day, when I set off for my parts—and often I arrive on a late train, and then I sit for a long time at night in an empty, ice-cold house—to this day, in the morning, our neighbor, Mrs. Szarzec, asks me: "So why, Mr. Piotr, were the lights burning so late in your house?" And I humble myself and make explanations, and, tormented by Lutheran phantoms, I suffer pangs of conscience, and I make constant excuses.

If only I could find a way to free myself from the gruelling ritual of opening and closing the curtains, I could manage it. But at that time I wasn't aware that the green velvet shades were like the curtain in the sanctuary—they separate the holy from the most holy, and they part only once. You just had to do it. When the conditions were right, you just had to go out onto the balcony and jump. In the end, what difference did it make that I really didn't much feel like it during the day? What I needed to do was sink my head more boldly during the day, too, into that insect cloud and force my swarming thoughts to more intense swarming. Nowadays, a person knows how to do it. On the other hand, it's just as well, because I didn't yet know the suicide handbooks (at that time they hadn't been published—or even, I suppose, written; and even today, to tell the truth, I know of them only through hearsay), and I didn't know that it was only a jump from at least the ninth floor that comes with a guarantee.

Supposedly, it is only the ninth floor that provides absolute certainty. The eighth floor, according to the experts, is not a hundred-percent sure bet. And we lived on the sixth, and, to make matters worse, this was new (Gomułka-era) construction. In addition to the fact that it could be too low, I could have been too light: I was tall but frightfully skinny, and the energy of the fall—energy, as we all know, is mass (in this case 117 pounds) times its speed (in this case, on account of the insufficient height, of little momentum)—could have been too little. I might perish not entirely, but only partially. The cars standing beneath the apartment block—should I fall on one of them—could cushion the fall, and so forth, and so on. What's the point of constant speculation if a person is going to go on living?

One way or another, the night of the first attempt had arrived. The day preceding it had been rather good. I had succeeded in not saying a single word to anyone for fourteen hours. When a day of complete silence occurs, when a person, let's say, doesn't open his yap to anyone from morning to night, doesn't encounter anyone, when he takes pains not to exchange a word with any salesperson or mailman, doesn't answer the telephone (calling anyone is out of the question), and doesn't drown out this state of affairs by flipping on some radio or television set, then it starts to get interesting toward evening. The air that surrounds your head becomes thicker and thicker—it becomes an insect cloud. The insect cloud stiffens like glass. The insect glass (though it would be better to say: the glass of insects) becomes stiffer and stiffer and more and more opaque, as if an icy breath had settled on it. The dead silence becomes more and more deafening; you hear your own entrails more and more loudly—the blood flowing through the heart, the gasses gathering in the belly, the urine filtered by the kidneys. When I add to this the astonishment that I am eternally chained to my own body, that I will gaze for all time and at everything from the depths of my own skull, that everything I see, hear, and smell sinks somewhere in the brutish lump that has my legs and arms—then it is time to go out onto the balcony. It's that way with me even today. Basically, I don't know what gives me the bigger thrill—the thought that I am finally going to kill myself, or the absolute and breathtaking void of many hours after which one *can* kill oneself.

I had succeeded in not saying a single word to anyone because we were in the grip of a severe cold spell. For several days, I had been going to and coming from school through air that was stiffening with icy explosions. Minus-four-degree labyrinths were becoming ever longer, ever more intricate and stuffy. That day, when, having passed through the Square at the Ponds, Filarecka Street, the Commons, I finally made it to the North Pole, a document with seals affixed to it was hanging on the closed doors stating that, on account of atmospheric conditions that threaten to disturb the learning process, classes—by decision of the board of education—were cancelled. I remember that this didn't particularly please me, or upset me. In general, school was a matter of indifference to me. Mrs. Prosciutko, the handcrafts teacher, a heavily made up thirty-year-old, got me a little hot, but that was it. I had neither any particular troubles, nor any particular satisfactions. Now the only good thing was that I had been one of the first to read the flowery document announcing the sudden holiday. I always got to school very early. Nobody at all was there yet from my class. I didn't have to pretend to participate in the cattle herd's joy that *school's out!*

I set off for home as quickly as possible. The labyrinths had gotten so thick by now that it seemed to me that I was climbing, as in a dream, higher and higher. Down below I saw the city submerged in a yellow crystal—black roofs, pigeons turned into ice, the dead and empty canals of the alleyways. My celestial roaming went on for a bit, but finally I dragged myself home. In the stairwell, with my heart in my throat, I passed by a famous local beggar. He had supposedly once been a commander in the White Army. And indeed, as he glided through the streets of Krakow, he had in him the majesty of a scorched and wasted galleon, which nonetheless still maintained its daring profile. At his sight, I usually took to my heels; now I heroically stepped over the crutches lying crosswise, blackened and covered with fossilized hoar-frost. He mumbled something, but in my hurry and panic I didn't understand precisely what. Today I think that he said, *The moonlit grass has overgrown the Bay of St. Susanna. You must prepare for the coming of the Lord of Surges.* In any event, such are the sentences I hear when I recreate that day, pitilessly, minute by minute. The moonlit grass has overgrown the Bay of St. Susanna. You must prepare for the coming of the Lord of Surges. I opened the door with numb hands, and, frozen to death, slowly and systematically thawed myself out, so that in the evening I might be able to go out onto the balcony—efficiently and silently. I warmed my hands up particularly carefully; after all, I wouldn't be able to manage it with stiff fingers. That was all—hot water and finger gymnastics—nothing more. I no longer practiced the silent opening of the drapes. As a future first-league soccer player and a representative of Poland, I knew the principle that in the final hours before the match you were not allowed to devote your time to practice, but only and exclusively to relaxation.

First, I read *The Mysterious Island*, probably for the hundredth time. Then I took some condoms from Father's drawer, one of which I blew up, and I played a little soccer. The goal was between the dresser and the door to the little room; I made most of the goals with headers—I was Brazil, and I had won the World Cup. Then I made myself *kogel-mogel*. I couldn't find powdered sugar, so I beat two egg yolks with regular sugar, sprinkled in some cocoa—it wasn't bad. Then I wanted to play shove halfpenny on the windowsill, but I didn't have time, because Mother had returned, and you couldn't play shove halfpenny in her presence, because she thought it was a game of chance played for money, and—deaf to all persuasion—she positively forbade it. For obvious reasons I gave it up right away. I didn't want to get into sterile debates. I didn't want to talk at all.

Mother declared, in the doorway already, that my old man would most likely return late, since she was more dead than alive and full of premonitions. Moreover, she had had terrible dreams the night before, and her dreams and premonitions always came true. My prospects were looking up. Since Mother was more dead than alive

Jerzy Pilch

and full of bad dreams and premonitions, she ceased speaking after a certain time. All indications were for a stiflingly quiet afternoon. Incidentally, even when her dreams and premonitions did not come true, she maintained that *they had come true in a certain sense*, that, at the worst, *they would come true sooner or later.* And besides, with time, the quantity and frequency of her bad dreams and premonitions grew; therefore, naturally, their accuracy also grew. If a person has evil premonitions on a daily basis, he experiences nothing but the expected evil.

In any event, on the day of my first suicide attempt, my old man didn't come home for a long time indeed, and there is no need to add that if he wasn't there, he didn't speak up. The insect glass (although one should say: the glass of insects) grew thicker. My kidneys began to hum a mournful little song. With a feeling of acute absurdity (I didn't know at the time that I *had* a feeling of acute absurdity), I did my homework. I was aware that I was doing the last homework assignments of my life, and I took pains—as if I were sending them off on a final journey—that they be perfect. I did them with unusual care. Later I felt sorry for the calligraphic Polish essay, sorry for the perfectly solved mathematical problem, sorry for the lined notebook, and sorry for the quadrille notebook. I imagined that neither my homework nor my notebooks would find their way to school ever again. By morning, I would be dead, and my book bag would be lying next to the bookshelf, and nobody would look into it. Unless it was the police (at that time called the *militia*), in order to check whether I had left a farewell letter, or whether, in one of the notebooks, there were notes of some sort explaining my desperate step.

I felt like crying, but my mood lifted at the thought that, in the morning, when my corpse would be lying at the bottom of the apartment block, our apartment would be swarming with uniformed functionaries. I knew that my old man would fear them like the devil. Not that he would have anything on his conscience, but just on account of his basic fearfulness. My old man went to pieces before every person of higher rank. He cracked before his bosses, the professors and directors of departments at the Academy; he cracked before officials in offices; he was even afraid of the custodian of our apartment block, Mr. Markiewicz, who was eternally tipsy and eternally cursed women and Communism. In a word, my old man was afraid of practically everyone, but in the face of all those who wore uniforms (including conductors on trains or trams—in those days there were still conductors on trams), he suffered from blind animal fear.

To tell the truth, my old man—short, born in Cieszyn Silesia, a Lutheran, not very bright, but industrious as an ant; who had been drafted into the Wehrmacht during the war, and after the war became a Party member—had his reasons for having numerous complexes. I do not wish to suggest that he despaired in vain, and for all his life, that he was not born in Wilno, a tall non-Party Catholic, full of panache, of broad talents, who had served with Anders during the war, and embarked upon internal emigration after the war. I don't wish to suggest this, but the poor devil unquestionably paid a price for being who he was.

Once, I recall, I was riding with him in our Fiat 125, and a militiaman from the traffic patrol pulled us over on account of one or another of the most banal violations in the world—failure to use a turn signal, or something like that. Jesus Christ! What a scene that was! My old man! God the Father! The Patriarch! King Solomon! David and Goliath in one person! Jesus—now that I think of it— Christ!—shook with fear, was close to messing his pants, and tearfully explained himself to the twenty-year-old sergeant, who himself was embarrassed by the inhuman horror he had aroused in this—as his identity card made clear—engineer from the Academy of Mining and Metallurgy, who was more than twice his age.

And what would it be like tomorrow morning! Not just one youngster from the traffic patrol, but a few higher officers from the criminal division would put the old man through the paces! And it would not be on account of neglecting to use the turn signal that they would put the screws to him, but on account of the corpse of a child! As God is my witness, it was a pity to kill yourself and not be around to watch the old man die of fear! But then again, to put this all in play, you had to kill yourself. One paradox, you might say, after another.

After my suicide—my mood was getting better and better—my old man would have the biggest mess of it. Everybody would blame him. Mother would accuse him to the end of his days of tormenting me with biblical sayings, of forcing me to learn German and gymnastics, of barking at me, of tyrannizing me with the copying of notebooks, and of placing bans on watching television.

Grandpa and Grandma would tell everyone to the end of their lives that it was all on account of him, that he was responsible, because he had insisted on moving to Krakow. Because he had forced, that's right, *forced* Mother and me to abandon our Lutheran parts and move to Babylon! That's right, Babylon! Krakow is Babylon! It's even worse, because, in the biblical Babylon, they didn't use gas to heat the stoves and the baths, but in Krakow they do! In Krakow, at any moment everything might be blown sky high! They had warned, and they had cautioned! A thousand times they warned and cautioned! And the other dangers? Did they not caution against them? Did they not warn about the numerous cars, under which I could fall at any moment? About the bandits and murderers who could attack me at any moment? About the Catholics, who at any moment could plant confusion in my head? They cautioned and warned about a thousand—what thousand? a million!—yes, about a *million* other dangers that threatened me, the very potential presence of which my mind had most clearly been incapable of withstanding. Not bad. After my death, the world will not look bad at all.

As was always the case when my old man was late, Mother cranked up various domestic chores to full blast: she baked, she put wash into the washing machine, she got out the vacuum cleaner. The point was so that the old man, when he finally did come home, would find her in full domestic fervor and have even greater feelings of guilt over the fact that he was late, and drunk, and that there was so much to be done at home, and it was all on her shoulders. The complete innovation, the original embellishment, the genuine pearl of my suicide, was the thought that, this time, Mother would also be harshly punished for preying on my old man's sense of guilt. After all, when I kill myself she, too, will have a terrible sense of guilt. All the more terrible in that it would begin with the simplest question in the world: How could she not have woken up? How could she not have woken up when I got up from the sofa bed at night? How could she not have woken up when I pulled back the drapes? How could she not have woken up when I went out onto the balcony in nothing but my pajamas? In nothing—during such a cold spell—but my pajamas! I am not saying that Mother, like the figure of a mother taken from a derisive autobiography, would have been significantly more horrified by my possibly taking cold than by the suicide I had committed. No. I am describing the situation in her categories. And in her categories, my going out onto the balcony in pajamas was the height of everything: recklessness, stupidity, crime, and nonsense. My jump from the balcony was beyond her categories, and even beyond her language.

I knew that she probably would not try to discover—because she would be incapable of doing it—why I had killed myself; but she would try, to her last breath, to discover why she hadn't woken up. And that the question why she hadn't woken up would be repeated many times, and answered in a thousand ways, so that the question why I had committed suicide could be pushed aside, and the answer to it hidden from sight. It was also certain that the odium would again fall upon my old man, for after all, if he had returned earlier, then he would have helped her out a little, and she would not have been so tired, and she would not have gone to sleep on her last legs, and she would not have slept the sleep of the dead, so exhausted and unconscious that she didn't hear a thing.

When my old man, devastated and up to his neck in guilt, had roused a little and begun to come around, he would surely begin to console her with the prospect of another child. Maybe not from the first moment, maybe not on the day of my death, nor on the day of my funeral, but sooner or later—yes, he would do it. You didn't have to be a prophet, or even a writer possessed of the ability to compose in someone else's voice, to be able to hear that it is difficult, a terrible tragedy, that they would have to bear its burden all their lives, but that it cannot put a veil on life, for life goes on, and, after all, both are still young and strong, and they could still, and probably they even ought to, try to have a child . . .

On the merits, and given their ages, it was possible. When I was born, Mother was twenty years old, and when I decided to kill myself the first time—it is easy to calculate—she had barely turned thirty. Thus, if I had succeeded that time in committing suicide, and if they had decided to have a new baby soon thereafter, there would not have been any contraindications.

And yet, for Mother, driving my old man to guilt was a narcotic without which she did not know how to live. Her instinct to harass the poor wretch—who, as it was, lived with a constant feeling of guilt—was stronger than all her other instincts. In this, she had the diabolical gift of making exceptionally surprising and venomous retorts. I was certain that she would hear out the old man's procreational arguments—in silence, and even with feigned goodwill—and then, with studied calm, making numerous and excessive pauses, she would say that this is all fine and good, but she is very curious about one thing, she is very curious, namely, whether, when they get a baby, she is exceedingly curious whether, when that baby grows up a bit, when it reaches the twelfth, or perhaps even the tenth year of its life, well, she is exceedingly curious whether Father would again drive it to commit suicide? Whether once again—by his habit of returning home late—he would kill it? She is very curious. Very.

It was getting later and later. Mother bustled about the kitchen more and more zealously. The old man still wasn't home, and now it wasn't about his feeling of guilt, in any event, not *only* about his feeling guilty.

Now it was already so late that all of life slipped through one's hands and scattered to the winds. And Mother cooked, and she fried, and she baked everything that formed the rock upon which our house was built: mushroom soup with homemade noodles, breaded veal cutlets, Christmas Eve cabbage, potato pancakes, apple dumplings, vanilla pudding, crêpes with cheese. A house erected on a rock is lasting, but a house erected on a rock composed of Mother's dishes will outlast everything. The crêpes were indeed timeless. Not even my imminent suicide was able to diminish their quality. I think I ate about eight of them. Then I didn't wash—with absolute impunity—didn't undress, didn't go to bed. Running amuck in my freedom, I sat in the armchair and stared at the television. I could do whatever my heart desired. I could play shove halfpenny on the windowsill, I could take out the copy of *The Biology of Love*, which was hidden at the bottom of the cupboard, I could stare through binoculars at the neighboring apartment block. On television, a film for adults called *The Small World of Sammy Lee* was starting, and I had a good chance of seeing something forbidden before I died. Mother was in the kitchen getting ready to bake a three-layer cheesecake with icing, and she was pretending that she didn't notice my debauchery. Everything, it goes without saying, within the framework of that same vengeful strategy. Everything so that she would be able to rebuke the old man, once he had returned, for leaving me prey to forbidden obscenities on television, when she doesn't have the strength, she truly doesn't have the strength, to look after everything, absolutely everything.

Unfortunately, in those days there were very few forbidden obscenities on television, and in fact, on the evening preceding my first suicide, I had incredible fortune. Fortune, one could say, in misfortune, since, when the scene in *The Small World of Sammy Lee* began, in which the owner of the bar ordered the newly hired stripper to do a trial run, the doorbell rang in the hallway, the door opened, and there—stiff from the cold, and the vodka—staggered in Father.

•

Mother and Father stood facing each other for a long time in total silence. Then the old man, rocking and giving off steaming clouds of hoarfrost and rectified spirits, managed to stammer out that, at the Academy of Mining and Metallurgy, they had held a ping-pong tournament, and that he had once again won. At that point Mother waited a good minute more. Then she grabbed the pot of mushroom soup with homemade noodles, which was standing on the table and had already cooled off somewhat, and she poured it all over my old man. Father reeled, but he didn't fall down. He began, at first with uncoordinated motions, then more and more precisely, to remove handfuls of the homemade noodles with which he was plastered and to fling them at Mother, but she was already in the depths of the kitchen, beyond the reach of his feckless blows. She stood at the huge skillet full of breaded veal cutlets and aimed at his head in a great rage, and she hit her mark almost every time. The old man, like a wounded bear, trundled along in her direction. On the way, his splayed fingers happened upon a pot of something that, once he had emptied it, turned out to be Christmas Eve cabbage, and now Mother was like a sea monster overgrown with greenish scales. Time and again she reached for the potato pancakes piled up next to the now empty cutlet skillet, and she furiously placed them, one layer after another, on Father's head. Then she poured portions of half-set pudding on him. He broke off a piece of apple dumpling and took aim at her, but before he threw it he fell into a reverie and instinctively, as if he wished to check how it tasted, bit off a little piece. Mother ruthlessly exploited this moment of inattention and attacked him with her whole body. The old man began to retreat. She dexterously opened the refrigerator and extracted a bunch of frankfurters, obtained by God knows what sort of miracle, and began to flog Father with them like a mad woman. He, in turn, raving with pain, blindly felt around for the jars of compote standing on the shelves in the hallway, grabbed one of them (it turned out to be greengage plums), and with an automatic motion, practiced during a thousand Sunday dinners, pulled the rubber seal, opened it, and poured it on her, as if in the hope that this would sober her up. But no, she went on flogging him. He shook the empty jar like a tambourine, or perhaps like the flag of defeat.

In a more and more powerful and spasmodic clench, like a couple of avant-garde performers, or wrestlers of equal strength, they sailed through the hallway and rolled into the bedroom. The door, as if touched by an invisible force, closed behind them. For a moment you could still hear the lashing of frankfurters, then silence set in, then the lights went out.

The scene of the auditioning stripper had passed irrevocably. There wasn't any point in comforting myself with the thought that, when I grew up, in addition to being a famous soccer player, I would also be the manager of a strip joint. I had to accept the more tragic truth: namely, that I would die without seeing a naked woman. That not even on the screen of a Nefryt television set would it be given unto me to verify whether there was even a grain of sense in Pastor Kalinowski's exceptionally enchanting biblical metaphor of the *roe-deer twins that feedeth amongst the lilies.*[*]

I did my best to bypass the warpath marked out by the shreds of frankfurters, pancakes, cutlets, and other minerals that formed the rock of our house. Once, twice, maybe three times, I made the leap back and forth, but I wasn't drawn by this new Olympic discipline. There wasn't any call for it, but in the face of the final prospect I made my way to the bathroom. I didn't have a particularly keen awareness that I was washing a body that, in a few hours, would become the body of a corpse, but it could be that I was genetically burdened with that sort of awareness.

For ages, Grandma Pech had been a well known Wisła virtuoso in the art of washing and dressing corpses. Tens, or perhaps hundreds, of the deceased passed through her hands in the strict sense of the phrase. In the next to last year of the First World War—when her

---

*There isn't.

mother and three of her brothers died from the Spanish flu almost simultaneously—my eleven-year-old Grandma was initiated into the arcana of the lightning-fast washing and dressing of corpses before they could grow stiff. For years and decades thereafter people sent for her from households with suddenly closed drapes. She never refused, she was always ready. She would get up in the middle of the night, put on the gray-black dress that was like her service uniform, pack a kitchen apron, a supply of flannel, cotton wool, and a bottle of rectified spirits into an oilcloth bag, and, either on foot or with the horses sent for her, she would hasten to the house surrounded by a different light, and she would wash and comb the bodies as they were losing softness, and wipe the faces with spirits. She would plait the tresses of the deceased women, and hundreds of times she would hear and see the signs left by the departing souls.

The atavistic nature of the thing forced me to repeat her motions. I glided the sponge over my shoulders with the same solicitude with which she touched the deceased Lutherans with cotton wool soaked in spirits. I was finally ready. I opened the sofa, made my bed, lay down. I kept constant vigil. I didn't fall asleep. Time passed slowly, but it passed, and after at least two, and perhaps three penultimate hours, the final hour rang. I got up cautiously, brought the chair over, got on it, and began to move hook after hook to perfection. After moving the seventh, when in the first drape I had only four hooks left to the end, the light went on in my folks' room. The door there opened abruptly, Father flashed through the hallway like a shot, then he fell into the bathroom like an exploding artillery shell, and immediately there resounded from that direction the sonorous rumble of bestial hurling.

I jumped down off the chair, put it back in its place, and returned to bed. I heard Mother's delicate steps. She came into my room; she smelled of raw meat; from under half-shut eyes I saw that smile of hers, bizarre and not of this world. A streak of food, rubbed to a tawny mucous, cut across her cheek. She went up to the window in absolute somnambulistic absence and mechanically closed the drapes.

Only now do I understand that the history of my first suicide is also a story about how alcohol, for the first time in my life, deprived me of my freedom. I mean, of course, the alcohol that was making its presence known in my old man's entrails. The poor guy puked almost to the break of dawn. He had a weak head.

All the Stories

I

In the environs of the little Austro-Hungarian town in which we performed our Socialist Student Workers' Traineeship there prowled a Silesian vampire, and from the very beginning the girls from the local Dressmakers' Technical College looked upon us with fear. They would turn tail, pick up the pace, respond badly to even the most sophisticated attempts at striking up a conversation. And we really knew how to strike up a conversation—not all of us, of course; not all of our five-man brigade knew how to strike up a conversation—but Wittenberg and I had an innate expertise. We strove for the maximal effect, elaborated on the plenitude of possibilities, turned cartwheels to construct tempting persuasions—all for nothing. The splendidly dressed misses from the clothiers' school wouldn't even pretend that they were making a date, that they would come for coffee, that they would say yes to an invitation to the dance. Not even as a form of good riddance would they say that they would see, they would make an effort, they would give it a try, and if they could find a moment, they would drop by.

Every day, after knocking off work, we would go to the local dive called *Europa* and one of seven indistinguishable local alcoholics would tell us the next in the series of stories about the vampire; we would each drink two beers and then go over to the Technical College building, which was beautifully situated in the depths of a park that had run wild. These expeditions were conducted in vain. Almost all the windows were closed, in spite of the September heat wave; the massive crowns of the oaks, and the equally massive clouds were reflected in the panes—and not a living soul.

Out back, on the playing field, there was no one; in the residential wing—no one; in the quite visible corridors—no one. Not a trace of a figure running by, not a shadow of shoulders, hair, feet. No billowing frock, cast off scarf, brooch, bracelet, ribbon. There was the barely perceptible scent of perfume—but even this might have been a pious wish. No song, no laughter, no giggles. Once, it seemed to us that we heard the murmur of a hair dryer; but this could just as well have been the distant drone of a biplane flying south. Other than that, neither hide nor hair. A complete void, wilderness, and, what follows from this, the complete absence of civilized customs.

It goes without saying, Poland at that time—*anno Domini* 1971—was under the Muscovite yoke, but regardless of the yoke, and regardless of the political system, it is accepted in all of human civilization that when, outside a woman's boarding house, school, dormitory, workers' hotel, convent, or even, for that matter, prison, there stands a group of starving men, and even if they are not granted entrance, they will at least receive an answer. Sooner or later, a window is cracked, and at first in the cracked window, and later in the wide open window, the boldest of the inhabitants (usually the chorus leader of middling looks) appears, and the exciting dialogue—although usually full of every sort of idiocy—begins.

"Are the gentlemen seeking something? Have they perhaps lost something?"

"We haven't lost anything, but we *are* seeking."

"If you haven't lost anything, you can't be seeking it."

"We are seeking in order to find it."

"I wonder what that could be? What do you wish to find?"

"We can't say it out loud."

"If you can't say it out loud, you can't say it at all."

"If you can't say it quietly, you don't say it out loud."

"Too bad. Either out loud, or not at all."

"OK. In that case, we'll say what we are seeking."

"But we no longer care about that. We are no longer interested in what you are seeking. Seek and ye shall find. Farewell."

"Knock, and it shall be opened unto you."

"Well my, my! Which of you is so pious?"

"We are *all* pious."

"Girls! We have a group of pilgrims under our windows!"

"Don't ridicule our faith, sister. We have among us one who has felt the calling and intends to enter the seminary."

"Girls! We have pilgrims under our windows! With a future clergy-man!"

"Sisters! Receive the weary wayfarers under your roof!"

"We can't today, because we already have a group of pilgrims spending the night with us. But give it a try again tomorrow. Knock, and it shall be opened unto you. But not on the first try." Etc., etc.

Wittenberg and I were experts at such dialogues. We had tens, and perhaps hundreds of balcony scenes under our belts. We had spent tens, and perhaps hundreds of hours under the walls of castles conducting unending conversations with imprisoned virgins. We knew how to put on performances like these and how to play them out. With the virtuosity of old actors, making skillful pauses for applause, we foresaw at what moment more and more numerous giggles would begin to emerge from within, gradually turning into generalized laughter; and after which line *beautiful little girls' heads* would begin to appear in the windows—at first bashfully, but then more and more boldly and *en masse*. It was always obvious, more or less, when other voices would join the voice of the leader of the chorus, and when we could begin to establish eye contact with the chosen beauties who would relentlessly stand in the windows. (The rule is this: you must establish eye contact with those who disappear every little bit and return after a moment; it is common knowledge that they disappear to put their hair in order, remove their glasses, throw a flattering shawl over their shoulders. This is the group from which the final recruitment will be made.) Even then we had all this knowledge at our fingertips, and every day, with dull stubbornness—like a person doggedly turning a broken television set on and off in the hope that it will repair itself—we would traipse over to the deserted Dressmakers' Technical School, expecting that finally a window would be cracked, the saucy leader would appear, and the ritual spectacle would begin. And yet, day after day, nothing, nothing, nothing. It seemed that the Silesian vampire had indeed murdered all the girl students, or as if, in a total panic, they had all fled into the depths of the forest, into which the park was gradually being transformed.

II

PERSONALLY, I DIDN'T MAKE A TRAGEDY OF THE THING, NOR DID I even complain very much. I was madly in love. To be sure, I traipsed over to the Technical School with full conviction, and—with deep faith—I looked for a miracle. When some young lady would make an appearance in the Austro-Hungarian lanes—thereby irrefutably proving that they nonetheless are, that they live, that they exist—or rather a couple young ladies from the clothiers' school (they always went to town in groups of no less than two), with eager enthusiasm, by myself or with our entire five-person brigade, I would set off following her, and I would attempt to strike up a conversation—masterfully, although fruitlessly. I reacted intensely to the strong bodies of the four female bricklayer's assistants who worked with us, hidden

Jerzy Pilch

though they were under overalls stiffened from lime. Thousands of temptations and licentious scenes swarmed in my head. The most important, however, was Gocha.

Our love had erupted in the second year of the *lyceum*, lasted through the third and fourth, and now, after the *matura* and the entrance exams (Gocha had passed the exam for the school of dentistry), it not only lasted and lasted, but it exploded more and more forcefully, with a volcanic force unknown in our latitudes. Gocha. Gocha of Gochas. Gocha like the *Lausanne Lyrics*! Gocha like a *flowering poem*! Gocha like the *Duino Elegies*! Gocha like *The Shadowy Drink*! Almost every day I wrote letters full of quotations, plagiarisms, and every sort of amatory graphomania, and every weekend I rode up into the mountains to see her. Those trips, like everything in life, required me to deceive my folks.

III

Anno Domini 1971 was the nineteenth year of my life, and, in that year, telling my forty-year-old Mother and my forty-five-year-old Father that I went to see a girl on Saturdays and Sundays was out of the question. Even worse, I had to head off an attack on their part. For a few months by that time, my folks had been in possession of the first and—as it would later turn out—only car of their lives, and there was a permanent threat that they would drop by and make an unexpected visit. My old man was the worst driver in the world, but his pathological pride wouldn't allow him to turn the driving over to Mother, to say nothing of me. By taking thousands of additional lessons, by paying thousands of złotys extra, and by practicing changing gears for hours at a time with dry runs, he passed the driving exam with the greatest difficulty. He hated driving, and he hated the car—a Fiat 125 purchased, with difficulty, using money borrowed from Pastor Kalinowski—and, it goes without saying, he drove with heroic perserverence. Reproofs of instruction are the way of life. Every trip was an inhuman torture and humiliation. In addition, every trip had to have some definite and edifying geographical goal. The possibility that one might drive a car solely for the purpose of improving their driving technique, and without a destinational, geographical, or, best of all, geo-historical reason, didn't come into consideration. A Lutheran—even if he is driving solely for the purpose of perfecting his driving technique—must drive *somewhere*. And not just *somewhere*, but to some fundamental, or at any rate useful, place. To drive who knows where, to take who knows what turn—this is impossible. There is no such thing as a sudden hankering for a left or a right turn. Sudden, and unfounded hankerings are beyond the Lutheran anatomy.

Before every training excursion, my old man pored over the road map of the Krakow environs, and he scrupulously laid out the route so that it would contain as many cognitively useful monuments as possible—ruins, churches, castles, or, at worst, factories, bridges, or tributaries of rivers. A drive to the little Austro-Hungarian town in which we were performing our Workers' Traineeship was a dream route: on the numerous straight sections he had perfect opportunities to practice changing lanes; he could bring me the cake that Mother had baked; he could take my dirty laundry back home; and above all, he could propose to at least part of the brigade—all of them, unfortunately, would not fit—a drive around the environs.

"Gentlemen, I propose a small expedition around the environs. I am at your service in the role of free driver and guide. And not entirely free, for if, after the trip, we make a rest stop at a certain well-known local confectioner's, I will be counting on a large ice cream! Ha! Ha! Ha! I know that the gentlemen would prefer a large beer, but nothing doing today. We set forth without delay! Contrary to appearances, there are several things in the vicinity worth seeing! A young man, especially a freshly minted student of Polish literature, in other words, a man of letters *in spe*, should constantly be looking around in the world! You are certainly aware that the great Polish writer, the Nobel laureate Władysław Reymont, had a photographic memory! Whatever he saw was fixed in the head of that writer of realist epics, and with all the details! He had a great gift! And more importantly, he constantly perfected and developed it! Every gift, every talent must be perfected! Even the greatest perfect their gifts! Reymont perfected his! He instructed his memory and his gaze! We will take a trip together through the environs, and we will train the realism of our gazes! Reproofs of instruction are the way of life!"

The closer the weekend came, the more severe the nightmare became, the more distinctly I heard the bombastic voice of my old man. Quite often I didn't so much imagine as *see*, with terrifying realism, how he would barge into our billet, which was full of empty bottles and reeked of cigarettes; how he would pale and stand stock still from horror, but not betray any of this; how, full of pride in the art of self-control, which he had mastered to perfection, he would smother the spirit of fury, summon the spirit of gentlemanly courtesy and Lutheran humility, and get down to putting things in order; how he would hold a manly conversation with our landlady and request— categorically request—that she keep him up to date about everything that is going on, and to this end, he would leave certain funds to cover the costs of telephone calls. And I saw how he would return and get down to making the beds, to a highly ostentatious—like in the army—making of the beds, and I heard Wittenberg's laugh, which was full of savage derision, and I saw the spirits of humility and courtesy evaporate like steam from Father, who became stupefied and as pale as paste, and I saw him attack my best friend with orgiastic relief, subject to the black spirit of a white-hot rage, and I saw Wittenberg, strong as a tiger and a judo expert, grab my old man and either first break his back and then smash his head against the wall, or the other way around. I couldn't let it come to this. Before every weekend, I called home, and I said that I had an obligatory excursion to the dam in Porąbka, to the camp in Auschwitz, or to the Błędów Desert.

•

IV

WHEN, NOT LONG AGO AT ALL, ON THE OCCASION OF MY FOLKS' SIX-
tieth wedding anniversary, I delivered an embarrassing speech, into
which—who knows why, probably at the instigation of the devil—I
wove in those old lies, both of them, Mother and Father, stiffened.

Theoretically, they had another reason to stiffen, since I had appeared at the celebration in the company of a certain fledgling singer
who was dressed in a lizard green dress with a daring décolletage
but my folks had been stiffening for those sorts of reasons for so long
that they were by then almost nonchalant about it.

I just couldn't resist, and I invited and brought to Wisła, for all
of the most exalted of family events, each successive woman of my
life. I always introduced them as ambitious television journalists,
who were collecting material for a documentary film about Lutheran
customs. Only such a fiction—uniting elements of work, mission,
proselytizing, a laudable interest in our exceptionalism, and the hope
for television fame that would satisfy Lutheran pride—gave them the
chance of legitimization. On the whole, hand on my heart, I don't
know whether or how that worked. Supposedly everything was in
order, supposedly my folks took note of it, supposedly they accepted
it, but how it was in truth—I don't know. Perhaps they were putting
a brave face on it? Perhaps they expected that one of these times I
would settle down, and they weren't ruling out the chance? Perhaps
they hoped that one of these Venuses would indeed turn out to be a
reporter interested in the Lutheran life? Perhaps they took them for
specters? Shrugged it all off? I don't know.

My tragedy is the fact that I always nurture serious intentions. Granted, I like to have a woman near me, whose sight even Lutherans find
breathtaking, but, after all, it is not because of such snobbery that I
drag these unfortunates up to Ram Mountain. I take them because
I love them. I want to be with them to the end of my life. I want to
live with them in a house eternally buried in snow, feed dogs and

cats, keep the stoves burning, watch movies in the evenings on HBO, drink tea with raspberry juice, etc.

And that is how it was this time as well. Everything went like clockwork. I introduced the fledgling singer in her lizard-green dress as an ambitious journalist who was collecting material about our customs, my folks put a brave face on it, took her for a specter, shrugged it off, or whatever. At her sight, the gathered Protestants had their breath taken away. She greeted everyone politely and modestly, she bowed and curtsied, which, given her décolletage, was something straight out of Babylon, but for my co-religionists a proper girl's *Kinderstube* makes a thunderous impression, even if a tit surfaces in the process. Then my current love began to converse with this one and that one, and—so it seems to me—she didn't even especially make a fool of herself through a lack of substance. True, I heard her ask Mr. Trąba, who was sitting next to her, whether Lutherans celebrate Christmas, and if so, when. But without any hysteria—this wasn't any sort of exceptional or especially bloody *faux pas*. The majority of the alleged experts on, and enthusiasts of, Protestantism that I brought there posed similar questions.

Besides, Mr. Trąba began to answer, favorably inclined—in my opinion, *excessively* inclined. He began to answer eagerly, but chaotically, which was no wonder—the visible range of her solarium suntan shattered not only his concentration. Even Father Kalinowski had problems with the welcoming homily. At least he didn't get tripped up on the *Our Father*.

The first hymn was sung, food served at the table, glasses filled. Eat and drink, and make merry, brothers and sisters! Quickly the company began to raise toasts based on cheerful biblical citations and deliver speeches composed on the model of sermons. I was delighted. I was delighted by the entire event. I was delighted by the speeches and the toasts. I was delighted by the fledgling singer in the lizard-green dress. I believed deeply that we would remain forever in my parts, and that in the evenings, in a house buried in snow, we would drink tea, watch films on HBO, etc. I was totally moved, and I was crazy about the absolute grandeur of the thing. When my turn came, or when I had the impression that my turn had come, I was close to tears from emotion. I tapped on my glass with the knife, I stood up, and I let 'er rip. It seemed to me that I was speaking incredibly fluently, that I was master of the form, and that I was faultlessly making my way to the conclusion, and I was simultaneously conscious that some force beyond my control was leading me astray, and that at any moment I would say something I shouldn't, but which, at the prompting of the darknesses gathering in me, was becoming necessary.

At first, I told them some bullshit from my childhood. Then I began, with bootlicking servility, to assure everyone present that all my life I had emulated my folks, that I had striven to live as they do—according to God's commandments. And even when it happened that I sinned, it was also—a paradox, but nonetheless—in emulation of them. And here I veered off into muddiness, or more precisely, I got carried away in absolute muddiness. I really must have heard Satan's whisper, since I suddenly began to blather embarrassingly about how, after passing the *matura*, at the threshold of my university studies, I didn't go to the dam in Porąbka, or to the camp in Auschwitz, or even to the Błędów Desert, but to my girlfriend at the time . . . to my girlfriend at the time . . . to my girlfriend at the time . . . I got flustered, since I sensed, after all, how terrible it was. I glanced in the direction of the fledgling singer, who was like a half-naked and emerald-winged angel among the Puritans enshrouded in their blacks; I glanced at her, and I didn't want to say what I was just about to say; I didn't want to say what I said, but my speech was now coming like a hemorrhage, as if I had been shot through the head. I didn't go then to the dam in Porąbka, or to the camp in Auschwitz, or to the Błędów Desert, but to my girlfriend of the time, and my current wife. I added this unexpectedly, and I bowed in the direction of the fledgling singer, who sat quietly and didn't even laugh; quite clearly she was thinking that it had to do with some Lutheran custom that was unknown to her—and my current wife, with whom I have been for nearly thirty years now, and with whom, I trust, I will live to see an anniversary like yours, dearest parents. Amen. God help me! God hear me! God forgive me!

I strove for grandeur, but I flew down into the depths of the abyss. I raised my glass, I turned toward the *venerable celebrants*, and, no amazement on my part, I saw a couple of elegantly dressed oldsters, frozen in horror (he in his best steel gray suit from the seventies, she in a fancy navy blue dress from the eighties), their heads hanging low, almost on the table cloth. Everyone, it goes without saying, grasped at once what a truly terrible gaffe I had committed, and no one—not even Father Kalinowski—hastened to smooth the situation over or to give me some sort of light-hearted support. I instantly understood what was going on. I returned to lucidity. I stood for another moment like the typical class dunce, who is still standing, although he ought to have taken his seat long ago. I stood for about another half a minute, and finally, in deathlike silence, I sat down on my chair. Copious sweat appeared on my forehead—I knew that I would have to suffer punishment.

The cooks brought in the second course, but the beef roulades and the veal cutlets were not salvation, they signified only a delay full of torment. Anyway, I didn't have to wait long. My old man didn't even try the second meat dish, he chewed a bit of the first (in other words, the roulade), stood up from the table, and went to change into his work clothes. A first, a second, a third slamming of doors reached us from the depths of the house, and after a moment the rhythmic pounding of a hammer resounded from the garage. The Lutherans, who were gathered around the table, relaxed a bit, began to glance at each other with recognition, and they smiled with pride: it is well known that when something bad happens, when the demons come, the best thing to do is to get to work. In spite of the horror of the situation, or perhaps on account of that horror, the question suddenly began to torment me: What sort of task had my old man set himself, and what was he so rabidly hammering?

Mother bustled over to the kitchen. I flew after her, I stood by the window, and I glanced at the snow-covered garden. "Mama," I said quietly, "I'm sorry. I didn't realize." She turned toward me, a monstrous fury—all the more monstrous, because it was silent—contorted her face. She began to threaten me in silence, to make signs—toward the garage, in which my old man might die any moment from overwork; toward the dining room, in which the guests now sat, left to themselves—and she threatened me with all her might. For a good two, three minutes she didn't say a thing; in the end, however, she couldn't stand the pressure of the silence; she stood on tiptoe, and she hissed. "How could you lie! How could you lie about going on an excursion to the dam in Porąbka, to the camp in Auschwitz, or to the Błędów Desert, when you went who knows where!" "Mama," I said with a trembling voice, "that was more than thirty years ago." "And what if something had happened to anyone, how were we supposed to let you know? Where were we supposed to look for you. What if someone had died? What then? Everybody at home is certain that you are at the dam in Porąbka, in the camp in Auschwitz, or in the Błędów Desert, and you are who knows where! Alone to boot! And what if something had happened to you? Where did you go? To the mountains? By bus? But we had a car! Father would have driven you everywhere! I would have been glad to go myself! But you, you arrogant egotist, preferred to go alone! By bus! In the crush! Paying money for it! Instead of comfortably and for free! An entire life of worry!"

Mother covered her face with her hands and tried to summon up tears of despair—she wasn't having much luck. The hubbub in the dining room was increasing. I didn't have to be there to know that the fledgling singer in the lizard-green dress was beginning to figure out that something wasn't right, that she was getting up from her place, that the remaining guests were interpreting this gesture as a demonstrative desire to leave the dinner, and they are attempting to stop her almost by force, that the amber suntan of my current love is turning pale as paper, and suddenly the terrified girl begins to assure them spasmodically that she doesn't know what is going on here, and that she doesn't know where she is at all; or what it is about; and she doesn't have a clue where, and to whom, I travelled after my *matura*, because it certainly wasn't to her! Perhaps I didn't travel to the dam in Porąbka, to the camp in Auschwitz, or to the Błędów Desert, but it wasn't to her either, because she wasn't even born then! And she hasn't been with me for thirty years, because she is only twenty-four years old, and why these absurd lies? Lutheran customs are one thing, but absurd lies are quite another matter!

Through four, five, and perhaps even six walls you could hear that the fledgling singer in the lizard-green dress was beginning to cry, that the Protestants surrounding her in ever tighter circles are first seized by agitation, but they immediately begin to calm down, and they attempt to calm her, too, and they defend me with all their might. They assure her emphatically that I hadn't lied, and that I'm not lying, because Lutherans never lie, but that I speak the truth, and I pray for the truth, because what I had said was a prayer for truth, the prayer of a person who had strayed in a moment of weakness from the path of truth but prays for a return to that path, and my prayer was heard, and it became the truth. And through the walls I heard my current love's scream, full of animal fear, and, on my word, I absolutely intended to return there as quickly as possible, and to explain everything, perhaps even to defuse the situation with some sort of joke—although I didn't yet know what sort. But first I had to run to Father. I left Mother, who was still having difficulty—this was altogether odd—trying to get a good lament going, and in a sprint, skipping two, three steps, I flew to the garage.

At first, I was horrified in good earnest, for it seemed that Father had gone utterly mad on my account. In canvas pants lowered to his knees, he stood next to an enormous oak table, which served him as a workbench, and he pounded—extremely methodically—an enormous steel nail into the table-top. He pounded it in methodically, but very shallowly—a half centimeter—then he tore it out, furiously and with superhuman effort, moved it over some three centimeters with incredible precision, and pounded it in again, and again tore it out, and again moved it over. Terrible was my horror, and equally great the relief, when I realized that my old man had not gone mad after all; rather, as normally as could be, with all precision and solidity, he was pounding extra holes in the pants belt that was lying on the table. I stood in the doorway. The table was high, and what is more it was outfitted on two sides with a slat that stuck up above the table-top, so that screws, nails, and all sorts of miniature elements wouldn't fall on the ground, and quite simply—and my agitation was not without its significance here—at first I hadn't noticed the belt carefully laid out on the table. "Papa," I said in a panicky attempt to pretend at being matter of fact, "can I help you with anything? Or can I bring you something to drink?" Father stopped pounding extra holes and looked at me the way he was accustomed to look at all intruders and spongers who interrupt his work—motionlessly and heavily. The hammer hung in the raised hand equally motionlessly and equally heavily, while the belt, as if the spirit of a snake had entered it, began slowly, then ever more quickly, to slide off the table. With an elemental reflex, I jumped up. I was unable, however, to grab it in flight. It fell on the cement floor. I bent over to pick it up, and again I was unable to do it, for I felt a light—I emphasize—*very light* blow to my head.

The fledgling singer claims to this day that she found me lying under the table, unconscious and covered with blood, but this is rather a schoolgirl's and—if I may say so—non-ecumenical and typically Catholic hysteria. Father had tapped me very lightly also because, at his age, he was simply incapable of tapping forcefully. In addition to that, he was standing there—I remind you—with his pants down, and it is well known that a man with his pants down is totally self-conscious, and all his movements, including movements of the hands, are self-conscious and limited. (A man with his pants down—to forge a dazzling aphorism on the fly—has no other goal in life than to pull his pants up.) True, an insignificant splitting of the skin and some bleeding, incommensurately abundant for the small wound, had ensued, but *all* the further results—that is to say: the trip to the emergency room; the examination; the obstinacy of the mean-sprited doctor, who stubbornly insisted that, as a result of the blow to the head from a blunt instrument, I had received a concussion; the narrow-minded phone call to the police; the arrival of the policemen at home; Father's arrest and detention at the police-station for forty-eight hours—*these* were all absolutely unnecessary things.

Although, on the other hand, maybe they *were* necessary. In some non-superficial and—if I can put it this way—deeply familial and genuinely communal sense, perhaps they were downright indispensable. For after that, whenever I would meet with my parents, we would laugh ourselves to tears over those events. We especially split our sides over the memory of the guests, a portion of whom—upon hearing that Father had murdered me with a hammer in the garage—couldn't measure up to the demands of Lutheran toughness and rushed into panicky flight. While the other portion—Father adored precisely that episode, and when he recalled it, he cried, in the strict sense, he cried from laughter; for the portion of the guests that didn't rush into panicky flight, but rather remained at the post of Lutheran toughness, true, they did meet those demands, but—give me a break, for I myself will die laughing—they, in turn, did not meet the demands of the Lutheran ethos, as they all got blind drunk and came out looking like corpses. "Those corpses!" Father would laugh. "The corpses! One corpse in the garage! But in the dining room . . . ! In the dining room, so many corpses! Nothing but corpses lying like trophies of the chase. Mr. Trąba—a corpse! Young Messerschmidt—a corpse! Doctor Granada and Kohoutek—corpses! Master Sztwiertnia and Father Kalinowski—both corpses! Even Małgosia Snajperek—a corpsette!" Supposedly all of them truly—I wasn't present for this, I lay with a bandaged head in the clinic—absolutely all of them had fallen fast asleep, and they slept not one, but many hours, until the break of dawn. "Instead of keeping watch and praying for the removal of suffering, we fell asleep like the Disciples in the Garden of Gethsemane," said Father Kalinowski, when Mother finally managed to wake him at daybreak. "I myself, overcome with wine, fell asleep like Christ in the tomb, and if it weren't for you, Mrs. Engineer, I would not have risen from the dead." With lightning speed, according to Mother's tale, he braced himself; to her horror, with a shameless motion, he reached for the unfinished bottle of cherry vodka that was standing on the table, and he took a hefty swig straight from the bottle. Then he fell into a pensive mood for a moment, and after a while, with a gesture well known from the pulpit, he raised up his hand and said: "But both the sleep of the Disciples in the Garden, and His sleep in the tomb—although they were needless events that to this day arouse opposition—would turn out to be, in fact, unusually necessary and, in God's plan, irrefutably needful!"

V

In September of the year 1971, I knew perfectly well which events are, both in life and in God's plan, irrefutably needful, and which are completely needless. Without giving it a second thought— especially, I would say, without giving it any theological thought—I would call up my folks, and I would tell them that our entire brigade had, on the coming weekend, an obligatory excursion to the camp in Auschwitz, to the Błędów Desert, or to the dam in Porąbka, and every weekend I would make the trip to see Gocha in the mountains, and those were unusual trips.

First of all—crouching down the whole time and ready the whole time for the sudden drop that would render me invisible—I would take the local bus to Krakow. With my eye, with the corner of my eye, glued the whole time to the glass in utmost vigilance, looking to see whether my folks' white Fiat wasn't crawling along in the opposite direction like a tortoise. The attack had been forestalled, the telephone call had been placed, but there remained unforeseen circumstances to be foreseen. To tell the truth, when it had to do with my folks, you always had to—you had nothing else to do but—foresee unforeseen circumstances. It could always happen that my incredibly convincing story about an excursion to the dam in Porąbka, to the camp in Auschwitz, or to the Błędów Desert would seem to Mother *somewhat odd.* My folks could always come up with the idea that *they would manage to drop off something to eat before my departure, if only a couple sandwiches with home-made butter, which strengthens the eyes.* They could always come to the conclusion that *I must have a cold, because I speak in such a dreadfully hoarse voice on the phone, and if I go on the excursion I will fix myself for good.* They could always make the desperate attempt to drive over in the early morning with a note, written in advance in their own calligraphy, *a justification of the absence of our son from the tourist activities.* Always, always, always. I was never able to foresee everything. Beginning in the deepest depths of childhood, I practiced decoding the unpredictability of my folks. I was really not bad at this. I could foresee practically everything, but, all the same, they always managed to surprise me.

I sat in the bus, crouching and ready to drop, and I quailed at the sight of every white Fiat, and at the sight of a white Fiat that was traveling somewhat more slowly than the rest—my heart stopped beating. Two times or so, I was certain it was them. On the first Friday one, on the second Friday a second white Fiat barreled along in the opposite direction on the deserted chalky road at wheelchair velocity. In hallucinogenic panic, I saw the silhouettes of my folks inside: Father frozen in a catatonic stupor over the steering wheel, Mother thrashing about with incessant exhortations to *slow down.* I knew that as soon as they got there, and didn't find me, they would set out in hot pursuit. First, it goes without saying, by requests, threats, force, money, whatever they could muster, they would extort, that's right, they would *extort*—even from Wittenberg, they would extort—a confession of where I was, and immediately thereafter they would set out in hot pursuit. I looked around me for some time to see whether, from behind, from beyond a white hill, from beyond a sandy turn, they would appear with lights and sirens blazing, but these were already much too surrealistic visions.

The closer I got to Krakow, the more the apparitions faded, and once I got there, at the bus terminal, they vanished completely. A biblical throng teemed there. The voice of God, roaring as on Mount

Sinai, announced the next departures. An azure pillar of exhaust fumes rose to the heavens like the sign of an accepted offering. I didn't have any luggage, and probably that advantage allowed me to make my way through the throng every time. God knows by what miracle, standing on one leg, in an exceptionally reckless position, but every time, suddenly I would find myself on the regional bus to Zakopane—crammed beyond human endurance—and my soul sang. Actually, I know by what miracle. In a couple hours, my body would be clinging to Gocha's dusky body, and on the face of the entire earth there wasn't a bus so crammed full that I wouldn't get on it in order to reach her.

Over the Zakopane High Road, the September air grew dark. Not even for a moment did I forget that I was a young poet, and with all my might I watched for the moment when the low clouds would turn into high mountains. I never managed it. Just as in childhood I attempted to grasp the moment of falling asleep, and I always fell into a dark sleep as into a deep well, so now, always, after the next glance at the horizon, the clouds were already gone, and there were the Tatras.

In the darkness I would reach the gigantic garden that had gone wild like a desert island, which surrounded the pension that Gocha's parents rented out. I would sit on a bench hidden in the hazel groves. I would light a cigarette and wait for the moment when, in the second window from the left, a sepia-toned light would flash, and a supple, long-haired shadow would appear. The shadow would appear, Gocha would open the window, look around, disappear for a moment, then she would appear again and give the sign. Off I went. The massive, and, at the same time, light house designed by Witkiewicz *père* had to it something of the sailboat scudding over the waves, and something of the fortified castle. I swam across moats, I climbed over walls, I confused the guards. Well, no need to exaggerate here about the guards—Gocha's parents were quite advanced in years and lived as if in a half-sleep. It sometimes even seemed to me that they had died long ago, and it was their indistinct specters that were wandering about the pension, but most of the time just sitting in wicker chairs on the veranda.

Sometimes the impression that one is dealing with the dead, or that the dead are still living in their former apartments, which are now deserted or have been occupied by others, is as disabling as an attack of madness. When it comes over me, it often seems to me that I myself have been dead for some time, and that, in the empty apartment on Sienna Street, the traces and scents left by me take on my shape, the shadow of my shape. Or, for instance, I am absolutely certain that my folks, even though they haven't been there for a long time, continue their spectral vegetation in the two rooms on Syrokomla Street. Through the smudged window, which probably hasn't been washed in a year, you can see Mother, in the pleated skirt, now worn and frayed, which she had once bought in Cepelia, cooking mushroom soup with home-made noodles in the icy kitchen; Father, in a track suit that is as transparent as a spider web, assembling on the ruined balcony a system for watering flowers based on the principle of communicating vessels.

Gocha's parents could be specters, spirits, phantoms—fine by me. The main thing was that they not notice how, in the late evening, I flit through the lobby illumined by the cadaverous gleam of the television, and then climb the creaking steps and slip into their daughter's room. For some time, I had fancy thoughts that they noticed me, but that they took me for a specter. Today, I think that they noticed me—and that they just shrugged it all off. Perhaps they weren't the only specters in the pension. Perhaps this was, in general, a pension of specters. I never left the room. I had a heightened sense of the oneiric quality of what was going on beyond the walls. It seemed to me that the waitresses gliding along the corridor, the chamber maids, the cleaning women—that all of them move extremely somnolently, that they speak indistinctly as if they are asleep, and that they are constantly surprised at something, as if they had been rudely awakened.

Even Hela, who was friends with Gocha and privy to our affairs, and who brought me dinners from the kitchen—in spite of the fact that she carried out a conspiratorial assignment that demanded quick wits and physical dexterity—made the impression of a somnolent ghost.

She was pretty, white-skinned, white-haired, and most certainly soft, very soft, to the touch. As soon as she had flitted from the kitchen to our room with an abundantly laden tray, the hurry was gone. She would sit drowsily on the bed, her carelessly braided tress would come undone, the carelessly buttoned sky blue blouse would come open. Gocha would sit next to her and say something in an undertone. I would eat in silence, *and quickly*—I wanted Hela to take the dishes and go away as soon as possible. But when I had finished, when I hastily drank the rest of the compote, and even when I demonstratively gathered up the plates and utensils—nothing changed. Hela would sit there, Gocha whispered, I waited. As time passed—and I have a great desire to write that such siestas lasted *for hours*—Hela would sit there more and more drowsily, with now, I suppose, hair completely unbraided and blouse completely unbuttoned. As time passed, Gocha would whisper more and more tenderly and quietly. As time passed, I didn't know what was happening, and maybe I wasn't there at all. Finally, Hela would get up with complete indifference, without consent—but also without objection—to the fact that she had to get up. Just as women do after amatory frenzies, she would stand before the mirror, button up her blouse, put her hair in order. With a perfectly neutral voice, without a hint of irony or ambiguity, she would ask me whether it had been to my liking, and she would collect the tray with the dinnerware. Gocha would see her to the door and stroke her back in farewell.

We would then remain alone, the air over the mountains would lighten and darken, we practically didn't sleep at all, we would embrace until the last spasms, to the last drop of sweat, to the first pain. Our bodies and our voices said much to each other, not a word was ever uttered on the topic of Hela. Nor did I ever notice later on that Gocha would see any girl to the door and tenderly stroke her back in farewell.

VI

On Sunday, I would set off on the return trip in a night bus that was usually entirely empty. The Jelcz, so corroded that it was as if it had been moulded out of rust, drove along unknown dirt and side roads. Frequently, it seemed that it flew straight across the hill tops. Sometimes it would halt at strange stops, in secret places, doubtless agreed upon in advance. Someone perfectly well known to the driver would get on or off the bus there. Time and again we would arrive at village courtyards, as if they were important stations, at which peculiar nocturnal commotions were in progress—wedding feasts, festivities, hog-slaughterings. The band was playing, campfires were glowing, drunken girls in stained wedding dresses knocked on the pane over which my unconscious head rolled—take me with you, they would whisper. With a flash of the headlights and a wail of the horn, we would set off further. Except for the camp-fire circles, an absolute silence reigned. Black forests, brown, unmown grain, mouldering haystacks, God knows where the road led. And yet, I would awake unexpectedly from the next slumber, filled with a scent as thick as slime, in the very heart of the little Austro-Hungarian town. The driver would smile broadly, say that he hadn't even gone that far out of his way. Every week, I would search for some small change; every week, it seemed too little to me. He would count the coins scrupulously, and always at the end, with a consciousness of the aphoristic gravity, he would say: "It isn't a lot, but sometimes that's everything."

VII

The road from the station to the billet led through the center of town, then across the castle hill—on both sides, forests and darkness. Every week I attempted to believe that I felt upon me a wild, phosphorescent glance—bull crap. Surely he could be lying in wait among the trees, in the high grass, along the path leading to the stream. It was there, in any case, that the bodies of his victims were most often found. But I couldn't fully believe in his presence. I was sort of afraid, but I didn't believe. Fear without belief counts for little. On the other hand, in the high grass itself, but nearer, significantly nearer, I imagined every time that I saw a longish, dark, coffin-like shape. On every return I saw the same body lying on the side of the path, the white shirt it had on was darker each time, the pillar of flies droning over the ripped throat thicker and thicker, the spread arms were arranged slightly differently each time. And the smell—the smell of a stuffy chamber full of flowers.

I tried to persuade myself that I was shaking from the cold, and I sprinted the last hundred meters to the unplastered villa in which we had our billet. I didn't measure it, but my time must have gotten better with every week.

In the room rose the smell of an encampment, barracks, prison cells. In any event, such was the direction of the equally firm and subtle evolution of sensations: from dirty socks to foot cloths, from vodka and beer to moonshine, from brand-name cigarettes to ever meaner tobacco. And the profound slumber of my sleeping colleagues was ever deeper and ever more eloquent. During the first week, they slept the euphoric sleep of young poets who had everything ahead of them; during the second, you could detect the first disenchantment in their sleep; in the third—bitterness.

The number of books on Wittenberg's bed grew; in the end, he slept under all seven volumes of Proust, under Eliot's verses, under little volumes of Herbert, Grochowiak, and Szymborska, under a notebook with hand-copied Miłosz, under a copy of *Trans-Atlantyk* covered in *The People's Tribune*, under Konwicki, Parnicki, Camus, Fromm, Freud, Jung, young Marx, late Mann, under Kołakowski's *Religious Consciousness and the Bond of the Church*, under Michelet's *The Sorceress*, under Frazer's *Golden Bough*, under Bulgakov, Babel, Broch, Faulkner, under three one-hundred-page notebooks, in which he had the beginnings of two novels, full of the highest philosophical tension, and one poem, full of the highest linguistic temperament.

And Wittenberg was covered with numerous other books, as with a blanket, or rather as with a net, for, from between the covers, his dark Levantine skin shined through. His right arm always hung from the bed, as if searching for the empty bottle that was standing there; the left rose in the direction of his head; his head rested in the proper place—in the center of the pillow—all around there were long, thick, curly locks, of which we were all madly envious. And with good cause. The hair style—a daring imitation and successful rival for the most expressive creations of Jimi Hendrix, who had been dead for a year at that time—exerted a magnetic attraction upon the girls' gazes.

Unfortunately, it was as ineffective as it was magnetic. Everything indicated that on that weekend, too, the biblical/rock-and-roll magnetism of Wittenberg's hair had attracted no Delilah. I didn't have to look around too carefully to ascertain that the eternal hunger for a woman, felt not only by him, not only by us, not only during Workers' Traineeship, but always and by all poets of the world, remained unsatisfied this time as well. In a room marked by each and every sort of transgression, once again all traces of any sort of female presence were lacking. Exclusively invisible muses were rising above the heads of the sleeping poets. No one from the Dressmakers' Technical College had left a handkerchief, comb, lipstick, not to mention any more intimate sort of prop. There weren't any extra cups, glasses, empty bottles of sweet wine. During the preceding evening, no girlish hand had cut elegant little wedges of yellow cheese on the copy of *Literary Life* that was spread out on the table. The nibbled pickle that was lying there, the hunk of bread, and the pyramid of cigarette butts created a sufficiently eloquent still life.

Clearly, not even the female bricklayer's assistants, who were working with us, had been persuaded to join them. Already the week before, having grown impatient with standing around in vain outside the Dressmakers' Technical College, we decided to approach our athletically built female comrades in labor and ask them: would they have a beer with us in *Europa* after work, and then we'll see. We laughed at the idea, with alleged self-irony. With a vague sense of shame, we feared—as Wittenberg put it—loss of sexual caste. But in our heart of hearts, we rejoiced and were insanely excited. This seemed easy pickings, a sure thing, and—to tell the truth—ideal for our riotous and exclusively corporeal yearnings. And so, when the girls from the construction site reacted to our proposition unenthusiastically at first, and then began to try to wiggle out—saying that they probably couldn't make it—we fell into a rather deep frustration. The girls from the clothiers' school were almost entirely unattainable, and that, paradoxically wasn't half bad: in the final analysis, we had no idea what we were missing. But here were walking, right under our noses, four female Titans, each carrying a sack of cement, as if it were a feather, on their Athenian shoulders, each in a blouse half-opened on statuesque breasts, each in canvas trousers draping a marble behind— painful and irreclaimable losses. In any event, the reclamation of four pairs of unbelievable tits dusted with lime powder, plus the rest, had not come about during my absence. I got undressed with the speed of lightning, I jumped into the marital bed, in the other part of which snored Wittenberg, overcome with vodka and literature, and I slept for three hours (which seemed like three seconds).

VIII

THE NEXT DAY, WE SENT OUR WOULD-BE MISTRESSES FIRST WISTFUL, then scornful glances. They, as usual, carried cement and bricks, as usual they whispered to each other, as usual they giggled. Once we had knocked off work, we sat longer than usual in *Europa*. No one felt like going to the College. It was clear by now that nothing was going to happen. The traineeship was ending in three days, and with graphomaniac zeal we attempted to kindle the nostalgic mood of *taking leave of the little Austro-Hungarian town, where, no doubt, none of us would again set foot for the rest of our lives.* One of the seven indistinguishable local alcoholics (it's quite a different matter that, in those days, unaware of the nightmare that awaited me, I behaved like a racist toward alcoholics: I made no distinctions among them, and I considered them half corpses, half animals) joined our table and began to spin the next version of the tale about the vampire. There was no reason to marvel at the abundance and vitality of this topic. The vampire (in those days the term "serial murderer," to say nothing of "*serial killer*," was unknown) had been murdering for years. Every few weeks—in the high grass, next to the path to the stream—the bodies of the next victims would be found, their combined number already allegedly reaching into the hundreds.

This time—if I may put it this way—it was the Party version. "All the stories about the vampire that the gentlemen students have heard up to now are not worth a hill of beans," one of the seven indistinguishable alcoholics skillfully suspended his voice and performed the four ritual acts that the entire seven would repeat with identical precision during their own narrations: he adjusted his beret, drank a tiny sip of beer, wiped his lips with the back of his blackened hand, and lit up a Sport. "All the stories you know about the vampire are false; the true one is the one that I know. It is, if it please the gentlemen students, kept strictly secret for political reasons."

One of the seven indistinguishable alcoholics exaggerated his own revelation. Either one of his brethren, or perhaps even he himself, had already, at least two or three times—at this same laminate table top always drenched with beer, in the same cadaverous glare of the fluorescent lamp hanging over our heads—told the version that asserted that the Silesian vampire was the deranged son of a Party secretary, that he has special protection, that the office of the Secret Police helps him pick out his victims, that the father, depraved by the exercise of power, but also desperate and broken-hearted, even in spite of the pressures exerted by Moscow, is unable to make the decision to have the degenerate locked up, and that, because of this, the blood-thirsty *secretarovich* will murder and rape who knows how long, perhaps even to the end of his life.

We knew this tale, and we listened wearily to the irrefutable pieces of evidence: that, namely, if the Party secretary looks bad when he appears on television and delivers a speech full of pessimism and veiled threats toward Moscow, this is an infallible sign that his son is again demanding victims, that he can't hold out any longer, that any time now he will escape, that the members of the Secret Police who are watching over him, if they won't help him, then they will certainly turn a blind eye, and that in a few days, in a week, two at the most, next to the path leading from the Castle Hill to the stream, the corpse of a girl will again be found.

At this moment—precisely at this moment, when the words "corpse of a girl" were uttered, and when one of the seven indistinguishable narrators made a pause and adjusted his beret, and drank a tiny sip of beer, and wiped his lips with the back of his blackened hand, and lit up a Sport—at precisely this moment, the doors of *Europa* opened, and there appeared not the corpse of a girl, but a living, flesh-and-blood girl in a yellow bouclé blouse and a sky blue Perlon miniskirt, and she crossed the threshold. And after her, there appeared a second and a third and a fourth. And all of them crossed the threshold, and all of them walked in our direction, and all of them sat down at our table, and all of them—amused by our absolute dumbfoundedness—each and every one of them, ordered a small beer with raspberry juice.

"The entire matter is a political game of the Party," one of the seven indistinguishable alcoholics continued his tale, but by then we were entirely uninterested in listening, or rather—now reconstructing those events and moods precisely—we began to listen with a delight that invalidated what we were listening to, for the delight that seized us—that, after all, the girls from the construction site had come, and not only had they come, but they had come decked out in their best, sexiest outfits; that they had put on their shortest skirts and their tightest blouses—the delight that seized us at their sight was so all-encompassing, that we listened, delighted, to the next installment of the story about the vampire. We were simply delighted by the fact that an irrefutable link between the bad appearance of the Party secretary and the later attacks of the vampire—always one, at most two, weeks later—had been established. We were in seventh heaven over the fact that the Party faction that was opposed to the secretary was spreading rumors that his son was a serial murderer. It pleased us no end that the faction that favored the secretary didn't deny that, granted, his son is mentally ill and dangerous, but the secretary did not succumb to the pressures from Moscow and did not have him locked up in the loony bin; what is more, the one and the other thing are provocations of former members of the NKVD. We were fired with enthusiasm for the former members of the NKVD. We bought the narrator—who was amazed at our unexpected applause—beer after beer. We ourselves lost all sense of moderation. Nor was it necessary to try to persuade the girls—the small beer with juice was a thing of the past. They put it away like they really did have some sort of Dionysian genes, they laughed at our every word, a constant neon light arrested the turning of the earth.

Just as delicately as could be, I glided my hand along the thigh of the Goddess of Large-Slab Construction who was sitting next to me, I felt the hint of lime dust that inhered in her skin, I plunged my mouth into hair that smelled of sweet flag and hop shampoo. If at that moment someone should have made me choose between Gocha and her, I would probably have chosen Gocha, but I would have been in a quandary. I would have chosen Gocha, but it wouldn't have been easy for me. I would have chosen Gocha, but with a heavy heart.

To this day, I have a hard time distinguishing—or rather, to tell the truth, I simply don't distinguish at all—between eroticism and love, let along back then. When I finally write a *Dictionary of Erotic Superstitions*, the superstition about the necessity of distinguishing sex from love will occupy a prominent position. There is no such thing. Sex without love makes no sense and is—at least in my case—impossible. Sex without love is an unnecessary event. And don't let anyone try to tell me that I simply ennoble copulation in a comic and naïve fashion. As far as I am concerned, there is no copulation that is not noble. Copulation is love. Love can last for years, and it can be like a lightning flash, and let no one remain in the delusion that the first is worth more than the second. All the more because it is usually the other way around. *Ergo*, you must love all the women with whom you wish to go to bed. You must fall in love with them, and you must make them fall in love with you. Whoever should have all the women in the world, but have not love, will be as sounding brass, or a tinkling cymbal. Even if you want to have a paid tart, you still have to love her, and it is no phony high-mindedness that speaks through me, rather a knowledge of the force of experiences.

Minute by minute, I was falling in love with the beautiful lady bricklayer sitting next to me. After an hour, two, or perhaps three— on the one hand, it is impossible to say precisely, since, as is well known, love stops, or perhaps even cancels time (after all, in writing metaphorically that the dead light of a dirty neon had stopped the turning of the Earth, I had already taken note of this fact); on the other hand, I think that I had fallen in love after more or less an hour—after two hours, that heroine of socialist labor was reciprocating my feelings; after three, we began to search for some secluded place. Actually, we didn't have to make any decisions. Our feverish bodies and our intoxicated souls knew perfectly well by themselves that the most discrete place would be next to the path to the stream. The corpse that had been lying there for weeks had dissolved entirely and been eaten by the earth. Zero visibility, grass as high as a wall. Trembling bodies flowed into the depths of their own depths. The sky darkened over the dark brown globe, a red star flew in our direction, I felt the shiver of cold. "We lost so much time," I said in a low voice, since, in spite of all, a whisper seemed to me too sentimental, "we lost so much time. The entire traineeship has passed . . . Why didn't you want to go on a date with us earlier?" "We were afraid," she said, smothering a laugh, and she hugged me by the neck, and she began, panting and laughing, to whisper into my ear. As she whispered to me, I recalled the beginning of the story, the first sentence, and the first day of the traineeship. We were driving to the construction site on an open truck. A fantastic, still summery day was rising. They sat across from us in a strange sort of tension, not saying a word. It was the beginning of a spectral September. In the environs of the little Austro-Hungarian town in which we performed our Workers' Traineeship, a Silesian vampire was prowling, and at first the four female bricklayer's assistants looked upon us with fear. Supposedly, of our entire five-some, the one who most looked like a vampire was Wittenberg (1953–1979).

The Double of
Tolstoy's Son-in-Law

I

WHEN, IN THE AUTUMN OF 2002, I CAME UPON A REPRODUCTION
in the newspaper of an old photograph showing Lev Tolstoy playing
chess, I had the feeling that something just wasn't right. It is easy to
say now that the icy shaft of a mystery had run through me, or that
the goddess of incomprehensible coincidences had placed a significant kiss upon my brow, or that the sulfurous wings of the angel of
darkness had brushed me—or something like that. Today it is easy,
exceedingly easy, and, given my stylistic impulses, shockingly easy to
say so. But at that time, none of these far reaching metaphors came to
my mind. Every sepia-toned millimeter was exceedingly intense, but
intensity is too little for a mystery.

As if for fear that I might disturb some sort of integrity, I didn't
cut the picture out; instead, I kept the entire newspaper. I put it into
the drawer in which I keep the shot for my air rifle, and from time
to time—decidedly too often—I would take it out and stare at it with
fascination, and I would study it through a magnifying glass, and I

looked at it under the light, and I probed the texture with my fingers, and I considered entirely seriously how to get to the laboratories where they could take an X-ray of it, magnify it to unparalleled graininess, out of which a secret sign would loom and establish the crucial, all-revealing DNA of the paper on which it was printed.

At all costs, and in vain, I attempted to decode the sudden and obsessive presence of Tolstoy's chessboard in my brain.

You all know such situations: an inconceivably distinct detail of a distant landscape; a strange light, nobody knows from where; a house, seen from the window of a train, toward which someone is running along a sandy path; the shadow of the suddenly turned head of a passer-by; the arrangement of objects on a table—someone, something, nobody knows what, suddenly comes to mind and gives you no peace.

The photograph of Tolstoy playing chess gave me no peace for three years. To this day, I don't have total peace, perhaps even quite the contrary, but at least I have been able to formulate certain suppositions. If I were the narrator of a detective novel, I would say that I have established the direction of the investigation.

I suppose it would not be beside the point to emphasize that I am not an especially ardent fan—either of chess or of Tolstoy. There is nothing frivolous in this confession. Especially as far as Tolstoy is concerned. I admire the author of *War and Peace*. I admire him inor-dinately and devoutly. Perhaps even, if someone were to force me to name the greatest novelist in history—a little bit shooting in the dark, but with inexorable intuition—I would name him. After all, if a novel is supposed to create a world—or even a universe—he was the most fully successful at it. I say that I am not an ardent fan, only because I don't know him well. You can't be an ardent fan of something you don't know inside and out. Fanaticism presupposes cognitive perfec-tion. And I know well, I even know very well, only one of his texts. Most certainly, I can confess with a pure conscience that I am an ardent fan of that one text. I'm an ardent fan of "The Death of Ivan Ilych." I consider this story the masterpiece of all masterpieces, the limit of human possibilities in the art of narration. All Tolstoy's other things I esteem and admire. I esteem and admire, but—please understand me well—I don't catch their scent.

Truly great, truly near, and truly intense writers have a scent. Nabokov smells of sea salt, Erofeev of honeysuckle, Márquez of saltpeter, Zweig of a November sky. Iwaszkiewicz of pine needles. Broch of glacial waters flowing down into a valley, Platonov of a burning-hot smithy.

Tolstoy doesn't have a smell. Unless prose has the smell of dying, and death is like air.

A few years ago I bought a fourteen-volume edition of his works in a used book store; of course, I didn't read everything, but I read *War and Peace* once, *Anna Karenina* and *Resurrection* twice, "Kreutzer Sonata" three, or perhaps even four times. I return to "Ilych" frequently, and always, as I read the last sentence—about "the death that is finished"—I get goosebumps. But I never had any sort of "Tolstoy phase," some sort of Tolstoyan preoccupation or obsession. And it is not a matter of common platitudes: *that the adoration of a great genius whose works have been published in the form of "Collected Works" is always marked by a certain coolness; that, granted, one admires Shakespeare, Goethe, or Dante, but that one doesn't go mad over them; and even—to tell the truth—that one rarely reads them before going to sleep.* Such bullshit doesn't apply to me. I read the classics before going to sleep. Or rather at dawn, for in the evening, whatever I pick up, whatever classic, whatever Flaubert, whatever Dickens, before I get to the end of the first page—I fall asleep. But I awake at dawn, and then I read the classics. With admiration and without any madness. Apparently, once a person is of an age when he reads only at dawn, and only classics, it is too late for great obsessions. Even the obsession—and it was an obsession—with the picture in the newspaper, in which Tolstoy plays chess, didn't incline me to obsessive reading of his collected works.

•

The caption under the photograph declared that in his old age his favorite game was chess; but if this was the case, did he write even one sentence about chess? It seemed, more or less, that, in the cosmos created by him, there ought also to be a place for chess, but where should one look for it? It seems to me that neither in *Karenina*, nor in *Resurrection*, and absolutely not in "The Death of Ivan Ilych," is there a single word about chess. Granted, the idea of thoroughly studying his remaining works—from the point of view of the presence of chess motifs—occurred to me, but nothing more. That intriguing idea did not become deed in the least. Of course, when you can't establish something, you have to invent it. That's what experiencing the world through literature is about. The foolishly beautiful idea that I myself might compose a mysterious story about the *unknown chess episode* in the life of Tolstoy was, however, entirely beyond my reach.

I didn't have even a preliminary intuition whether the magnetism that drew me to this picture was hidden in the writer himself, who was bent over the chessboard, or in his opponent, who was dressed in the fashion of the landed gentry (and whose face, incidentally, seemed to me strangely familiar), or in the members of the household, gathered in great numbers around them, who were seemingly cheering on one or the other, but who were actually posing for the photograph. (Although Sophia Tolstoy seems to have been genuinely cheering—in any case, she is looking intently at the black figures with which her husband is playing.)

Finally, I made the effort, and with the help of a certain petite, but inordinately enterprising Russianist, vintage 1968, I established who is who on the daguerreotype. Incidentally, the petite, but inordinately enterprising Russianist, vintage 1968, who, at first, thought I had come up with a subtle pretext for you-know-what, then, that I was a maniacal nutcase, finally herself became excited about the topic and assembled an extensive group of materials proving that, after all, chess played no trivial role in Tolstoy's life. She even obtained a special book from Moscow, published in the sixties, entitled *Tolstoy i shakhmaty* [*Tolstoy and Chess*]. I looked everything over carefully, I made notes, but I knew from the beginning that these were only formal activities, which would by no means push anything forward. And indeed—they did not.

The secret was probably in chess itself. But—to repeat—I'm a mediocre chess player. Of course, it is possible to speak here of more intense emotions and greater proficiency. The fact, however, that I know more about chess than about the life and works of Lev Tolstoy does not mean that I know a lot about chess. Granted, I used to have a few strong opening moves. Now it is up and down. Now, even that ability, if it's not fading, certainly doesn't show any sparks; but I used to have a few strong opening moves. Perhaps even excellent. Nothing but grandmasters were my teachers. That's right. Each was a grandmaster, and each had his own distinct and unforgettable style of play: Grandpa Pech—bawdy renaissance style; Grandma Pech—fierce style; Uncle Ableger—lightning fast style; Uncle Paweł—devout style. With the exception of Mother, all the members of the household played chess.

The chessboard, which we would place on the table covered with a sky blue oilcloth in our gigantic kitchen, was similar to Tolstoy's. I don't wish to say anything by this. Nor do I multiply cheap effects, nor do I make second-rate jokes. I simply state that our chess set in the old house in Wisła originated—like the chess set they played on in Yasnaya Polyana—in those mythic epochs when the chessboard and the box were separate. Granted, the genius who came up with the idea that the box, after it was opened out, could become the chessboard, had made his discovery. And in fact—as is evident from old prints, at the least—he had made his discovery ages ago. But luckily this discovery hadn't made it to Cieszyn Silesia by the fifties of the twentieth century. And if it had made it to Cieszyn Silesia, it hadn't made it to Wisła. And if it had made it to Wisła, it hadn't made it to our house.

An atavistic-sentimental antipathy, stemming from those times, toward *the box that becomes a chessboard once it is unfolded*, does not—of course—keep me awake at night. I am not consumed day and night by that hatred, but it equals my antipathy to magnetic chess pieces. On the whole, I try to fight my own neuroses. But that one I cultivate.

First (first!) you have to lay out the chessboard. Then (then!) pour out the chess pieces from the box. Pour them out on the chessboard! Not onto the table! No pouring out onto the table! And while placing the pieces, and while putting the pieces away, the chessboard must be in place! Before play, the pieces are to be in the box; during play, on the chessboard. Outside the chessboard stand only dead chess pieces!

Father must have had the same phobias. That's why he insisted on the drawer, and at first even on two drawers. He played pretty well. Not as lightning fast as Uncle Ableger, who adored playing tournament chess and imposed a frightful tempo, drove his opponent on, and—I have to admit—mostly won, although sometimes in his frantic rush he committed blunders you wouldn't believe. And not as fiercely as Grandma Pech, who couldn't stand to lose. And not as hedonistically and generously as Grandpa Pech, who, for the sake of beauty and amusement, forgot about results and, to a certain extent, specialized in losing. And not so prayerfully as Uncle Paweł, who thanked God after each successful move.

Father didn't play either so lightning fast, or so fiercely, or so sybaritically, or so piously—but efficiently and mercilessly enough. After all, chess is merciless by its very nature. In the art of moving chess pieces, there can be no mercy—at most, there can be an error in the art.

I think that, as a child, I must truly have been not so bad. I must have been—because I don't remember anything. And I remember all the ruined games: the crumbling dam we had made out of stones over the stream in Partecznik; a lost match with a IIc team; the disaster in the church trivia contest—when I said that it was Cain and Abel who were twins, rather than Jacob and Esau; lost points during ping-pong tournaments in the Lutheran Church House. I remember all the blocks in the evening games of dominoes; all the disturbed oars and boat-hooks in the pile of pick-up-sticks; all the un-cast sixes in games of Sorry! on holiday evenings; and all the unnamed mountains and rivers in States, Cities—but I don't recall any lost chess games. In other words, I must have won. And won for real, because there was no custom of allowing a young person to win for encouragement—not in our house, nor in Lutheran houses in general. On the contrary—there was the principle of humiliating, from the very beginning, the young person's every ability, grinding him down, kicking him in the ass. If he manages to cope, there is hope for him, if not—oh, well—the Lord God welcomes various sorts at His table.

I remember the flow and the musical naturalness of play. I didn't have the sense of the infallibility of any move—I had the sense that there simply wasn't any other move. Probably, in my case, the famous cognitive innocence had to do with chess, and not with drawing. Most children, as is well known, draw in interesting ways at the beginning; once they grow up a little and begin to draw more consciously, that is to say, to lie, to contrive—the gift vanishes. I grew up a little, began to contrive, the gift vanished. Nowadays I rarely play, and for the last five years all the more rarely, since I play exclusively with myself. If I come upon a chess puzzle in some journal, I am usually able to solve it, and usually—without bragging—it doesn't take me more than a quarter of an hour.

Today's newspapers rarely publish chess puzzles. I don't intend in the least to whine about the fact that we have come to live in evil times, in which lamentable computer games have supplanted the game of kings, or anything of that sort. Absolutely not. I don't have inclinations toward those sorts of banalities, and when, in moments of weakness, they come over me, I summon up the rest of my mental forces, and I fight them in their infancy. Besides all that, I believe that all "games and entertainments of kings" ought to be limited to the elite, and that, in general, only those things that a small, the smallest number of persons cultivates and practices are worthy of note.

I remark upon the sporadic presence of chess problems in today's journals in order to make excuses for a certain eccentricity. Namely, browsing through the newspapers and magazines at the Empik book-store—not with the goal of finding a chess puzzle, in any case, not exclusively with that goal—I noticed that a weekly called *New State*, which is completely unknown to me and always just takes up space on the shelves, publishes not so much chess puzzles as a special chess rubric, even on a decent level, and that, in addition, those half columns (true, they are of a small size) were edited by a rather—judging by the picture—attractive female chess-master with the exotic name of Iweta. I began to buy it rather regularly. I cut out the descriptions of the games and the commentaries by the attractive female chess-master with the exotic name; the rest of *New State* I throw away without reading—so much for my eccentricity.

I have three chess sets. A large one ("Classic?" "Royal?" "Olympic?")—clearly I'm not certain of even the basic terminology; in any case—the chess board measures sixteen inches on a side—it is significantly bigger than the one in Wisła, but the shape of the figures is identical to those that perished together with the house, which has turned into ruin and dust. Pawn, rook, horse, runner, lady, king. The ancient pattern and—since they are taken from my world—the ancient names. No completely unfamiliar knight, bishop, queen. Whenever I hear or read that someone makes a move with his knight, bishop, or queen, I'm not certain at first what game we're talking about. I'm exaggerating—but only slightly and for symbolic effect. Further—I'm ashamed to admit it—I also have magnetic chess pieces. Yes, it's true. Small, classical, but, nonetheless—magnetic. It is—it goes without saying—a piece of shoddy barbarity.

Just as the genuine art of carpentry should be practiced without a single nail, so in genuine chess there is no place for any metal elements. Far greater principles than these are regularly broken for the mother of all shoddiness: human convenience. Alleged convenience. Supposedly in certain situations—for instance, on a trip—it is extremely convenient to play with magnetic chess pieces. I don't know. I avoid travel. Supposedly not only in certain, but in absolutely all situations, computerized chess is even more convenient than the magnetic version. Here I know even less. I use a computer exclusively as a typewriter. For me, the first is worse than the second, and the second is worse than the first. Magnetic chess is worse than the computerized version, but also the computerized is worse than the magnetic. As in life: all scales are in sharp decline. All scenarios are black. True, computerized pieces of shit will supplant magnetic pieces of shit, but this is small consolation, because, seemingly annihilated by the new thing, the slightly magnetized freaks won't disappear at all; rather they will take on a venerable patina and will become rarities sought after by collectors of twentieth-century design, and perhaps even of twentieth-century art. The circle is closing. The loop is tightening. But I give my word of honor: it wasn't for the patina that I bought the magnetic chess set.

I bought it—in a men's gift shop on Krucza Street—because it constantly seemed to me that a bizarre instability reigned over my usual chess set, on which I incessantly played the Tolstoyan game. I suppose I don't have to emphasize, or even point out, that I set up the pieces as soon as I saw the photo. I examined them carefully, I played out successive variants, I returned to the starting point, etc. But with time—this lasted a good couple of months—I began to get the bizarre, though in this case perhaps only too justified, impression that something, someone, some sort of spirit or some other demon was changing the positions of the pawns and other figures, that they were gliding over the chessboard by themselves—the devil only knows.

The solution turned out to be highly disappointing. The Ukrainian woman who cleans for me once a week, and who is—incidentally—amazingly pedantic, wasn't able to resist, and she dusted the chessboard as well. Once I figured out what was going on, I reprimanded her severely, and I absolutely forbade her to go anywhere near the chessboard. But as is usually the case with threats, I felt a lack of security, and so, with the goal of at least minimally strengthening the stability of the position, I bought the magnetic chess set.

True, as soon as I saw, while still in the store, the shocking English inscription on the box—"*Made without child labour*"—I hesitated for a moment. After all, as soon as a person of my generation hears *that it is not true that we put children to work*, there naturally appears a vision of millions of little, emaciated Chinese, hungry and cold, milling or even sculpting the pawns, bishops, and rooks. Such a vision presented itself to me, but it quickly vanished. I'll say it honestly: it vanished before it appeared.

My third chess set is a present from a woman I would like to forget. Clearly, however, that wish is weaker than the desire of possession. I haven't gotten rid of this souvenir, which is all the stranger in that it is a trashy curio to boot. Only—to vent ungentlemanly disdain—a calamitous woman, or rather, only a catastrophic woman, only a woman that catastrophic could hope that anyone would believe that the pseudo-Indian imitation of wood, marble, ivory, copper, ceramic—and whatever else have you—was imported from Bombay, when it was most certainly acquired in the underground passageway under Central Station. And that's in the best case scenario.

As to literature about chess, I have an anthology of all the matches of Bobby Fischer, three volumes of the *Biographical Dictionary of Polish Chess Players*, an English-language monograph on the "Sicilian defense," as well as a fundamental and, frankly speaking, totally insane work entitled *With Chess Through the Ages and History*. I haven't read any of these titles even superficially, but then, the number of the books I put off for reading during more peaceful times is much more considerable and their topics wider. By more peaceful times, I mean days, nights, weeks, and months, the lion's share of which will not be consumed by the passionate chasing of girls. When this happens, when I awake at dawn and begin to read some classic, I will read until the afternoon, and perhaps even—if I feel like it—until dusk. Something tells me I won't live to see this epoch of peace and quiet, but this doesn't mean you shouldn't collect books.

•

II

Someone might say that, by constantly emphasizing that I supposedly don't know much about chess, I am being coy and am obscuring things, since it irrefutably follows from the story I am telling that I must be an entirely decent chess player. Well, without a shadow of a doubt and with deadly solemnity, I declare that I am a miserable chess player, not to say no player at all. And one fundamental detail disqualifies me: I don't know, and I have never completely mastered, the art of chess description. I have mastered it only to the point where I can decode the notation of the newspaper chess riddle without making embarrassing errors, and this is truly little.* The chessboard of my childhood was composed of wooden cream- and dark-brown-colored fields, called "white" and "black," glued onto canvas; and the paradox of the terminology ended here for us. Not I, nor a single one of the house's grandmasters, had the least inkling that there existed some sort of a7s, c5s, f3s. I wouldn't bet my life on it that they could answer without consideration just how many fields and how many pieces there were. And if anyone should tell them that it is possible to play on a scrap of paper, they would be laughed at. Sensual pleasures weren't their strong suit, but there was no point in playing without touching the pieces, without their leisurely or impetuous movement, without permanent staring at the position of the pieces, which slowly dissolves (and yet entrances to the end in its mysterious symmetries). Professional arguments—that if you haven't mastered description, you will also have trouble with chess memory; that, granted, you will remember the position of the pieces, but a memory like that is not very capacious, because the pieces are spatial, and not very many of them will stick in your head—these professional arguments were not for us, and to this day they make no impression upon me.

---

*It is little, but it is intense. If you know Zweig's *Chess Story*, and you must know it, you will understand: I always was, and am, on the side of Czentowic.

Supposedly the mind of the professional chess player is filled with hundreds of thousands of combinations. I have only a couple of them in my head. Although, without a doubt, in the untangling of precisely this history, a few more might come in handy. Just a dozen, just a few tens, just a hundred.

Perhaps I wouldn't stare for months and years at the position of the pieces on Tolstoy's chessboard like there's no tomorrow. Perhaps the position of the pieces itself would open up some sort of secret trap-door in my mind. But I stared, and I didn't have a chance, since even if I had seen such a position at some point, I didn't recall it. Even if I had heard this melody at some point, with my wretched ear for music, I didn't have a chance of repeating it. A classic says: if you remember—you need only connect; but I couldn't connect, because I didn't remember. I didn't have a clue what to connect with what.

Today, I see clearly that I was also afflicted with a peculiar blindness. I carefully examined every square millimeter of the photograph, but I didn't see the stylish little table on which the chessboard was standing. No: it wasn't that I didn't notice, or I didn't attach sufficient importance to it—I simply didn't see. I had a bizarre, or perhaps not at all bizarre, but rather a well-justified block. I didn't see what was in front of my nose, and I didn't remember the first storyline. I pounded my blind head on the photo of Lev Tolstoy playing chess, as if on the Great Wall of China, or on the Berlin Wall. And I stood before that photograph, as if at the Wailing Wall or at the Iron Curtain. And nothing. No move, not a hand, nor a foot. Neither a bishop, nor a rook.

Until once, in one of my common and daily-experienced epiphanies; once, namely, after glimpsing, at the intersection of Krucza and Żurawia Streets, the most perfect suntan in the world; once—to put it more precisely—on a certain November afternoon, when I was just about to chase after the shoulders emerging from a lizard-green dress and opalescing like Nestlé milk chocolate; when I was already—I'll say it honestly—chasing after them; when at any moment I was about to change my shape and state of concentration and become a drop of sweat on the withdrawing back of the super babe I had glimpsed by chance—it suddenly dawned on me. Suddenly I stood as if rooted in the ground, suddenly I gave up the chase, suddenly I became myself again. Suddenly the torment caused by this ill-fated photograph vanished; suddenly I realized whom the fellow playing chess with Tolstoy resembled.

He had reminded me of someone the entire time, but this was—so to say—a side uncertainty. An ornamental uncertainty. And so, taken as a whole, the picture was troubling from A to Z, and in it—on top of all that—someone reminds me of somebody. But the fact that he reminds me of someone seems unimportant: it is too ostentatious, it is too much on the surface, and it also looks like a mysterious, although trite, addendum. The main hieroglyphs were almost certainly registered on the chessboard; the match, which had barely begun, might go in any direction, and hundreds of possible combinations could be puzzles and their solutions. Thousands of pages and stories recorded by the brilliant writer might contain entries and exits from the labyrinths. In the end, probably it is in them that we will find the beautiful and intricate crux of the matter, and not in the fact that someone here resembles someone else. Someone always resembles someone else; and when you set off from a small town into the great world, you constantly come upon people in this world who are doubles of people who lived in the neighborhood, and—outside of anatomic pranks—there are no secrets here. I could write a whole book about the doubles of old citizens of Wisła I have met in the world, and it would be a superficial work. Even the similarity of old Lazar to Winston Churchill or of Szarzec from Partecznik to Paul VI is of little significance, to say nothing of the lesser cases of similarity.

It appears that I myself am disappointed with my own solution. Yes and no. I am, because it turned out that the key to the mystery is to be found in the addendum to the mystery that was lying on the very surface. And I'm not disappointed, because the principle that a good horror contains answers to fundamental questions—the nature of evil, the devil, and the other world—proved true as gold in my own thriller.

III

THE LANDED GENTRYMAN PLAYING CHESS WITH LEV NIKOLAEVICH Tolstoy reminded me of a certain driver from the Academy of Mining and Metallurgy. We saw him a total of one time, and although both Mother and I, and the other members of the household, well remembered his feats, his face and external appearance were completely erased. And here you have it, after staring at the photograph for three years, on its surface appeared that same—the spitting image of that—good-natured, but essentially hypocritical smile; that same high forehead passing over into a bald spot; that same slovenly and disheveled beard. I had found it. The truth lay on the surface. It was darkest under the lantern. I had for the telling one of the basic and, for a short time, frequently recalled family stories. What is more, a thoroughly family *chess* story. Recalled frequently, but for a short time, for it soon turned out that all of us preferred to forget these not entirely understandable events from—today it will already be—more than forty years ago.

For an engineer at the Academy of Mining and Metallurgy, Father disappeared without a trace decidedly too frequently. He always returned, however, and there is no point in hiding it: these were sorry returns. Always sozzled, always the worse for wear, and always with that same old story: namely, that he had been playing ping-pong with his colleagues until the break of dawn.

When he got lost during the move to Krakow, however, the matter looked ominous. For the first time, we were certain that he was no longer alive.

It was a sweltering August in the year 1962. I was ten years old, and I was at the apogee of all possibilities. After some dozen months of incessant soccer playing, I had become a consummate forward. In a thick journal with a green binding, which I had received for my birthday, I was writing a detective/romance novel. In the expectation of God knows what sort of mystery, I traipsed around after a certain oddly dressed female vacationer. Almost every night, I dreamed of great flights over the Earth and breath-taking landings in yellow grass. I was in love with Claudia Cardinale and—as befitted a true man—I didn't care in the least about reciprocity on her part. Beginning in the fall, we were to be living in Krakow, and each day of that summer had the taste of final things.

Father placed an order with Master Sztwertnia for bookshelves that were to occupy one whole wall in the Krakow apartment, a hanging kitchen cabinet, and a special little table for playing chess.

"What do you mean, a little table for playing chess?" Mother wrung her hands. "A little table for chess? It's a disgrace to order something like that. Master Sztwertnia is a serious craftsman! He isn't going to make any absurdities! What's the point of a little chess table!" Mother screamed. "Can't you play on a normal table?"

"No," Father responded dully.

"You are Newton!" Mother raised her gaze to the heavens. "You are the great scientist Isaac Newton!"

Probably for the hundredth time, for there was no lack of opportunities, she cited the anecdote about Sir Isaac Newton, who, so they say, weary of constantly opening the door for the cat and her kittens as they sauntered back and forth, ordered two openings to be cut over the threshold—a large one for the cat and a smaller one for the kittens—"as if," she choked, "as if the small cats couldn't manage to pass through the large hole! Newton! A genuine Isaac Newton! And besides, when are you going to play that chess? When? Since you are never home."

"On Sunday," Father answered arrogantly, and Mother capitulated and glanced in the direction of Grandma Pech, as if seeking comfort and understanding. Every time Grandma heard about the little chess table, she would shudder, as if it were a matter of deviltry in the strict sense; she didn't cross herself, she didn't make the sign of the cross, since we don't do that on a daily basis; but she would wave it off in despair and immediately, from the spot where she happened to be standing at the moment, rush off, as if she were rushing into panicky flight that would take her as far as the eye could see, and after a few steps she would suddenly halt and glance furtively at the old man to see whether he had come to his senses, and seeing that he hadn't come to his senses, she would lend her features an expression that said: Get thee hence, Satan!

Grandpa gave a faint smile, chuckled quietly, laughed in the depths of his soul. It wasn't so much the little chess table that delighted him as the panic into which the women fell on account of this piece of equipment. But even he, after a certain time, lost his composure, became morose, drew Father aside, and tried to reason with him:

"Think this over, Józef. Just think it over. I myself, as you know, adore chess, but why go overboard? We play chess, but we aren't real chess players. All of us, almost all of us in this house, play chess, but our house is not a house of real chess players. To say nothing of a house of chess playing professionals, chess playing gamblers, or chess playing addicts. We play the way the Lord God commanded: on Sunday afternoons, on long winter evenings, on holidays. And we play with the sort of chess set He commanded, and on the sort of chess board that is pleasing to Him. Why do you want more, Józef? Why do you need this little chess table?"

"In order to play chess on it," Father answered dully. "In order to play chess on it in Krakow. On Sunday afternoons. On long winter evenings and on holidays."

"On holidays," Grandpa responded, "I hope you will come visit us. And then we will play as we always have. I don't understand you, Józef. Take, for example, beds. We all sleep in normal beds, *all* people in general sleep in normal beds: wooden, with straw pallets and mattresses, and under eiderdown. And that is how it should be. But you, Józef, with that little chess table of yours, you are behaving as if, for unknown reasons, you wished for yourself who knows what sort of bed. Air mattresses like at the swimming pool, silk bedspreads like in a brothel, and bamboo frames like in the Congo. Think this over, Józef. After all, this is, basically, deviltry."

"No," Father responded, "it isn't the same thing. An air mattress is not a little chess table. The chess board glued to the table top isn't a coverlet in a brothel. The Congo isn't Krakow. The entire problem," Father paled, and drops of sweat broke out on his forehead, "the entire problem stems from the confusion of concepts. The confusion of everything with everything else—*that's* the deviltry. The muddling of everything with everything else—*that's* demonism. There's no point discussing it. I won't give in."

IV

THE TENSION GREW. WE AWAITED MASTER SZTWIERTNIA AS IF FOR the Second Coming of the Lord, who will judge the advocates and enemies of eccentricity. When, at long last, the drone of his dilapidated Willys resounded in the courtyard, when he himself appeared in the doorway in an ancient collarless shirt, in a worn out brown suit marked here and there with streaks of sawdust; when he sat down at the table in our huge kitchen, and when, after a discussion, or rather, after a cursory review of the structural details of the bookshelves, which were to cover the entire wall, and of the hanging kitchen cabinet; when, self-conscious and the object of the glares of Mother and Grandmother, Father removed from his breast pocket a folded piece of paper with a carefully sketched project for a little chess table—at this point a terrible, explosion-pregnant quiet fell over the kitchen. The master carpenter placed the paper on the table, his silver head inclined ever lower, the women standing at the stove looked at my old man with disgust. It can't be helped; since he didn't want to listen to our warnings, since in spite of our admonitions he insisted on committing this prank, now he'll get what's coming to him. The master will give him a thorough chewing-out out on the spot and tell him not to bother a serious professional with such caprices. Grandfather sat on the opposite side of the table and smiled cheerfully—for him, every solution was attractive from the narrational point of view. He had said his bit, given his warning—OK, he had a clean conscience, and now, somewhat excited and light of heart, he awaited a hell of a lark.

The master bent ever lower over the page, then he suddenly straightened up and said: "Wait, wait a minute." And he reached into the side pocket of his jacket and extracted, first, a massive carpenter's pencil and then—smiling apologetically—an equally massive case holding round glasses in a wire frame, and he put those glasses on his nose and looked at the drawing a good while longer, and he tapped it with his pencil, and it seemed to us all that he was definitively putting a nail in the misguided construction, and he tapped one more time and said: "Wait, wait a minute. One drawer will suffice, but it should be on the side."

Jesus Christ! Master Sztwiertnia hadn't put a nail in it, he had only pointed out a flaw in the construction.

Few, very few times in my life have I seen my old man completely happy. Three, perhaps four times. Once, when we were coming down from Partecznik and suddenly, as we came around the bend, our just finished house came into view on the opposing slope in the yellowish radiance of the sun that was setting over Czantoria—perhaps then he was happy. Perhaps he was happy when, a year before he died, he returned home from the hospital, opened the gate, went up the stairs, and life, so it seemed, was before him. Perhaps when, forty years earlier, at the parent-teachers meeting, Mr. Kogutko told him that I was the best mathematician in the class, he was happy, because he didn't yet know that my career as a mathematical genius would end soon, and hopelessly. Perhaps he was happy when, with superhuman effort in inhuman conditions, he completed work on his greatest invention: a machine that automatically watered balcony flower boxes. Perhaps he was, perhaps he wasn't. But then, when Master Sztwiertnia treated his project for a little chess table with dignity and curiosity, he was absolutely euphoric.

At first, like a student made self-conscious by unexpected recognition, he didn't really know what to do. But he quickly overcame his triumphal abashment, and—not favoring either his female antagonists (who were suddenly intently focused on the tea kettle with its sluggishly boiling water) or his ally (which, immediately, judging by his euphoric countenance, Grandfather had become) with even a single glance—he launched upon detailed inquiries with Master Sztwiertnia.

One drawer for the figures and pawns will suffice, but it must be on the side, because that is both convenient, and it maintains the principle of impartiality. Chess is a game in which, before the beginning of the match, the pieces must not be kept on the side of any one of the players. Two drawers, one on each side—OK; but if there is one, then it must be in the middle. Sufficiently deep in order not to unsettle the balance; which is all to the good, since it will be firmly planted. And it won't be necessary to pull it out the whole way; so that it will be possible to keep something important in its depths. For instance, photographs that you rarely look at or other paraphernalia intended for a man's use. Sztwiertnia winked knowingly. Panicky hisses began to reach us immediately from the direction of the kitchen stove, but those were already a different sort of indignation. This was ritualistic indignation, and full, for that reason, of a peculiar relief. An indignation that was prepared, practiced, and even studied. An indignation expected by those who were going to feel indignant. An indignation that itself was anticipating its own venting. Not deprived of genuine excitement, but not sensational.

It was universally known that master Sztwiertnia was a rabid sex maniac and would shift every conversation, sentence, and situation in his favorite direction. The fact, however, that the master, in exploiting his uncommon talents, left signs of his obsession everywhere he could—this aroused genuine panic. Sztwiertnia had hands of gold, he could do practically everything, he dabbled in every craft and every art, he played numerous instruments, he also drew and painted magnificently. And it was well known that when you ordered from Sztwiertnia—for instance, a cabinet—it would be a cabinet slightly surpassing in beauty and solidity all the Kalwaria, Gdańsk, and other cabinets of the world; but it was also well known that, somewhere in its nooks and corners, the master—as if it were the author's signature—would hide a troublesome detail, a lascivious ornament, an obscene bit. And that it wouldn't be some bare ass with a huge tit tossed off with his carpenter's pencil. No way! The master would produce perfect mythological scenes, nudes worthy of Titian, Rubenesque shapes; he was realistic like Ingres, sensual like Renoir, perverse like Manet, distinctive—and particularly irremovable—like a Japanese woodcut. No need to add that, following the model of the old masters, Sztwiertnia often gave his nudes faces known to everyone in the neighborhood. The most notorious was the image of a muscular satyr with the head of Pastor Kalinowski embracing a buck-naked nymph, with the face of Ryfka Deresewicz, frozen in a spasm of absolute transport—oil on wood. The wood was the bottom of a huge feast table ordered by the parish for the Church House in commemoration of the founding of our church. The history of the origin of this masterpiece, its concealment, revelation, and destruction—this is a topic for another story.

It was clear what the studied hisses of the women signified and what they concerned. Bad enough that there was to be a little chess table, but now with pornography inside it to boot. But the Master, who adored reactions full of more or less feigned indignation, this time didn't even twitch.

"Wait, wait a minute." On his pale countenance appeared what seemed to be a truly erotic flush. "Wait, wait a minute. It isn't fitting that the chessboard be glued onto the tabletop. I'll say more, Mr. Engineer, it isn't fitting either that it be glued in, recessed. That is, it must be recessed, but it can't be any chessboard taken from some sort of factory-made chess sets. It must be an original chessboard. And we will have to make it, cut sixty-four squares, half with dark veneer, half colorless. Or it would be even better if we make the dark squares of walnut, or even better, black oak, and the white of sycamore. This will harmonize with the pine and be elegant. Wait! Wait a minute!"

V

WAIT, WAIT A MINUTE. TOWARD THE END OF AUGUST, MASTER Sztwiertnia appeared with the finished miracle under his arm. He set it down carefully in our fieldstone-covered courtyard and began to unwrap it from under numerous layers of *The Workers' Tribune*. The removal of the successive veils ought to have been like the baring of a body, like a striptease, but it wasn't. That is, on the one hand it was something more, on the other something less. More, because the solicitude with which Sztwiertnia removed the subsequent sheets of *The Workers' Tribune* was some sort of hyper-solicitude and hyper-tenderness. With such extreme delicacy one doesn't disrobe a woman, with such extreme delicacy one doesn't even dismantle an atomic bomb. Less, because the languor of the Master's movements also flowed from the fact that he was drunk as a lord—a sensation in itself, since Sztwiertnia practically didn't drink at all.

Finally, the incomprehensible architecture was made visible, finally there spread before us the view of a cathedral in the desert, of a statue extracted from the swamps, of a fresco unveiled from under layers of Roman plasters, and slowly we approached its curves, symmetries, and radiance, and nobody knew what to say, for none of us had known such beauty and such selflessness before. And no one knew that such a thing existed, that it even could exist. Even the women had delight in their eyes, because you could feel that, without the help of God, it was impossible to bring something like that into existence. And then we began to touch it, test it, push and pull the drawer, count the squares; to examine what sort of luster the chessboard had when viewed from an angle. And we examined Master Sztwiertnia's masterpiece more and more conscientiously, more and more carefully did we follow its turns, leaps, and perspectives, and then we just stopped pretending that we were looking at it for the beauty of the construction, for the color, for the play of lights. Ever more impatiently and entirely openly and—that's right—shamelessly did we investigate it, inch by inch, in search of the seal of love, which, on an object that perverse, must have been infinitely perverse. We pulled out the drawer and examined the bottom and the underside of the drawer, and the bay for the drawer, and we looked under the tabletop and everywhere. And there wasn't anything anywhere, and we glanced with uncertainty at the Master, who stood nearby and smoked Extra Strongs. We looked at him in the hope that he would give us some hint, if only the path leading to the erotic miniature, which perhaps it would be necessary to study through a magnifying glass, but those studies would be well worth the trouble. The Master, however, didn't say anything; he smoked, reeled slightly, came to, and once he had come to, and once he had finished smoking, he shook his head and said: "There isn't anything there; that little table is the very essence of screwing in and of itself."

VI

EVERYTHING WAS NOW READY—THE HANGING KITCHEN CABINET, the bookshelves that were to fill an entire wall—and innumerable boxes stood in the courtyard in a covered spot, where, supposedly, even after the war there had stood an ancient coach, and where its scattered and corroded specter still roamed. Services, sets of knives and forks, towels, three wedding presents that hadn't been opened in ten years, a vacuum cleaner, photograph albums, books, a floor lamp, an exceptionally beautiful étagère, a gigantic couch, an even larger armchair (a present from the bishop), pieces of crystal, a *Capital City* radio, several bales of material for window curtains—all this was supposed to fit into the two Krakow rooms, in which we would finally start living like human beings.

"You don't live like human beings here?" Grandma Pech asked. "Is rain pouring on your heads?"

"Rain isn't pouring on our heads, but that doesn't mean that we live like human beings. We have no life here at all. We are dying here. In any case, I will die here any moment now."

Mother's voice shook strangely and childishly. I didn't really understand in any detail what was going on, but that it was a contest between life and death—this much was clear. In any case, it was clear at least once a week. Once a week, Father would come home from Krakow. Then my bed linen would be transferred from the great marital bed, where I slept excellently, to the hard couch against the wall, on which bad dreams tormented me and on which I always woke up in the middle of the night. The lamps at the head of my parents' bed would be lit, Father would wander around the room in nothing but his pajama bottoms, shifting objects from place to place, poking around the books, and repeating—practically shouting—spasmodically: "Forgive me for living, just forgive me for living! Forgive me for living, but this doesn't depend on me, although who knows, who knows!" Mother would follow my old man with a tired and hostile glance; on the other side of the wall, in the small room in which my grandparents slept, there would resound a cough, the floor would creak, you could hear shuffling, the door would open, Grandpa would appear in it in remarkable underclothes, and say: "Calm down, we beg you, calm down. Calm down. After all, you both have higher educations!" Father would find some book, put a jacket on his naked body, and go to the kitchen. Mother would turn out the light. I could still hear her spasmodic and despairing whisper. I would begin to fall off to sleep. The nightmares would return.

In the morning at breakfast, the talk was always about engineer Kowala, who had already made plans for the entire attic; the walls would be raised and brightened, there would be five rooms there and enough space that Józek would be able to set up even *two* ping-pong tables for himself. Father, pale and sleepy, would respond furiously that they should stop bothering him with ping-pong tables, because positing ping-pong tables as an element of a life-plan is a muddling of everything with everything else, it's demonism. He doesn't intend to play ping-pong, he intends to do something yet in life. "I have this capricious desire to do something yet in life that is in keeping with my education and interests. I know that this is incomprehensible for you, and that, in your opinion, I ought to just sit here and fart around, but I, unfortunately, am not interested. I want to do something in science. I won't become an Einstein, because the war took away a good bit of my life, and you can't get that back, but at least I want to try. Do you all understand? And he," Father pointed with a nod of his head in my direction, "he also deserves a different start in life. Different from the one I got. I can't do *much* for him, but at least I can provide him with a different start."

VII

I PACKED MY BAGS DAILY. EVERY DAY, I PLACED MY BOOKS AND TOYS anew in an old, navy blue suitcase. Depending on my mood, I would promise them a trip to Krakow or condemn them to stay forever in Wisła. "You didn't acquit yourself today," I would say to my Piko model train set, "the move to Krakow is an honor, and you haven't earned it," and I would remove the little cars and tracks, and I would close the suitcase ostentatiously, so that the victim was conscious of the irreversibility of its fate. "Do I make excessive demands upon you?" I asked my Finnish knife. "No, I demand of you elementary effort. I repeat: elementary effort. But you can't even manage that. Unfortunately, Krakow is a city for tough people, not for wimps. Everybody off! Be my guest," I would say to my stamp albums in an icy tone, "be my guest. If you don't like it, just go on sitting here. Be my guest, sit here to the end of the world and fart around!" The following day I would return to grace those I had spurned, and I would cast into the abyss the Czech crayons, the East German sets of miniature tools, periscopes, slide projectors, magnets, adventure and fantasy novels, which were already feeling like they were practically in Krakow (you rested on your laurels too early, lazy bones!); and so on, over and over. I strutted about like a madman. I was an absolute ruler and absolutely capricious. I deserted my world, and with the ghastly delight of an underage emperor I cast it into the abyss.

The motionless, green surface of water in the swimming pool, the triangulation tower on Czantoria excellently visible in the russet radiance, the ball turning dark from the wet grass on the soccer field *Start*, the smell of mown hay at the villa *Almira*, the dark radiance of the skin of the girl sitting in front of me at the movie theater, the air thickening in the afternoons like a magnifying glass—all of this was to be abandoned here forevermore, deprived of my presence, my glances, and my touch. My absence was punishment, and the punishing was sweet.

But in the evening, Chowderhead the cat would jump on my bed. I felt the beating of his heart, I petted his head, trustingly nestled in the eiderdown, and I bawled, and I howled from despair. It was perfectly clear that here, in the gigantic house with a garden and courtyard, it will be a million times better for him than in two rooms in Krakow, and it was perfectly clear that we would come for holidays and vacations; and I would be with him then to my heart's content; and everything fell to pieces, and the entire incredible summer of the year 1962 was so distinct that it drew a curtain over my despair, and to this day I am certain that the entire evil of my life and all my ordeals are retribution for abandoning Chowderhead the cat. I am paying for his year of solitude with my ghastly and unbearable solitude. For the last year of his life—when he looked for me in empty rooms, when he would jump up onto cold sheets, when he would sniff abandoned objects, when, in the hope that, when he woke up, everything would be as before—he would go to sleep and wake up, and I still wasn't there with him. The path of my life was recorded in the animal heart of Chowderhead the cat. I didn't choose that path. Father went missing during the move—that was a sign of doom. But abandoning Chowderhead—this was the choice of doom.

VIII

The oddly dressed female vacationer walked in the direction of *Oasis*. With the light heart of the chosen one, I hastened after her. She turned toward the Dziechcinka; today she was wearing a violet, long-sleeved dress with gigantic, russet fern fronds. When she was under the viaduct, she disappeared; this time, more than usual, it appeared that she had vanished in thin air. I looked around for a while, without panic, and without great nervousness; her sudden disappearance belonged to the order of things. I returned home. In the courtyard stood a special truck with a special tarp.

Father had been announcing all summer long that a special truck from the Academy of Mining and Metallurgy, covered with a special tarp, driven by a special driver, would come to collect our belongings. It had finally arrived and—no big deal. I was disappointed. Not by the truck itself, for, after all, I knew my old man's excesses well enough not to imagine some sort of heavenly chassis or golden tarps, but by the fact that the world had moved. The pieces of furniture, boxes, objects heaped under the shed had been more unusual in their immobility than they were now as—one after another—they were set in place under the tarp. All the men were working, but on the back of the truck stood a slovenly unshaved guy, with a high forehead that was verging on a bald spot, and he directed the work imperiously and with a false smile.

IX

It goes without saying that I didn't have a clue that he was deceptively similar to someone with whom Lev Tolstoy had played chess more than half a century before. I didn't have a shadow of any sort of forebodings, no divine intuitions whatsoever; no otherworldly missives reached me that the special driver of the special truck from the Academy of Mining and Metallurgy—who was bestowed with the inclinations of a leader, and who had just arrived from Krakow for our possessions—was similar to the son-in-law of Lev Nikolaevich Tolstoy.

It seems that I didn't mention this yet, but the petite, and yet inordinately enterprising Russianist, vintage 1968, had in the end established irrefutably that, on the photograph that had so absorbed me, the author of *Anna Karenina* was playing chess with his son-in-law, Mikhail Sergeyevich Sukhotin. I couldn't mention it, because when I began to write and to look into the matter, I didn't know this yet. Now I know, and I am supplementing the data. A friend and disciple of Tolstoy, Vladimir Grigoryevich Chertkov, also came into question, since, as my Russianist claims, he likewise played chess with Tolstoy, and he, too, was photographed in the course of such a game.

But there is no doubt that in the photo, the story of which I have been telling all this time, it is the son-in-law. Arguments of a—I would say—spiritual nature also speak in favor of this: the guy at the chessboard has struck a submissive and flattering pose, as if he were apologizing for not losing straight-away, on the first move. Most likely, everyone who played with Tolstoy struck such a pose, but with the player for whom Tolstoy was also a father-in-law, such a pose could without a doubt be more distinct. After all, if you are rolling the daughter of the author of *Resurrection*, you have to show some humility. Something for something.

X

Neither I, nor Father, nor Grandpa, nor either uncle, nor the Nikandy boys, who were helping us load our sticks of furniture onto the truck—none of us knew that the guy was a double for Tolstoy's son-in-law, but all of us could see only too well that something wasn't right about him.

He rushed about the platform like a madman, shouted out commands in the most genuine fury, in a moment he would restrain himself and pretend that it was all jokes and playacting, that he viewed these incidents from an infinite distance. A second later the fury would possess him again, and he would rage, and he would go at it hammer and tongs, the virtuoso of every sort of packing, loading, and arranging of objects. It was absolutely clear that he was giving us stupid commands and superfluous orders, that he was pretending to be God knows who, and he sweated atrociously while doing it. *"Wet as a drowned rat, and there he goes giving commands,"* Uncle Ableger finally said under his breath, and as is usual in such situations, a silly, coarse, perhaps even vulgar sentence—after all, it wasn't entirely clear what it meant—defused the situation and, at the same time, took on the characteristic of some sort of aphorism, or perhaps incantation. *"Wet as a drowned rat, and there he goes giving commands,"* we repeated, lifting boxes, and we split our sides laughing. *"Wet as a drowned rat, and there he goes giving commands!"* Tolstoy's son-in-law—helpless in the face of our laughter and wishing to use the classic method to blur the lines of our laughter—laughed along with us. The results were ghastly, since he laughed with the zeal of the class dunce who was pretending that *he* best understood the joke he didn't get. But also, slowly, both his and our laughter died down. Slowly we neared the grand finale—everything was already under the tarp, arranged with the more or less alleged perfection, secured, tied down, wedged in. The little chess table, wrapped in so many layers of *The Worker's Tribune* that it looked like a miniature Orthodox church or an atomic mushroom cloud, stood—I remember—almost in the middle, tightly fortified by boxes. Grandma Pech still gave them a bag of apples. She still ran across the courtyard with a package of cutlets for the entire week, wrapped in paper that was already beginning to leak grease. Still, at the last minute, I came to the decision that I would pardon its laziness, and that, after all, I would take *The Mysterious Island* with me to Krakow, and I threw it into the truck, and—Bombs Away! The final chapter of The Book of Exodus had been composed.

·

It was getting toward one o'clock. It was probably the most torrid day of the summer. We washed under a black rubber hose pulled out from the laundry room, from which flowed fantastic water, icy and fragrant of fecund meadows. Grandma was preparing dinner in the kitchen, and it suddenly turned out that Tolstoy's son-in-law had vanished. Just a moment ago he had been by the vehicle, just a moment ago, naked to the waist, he was pouring water on himself like a maniac and boasting of some sort of infinite knowledge concerning the art of pouring water, just a moment ago he was sitting in the cab, just a moment ago he was bustling about, here and there—and now he's gone. The guy's gone. He's not in the can, he's not under the tarp, he isn't in the courtyard, he's not in front of the house. Jesus Christ! Stung by our laughter, our constantly repeated "*Wet as a drowned rat, and there he goes giving commands,*" he took offense and ran off further than the eye can see! We had gone too far; after all, the guy worked like a dog, was busy as a bee, worked his ass off with the rest of us. So what if he was a bit strange? Better strange and industrious, than normal and a lazy bum. He couldn't stand it, and he disappeared into thin air. We knew of such reactions. Disappearing without a trace— that was a constant custom of Grandma Pech. Whenever so much was going on all around that she couldn't stand it, she would up and vanish, hide away somewhere in the depths of the house, and often it was necessary to search for her for a long time, and with our hearts in our throats. Yet another peculiar and complicated story. How were we supposed to know that he had the same habit? But, after all, he didn't disappear in the house, he didn't hide away in our loft, he didn't climb up into the attic. He took off somewhere, and that was the last we saw of him. A fine state of affairs. Mother had been in Krakow for a few days already, getting the new apartment ready, making space between the new super sofa beds for our Wisła stuff, and now we didn't know whether there is any point to any of it. My old man wouldn't go by himself—he doesn't have a driver's license. In our house, nobody at all has a driver's license. The Nikandy boys can probably drive anything, but none of them has a driver's license either. A tragedy. Simply a

Jerzy Pilch

tragedy. Or rather—as it was to turn out—the subtle prologue to a tragedy.

Because Grandpa Pech had also vanished. He had vanished, but only for a short time. For—let's say—a quarter of an hour. He returned after a quarter of an hour, leading Tolstoy's ashamed, and highly abashed, son-in-law. He hadn't wanted to cause any trouble during the family dinner, which, as he understood, was also in a certain sense a farewell dinner. He hadn't wanted to cause any inconvenience. He wasn't a guest here, he was here to work. He had run out to town for a moment for a cold lemonade. For a cold lemonade before the trip, and for strengthening. Grandpa shrugged it all off, especially upon hearing the words *lemonade* and *strengthening*, but all ambiguity was immediately hushed up by the peals of laughter and the spasmodic cries of the women. How could he go for lemonade when there is so much compote stored up in the house! Hundreds of gallons! From our own apples! From our own garden! You can drink and drink, and even so, you'll never drink it all up. And even if—a new batch will be ready in a flash! Or we can open last year's! Whatever kind you like! Cherry! Plum! Pear! Please, drink, be our guest! And no need to ask—feel right at home and help yourself! But now you must sit down to the table! You've got to eat dinner before the trip! Compote is one thing, but dinner is quite another!

Tolstoy's son-in-law did indeed soak up whole jugs of compote, but the rest didn't go down so well. Maybe two spoonfuls of chicken noodle soup, the meat barely at all, the potatoes and cucumber salad scattered about on the plate. Basically, this was unfathomable. It never happened in our parts that a grown man wouldn't wipe his plate clean. So something wasn't quite right with him after all. Stomach ulcers? Something even worse? God forbid!

He excused himself constantly and in a roundabout way, saying that he was very sorry, but before a trip—especially such a difficult trip—he eats little, because an abundant meal lowers his psychophysical efficiency. It wasn't very clear what he was talking about. This was the first time we had ever heard about the harmful effects of eating. But it seemed that pangs of conscience were still consuming us, because everyone zealously nodded in agreement with everything he said—besides, what was there to talk about, now that it was time to set off? The bells call us to devotions from the tower, Mother from the doorway to supper. They're already calling, it's time. Time to go home, time.

Just before starting out, Tolstoy's son-in-law announced that he had to stretch his legs, and especially straighten his back, and walk a bit. And again he disappeared beyond the gate; this time, however, he returned lightning fast and in a suddenly fine mood. Grandpa again shrugged it off, but they were already leaving. Father sat on the right. I opened the gate. The Star, as huge as a hill, rolled along over the field rocks, drove out onto the road in a blue cloud of exhaust, turned left, set off toward the center of town, disappeared in the darkening perspective, and vanished for the ages. Like a stone in water. For ever and ever. Not a trace, not a peep. Now you see them, now you don't.

I traipsed about the house; from the window in the attic you could see everything, as if it were on the palm of your hand. Suddenly, everything became so near and so distinct, like I was staring through binoculars: female sprinters ran around the playing field, frontier guards walked along the border on Stożek Mountain, the cat walked through the garden on a precise diagonal, there was something terrible in the clouds over the Jarzębata, the bridge groaned under a black Wartburg. In the desolate room, I opened the green-bound notebook with my detective/romance novel, but I didn't have any ideas. I thought that in a couple days—when I finally landed in the new apartment, about which Father told such miraculous things, when I went out on the high balcony and saw *Cracovia* stadium down below, when, from the other room, I caught sight of the roofs of the city heaped up and overlapping like wings of a biplane—then I would certainly begin to write up a storm. I would go by train on Saturday with Grandpa Pech: Wisła—Goleszów—Skoczów—Czechowice—Chybie—Trzebinia—Krakow Main Station; on Sunday I would look around a bit, and on Monday I would get going with the book. As you

Jerzy Pilch

can see: at an exceptionally early age, I found myself in the clutches of the old writer's superstition—that supposedly a change of place will help. And I remained stuck in it for a long time. Until recently, to tell the truth.

I closed the notebook, and I was just about to dash out onto the soccer field. Any day now, Poland's national team was supposed to arrive, perhaps it was already there and was having its first practice. I laced up my tennis shoes—probably on the way I would come upon the female vacationer in her next incredible long sleeve dress; I was already in the doorway, I was already turning the door handle, when Mother telephoned from Krakow: "What's going on? When did they leave? They still aren't here! They left around two, and it's already seven! What's going on?"

Grandpa, usually the calmest member of the household, immediately began to swear under his breath that it's no wonder. It's no wonder that they haven't arrived, because if the driver has to have a lemonade in every roadhouse along the way, lemonade, cold lemonade, they won't get there even by tomorrow. He spoke too soon. They didn't get there by the next day. They didn't get there at all. They never got there. A thunderbolt struck out of the clear blue sky, and everything burned up.

All evening—telephone calls. From Krakow, and to Krakow. There and back again. Through the intercity exchange. Except that Mrs. Gertruda—who had been the telephone operator forever, and who had been hopelessly in love with Grandpa forever—connected us without our having to wait our turn, and quickly. But what good are quick connections when there is nothing to talk about. They aren't there, and that's that. Are they there? No. An hour later—are they there? No. All night long—are they there? No. In the morning—are they there? No.

Before noon, Grandma locked herself in the back room, and there resounded the creaking of a wardrobe that was almost never opened. I was afraid. I was afraid that funeral dresses were hanging in the never-opened wardrobe. I feared preparations for Father's funeral. I didn't want him—once they had finally found him—to lie in an open coffin in the biggest room. I didn't want Grandma to wipe his parchment face with spirits. I didn't want to sleep under the same roof with his corpse. Of the two evils, it would be better that he never be found; that he land—together with the special truck driven by the special driver from the Academy of Mining and Metallurgy—in America, or on the Moon.

Today, when the most diverse *attacks on long-distance freight trucks* are our daily bread, when almost on a daily basis entire columns of trucks or entire segments of train cars disappear without a trace, as if they had evaporated—this causes no sensation whatsoever. But back then? A gigantic Star loaded to the hilt has vanished without a trace? Impossible. In any case, the *militia* didn't believe it. Neither the Wisła nor the Krakow militia officers believed it. They shook their heads doubtfully, they observed us with a flicker of compassion, and they continually asked whether Father perhaps had had some plans. And whether, before the current disappearance, it had previously happened that he would disappear? And whether, before the current ill-fated trip, he had also recently taken a trip somewhere? Where do you have in mind? That's just it, where? Perhaps he had taken some unusual business trips lately? Perhaps he had made some calls? Using the intercity exchange? Perhaps international? Perhaps he had submitted the paperwork for a passport? Do we understand correctly that you have acquaintances in London? Were there any letters from them recently? We aren't suggesting anything. Nothing at all. But whenever someone vanishes with all his belongings, he usually knows what he is doing. And usually, after a certain amount of time, he turns up. In London, or in Munich, or in West Berlin. Absolutely not? Are you sure? Well, in that case, let's hope for the best. Patrols are on the road, and as soon as we know anything, we'll let you know. Sooner or later he'll turn up. After all, he's not a needle. If he isn't on a ship sailing for America, he'll turn up. He'll turn up. The ill-fated vehicle will turn up. The unlucky Star will turn up. It will turn up. In the middle of the road, in the middle of life, in the open field. Covered by a yellow hill and a hazelnut grove. With an almost entirely burned tarp.

On the morning of the third day, Master Sztwiertnia will drive down in his famous Willys that still remembers the war, he will take Grandpa, without a word they will set off, and, after not quite three hours of careful driving, they will find the place as if drawn straight to it. Suddenly, from the right-hand side, some sort of stench will come to them, the smell of burning, barely perceptible smoke, and they will turn, although there won't be a road there. Only after a moment will tire tracks appear in the grass. Father, unshaven and battered, will be sitting on a ripped open box, which had been removed from the back of the truck, and out of which were pouring dictionaries and encyclopedias; his face covered in his hand, elbows resting on the little chess table.

In the first moment, they didn't even notice the crack, because the base and the table top were incredibly strongly and intricately bound with twine, and it seemed that those pieces of twine still came from the packing, that the innumerable layers of *The Worker's Tribune* had been removed, but the pieces of twine had been left. Only later did it turn out that he must have spent the entire three days that he had been in the field attempting every which way to put the severed table back together.

Master Sztwiertnia's masterpiece had been precisely—absolutely precisely—split in two, as if from the blow of a blade that was incredibly forceful and precise. On the split chessboard: a greasy paper that had once contained the cutlets, a gnawed-at apple, a partly burned scrap of *The Worker's Tribune*. Besides, everywhere around there were burnt pages of *The Worker's Tribune*—was he sending signals with the lit newspapers, or what? Of Tolstoy's son-in-law—it goes without saying—not a trace, which perhaps was only for the better.

Suddenly, it was swarming, the local inhabitants were running through the fields, the *militia* Nyska drove up with bravado, a fire-truck with the siren going, with its crew ready to act, neared from the horizon, from the nearest cottage a woman was bringing bread and milk, the heavens were parting.

The keys—left behind by Tolstoy's son-in-law, as it turned out— were in the ignition. With the exception of the burnt tarp, the vehicle was lacking nothing; the things were completely untouched by the fire, even the ties and the reinforcements were still there; there would be no problem in setting off for Krakow with everything. With a parade, to the accompaniment of car horns, escorted by the highway patrol, volunteer escort cars at the front. The triumphal entry upon the Dębnicki Bridge was in preparation. With everything, perhaps even with an orchestra. With everything, with the exception of the little chess table, which had been split in two and was tied up with pieces of twine.

XI

WHAT CATACLYSMS HAD COME UPON THEM? WHAT STORMS? WHAT apocalypses? What was their sequence? Had Tolstoy's son-in-law suddenly felt faint and decided to take a bit of a nap on the shoulder of the road? Had the earth opened up beneath him? Had he dashed off for the next, this time irrevocable, cold lemonade? Had they decided to arrange an eccentric picnic with cutlets and chess pieces in a meadow at the side of the road? Had a phenomenal Syrena with shining arms suddenly appeared before their hood and lead them astray? Had the Star caught fire out of the blue, and, in the panic of the flames, had they turned off the road wherever they could? Had the mysterious driver set off for help, but hell had swallowed him up somewhere on the way? Had a lightning bolt of mysterious vengeance fallen out of the sky and sliced the chess table in half? All these possibilities and all these events mixed up together at once?

Father remained silent. "You'll never find out," he would answer Mother's pesterings, which went on for years. "You'll never find out. By my word, never." And indeed—he never breathed even a word.

Then, in the middle of the road, in the middle of life, beyond the yellow hill—when it came to the little chess table, what to do with it, whether to take it to Krakow, or rather have Master Sztwiertnia take it back with him to Wisła and try to salvage it—not so much did he not say anything as, simply, he couldn't say anything. Even when he wanted to, he couldn't get a word out—his throat had entirely stiffened. Was he crying?

Moreover, the Master was not inclined to attempt to salvage it. He didn't like this story. He examined the suspiciously even break—it looked as if it had been made by a scroll saw—he studied it precisely, and he shook his head with a sense of the absolutely unfathomable. He glanced at the sky, as if only up there could there be saws that cut so diabolically.

He agreed to take it back with him, he brought it back, but that was that—it is no problem to fit a little chess table into a terrain vehicle. Especially in two pieces. He brought it back, but he didn't take it to his workshop. He didn't hasten to start gluing or to make any other repair. He most clearly didn't wish to engage the forces that could work so thunderously. He brought it back and placed it on a spot next to the shed, next to the specter of an ancient coach. Wait, wait a minute. Now's not a good time for me. I'll take it and repair it when the right moment comes. Nine years later, Master Sztwiertnia died. The great funeral procession went through all of Wisła, from the church to Gróniczek. Over the grave we sang to him of eternal light: "Dear light, dear light, that scatters the malevolent blight . . ." We sang beautifully, and from the depths of our hearts, for it was clear that Master Sztwiertnia was in God's lights.

The little table leaning against the wall slowly turned into who knows what. Over the next decades it became overgrown with a crust of bird excrement, woody roots, and fossilized dust. Anyone who didn't know would never guess the sense of its formlessness.

Sometimes, in my dreams, I see the great Star turning into the dark field. The tarp on it is burning, and in the yellow glow Father is setting up chess pieces on the most beautiful chessboard in the world. He begins to play with someone, but I don't know with whom, because the other one is in darkness.

XII

AFTER WRITING THIS STORY, I COULDN'T RESIST GIVING IN TO SENtimentalism: I collected the remains that had been consumed by heat waves, frosts, and bark beetles; I brought them to Warsaw, and I took them for renovation to famous masters from the gallery of old furniture on Ząbkowska Street. Last week—once the construction had regained its former radiance and splendor, once it had again become beautiful like music (more beautiful, because music ages beautifully), and once I had placed it with great pomp in the large room on Sienna Street—I discovered two pawns in the drawer, one white and one black. I was certain that they hadn't been there. I call the masters: "Where'd the pawns come from. They certainly weren't there before." "They were there, but immovable and almost invisible, sunk into the mass of the wood, overgrown with fossilized cobweb."

Two dead pawns. The beginning of every chess match. The beginning of every match in the world. The beginning of Lev Tolstoy's match with his son-in-law. In the photograph you can clearly see that they had just begun. They have behind them the first exchange of pawns. The white pawn in the drawer, and the black pawn in the drawer. From here on, everything is possible. The game can go in any direction.

Manuscripts of a
Person from My Parts

IN THE NAME OF THE MOST HOLY TRINITY—AMEN. IF SATAN CAST out Satan, he is divided against himself; how shall then his kingdom stand? If the light that is in thee be darkness, how great is that darkness? Once fanatical prophets start writing you, the ball is over. Once gloomy psychopaths start writing, it begins to be unpleasant. For the last two, maybe three years I have been receiving more and more letters that are—to put it delicately—odd. Supposedly, this is a sign and the price of genuine popularity. The measure of genuine fame is not the number of female admirers and fans. The measure of genuine fame is the number of enemies and the presence of loonies. As soon as a dragnet of hate-filled people begins observing your every move, and as soon as even a small cortège of hebephreniacs begins to follow you, only then do you mean something—or so a certain, now deceased, but highly insightful friend used to say. Without a doubt, he knew what he was talking about: for quite a few years he was famous, even very famous. Psychopaths conducted copious correspondence with him. I don't know. I'm unable to assess my own situation. Just today I see the following aphorism on the wall calendar: "Popularity—the punishment that looks like an award" (Ingmar Bergman). It seems that hundreds of similar aphorisms have been composed on this topic. Basically, it's a trifle. But I realize that Bergman's old man was a pastor, and I begin to feel a little awkward. Within reasonable limits, it goes without saying. Let's not go overboard here about any sort of psychoses, obsessions, fears. I'm not saying that now I cut open each envelope with my heart in my mouth, but the time of envelopes containing nothing but letters from enraptured owners of yellow dresses; from passionate male and female admirers of cats; from faithful fans who, although they have regard for me, will still never be able to understand how I could move from magical Krakow to soulless Warsaw; and even the time of incoherent epistles from failed poets with whom I supposedly once drank vodka—all this has past. The time has dawned for bloody exhibitionists who are fond of paradoxes: "Do you know that if I stick my tampon in too shallowly, it presses on the notorious G spot, and I wander about aroused all day long, although I basically don't realize it?" The time has dawned for bigoted aunties who are imbued with a will for converting people to faith in Jesus: "Do you know what Jesus gives to man? Wouldn't you like to taste how good Jesus is? Jesus tastes better than all the cutlets in the world! Jesus tastes better than all the cheesecakes, poppy-seed cakes, and tortes of this Earth!" The time has dawned for female *gymnasium* students who insightfully analyze domestic toxicities: "I interrupt my writing for today. Father has just thrown me out of the room, because he suddenly felt like screwing Mother. Believe me, nothing so discourages me from sex as my folks. I understand perfectly well that my folks are not there to encourage me to have sex, but mine don't spare me their sexuality. In our two rooms, they are in a difficult situation, all the more reason they shouldn't approach the matter frivolously and routinely." The time has dawned for risk-taking historiosophists who don't shun blackmail: "Perhaps someone in Poland could finally show some courage and praise the Partitions? After all, the Partitions were a splendid time—the economy was developing, we spoke foreign languages fluently, and our literature produced the greatest masterpieces of its history, and that was not just in the Emigration, but also precisely here at home. I am thinking, of course, of Bolesław Prus's unsurpassable *The Doll*." The time has dawned for metaphysical fundamentalists, who are truly worthy of considerable attention: "The single task of the writer, my dear sir, is to conduct a fictional proof for the existence of God; and what is more—only the writer (not the mathematician or the philosopher) can be effective here." The time has dawned for troublesome mistresses sending sepia photographs from the seventies, which they provide with tender dedications. The time has dawned for detox clinic brethren who live in their imaginations, and the time for Lutheran co-confessionals with liberated minds. The time for murky propositions, the time for troublesome requests, and the time for heavy insults. The time for madmen has dawned, wild like never-mown yellow grass. "Every normal person feels like killing someone once in a while. In my case that normalcy went further: in a special notebook, I keep a running list of persons whom I would be happy to kill," writes a guy who—as he assures me—is connected to me by a million bonds. Supposedly he comes from my parts, supposedly he is a Lutheran, supposedly my age. Sometimes he says that he is the omniscient Protestant narrator, and this does not seem to be a rhetorical device, but genuine mania. Sometimes he pretends to be a woman. Using feminine personal forms is one of the ritual dodges of internauts. I don't know whether he belongs to that tribe. His correspondence arrives by normal mail. The bulky envelopes contain constantly updated Xerox copies of lists of persons he would like to kill, as well as extensive, pathological "justifications of sentences," full of diverse digressions. The disgustingly familiar tone, full of pledges of brotherhood, is insufferable.* Just like you, I like to have a drink, and I'm

---

*Hence, for defensive purposes, I here edit and publish these letters. I am aware that their author might only now launch his attack, since I am giving him additional arguments; he might, for example, charge me with the theft of *his* texts and bring the case to court. (He himself, incidentally, doesn't mark quotes from

crazy about the girls. Just like you, I was battered by my sainted, I supposed accursed, family home, and in the best moments of life I am, at best, a female convalescent. "The father's home is a true paradise?" Did I hit the bull's eye? "Even if you were to travel the entire world, you won't find one more beautiful." You don't have to write back, we both know that I hit the bull's eye. We both know what we have in our minds. We wake up at the same time, and we get up at the same time. Do I exaggerate? Even if I exaggerate, it isn't by much. When did we get up last Thursday? I got up at seven past seven. I woke at seven past seven, and until half past seven, in other words for twenty-three whole minutes, I listened raptly to the solitude of my kidneys, my liver, and my heart. The previous evening, the spiritually twisted daughter of an organist from our parts had been at my place. The dusky body of a thirty-something discus thrower with an epic genotype. Even dressed, it took your breath away with its vastnesses; undressed, it drove you mad. My lonely and desolate hands are feverish even now. At half past seven, I drew back the Australian Merino bed cover and impulsively arranged the objects lying on the other side of the couch: a pencil, a notebook, the Bible, a box of chocolate-covered marshmallows, a pack of cigarettes (Davidoff Light), a cigarette lighter, a can of beer (Żywiec), a watch (Omega), a book (*Cancer Ward*), all four remote controls (TV, radio, DVD, Canal+), both cell phones, and the receiver from the home phone. On the whole, I don't eat, drink, smoke, write, talk on the phone, watch television, or even read in bed (once I begin to read, I fall asleep immediately)—but I

---

the Bible, or a fragment from a poem by Iwaszkiewicz—not even with quotation marks.) He might also—and this is the more threatening variant—feel himself the stronger partner in our alleged partnership, which he insistently emphasizes all the time, and attempt, in his imbalance, to recognize himself as the author of all my texts. He might attempt to become me, which, anyway, is difficult; I am myself only in a certain sense. The last letter, from a month ago, might also mean that he won't speak up again. We'll see. I assure you, however, with all my heart, that I'm not engaging here in any literary tricks, with a found—or, in this case, mailed-in—manuscript chief among them. I write this footnote not for literary effect, but out of genuine fear. The guy really exists, he really writes, and he really is hounding me.

Jerzy Pilch

like to have everything within reach. I checked the cell phone to see whether there were any messages—and sure enough: at dawn two strophes of love and longing had flowed onto the mysterious machinery. The first was from The Greatest Love of My Life; the second, from an unknown author. The number of idealists—who do not consider it fitting to sign their missives, since they are absolutely convinced that not only do I have their numbers registered in my phone, but also etched on my heart—is significant. God be with you. Every morning when I find the received messages, it seems to me that I slept like a log. An absurd illusion (at night I put it on "silent"), but irresistible. SMSes, silent like moths, deepen the nocturnal peace, such that—recalling the times when we used to write poetry—I express the matter in the form of a poetic aphorism. Long ago, I noticed that the first messages arrive around five in the morning. Completely as if the most virulent letter senders had, at that hour, their preliminary versions ready. After intoxicating and prolonged excesses with the organist's daughter—deliberately not leading to fulfillment and thereby always a bit destructive—I slept, perhaps not like a log (I got up once to go to the can), but quite well. I didn't have any nightmares, no deranged telephone call ripped me from my sleep (I don't unplug the home phone at night), no betrayed husband called to make threats, not a one of my abandoned girlfriends woke me up in a fit of hysteria. Nor were there any silent or ecstatic calls from old drinking buddies, no madman or murdered passerby howled on the street under my windows. The night hadn't been bad; so, too, the awakening. The sheets smelled of the sprinter's sweat of the organist's daughter. I didn't enter her name in the register. There wasn't any reason. For the moment there isn't any reason. She didn't do anything to make me angry. She didn't smoke in bed. She didn't jabber on the phone for hours on end. She didn't puff like a steam engine, she didn't bare her saliva covered teeth, and she didn't make any silly faces during orgasm. After which, she didn't cuddle spasmodically and devotedly. She quickly went to the bathroom and didn't sit there long. She didn't speak up very often. When she picked up the Bible, she didn't wink at me in a sign of Lutheran brotherhood. She glanced at *Cancer Ward*, but in her glance there wasn't any of the usual cognitive obtuseness indicating that this was the first time in her life she had seen that medical textbook. On the contrary—she knew what the book was. She stood for a long time facing the wall with the bookshelves—a risky venture in itself—but it didn't end in any whimpering. High marks! Whenever I hear whimpering—can I borrow this or that for a few days—I don't know myself what infuriates me more: the whimpering, the borrowing, or the assumption that our intoxicating acquaintance might last that long. Woman! After all, in a few more days you might—as far as I'm concerned—no longer be living. On the spot, now, immediately, I feel like killing you, and on the spot, now, immediately, I will frivolously enter your name in the register! In a few days! She would give it back in a few days! Or maybe in a week? Or in two weeks? Who will give it back? You? More likely your two-week old corpse with a rusty spoke still not removed from your aorta. We can't stand lending anything. Lending is the worst. When you are from the tribe of nut jobs who always have all their pairs of shoes polished, and all their pencils always sharpened—well, it's clear. All objects impeccable and in their place. A loaned object = a lost object. The principle that you don't lend objects of personal use arose, I think, in a kolkhoz. All objects are of personal use. Everybody touches objects in his own way, and in his own way prostitutes and thwarts them by his touch. People don't notice and don't discern that the neighbor who returns a borrowed umbrella returns an umbrella that is deformed and defiled. There are objects that are more and less prone to deformation and defilement. Books are unusually susceptible to such massacres. Just being picked up, just being read by someone else, defiles them, and then they also open them up, fold them back, make notes in the margin, flip the pages, close them, glance through them, check, look for the page, bring them closer to the eyes, shove them under somebody's nose, set them aside, etc. The manner of touching a book as an object contains an entire arsenal of gropings, defilements, and sullyings. Reading a borrowed book is like taking a paid woman. Except that taking a paid woman is better, to the extent that it is quick. Quick reading makes practically no sense. That is why I never have any borrowed books. Paid women—certainly. Because I treat literature with deadly seriousness, I go to the brothel, not to the library. Of the two evils, I would prefer to give someone a book than to lend it. My library isn't large, slightly more than one thousand five hundred titles. Predominately history, classics, dictionaries and encyclopedias, a lot of poetry. None of our holy books. No old hymnals or prewar Protestant almanacs. Luther's *Postil*, Kubala, Sr.'s *How to Protect Against the Deviltry of Daily Life*, as well as the *Illustrated History of the Protestant Church in Granatowe Góry*—they're on the bookshelf of specters. And way back, at that. I don't need to add that everything, especially the specters, are arranged in orderly fashion, according to size. The organist's daughter stood for a long time near that harmony, but she didn't disturb it. She didn't even take a volume off the shelf. She settled for communing with the spines. This is a commendable form of communing with a library—to tell the truth, for outsiders, even for young Lutheran girls, the only acceptable form. In a word, the organist's daughter didn't betray her spiritual poverty in this, or that, or any other manner. Which doesn't mean that I had come upon some sort of ideal. Not at all! She has a huge, cardinal defect, except that for now that defect looks like a virtue. For now. For now I don't feel like killing her. In what does that defect, which looks like a virtue, consist? Let's not pretend we don't know! Let's not make up stories! What's this all about? Haven't we had any Protestant girls? Haven't we cast a greedy eye on virginal confirmation class girls? Haven't we tried to put one over on charming pastors' wives? Haven't we analyzed the cut of Lutheran thongs? Hasty female parishioners haven't bickered with you sweetly that they won't kneel, because that's Catholic? So what defect, which looks like a virtue, did the organist's daughter have? Why, she had this defect, which looks like a virtue: that, in giving herself to a Lutheran from our parts, she did this with peculiar delight, because she felt that she was doing what was pleasing to Lord Jesus. And also to the Apostle

Paul, all four evangelists, and—of course—our Reformer, Dr. Martin Luther. As likewise to the organist, the organist's wife, the bishop, and all our pastors, and all our brethren. All of them surrounded our sack, and gave their blessing, and encouraged us to *get to it.* And I took that Protestant body—although, as far as its anatomic perfection was concerned, it was remarkably supraconfessional—and I saw the signs of the cross made over us by the Apostles, and I heard Luther as he cheered me on with his classic and original phrase: *Der alt böse Feind mit Ernst er's jetzt meint!* "Go to it, son!" shouted the blissful organist. "Come, my betrothed," whispered his daughter. And I won't try to hide it: this grabbed me and made me hot. In any case—for the time being. For the time being, I didn't enter her name. But that doesn't mean that I was idle. The massive Italian notebook, which was the main register of those I had condemned, the mother of the lists of all my victims, was in action. Every normal person feels like killing someone from time to time. But I developed this normalcy creatively—using an exquisite notebook, in which I record (and also cross out) the names of those I feel like killing. Today I entered the name of the female drug addict who accosted me on Sienna Street, I crossed out The Most Beautiful Woman in the World, I added Father Kalinowski (we all used to play cards—two walking skeletons, a certain female corpsette, Father Kalinowski, and I), I crossed out great-grandfather on Father's side (on the whole, he is blameless), and for the hundredth time I added and for the hundredth time I crossed out The Greatest Love of My Life. That's how it is. There is no begging for mercy here. Trouble is brewing on every page. I am constantly adding someone, crossing someone out, some appear for a few hours— when, in a surge of sudden frenzy, I enter the name, and when, in a moment, in a surge of equally sudden relief, I cross it out. Two weeks ago, in the twinkling of an eye, I entered and crossed out—and, to all intents and purposes, I crossed it out before I had time to enter it— the name of a certain, seemingly not bad, student of archeology. That's why I had made a date with her. I made a date with her because she seemed not bad. Anyway, it's all the same why I made a date—the affair was typical in its disastrousness. You know the pain I am talking about: the young lady, who seems not bad, turns out five minutes into the conversation to be as thick as a plank, which, if it automatically spelled the end, wouldn't be so bad. Unfortunately, she fiercely sought another date, made persistent attempts, sent sensuous SMSes. And so, once she had finally shown up, it was impossible to leave after ten minutes. You have to play the gentleman. You have to do your time. You have to put in at least an hour. I did my time, but after doing it, I was in such a fury that I didn't have a shadow of a doubt: immediately upon my return home, a bloody entry would follow! Very bloody! Executed venomously, with a purple felt-tip pen! But before I got home—and for me it was a bit of a hike, since the seemingly not bad student of archeology, instead of accepting my conditions and appearing either at the *Dezerter*, or at *Guliwer* on Bracka Street, insisted on *Singer* in the Kazimierz district, and I, guided by the obvious intentions, servilely agreed to this as well—and so, by the time I dragged myself home from that *Singer* located on the outskirts, my anger had passed. I smiled meditatively upon my own stupidity and upon my own unbridled sex drive, and I simply wrote the hinney off. First she was, then she wasn't, and she was there so briefly that it was as if she had never been. I didn't even have time to imagine ripping off her jeans, blouse, bra, and packing the first spoke that comes to hand into her heart. I don't rape, don't grope, but I do undress them before I kill them. It's good to undress the future corpse. Chiefly for the sake of polemical convenience. As a philosopher we revere likes to say: "In a dispute between the naked and the clothed, the naked will never be right." And if someone is never right, it is easier to get rid of him. Annihilating someone's shame and pathetic bodily shell— in places it is yellowish, in places a bit fatty, in places hairy, in places congested—is not such a big deal. It can be a favor. She trembles, her tits shake. Her tits aren't bad. I know the details. I know the details, because I am an omniscient Lutheran narrator. A Lutheran narrator, by the way, can be no other. He can only be omniscient, omnipotent, and chosen by Our Lord the One in the Trinity, Amen. Amen,

Amen, Amen, Jesus Christ is Lord! She trembles, her tits shake, her tits aren't bad, but for a moment, before entering her name in the register, this loses its significance. Besides, her tits are no longer not bad. Her tits weren't bad until she opened her yap in *Singer*. As soon as she opened her yap and began to blather, her not-bad tits immediately went flabby, her shapely legs immediately became crooked, cellulitis immediately began to cover her smooth ass, pustules began to erupt on her silken skin, the luxuriant shock of hair began to become oily. And she sweats, and she goes in her panties, and she is standing in a puddle of her own excrement, and, as quickly as possible I must shorten her, and especially my, horrible shame. And so, I produce the rusty spoke from my breast pocket, and poof! in her neck, and poof!—just in case—in the liver, and the seemingly not bad student of archeology is no more. Poof! in the aorta and poof! in the artery, and no more—the tramp from the Kotlarski Roundabout is no more. Poof! in the ear and poof! in the eye, and no more—The Most Beautiful Woman in the World is no more. Poof! in the spleen and poof! in the pancreas, and alcoholic auntie is no more. Poof! in the snout and poof! in the noodle, and Father, Mother, and the neighbor lady are no more. Poof! in the belly and poof! in the jelly, and The Greatest Love of My Life is no more. Poof! in the broom and poof! in the womb, and Viola Caracas is no more. Poof. Poof. Poof. Someone inhumanly tired and with a grave injury to the heart is running a thousand-kilometer obstacle course. Over the orange track there fall icy nights. Then the unending winter of the century. Women lying in the snow, in the ice, in the frosty grass, on the banks and the shoulders of the roads. Their patterned dresses, navy blue scarfs, and sunglasses. A lot of women. There is no point in trying to hide it: there are many, very many women on the list of persons I feel like killing. If I were to kill even half the people on my list, I would have decent chances at becoming the *serial killer* of the millennium. Hunger. Hunger and once again hunger. Insatiable hunger. Hunger that is there for one's whole life. Hunger for the body. Evening. Vacations after passing the *matura*. The short, violent, northern summer. The stuffy room in the wooden attic. The pain of sunburn. The rumble of the river. Hunger. All the women in the world. All of them from the beginning of history. All who died before us. Their buried skeletons and bodies, now eaten by the clay, which once were covered by skin created for our touch. All of them. Invented. Fantastic. To the end of your life you will regret that you didn't touch the woman created by Saul Bellow who was named Renata; that the mistress of the Frenchman was not your mistress; that you didn't take Kitty away from Levin; that you didn't undress Singer's sensuous Jewesses; Kundera's eccentric Czech women; Solzhenitsyn's labor camp prisoners, gaunt like models; Márquez's golden-skinned mulattoes; Bunin's impoverished gentrywomen; Kafka's pencil-pushers dressed in white blouses. Personally—I must confess—I even feel affection for the most frequently used of all the literary asses: Anna Karenina, Madame Bovary, and Clavdia Chauchat. I regret that I didn't unbutton the first one's corset; that I didn't treat the second with all the brutality she deserves; that the third didn't come to *my* room on New Year's Eve. OK, I'll say it frankly and bluntly, although at the same time thoroughly metaphorically: I regret that Isolde didn't blow me, that I didn't have anal sex with Shakespeare's Julia. And I even regret that it wasn't me, but Leverkühn, whom the mythic whore infected with syphilis. We have the same curse and dreadful fate: that, at the sight of bared shoulders in a summer dress, a daring décolletage in an evening gown, dark hair pulled back from the forehead, and a thousand other scenes and views, we will always lose consciousness. We will suffocate on account of the lack, we will be ready to strip off our own skin in order to be able to touch. Without that touch—death in agonies. The desire to kill is deeply justified in this context. When one feels like screwing ideal beings, it's no wonder that one feels like killing beings made of flesh and blood. But wait! Wait! Wait! There hasn't been anyone for a long time. I didn't enter the name of the student of archeology, and my charts, at which I am just now glancing with curiosity, show clearly that the last babe I wanted to kill, and had noted in the register, was Viola Caracas. What do you know!

The number of cows that a person feels like clubbing to death is diminishing at a terrifying rate. Apparently we are getting old. The acquaintance with Viola Caracas began in the manner typical for our times—through the Internet. She sent frequent emails, not badly written, although exceptionally vague. Almost no details about herself. This agreed, however, with her key confession, repeated in various versions, that, you know what, I don't feel too well in this world, because I generally spend my time in the sphere of ideal beings. I underestimated the danger of this admission, and I even, rashly, found it appealing. In addition to this, granted, there were almost no details about herself, but one essential detail finally came out: namely, the year of her birth. It was recent. Even—I would say—shockingly recent. I made a date with her. Seemingly interesting: a dainty little doll with the face of a Venezuelan whore. Hence the nickname—of little sophistication in its simplicity—Caracas. Well-groomed, tidy, scrubbed, coiffed, dressed inordinately perfectly. For such a young age—an excessive perfection, smelling of premature spinsterhood. There was no question, for example, that she would ever drop in on me right after classes. After classes, she always returned first to the student dorm on Piastowska Street, where she tarted herself up for at least two hours, and finally, in a New Year's Eve blouse, sizzling-hot make-up, and a fantastic hair-do, she would make her way to my place. It goes without saying: ideal beings. What she thought about during preparations was equally important to her as the actual next installments. The actual next installments with Viola Caracas were, as a matter of fact, not bad—really not bad. She had splendid—writers of old would write—alabaster skin and a truly Latin temperament. Unfortunately, she also had a certain insurmountable vice. She didn't speak up at all. There is no reason to laugh here. We know perfectly well that the silent woman is the ideal. But it depends on the quality of the silence. There is favorable silence, and there is hostile silence. To formulate the matter more precisely: Women who don't speak up are divided into those who don't speak up favorably and those who don't speak up hostilely. Viola didn't speak up—let's put it this way—in order to play to a draw. Not hostilely, but also not favorably. She kept silent and stared intensely and greedily, and her pitch-black eyes burned like the windows of the Miraflores Palace during a New Year's Eve ball. On more or less the third date, I understood that she was a victim of her own imagination. Her mind spent its time, indeed, in spheres so ideal that she was not capable of stammering out even one concrete sentence. In time—not even one concrete word. The acquaintance—you could say—melted into mists devoid of absolutely anything concrete. To put the matter precisely, one thing remained concrete: her name on the list. OK, I'll say it. I'll say it, although at first I didn't admit it. It was about something else. We entered Viola Caracas on the list, but our first impulse was to hide the genuine reason. Actually, it concerned contact lenses. This seemed petty to us. What nobility! What self-restraint! But such is the truth: ever since babes began, on a mass scale, to take out their contact lenses before going to bed, the enthusiasm has diminished. Immeasurably diminished. Sure, not all wear them, and thus not all of them remove contact lenses before they go to bed, but there are so many of them, and the ritual has become so distinctive, that its shadow is cast upon all the rest. I lie on the sheets, and even if I know for a certainty that the miss for whom I am waiting doesn't wear contact lenses, I have the traumatic sense that I will immediately hear the rattle of lenses coming from the bathroom. And Viola Caracas was probably the seventh babe in a row to wear contact lenses. Seventh! The seventh in a row! Three out of six of her predecessors were allowed to spend the night, and they rattled their contact lenses in the bathroom! She herself didn't stay for the night and didn't rattle, but she had them, she wore them, and that was enough. The trauma— God forbid—is not a matter of an aversion to nearsighted girls. Not at all! Quite the opposite! We love four-eyed girls! We have a thing for four-eyed girls! Our pathetic fetishism was born and shaped in the pediatric ophthalmalogy sanatorium in Witkowice. It couldn't be avoided, since there were no babes there other than those who *wore* glasses. To put it precisely, there weren't any other babes there than those who had just had their crossed-eye operations. That had its good sides. The oldest—the half-blind fourteen- and fifteen-year-olds (there was even a sixteen-year-old, but she was flat as a board), eyes plastered after the operation, pupils dilated from atropine—were in no position to notice that we were ogling them, and they changed clothes in the gigantic multi-bed rooms with exquisite slowness, practically feeling their way in and out of them; they bathed under showers in bathrooms as huge as factory floors; on scorching days, they lay down in the Austro-Hungarian garden, overgrown with Asiatic grasses, and, as if in a dream, not seeing and not knowing that all bounds had long ago been crossed, they rolled up their skirts and opened their blouses. It goes without saying that we, too, wore glasses; we, too, had just had operations to cure our crossed eyes; we, too, had gummed-up eyes and vision blurry from drops and creams. We were completely unfit for the role of voyeurs. All the more fervently, then, did we turn our countenances toward the light shining through our dressings. The foremost angels of our childhood were nearsighted. They all wore glasses. The first girls I saw undress in my life took off everything but their glasses. In any case—the glasses came at the end. After the panties. The indomitable subconsciousness that glasses are a natural element of the female anatomy stems from those times in Witkowice. To recapitulate: we are dealing here with fundamental matters, two fundamental doubts. First: contact lenses lead to the extermination of glasses-wearing women. After all, you almost don't see any women, especially young women, in glasses any more! Nowadays, a super babe in glasses is a deviant, brothel request! I'm serious. Nowadays, if you want to have a super babe in glasses, you have to set off for a super brothel, in which super secret desires are realized. And even there, if you say that you want a four-eyes, the personnel, well versed in excess, will look at you scandalized by the knowledge that such deviants still walk the earth. A four-eyes removes her glasses and most charmingly squints her nearsighted eyes! Oh, how irrevocably has such an enchanting sight vanished! Thousands of other scenes have vanished! The four-eyes have died off! The perversely narrowed eyelids buried in clay! When I think that I could have had glasses seven times in a row, and yet I had contact lenses seven times in a row, it makes my blood boil! That's it! That's absolutely it! I enter all the pieces of tail wearing contact lenses on the list *en bloc*! All of them! The great quantifications are to me like blood brothers. And just what do you think—as Friedrich Nietzsche would say—and just what do you think? That you have taken off your glasses, and so you will escape with impunity? You won't escape. Digging around in one's own innards will not go unpunished. And that's the second question. The breaking of a taboo. For the time being, it's OK. Seemingly OK. After all, removing contact lenses for the night differs in no way from removing an artificial jaw—I understand that this can be OK. Barely, but it can be OK. For the time being, no sign of danger. For the time being. I'm not exaggerating. I'm not exaggerating in the least. You yourselves will see. You will see what you will live to see. And you will live to see women who, for the purpose of elevating their hygiene, will remove their wombs for the night. You will see it. You will live to see it. You. Not us. Just so that everything is clear: there is no conservatism here as far as the development of bodily embellishments is concerned. We know perfectly well that there is no need to improve on the Lord God, and that Katharina von Bora didn't depilate her legs particularly carefully. We know this perfectly well, but we couldn't care less. At the current stage, we are in favor of depilation. We are in favor of depilation in its most inventive places and patterns. We say yes to the most radical make-ups, tattoos, hair streaks. Rivets, studs, fake nails, wigs, hair extensions, body painting—by all means. Even an artificial tan—if it really has to be—well, OK. Even slight surgical corrections, if they are of the superficial sort, are acceptable in a pinch. But going beneath the surface? Crossing through the gates that lead to the center of the body? Of course, once you have shaved, tattooed, shortened, lengthened, painted, enlarged, diminished, sealed up, trimmed, pierced, bedecked everything that is on the surface with jewelry; of course, once you have done everything possible and impossible on the surface, the reflex is to go below. Once you have done cosmetic operations upon everything that is on the outside, why not correct the profile of your liver? Do what you like. I don't reach any deeper than to the depth of contact lenses, and even so—I drown in that depth. I am lying on the sheets, waiting for her, and I can't get rid of the ghastly impression that I am about to embrace, and that for the whole night I will be embracing, a body composed of fewer elements than an hour ago. My hands glide apprehensively along her skin, as if in the fear that any moment they will come upon a ghastly gap or expanse—like the hole in a tortoise shell. The decided majority of my potential victims are ephemerids, meteors, may flies. They flash and vanish like the seemingly not bad student of archeology. The world is now marching full speed ahead, and there practically isn't a day when one doesn't feel like killing somebody. Somebody new, of course. Because I also have a group of highly distinguished veterans, who have been waiting for execution for a long time. There is even a certain record-holder—his name, once entered and never deleted. My poor old man—indefatigable in his striving for perfection. Be ye perfect, even as your Lord which is in heaven is perfect. Not long ago, when the faucet in my kitchen broke, and when, almost involuntarily, I cut out a leather gasket from the end of an old belt, I realized that the invention of the leather gasket—truly much more durable than a rubber one—and the art of changing it, is the single thing he taught me. He tried to teach me probably all the arts known to man. In all of these skills, which were to be mastered by the path of exercises and grueling effort, I was supposed to be, if not the best in the world, then decidedly better than all my peers. Nobody is an Einstein or an Edison, but if you adhere to Lutheran principles—who knows? During breakfast yesterday I came upon an article in the newspaper about one of this year's outstanding Polish *lyceum* graduates, who had learned to read and do sums when he was four years old, and from then on school went like clockwork. He won competitions and contests, he wrote works of scholarship, he had perfect mastery of five foreign languages, foreign schools were interested in him, and now he was setting off to study at a select university in

America. The roll stuck in my throat, the coffee burned my mouth, I read with a twinge in my heart. A gray old fart, heading toward sixty—I read in growing panic, I looked around, and I felt the reflex to destroy and conceal the article, so that it not, by chance, fall into my old man's mitts. Boy, what fortune you're no longer alive. You can strive for perfection in every situation. Instruction is the way of life. We would be traveling—let's say—wherever. We would be traveling—let's say—by PKS Bus to Wąwóz, to some pious auntie. We would be traveling—let's say—with this or that velocity, the road to be taken—let's say—was known, the time—let's say—was this or that. How many operations and calculations was it possible to perform on the basis of even such elementary parameters! And variations! And eventualities! And likelihoods! And what would happen if the bus moved at a uniformly accelerating pace? And, purely abstractly, let's suppose that, on the way to Wąwóz, we pass from the first to the second cosmic velocity; then how, in terms of the laws of physics, would the course of such an intellectual experiment look? It wouldn't be so bad if it were just those five kilometers to Wąwóz. But what about once the ritual roundtrips between Krakow and Granatowe Góry had begun, and it had become 145 kilometers one way? We made this journey a million, perhaps a billion times, and to this day I don't know its roadside sights, because the entire time I was solving the problems dictated by my indefatigable old man. And when, God forbid, it was raining, and there weren't any sights, then the real nightmare began. Then I had to determine which motions and which velocities gave the resultant that was the motion of the drops of rain gliding diagonally across the windowpane of the bus. And often it rained the whole way—and, with the PKS buses of those days, this was more than three hours. Poland is a rainy country. By the end, my head was thumping, I couldn't understand a thing, I wasn't able to solve the simplest operation. "Do I demand that you become an Edison or Einstein?" my old man seethed in a furious whisper. "Do I demand that you be a genius? No! The only thing I want is that you understand the basic things in the world around you!" Unfortunately, the world was in constant motion. Everything around me was moving. A dog of a specific mass ran with a specific velocity across a meadow with a specific surface area, trees swayed like a pendulum, clouds scudded according to vectors, the stone that had been cast sank, submitting to the force of gravity, even the seemingly motionless tea in the glass had a specific surface tension—the world was a ceaseless assignment for calculation and execution. I passionately cursed every movement of a reality that was in ceaseless flux. (*I was supposed to be an Einstein or an Edison, and I was—in the best case scenario—a grotesque antagonist of Heraclitus, but I didn't have a clue even about this. Oh, the bitterness!*) The last state of man is worse than the first. And in the end—there remained the cutting out of gaskets. Gaskets, indeed—*them* I cut with virtuosity and to perfection. In the cutting of gaskets, if I am not an Einstein, I am certainly an Edison. Or the other way around. I was able to master this art only because my old man, occupied with his feverish search for raw materials, paid significantly less attention to me than usual. In those days, and in those faucets, gaskets blew one after the other, belts of the appropriate thickness were scarce. All of our pants belts were already either completely massacred, or they were shortened to the limits of caricature. But Father was an intrepid inventor, and once, without hesitation, he cut a gasket out of Mother's practically new sandals. When she discovered this and made his life a hell, he responded by telling her to stop annoying him and to stop practicing mental monism. Because, after all, when you have a choice between sandals that are whole and a faucet that is leaky—and, as a consequence, a flood in the apartment—you have to make the proper choice and not practice mental monism. He had a weakness for foreign words. Once, he began to look through my stamp collection. With greater and greater disgust, he turned page after page, and finally he asked whether I was really amused by the practice of cognitive promiscuity and the collection of things that were as different as night and day. Wouldn't it be better to stop practicing cognitive promiscuity and introduce some sort of order to this bedlam? After all, I don't demand of you that you be a professional philatelist, but this at least should make some sense! From that time on, following his suggestion, I collected Polish stamps on exclusively historical topics and foreign stamps on exclusively sport topics. Anyway, my collecting was only so-so. The philatelist's passion quickly died out in me. I don't say that it was out of longing for cognitive promiscuity, but it did die out. These are my curses. I recently came to the conclusion that I buy too many classical music recordings on a whim. Not even silently did I utter the word promiscuity. I swear. I might think that I buy things as different as night and day, but the word promiscuity didn't come up. I am sure of it. And I decided that, from then on, I would buy nothing but compositions for piano in Polish music, nothing but compositions for cello in foreign music, exclusively compositions for cello. But then I understood the structure and the nature of my decision, and I lost my desire for music. Repetition upon repetitions, and even more: imitation upon imitations. The father figure taken from a sneeringly venomous autobiography. Our Father, who art just as massacred in heaven as Thou were on earth. Unfortunately, we are not specialists in disinterested avant-garde crimes. We are specialists in well-justified crimes within the family. We don't give a damn about other people. Although I can't get the tramp from the Kotlarski Roundabout out of my head. I felt like killing him three years ago, and to this day I haven't crossed him off the list. I would still be happy to kill him. At that time, I imagined that I would sink an eight-inch screwdriver, dripping with manure, under his diaphragm—this technology still suits me. He didn't do anything to me. Entirely submerged in delirious darkness, he described perfect circles around me, muttered apologies under his breath. It seemed to me that I heard: *The Siberian ice has frozen over the Bay of St. Susanna*, but this was too little remorse. I caught the stench of shit macerated in denatured alcohol, or perhaps the other way around. No dark brown lightning bolts, no murky illuminations on that account. I don't harbor any olfactory excessiveness. In general, I don't harbor any sort of excessiveness. My tactile excessiveness does not belong to the realm of exceptions. It belongs to the realm of rules.

I am a man of touch. Recording the names of those I would like to kill is not an example of excessiveness. Quite the opposite—it is the prevention of excessiveness. Criticism of a life does not have to be a praise of death, but it always comes out a bit that way. In my case, it comes out this way all the more, because I react to every attack of the world with the recording of a name. And since the world attacks ceaselessly, I ceaselessly record. With light blue ink. To write as in childhood with light blue ink. To write with the inks of by-gone days, in those smooth-paged "woodless-paper" notebooks, to describe those adventures, which at that time were not adventures at all, and now belong to the great Book of Canons. Objects that stand in my way. The light in the bathroom, which goes on and off according to its own rhythm, the eyeglasses, which are forever getting lost, the sofa bed, which falls apart every evening. The leaky radiator, which, if I could, I would blow to smithereens. The Coca-Cola spilled on the carpet, both it and the carpet, sticky from the sweetness—to be killed immediately. The late train—kill it. The broken cigarette lighter— kill it. A sudden rain—sudden death. Icy, yellow air over the city. Pigeons on the windowsill. A few times I took aim with my air rifle, I had them in my sights—and nothing. An absolute fiasco. Not only from the sniper's point of view. Complete disaster. I couldn't even risk a warning shot in the air. And what if a gray lump of fossilized lice takes flight and—there you have it—plonk! There was no question that I could survive the dull blow, the flying feathers, the trace of blood. As a matter of fact, I don't even write down the spectral corpses. I write down reactions. I write them down just in case, just in case it should come to something. But, truth be told, what should come to what? Death to the living. The living to the grave. The grave to the wall. After age fifty, our libraries gain in spectrality. Whenever I can't find some book, I start to write it. Every normal person, at least once in his life, feels like killing his father. I broadened that normality to the extent that I felt like killing him a few thousand times. He—me, hundreds of thousands of times. Mother—him, at least once a week. He—Mother, on a daily basis. We were a very loving family. The most ordinary family of monsters in the world. True, my folks would be reluctant to entertain the idea that they were monsters, and they wondered where such a monster like me had come from, but that is typical. All the monsters in the world wonder where their monstrous offspring have come from. Today both of them are already in the other world. I'll say honestly that I prefer to imagine that world impersonally. If anything distinguished us from other monsters, it was the observance of Lutheran principles and the reading of the Bible. Yes, sir—the Gospel According to Matthew. Yes, sir: Matthew 6:23, Matthew 12:26, Matthew 12:43–45. Yes, sir—our favorite verses. Sometimes it seems to me that I have a large butterfly net thrown over my head. Images and spaces, sounds and smells sink into me. They are like remnants of shrouds overgrown with sand and yellow bandages. I drag them to my sack, fall asleep, dream the same things, though deformed and vanishing, as if instant acid had consumed them in my unconscious head. I awake, and everything repeats from the beginning. Critique of life does not have to be a praise of death. But the defense of life has to be a praise of despair. I strip naked, stick a rusty spoke in my heart, and all of you are no more. The good God removed our minds from our weary heads and replaced them with two or three quotations from Scripture. But the heart of the matter is—which? Which quotations? It's not so bad if someone is allotted a tolerable phrase, but when someone gets a more—so to say—mysterious combination, it's game over. I'm not saying that he will find himself in the clutches of infernal powers, but the fact remains: as early as the sixties, my old man brought back a plaster figurine of Mephistopheles from a business trip to the GDR. True, this likeness of Satan didn't stand for long on the étagère. In the course of the very next squabble it went to smithereens, and not at all because there were any exorcisms in the house, but because Mother—it was she who hurled Mephistopheles at Father—didn't have anything else handy at the moment. All the same: a statue of Satan stood in our home. Sure, it was little; sure, it was plaster; sure, it was there briefly—but there it stood. There it stood under our roof: a silver calf.

There it stood upon our altar: Satan from the German Democratic Republic. That's how it is in life. One person has *Doctor Faustus* on his shelf, the other a plaster devil. One knows Leverkühn's conversation with the Prince of Darkness in the original, the other has the dust of a pathetic copy on his collar. One is mine, the other yours. One in a book, the other on the shelf. One is plaster, the other paper. Each has the one he fears. Do we understand each other, my curse? Our Satan was everywhere. He was in hard candies. He was in lemonade. He was in vanilla ice cream. He was in soccer, in chewing gum, and in music. In the radio and in the television set. There isn't any point in talking about cigarettes, beer, and short skirts—they were all his work. In the summer, he sunbathed at the swimming pool and swam in the river. In the evenings, he showed films in the summer movie theater. He played the electronic organ at the band shell. He danced at parties in the House of the Spa. He removed the chiffon blouses from the Czech strippers. At night, he rummaged through pieces of junk in the attic. He slept in the bogs. He lay in the empty, ice-cold entryway. He ran along the railway embankment. He stood on the bridge and brushed snow from his overcoat. The yellow light of his flashlight wandered along the dark blue slopes. On winter evenings, he gave us things to read that we were unable to put down. He would shove a pencil into our hands and tempt us to record random thoughts. Luther did battle with him his whole life and often lost. But in the final analysis Luther was a colossus. Luther stood in the same rank with the Prophets, with the Evangelists, he was near Lord Jesus Himself. He wished to marry Katharina von Bora—so he made a schism. And us? What were we supposed to do? What sort of schism were we supposed to make so that, without fear of the fires of hell, we might buy a bottle of lemonade or go to the movies? The matters of the world are simple. If you risked hell over a lemonade, then—let's party!—seven lemonades for me, please! If nothing but greedy (in the original: lustful) gazing upon a suntanned female vacationer is already adultery, then only a sucker would stop at gazing. If the devil is everywhere, that means that he doesn't exist at all, or, at best, he is made of plaster and comes from the GDR. If we blather on about Satan, over and over, and without cease, then there is no Satan—there is only blather. What were we supposed to do? For want of anything better, you could start up a soccer game on the grounds that it is supposedly good for your health. For want of anything better, music might praise God. The TV could spread knowledge about the world, and whoever lived to see the epoch of unpunished reception of foreign stations could watch them under the pretext of learning foreign languages. Toward the end, my folks were a pair of barely moving oldsters. All day long they tottered and rustled about the house, thought up for themselves some sort of absurd, but seemingly useful occupations: Mother ironed scarfs that had never been worn, Father punched additional holes into his pants belt; finally, as evening came, they would sit, dead tired, in front of the TV; they sat, however, with shame and in deliberately uncomfortable and fleeting poses, so that it would seem that they had sat down only for a moment and by chance; and once they had settled in for good, they would turn on SAT1 or CNN. They weren't watching TV, they weren't going easy on Satan: they were learning foreign languages. In daily life, Satan and Lutheran principles are sufficient. Father had significantly greater difficulty with this than Mother. Throughout all his life. He would take me to Cracovia matches, and he always had a toothache during those matches. Not metaphorically, on account of the pathetic play. It was in the strict sense that he would have tooth attacks during Cracovia matches, and he would light up a cigarette in order to soothe them. He would ask someone he knew, or didn't know, in any case, someone nearby who was smoking, and in those days, almost every fan smoked, so it wasn't a problem. My old man would ask them to give him one, or even two, because his teeth were hurting him horribly, and—pretending to inhale smoke especially intensively on the sore spots—he would smoke away. It seems to me that eventually, just in case of a sudden toothache, he started carrying with him a package of mentholated Giewonts. It really didn't happen soon, and in fact it was quite late, even very late, that I understood what was going on here. Quite another matter that the thing was, for the brain of a ten-year-old, quite complicated. My old man smoked, which was deviltry, and so, wishing to neutralize the deviltry, and even to rein it in entirely, through the observance of Lutheran principles, he pretended that his teeth ached, and that he smoked for the pain, which was a lie, in other words heightened deviltry. The truth was different, and *this* was the seven-fold deviltry, because my old man smoked out of fascination with the director of the personnel department at the polytechnic, Mrs. Przekrasicka. *She* smoked, but *he* wanted to give her a roll in the hay. When the unclean spirit is gone out of a man, he walketh through dry places, seeking rest, and findeth none. Then he saith, I will return into my house from whence I came out; and when he is come, he findeth it empty, swept, and garnished. Then goeth he, and taketh with himself seven other spirits more wicked than himself, and they enter in and dwell there: and the last state of that man is worse than the first. The steadfastness of Lutheran principles lies in their exclusivity. Beyond them there is nothing. There are, to put it succinctly, situations in which the observance of Lutheran principles turns out to be absolutely fatal. Father's undoing was the fact that, finally having given the director of the personnel department at the polytechnic, Mrs. Przekrasicka, a roll in the hay, he was incapable— once it was all over—of getting rid of the handkerchief, which had been soiled during the amatory frenzy. In a word, his undoing was the Lutheran principle that nothing is ever to be thrown away. I know what I'll hear now—that the principle of never throwing anything away is not only a Lutheran principle, that it is a supraconfessional principle, and even supracultural. Very well. But when the principle of never throwing anything away becomes a Lutheran principle, it takes on a special shape and and a special terror. Once he had given the director of the personnel department at the polytechnic, Mrs. Przekrasicka, a roll in the hay, my old man folded the handkerchief carefully, put it in his pocket, and set off for home. I know the details. I know the details, because I am an omniscient Lutheran narrator. A Lutheran narrator can be no other. Even when the narrator is a Lutheran child, then it, too, is omnipotent, omniscient, and chosen by Our Lord, the One in the Trinity, Amen. Father was intoxicated by his amorous success. He was especially intoxicated by the class aspect of his amorous success. Przekrasicka—this wasn't just anything! And it absolutely wasn't a matter of the fact that she was the director of personnel at the polytechnic. The position, of course, was important and key, but it was nonetheless in the administrative sector. Father, as a researcher, a doctoral student, lecturer, etc., etc., was, in this regard, of infinitely higher standing. But Przekrasicka was a well known Krakow name! Her husband, Mr. Przekrasicki—he was a well known Krakow figure! To tell the truth, an artist! In a certain sense, a painter! A poet, who had his verses printed in *The Catholic Weekly*! Fully a man of the world! Tadeusz Kantor himself attended receptions at the Przekrasickis! My old man couldn't even dream that he would be in attendance there! He couldn't dream that he would give the hostess of those sorts of banquets a roll in the hay! And at the very thought that maybe he might do so after all, and especially in the course of the thing, it seemed to him that glory after glory, honor after honor was flowing down upon him. And the very fact that Przekrasicka smoked drove Father mad! According to our Lutheran principles, the smoking woman was beyond all categories. Only a man could smoke, and that only under the condition that he had become addicted to tobacco in a concentration camp. Smoking because of toothache? Smoking because of—as St. Paul would say—burning of the body? Forget it. As far as women were concerned, there could be no justifications. Not even a concentration camp, not even the Gulag, not even death row was justification. Women didn't smoke, and that was that. The only ones who smoked were basically no longer women: whores or creatures from another planet. Father rolled Mrs. Przekrasicka, and he had the impression that he was rolling a whore from another planet. Dwelling on such satisfactions caused him to forget the handkerchief in his pocket. That is, he didn't forget, there was no way he forgot, but he was incapable of throwing it out. On his way home, he passed a thousand places where he could have done it, even if there weren't any trash cans, even if there wasn't a single can, which is possible, although not very likely, after all there were the Commons, the park, dark squares, the grates of street sewers, it would have been perfectly easy to be rid of the ill-fated handkerchief, but not my old man, he didn't throw it away. He carried it home. Maybe he thought that he would quietly slip it into Mother's laundry? I don't know what he was thinking, even as an omniscient Lutheran narrator I don't know what he was thinking, maybe he wasn't thinking at all, because to think that it would be possible to slip something quietly into Mother's laundry is the height of naïveté! That was a naïveté much greater than bringing the soiled handkerchief home. After all, before washing, and after washing but before drying, as well as after drying, Mother examined each thing under the light a thousand times, each set of knickers, each rag, each piece of tattered clothing! Nothing could go to waste! Damage! Rip! Wear out! You had to know when to sew! Patch! Darn! After washing? Or before? Or should you even risk washing? Will that shirt be suitable for going out any more? Or should you wear it only around the house? And why are those pants so grimy? And where? And when? And even if they are so grimy that they are no longer suitable for going out or wearing around the house, you still don't throw them away, because they will be good if we have to paint the apartment, and if not, then they will be ideal for weather-stripping the windows in the winter. In this fashion, after decades of collecting rags, our apartment was filled and overgrown with rags, it became the world's only rag museum, rag mausoleum, rag labyrinth. We were surrounded by such fortified rag walls that not even nuclear radiation could pass through them. When Chernobyl exploded, my folks' apartment, so overgrown with rags, was the safest bunker in all of Europe. But to return to the main thread of the narration: on my word, I am probably maligning my own Father by ascribing to him the idea of slipping the handkerchief into the family wash. That was out of the question. So what, in that case, did he wish to do? Did he wish to wash and dry it himself on the sly? In our two rooms? In the face of Mother's ceaseless presence and eternal

Jerzy Pilch

bustling? That would be absolute and criminal idiocy. Was he suddenly aware just how low he had fallen and to what end he had come,
and had he decided that—tough—what had happened had happened,
he was not going to wade further into the bog, and he would no
longer make the next step into the abyss—which would be to throw
away a perfectly good handkerchief? Had the physical act with the
director of personnel at the polytechnic, Mrs. Przekrasicka, swept out
of his head all thoughts and remnants of the instinct for self-preser-
vation, and therefore he especially heightened the old principle of not
throwing anything away, and especially, God forbid, of not throwing
away things that were perfectly good, and the handkerchief was not
only perfectly good, it was almost new? Did he, having the choice
between the risk of exposure and the certainty of breaking principles,
decide not to break principles? Was he taking a risk? Having considered all the parameters and variations, was he taking a risk? Had he
calculated the risk? Had he not calculated anything, because he was
plunged in absolute chaos and helplessness? One way or the other,
everything inexorably made its way toward a horror-filled finale. My
old man entered the apartment, removed his overcoat in the entryway,
and with the help of embarrassing theatrical gestures, he began to
make it known that he was hungry as a wolf. The sight of Father—
rubbing his belly with feigned grief, desperately smacking his lips and
winking at me conspiratorially, as if to say that if I would support his
efforts, Mommy Dearest would fry us up some up some pancakes—
was *un*bearable. Today—when I am clearly aware that my old man
rubbed his belly, pitifully smacked his lips, and pretended to be a
hungry little boy less than an hour after the copulatory frenzy to
which he had surrendered in the personnel department office of the
polytechnic, which they had locked from within—I turn my attention
with due consideration to human nature, full as it is of contradictions;
but at that time, I was convulsed with desperately diabolical snickering. But the laughter, the snickering didn't last long; almost immediately the great terror ensued. I don't recall whether searching through
the old man's pockets was already one of Mother's constant customs

those days, or whether it arose precisely at that time. Besides, it isn't so important whether Mother reached into the old man's pockets as a matter of routine, or whether she was led by a sudden intuition—it is enough that she reached in there. She reached there immediately, and immediately she extracted a handkerchief embroidered with pearls, adorned with intricate needlework, no need to mention the name of the overcast stitching on the edges. An immediate reaching, immediate extraction, and an immediate leap for his throat. The flame of the panther's coat rising in the air, and the beginning of the immortal aria: I'll kill you! I'll kill you! I'll kill you! The old man didn't try to defend himself at all, he laid down his weapons and folded his wings, and for a good hour he was a corpse in the strict sense of the word. Only when he had recovered from the shock of being the culprit caught with the evident proof of guilt in his pocket did he begin to defend himself, aggressively and desperately; he stubbornly dug in his heels and insisted that Mother was engaging in trivial investigative inductionism. "Time to be done with trivial investigative inductionism!" he yelled. "Stop engaging in trivial investigative inductionism! We won't get anywhere this way! Do I demand any sort of great things? I don't demand any great things! I demand common understanding! Common human understanding!" Mother's rage was, from the beginning, mighty and impotent. All the mightier and the more impotent because she, too, was incapable of throwing the disastrous handkerchief away, and what is more, she realized that sooner or later she would launder it herself by hand and iron it. True, she repeated in the depth of her soul—"What fault is this of the handkerchief? What fault, finally, is this of the handkerchief? What fault, finally is this, in the least, of this handkerchief?"—but those seemingly thoroughly rational questions didn't extinguish her rage and pain, quite the opposite. That very evening, she moved into my room, to the green sofa bed for guests. For months on end they slept apart, got up in the morning, ate breakfast, went to work, returned home in the afternoon, rested a moment, and from early evening on, with voices horse from yelling, solemnly promised each other that they would kill each other during the night. "With this knife, with this very knife, I'll slit your throat!" Mother would bellow and wave about a huge butcher's blade that we had brought with us from our parts. "With this hammer, with this very hammer, I'll smash your head in!" my old man would wheeze and show her the great bricklayer's hammer that he had bought at the time of our move. "As soon as you fall asleep, you're a goner!" "Sweet dreams, you won't wake up anyway!" So tenderly did they part before falling asleep, and dead tired they fell into truly sound sleep. The notion that Mother would get up in the night and go, all the same, to butcher Father didn't especially disturb me. But the notion that the old man would get up and come to my room and start to pound Mother's head with a gigantic bricklayer's hammer was unpleasant. I'm not saying that I imagined the sound of the cracking skull and the splash of the spraying brain, because I didn't know such realities, but the possibility that the old man might bash me with the hammer as well really did come into consideration. Even if it was only because of normal momentum. And if it was not because of momentum, then it would be after giving it some thought, out of a desire to spare me the fate of being a half-orphan. Or with premeditation, wishing to liquidate me as an eye witness. This was relatively unlikely; I doubted on the whole that he would wish to liquidate me for precisely that reason. I supposed that, if it came to that, he would attempt to reach an agreement with me; still, you have to be prepared for all variations. Every evening, as the tragic opera was nearing its close, I played on the floor, as if casually, but in truth I was assembling a special alarm. It wasn't difficult. I had all the necessary elements: I had "The Little Electrician," and "The Little Engineer," and "The Little Architect." The construction of a simple system, which, with the slightest opening of the door, turned on a piercing bell, was truly childishly simple. Moreover, every day I perfected the construction. I had an innumerable quantity of toys, I had bells, lights, miniature motors, moving semaphores, fire trucks and ambulances with sirens, special flood lights, three electric trains, batteries, hundreds, perhaps thousands of useful objects. There was something to choose from and something to plot with. It came easily to me. I was a young Einstein and a budding Edison, or maybe the other way around, and I was overflowing with concepts. I was able to link the wires and set up the construction in such a way that, when the door was opened, the train was set in motion, the bell rang, the lights shone, the cars drove. I truly was able to do everything, and I truly had everything. How often—and with pride!—was Father wont to say that I had whatever my heart desired, and that I didn't lack for any treats. The first state of man is worse than the last, and the other way around. The last is worse than the first. All our sentences and all our quotations go into darkness. The organists' daughters. The pastors' sons. Death playing chess. A scarf embroidered with pearls. The growing pile of dark writings. An Italian notebook. Seven seals. And if I by Beelzebub cast out devils, by whom do your sons cast them out?

The Spirit of
Miraculous Discoveries

I

The bizarrely dressed female vacationer was Mother's age, or perhaps even older. We pursued her, but we were unable to focus on her. She traversed the center of town and the neighboring valleys by paths just as bizarre as her outfits. She would suddenly emerge from beyond the bend; it wasn't clear whether the dark colorations on her fantastic dresses were a pattern or a sweat stain; but it was clear that it was necessary to drop everything and set off after her. Sometimes, when we were playing soccer, her tall and dreadfully thin silhouette would appear on the road to Almira, which ran above the playing field; something would then force us to interrupt the match; in panicky haste we would wash in the stream, get dressed, and rush around. Janek always slowed everything down, because, first, he wanted to keep playing, and then, he would wash as if he were going to the ball. He would pull the faded baggy pants from his hips, jump into the deepest part of the stream, and swim endlessly in the dark green water. He would climb out, comb his hair with inordinate care, drowsily put on his black pants and white shirt—he made a point of getting on our nerves.

The bizarrely dressed vacationer constantly turned back, and here was the entire hope and terror of the chase: we were on the trail of a specter that would suddenly cease to flee, turn back around, and vengefully set off in our direction. She would arrive at some place known only to her and turn around; she would suddenly back up, suddenly make violent and panicky reversals, as if lava from Etna or Vesuvius were flowing from the spot she had touched with her foot. Then there was no way out: we had to trudge on; she would approach relentlessly; we would have much preferred to turn tail and run, but, in the first place, we had our honor, and in the second, we were drawn to the high voltage. No two ways about it—the gamble was out of this world—it always seemed to us that, at the moment we passed, she would do something uncanny, scream or lunge at our necks with her long, carmine nails. Nothing of the sort ever happened, although always, when she was right there, we got the shivers. Janek would shake like jello.

She seemingly didn't do anything terrible, but all the same, what she did was sufficiently terrible. Always, when we were face to face, and when we cast furtive glances in her direction, she would bite her lips in a theatrical manner, make bizarre faces, as if she were choking with laughter. As if, by force of will, she were suppressing an attack of hysterical weeping or tubercular coughing. Her eyes were popping out of her head, her face flushed, her lips unnaturally twisted—it looked like she knew everything. Like she understood perfectly well that she was constantly being followed, and like she constantly laughed at the fact. This was disconcerting and horrifying in the extreme; we swore that, seeing that the old tart has such a high opinion of herself, we would not even glance in her direction again. But there was no escape from her fatal magnetism—after a couple days the rituals would begin anew.

In any case, it soon turned out that she was making bizarre faces the whole time, that, for the entire length of her walks, she fought back spasmodic laughter, weeping, coughs. Contrary to appearances, this mitigated the terror—it is always better when someone has some sort of permanent attack, and not only at our sight.

The most bizarre were her dresses, inappropriate for either the time of day or the season of the year. Some sort of sophisticated creations with long sleeves, made of heavy materials like brocade, mandarin collars under the neck, lace collars, some sort of gigantic embroideries, cream-colored on green, orange on dark blue—by that time, even then, nobody dressed like that, not for any occasion. Today, I think that Janek Nikandy—always in black pants and always in a white shirt—suited her perfectly.

II

HE PLAYED SOCCER AS IF HE WERE COMPOSING MUSIC TO ACCOMPANY his runs along the length of the field, to accompany the smell of the grass, the ball darkening from the dampness, always falling upon his foot as if from heaven. He swam in the deepest part of the river as if he were composing music to accompany swimming in the deepest part. He collected stamps as if he were composing music to accompany stamp collecting. He read everything he came upon, as if he heard song in everything that had been written. He would raise a mug of beer, throw back his head, and drink, just as the greatest composers in the world must have drunk.

He examined the girls at the swimming pool, and it was clear that he knew everything about them. *We* set our sights on the middling ones, *he* scorned even the best. He was waiting for the most beautiful one among the most beautiful; but even *she* couldn't be certain that she would be accepted. This didn't surprise anyone. It was clear to everyone that Janek could have any woman in the world at any moment, that he would go far: that he would complete the entire blacksmith's training course in a year, two at most; that he would then, likewise in a flash, complete a few majors, go abroad, go through Oxford, Harvard, fly into the cosmos, win the Chopin competition, be the first Pole to buy Real Madrid, discover new stars, construct an everlasting battery for a flashlight, discover a vaccination for cancer, or do other miracles.

Janek had everything: stacks of books in the attic; collections of incredible objects in the drawers; a one-eyed father who forbade him nothing; a mother as beautiful as an Egyptian priestess; two unbearable sisters; three dissolute brothers, who could fix anything; a mentally ill grandmother, who never left her room; and a grandfather, who had been dying for years, and who barely spoke Polish. Supposedly before one of the old wars he had had a different name and had been a famous Viennese tailor. It is uncertain whether Robert Musil had his suits sewn by him, whether Hermann Broch had his pants shortened, but it is possible.

III

THE NIKANDYS DIDN'T GO TO CHURCH, THEY HELD THEIR RELIGIOUS services at home. The entire family sat at the table every day, the one-eyed father read from the Bible, prayed with concentration, then he spoke about the presence of God in our lives and about various spirits, mostly about the Spirit of Light and the Spirit of Darkness.

I feared the God of the Nikandys—He was too near. The Spirit of Light would show himself and disappear, the Spirit of Darkness lurked in every corner. In our Church, God was at a safe distance, and there weren't any spirits at all.

But much worse than the Spirit of Light, than the Spirit of Darkness, than all the other spirits known to Janek, was the Spirit of Miraculous Discoveries. I think he kept it under his collar, I think it sat on his shoulder and whispered where he should look. Janek happened upon everything. I would be walking next to him on the banks of the same river, treading the same earth, but it was he who would bend down and pick up parts of Stalin-era motorbikes, feathers from Caribbean birds, cogwheels on quartz pivots, silver keys to God knows what safes. It was he who would pull out from the bottom of the deepest part of the river washed out dials from submerged clocks, fish skeletons coated with phosphorus, stones as symmetrical as octagons, brittle teacups without a single crack, bracelets of thick glass shining like green stars, Austrian, German, Russian, and even Swiss coins. I came upon nothing but unremarkable things: a tin cup, a smashed thermos, a penknife covered with rust, a fork with the inscription "Silesian Gastronomy." Nothing worth talking about.

You could beat him at soccer sometimes, especially when he had too many bush leaguers on his team. I swam almost as well as he did. I had the same sort of household, maybe even a gaudier mixture. I was definitely better at chess—except that this remained somewhat in the realm of theory, since, once he realized that he couldn't beat me, he ceased playing entirely. In any event, I had no complexes, I didn't suffer. I was in his shadow, but I rather admired than envied him. The harmony full of perfect lights that he had within him aroused my adoration, not my envy.

But whenever he found the next remarkable object, whenever he would bend down, and, the next time, pull out, literally from under my shoe, the moveable fragment of some sort of phenomenal mechanism, or the brass buckle from a Red Army belt, or a retort overgrown with moss, which a group of wandering alchemists must have lost on this spot centuries ago—then I hated him with all my heart. There was an abyss between us in the art of observation: he was a master, I an abject loser. I always lost that match and always by a score of something to zero. I lost for a time. Not so much until the time of my desired victory as until the time of the final disaster. Until the time of the disaster of disasters.

Janek would receive his discoveries with manly self-restraint: no leaps or euphoria—it was just the norm; and, in fact, it *was* the norm that he always found something. But one day, when we had traversed the length and breadth of Wisła in pursuit of the vacationer in brocade dresses; once we had accompanied her practically to the very doors of Villa Almira and then run back down and descended, next to the swimming pool, to the water of the river, warm after the sultry day, and we set off along its twists and turns toward the reddish-brown sky over Czantoria Mountain, and when, under the third bridge, Janek bent down and dug something up from the river's stone chippings—this time even he shouted, even he lifted his arms in victory. He held something very nondescript in his hand and waved it feverishly in my direction. I was in no hurry to celebrate his most recent triumph. I pretended that the water was offering greater resistance than it did. I approached slowly, but still—even when I was already quite near—I couldn't recognize what he had come upon this time. Finally, seeing that I still didn't get it, he put the thing to his eyes, and I understood that this was a pair of binoculars left behind by the Germans, similar to a fossilized crab, overgrown with gravel and algae. (And anyway, the number of binoculars left during the war by the retreating Wehrmacht is shocking. Sometimes it is impossible not to think that our earth, saturated with the blood of heroes and filled with the ashes of martyrs, is also overgrown with the lenses of Carl Zeiss.)

We began to scrub it while we were still in the water, then on the shore, then in our neighboring courtyards, and the more its original shape emerged out of the chaos, the higher my heart soared. And when, finally, it was entirely restored—that is, when, through one of its tubes, you could see some sort of image that was foggy, but brought nearer all the same—I became triumphally certain: this time I would be better. I didn't even need to summon the Spirit of Miraculous Discoveries. I knew where to look.

IV

I SEARCHED THE BACK ROOM INCH BY INCH. I LOOKED UNDER BOTH beds. I dug out everything that was under the beds, and there was quite a lot of it. I looked into each and every shoe. I checked the straw mattresses. Night stands—so filled with objects that they were practically inflated—took me a lot of time. Then I checked the interior of the clock, the hearth under the stove, the ash pan under the hearth, and finally I stood before Grandma Pech's wardrobe, heavy, deep, and dark as the ocean.

To say that no one but her had access to that wardrobe is to say nothing. Grandma herself seldom opened that wardrobe, and always with some sort of uncertainty or fear. She would then close the doors behind her; she would chase away anyone who just then happened to look in on the back room and ask her about something; just like in a film—she would block out the wardrobe with her own body, so that no one could even glance into it.

All the domestic furniture made themselves known: the table creaked, the stools were falling apart, the upholstery on the armchairs was tearing, the sideboard was headed for collapse, the stoves smoked—there was constant talk about pieces of equipment that were falling to pieces. We talked about them, and we talked to them; it was as if constant conversation with the dying objects was supposed to keep their spirits up. We talked especially frequently about all the cupboards: what to put in which one, what to bring from which one, in which one hymnals stand on the shelves, in which one Grandpa's postal uniform was hanging, in which one there was a box of winter socks, in which one the bottom was falling out, in which one the locks needed to be oiled, in which one mice had danced the night before; this, that, and the other thing. All the cupboards were constantly on our tongues. But about the wardrobe in the back room—never even a single word. As if it didn't exist, or rather, as if it were a wall-less specter, as if it didn't have hinges, as if no one knew what was in it. As if demons with unpronounceable names lived in it, or as if the path to the abyss opened up in the wall behind it.

I stood before that wardrobe as before the gates to a forbidden city; there was a terrible silence in the entire house. The spirits of the world's leading burglars sat on my shoulders and whispered advice about what I should do. My hands glided over the dark pear wood and correctly felt out the weak places. I guessed the most secret codes; invisible keys slipped into locks that had been oiled just a moment before; the tree rings in the wood were like a legible map leading straight to the treasure. The wardrobe in the back room, brittle like a decayed cork, or perhaps heavy like lead, opened slowly. I smelled the scent of silk blouses from the twenties. On hangers hung patterned and light dresses from those times—one with a deep décolletage in the back, a second made of pleated yellow crêpe de Chine; two satin jackets (one matte, the other shiny), a raincoat with circus designs, a jersey bathing suit—no ghosts, no werewolves: the spirit of a young girl lived in this wardrobe. The spirit of the young body of Grandma Pech, sprinkled with naphthalene as if with slaked lime, was imprisoned there. This was its kingdom, this was what was guarding—as if they were precious jewels—the brown suit and the green hunting outfit, which were hanging there on the other side; the yellowed curtains, which were lying on the shelves, and which, in their time, had hung in the windows; it watched over the bed linens, which fell apart in your hands; it dusted the stack of books from the bordeaux-colored series entitled *Library of Masterpieces*, which was hidden away in the depths; it was the spirit that looked through the album, wrapped in brittle oilcloth, with photographs from her first wedding; it had in its care all the ties, hats, neckerchiefs, scarfs; it was what hovered over the boxes that stood on the floor of the wardrobe.

I took into my hands object after object, opened box after box. In the first were tangles of fossilized yarn and a million buttons. In the second, promissory notes, bills, postcards. In the third, daguerreotypes—fragile as emigration—of old man Trzmielowski and old lady Mary, with Humphrey the cat in her hands; they stand, smiling broadly, before an iron gate leading to a gold mine in Nevada. No wonder they are laughing. They would return to Wisła soon thereafter, and, in addition to the eccentric custom of giving Anglo-Saxon names to the household animals, they would bring with them so many dollars that there would be enough for satin jackets and dresses with décolletage for Zuza. The fourth box was full of burned out prewar light bulbs. A collection that was not sorrowful or comical, but lofty and romantic. Who among you women has loved like this? What woman in the world got the idea of saving the light bulbs that had shined during the lifetime of her beloved? As a memento of that by-gone light over their heads; as a memento of those moments when they were gently extinguished over their bed?

A pair of hunting binoculars, which were older than World War II and had belonged to Grandma's first husband, were in the fifth box. I knew about their existence, because, from time to time, whenever unique astronomical phenomena occurred—when bizarre air vehicles glided over the mountains, or on a summer night something unusual happened in the sky: the Big Dipper made such a big dip that its handle cracked, or the North Star shined ever more strongly from minute to minute, as if it were flying straight toward our yard—whenever such spectacles occurred in the cosmos over our heads, Grandma Pech went to the back room, meticulously shut the door behind her, and returned after a moment with the binoculars.

Once, we observed a biplane circling over Wisła; once, a comet over Czantoria Mountain. The biplane circled desperately and in vain and couldn't find a way to straighten out its flight or make the decision to land; it looked tragic to the naked eye, but entirely different with the binoculars. The plates of the fuselage were about to drop off, its flight was about to end, but through the binoculars we saw the plane soaring calmly in the sky, the solid riveting of the wings, the equally shining dials on the control panels. Janek was even able to catch sight of the pilot's face. Supposedly he wasn't in a panic at all, supposedly—quite the opposite—he was in sovereign control of the rudders, and this was most likely accurate, for suddenly, after one of the circlings, he stepped hard on the gas and disappeared over Jarzębata Mountain. The motors fell silent; we were sure that he had landed on the peak. We rushed up there as if on wings, in an absolutely full sprint. Usually it takes at least an hour to walk to the peak of the Jarzębata—we were there in a few minutes. I will never forget the sudden silence of our thudding hearts and the yellow meadow, in the middle of which the biplane ought to have stood, its propeller still revolving, and yet there wasn't a trace—only the great calm of the Beskid peak, the warm breath of the sun, the gentle ocean of the blue sky, and a partridge suddenly shooting upward.

From a distance, the comet over Czantoria Mountain looked like normal fire, except that it was slowly floating through the air; but from up close, it looked like a red-hot bulldozer driving in first gear. The binoculars brought everything close: the pieces that were incessantly falling off the humming machinery, the meteors that were constantly revolving—as in a cauldron—in its very center, the blizzards of snow creating an ideal fan, the spotlights wandering across the peaks of the mixed forest.

V

I CAREFULLY ERASED THE TRACES OF A PLUNDERING EXPEDITION THAT had been crowned with complete success. I arranged all the boxes and all the objects in their proper places. Then, with the treasure hidden under my shirt, I flitted through the house; then, along the steep path up the railway embankment. I was the happiest person in the world: I was running toward certain victory; Janek didn't have a chance.

An image that was foggy, but nonetheless brought nearer? I had exaggerated in the first euphoric moment. The binoculars found on the river bottom didn't bring anything nearer, literally not a thing. They were suitable for placing on an altar. For the very peak of the old bureau, in which Janek kept all his discoveries. That is where he put it, and there—like the crown of miraculous discoveries—he worshipped it. I had a hard time believing it, but a few times I caught him casting glances that seemed uncanny to me, because I didn't know that they were tender. I swear. I was jealous of his love for the old German binoculars, and I offered him—I know that this will sound terrible—much more attractive goods. All of this took place blindly and in the dark, but I simply agreed that he could love his, while using mine. Blindly and in the dark, I attempted to convince him to commit infidelity. Everything I did, I did instinctively. He—as it would turn out—not only knew everything; he also knew how to give everything a name.

We stood on the embankment, and we turned in all directions, and we saw right in front of our noses the clock on the church tower, a swimmer jumping from the diving platform into the pool, the border patrols walking along the border on the top of Stożek Mountain, women sprinters practicing in the stadium, clouds on Ram Mountain, perhaps even the tower of the Cieszyn Castle. We saw everything! Everything at every moment could be brought near! Every meadow, every courtyard, every car, every swimming suit, every head, all the legs, all the shoulders. The carnival of unbridled close-up peeping had begun! Everything! With details! The unprecedented season of bringing near all that is far had begun!

It had begun, but we didn't give a damn. The binoculars, which were as rare as the comet over Czantoria Mountain, brought everything probably a thousand times nearer, but we were interested in bringing only one thing nearer. Only one. No couples disappearing into the woods, no girls changing clothes on the river bank, no women's dressing rooms at the swimming pool, no female athletes standing under the showers after practice, no rooms in which God knows who was doing what! No mythological meadows near Bukowa, on which nymphs from Gliwice danced with Chorzów satyrs! No wide open windows in the tourist hotels! None of them!

None—except for one! You smile, because you know right off the bat—just like us—what window we're talking about here. You smile, because—just like us—you don't know what sort of tragedy would immediately follow! That's right! The unprecedented season of looking at everything from up close basically never even got started. Or rather, strictly speaking, it ended before it could get started! That's right. It ended before we understood that it had dawned.

It goes without saying: among all those wide open Wisła windows, among all the wide open windows of the Principality of Cieszyn, among all the wide open windows in the world—only one window came into play. You guessed it. Her window. Under the very roof of the Almira, on the left side, a window that was open round the clock—even when summer downpours came—and lit up every evening with a thick, yellow luster, which didn't go out until late in the night. The window of the bizarrely dressed female vacationer. Who knows what sorts of secrets would finally be revealed! Finally, we would discover what that freak did in the evening! What she was up to! What her life consisted of! How many more dresses—and just how bizarre did she still have in her wardrobe!

I was overflowing with repeated waves of pride. Not only had I had enough courage and skill to break into a dresser that was, perhaps, inhabited by evil spirits. Not only did the discovery extracted from there slightly trump Janek's discovery. Not only did it give the gift of bringing everything near. Not only did it bestow the overwhelming power that all the peeping toms of the world savor. It was also the key to a fundamental secret. It allowed us to solve the greatest mystery of that summer! Janek could just go ahead and keep that optical ruin of his on the top of the dresser, he could venerate it, worship it like the golden calf. But just let him attempt to climb up the diving platform at the swimming pool, and just let him attempt to see from there into the depths of the yellow light under the roof of the Almira. Lord God! What preeminence You have finally given me supremacy over my always prevailing friend! Of what pride have You given me to drink! You have even permitted me to see humility—let's say: a certain humility—in his eyes and in his motions. For it was with humility, with the humility of the subordinate that Janek Nikandy climbed up the diving tower at the swimming pool that evening.

Granted, it was he who, one fine day, drew an ideal line in the air, connecting the top of the tower to the window in question; granted, it was he who forced me to climb that Mount Everest and pointed out the distant rectangle, entirely dark in the blinding sun; granted, it was under his leadership that we sneaked over to the swimming pool one evening and, trembling in the darkness, which was lit up by the leaden surface of the water, climbed up to the highest platform of our observatory and stared at the yellow light as if at a distant, motionless star; granted, it was he who said at that time: *If only we had a telescope, or at least the pair of binoculars*; granted, it was he who, about a week later, dug up from the bottom of the river his treasure of treasures; granted, granted, granted! All of it granted! But now, at the decisive moment, now, at the threshold of the night that was to settle everything; now—under *my* leadership—we climbed the tower! Now *I* had slung over my shoulder a set of Carl Zeiss lenses of the highest, prewar quality, which would allow us to see into—and this was no time for modesty—the fundamental mystery of existence.

I was the leader, and I knew that I was the leader, and I knew what sort of leader I wanted to be. Magnanimity—as befitted the greatest leaders of humanity—never left my heart. When we found ourselves at the top, when the delicate, dark blue breeze embraced our heads. And when we had turned our faces toward the yellow light, I took Gustaw Branny's hunting binoculars off my shoulder, and I passed them to Janek. He, in turn, took them without a word, lifted them to his eyes, and looked for a long time. A long time. A very long time. For an inordinately long time, he scrutinized the unfathomable lighthouse pulsating with yellow splendor. For a long time, he sought out the mysterious lighthouse keeper in brocade dresses who was living there. For a long time. A very long time. For a long time, he stared at the peak of Olympus covered with a yellow cloud, and for a long time, he waited for the figure of the goddess to emerge from the clouds of glory. For a long time. A very long time. An exceptionally long time.

"What, for fuck's sake? What do you see?" My nerves got the better of me, and I lost the dignity of the leader.

"Nothing."

"What do you mean, nothing?"

"Well, fucking nothing."

"What nothing?

"Nothing."

"You have to see something. Do you see her?"

"I do."

"So why are you bullshitting me that you're not seeing anything?"

"I'm not bullshitting. I'm not seeing anything."

"What do you mean you're not seeing anything, when you are?"

"I'm not seeing anything."

"Do you see her?

"I do."

"So what is she doing?

"Nothing, fuck it, she isn't doing anything. She's sitting at a table and writing."

I couldn't stand any more tension; my nerves were completely shot. I fell out of not only the role of leader, but out of all roles and all functions. And with some incomprehensible sorrow in my heart; with some sort of desperate grievance toward the world, that it doesn't have any mysteries; or perhaps with the terrible suspicion that my friend was lying, that he was deceiving me and didn't want to tell about the unprecedented things that he was seeing—with a sudden and violent motion, I reached for the binoculars. Too suddenly and too violently, a thousand times too suddenly and a thousand times too violently, because not only did I not manage to grasp them, lift them to my eyes; not only did I not manage to catch sight, dumbfounded, of the bizarrely dressed female vacationer sitting at the desk and writing; but I didn't manage to do anything. I didn't manage to do anything, because, suddenly, everything was over. Suddenly everything—speaking both metaphorically and literally—came crashing down. With a precise and strong blow—which, if I had really wanted to inflict it, I would never have been able to do with such precision and strength— with an unprecedented, and unintentional, simple boxer's punch, or perhaps a volleyball player's spike, I dislodged the binoculars from Janek Nikandy's hands, and they, like a flighty, nocturnal creature slipping through our fingers, flew to the ground. Unfortunately, this was not the desperate leap of the escapee attempting to regain his freedom, it was not the liberating leap into the water: it was a suicidal leap onto the cement.

I wasn't certain whether I was hearing the crack of the bursting casing, the crunching of the lenses as they were ground to dust, or Janek's diabolical snicker. Sometimes, in the famous *least appropriate moments*, a strange laughter came over him. Once, with precisely that same sort of snicker, he told us that one of his sisters, fourteen-year-old Regina, was pregnant, and that his father would probably kill her; or that May First was no holiday at all, but an invention of the Communists; or that his mother, Mrs. Nikandy, beautiful as a Grecian goddess, goes to the WC at night completely naked—in none of these stories was there anything comic. Nor was there even a hint of consolation over the smashed binoculars lying below the diving platform. I was too innocent and too young for the phrase—"it's so terrible that it's funny"; Janek, too—except that he laughed. He didn't know that it was so tragic that it was funny; but he had already been blessed by the household deity of the Nikandys with the gift of laughter that surpasses consciousness. And tragicomic events now followed with unprecedented speed, and one after another. First, in the glowing yellow window of the Almira there appeared—fear had sharpened our senses, for we could see it even without the binoculars—a dreadfully tall and thin silhouette, and right away thereafter, as if it had God knows what sort of volatility, it began, like a skier schussing in the darkness, to fly in our direction. Before we managed to climb down, on entirely wobbly legs, she was already there, shining a flashlight thin as a pencil, and gathering the glassy gravel, to which the binoculars had been reduced, into a plastic bag.

At first, we thought it wasn't her, that it was one of the female sprinters, who were at their training camp *Start*. For the bizarrely dressed female vacationer was not dressed bizarrely at all this time. She wasn't wearing any brocade dresses with incredible patterns, but a dark green sweatsuit, which made her look a hundred years younger. On her head—no curls, buns, or bouffants, instead her hair was drawn into a pony tail. From time to time, a lively beam of the flashlight illuminated her face, and then it became clear what beautiful, what expressive, and what—I have no better word for it—quick features she was hiding on a daily basis under vulgar make-up.

My God, how miraculous it would have been to have made all these discoveries through the binoculars! To peep at her every evening! To discover, every evening, a different secret—now the secret of the dress, now the secret of the hairdo, now the secret of the make-up! And You, Lord God, knocked the binoculars from my fingers, You commanded the bizarre angel, with make-up rinsed off and her hair combed out for sleep, to fly directly down to us. You commanded us to experience all the epiphanies at once. You commanded us to stare at her from right up close, without the binoculars. And You condemned—me at least—to a life-long mania for distinctively beautiful female loonies that are slightly past thirty!

We stood completely motionless, like a couple of complete dunces. The phantom in the green sweatsuit seemed not to pay us the least attention, and only once she had finished her work, once she had gathered up the smashed lenses, down to the last speck of dust, then she stood up straight and came up to us, and one by one she took first me, then Janek by the chin, and then shined the flashlight, first in our eyes, and then in her own—as if she were performing some sort of shamanist presentation—and she said, *Bandits, complete bandits*, with some sort of stifled and passionate voice. To this day, I remember that flash of light in her grey pupils, and I remember the intensity of those pupils, and I remember the dark hieroglyphs in their depths, and I am absolutely positive that in those signs were recorded the beginnings of all my amorous prayers.

"Now one of you bandits will follow me. I will give him the address in Katowice at which, after a certain time, the binoculars, like new, will be ready for pick-up. Whole and like new. Precisely the same. He, from whom you took them, he, from whom you borrowed them, and he, to whom you will return them, won't notice a thing."

Jerzy Pilch

She saved us, perhaps she even saved our lives, but—for the saving of life—she had a voice that was inappropriate. "Which of the bandits will follow me? Oh, of course, the more dangerous one. You'll come," she took Janek by the hand, "you're the dangerous one, perhaps even menacing. You've got an evil look in your eyes. And you," she turned to me, "you will wait here for your friend like a good boy. It won't take long."

With a fear that I didn't know how to name—it certainly wasn't fear for the smashed binoculars—I watched as the doubled shadow, hers and Janek's, receded from me, as it climbed the steep slope in the direction of the Almira, as it vanished among other shades—then a completely dark and very long night ensued. Someone ran, or perhaps fled, through the center of Wisła, you could hear his panicky foot patter; then someone's cry resounded, strangely joyous and triumphal; then the 11:23 train to Zawiercie gathered speed on the embankment. Had I fallen asleep? Was it the first time that I dreamed the best dream of my life, that I was walking through a gentle blizzard of butterflies?

I sat at the bridge table made of stone, at which deeply-tanned regulars played for unprecedented stakes, allegedly sometimes even for women. The surface of the water, permeated with suntan oils, gleamed like a roof that has just been tarred, or perhaps like the back of a Leviathan. It got colder and colder, my head kept nodding, and suddenly Janek stood next to me like a specter. I didn't know whether half the night had passed, or half an hour; most certainly less than half the night, but more than half an hour. At *The House of the Spa* the dance was still going on, but it seemed to be drawing to a close. You could hear a slightly relaxed version of Rossini's *Tarantella*—always toward the end, and always, when they were slightly relaxed, the Potulnik brothers played classical pieces from memory. Without a word, we set off home. When we were on the bridge, I asked:

"Do you have that address? When are we supposed to go there? To Katowice? Right?"

Janek remained silent; out of the corner of my eye I noticed the quick motion of his hand and a scrap of paper flying over the railing.

"Let it sail to the seas and the oceans?" I made sure I was understanding what he had done.

"Sail to all the seas of the world. To the Black Sea, the Yellow Sea, the White Sea, and the Red Sea," he pronounced the colors like incantations.

Suddenly I felt an incomprehensible feeling of relief. It was as if a warm, Caribbean sea current had passed over me from head to foot. Nothing bad had happened, my God! The world was now missing one object—granted, it was exceptional—but what of it? Nothing! My God, that is nothing! It wasn't certain whether Grandma would even notice the loss, whether she would ever look into the box where the binoculars were kept. She looks into the wardrobe in the back room two, three times a year, but into the box? When? I knew when. When a comet appears over Czantoria Mountain, or when the Big Dipper flies to pieces in the heavens. When would that be? Perhaps in twenty years, and perhaps never. Not only Grandma, not only we, but perhaps not even anyone in the whole world would live to see the next comet fly across the sky like a red-hot bulldozer.

"Did you fuck her?" I asked, when we were saying goodbye in front of our houses, and the question itself was proof of what soaring euphoria had seized me, and what mad boldness. I knew perfectly well that my friend couldn't stand intimate questions. "Did you fuck her?"

"I didn't feel like it," Janek Nikandy replied, and he disappeared behind the gate to the dark gardens surrounding our houses.

VI

LAST NIGHT, AFTER SEVERAL DECADES, I AGAIN DREAMED OF THE butterfly blizzard. Back then they were yellow, today's were white; this time my daughter Magda was with me in the dream, she held my hand, and I think she was coming to my rescue, because the number of butterflies was increasing, and they slowly began to suffocate me, but, all the same, it looked like it was going to be a beautiful death. All the more beautiful in that, just before dawn, in a flash of half-consciousness, it suddenly occurred to me that I am someone who understands the terrible randomness of the world. I suddenly saw that the world is a great field full of asymmetrically laid out campfires; you have to go incessantly from fire to fire; extinguish and kindle; go through the darkness, go through the light; someone tells of dangerous charges that could explode any moment. Suddenly it dawned on me that I knew how to write about—and how to take account of—the randomness, because other than that, there is nothing; how to show the campfires and the paths between them, and how to remember about the force of the charges planted everywhere, and how to liberate oneself from life for the sake of the spasm of love. I awoke slowly. The entire irrefutable transparency of the argument was vanishing. Grandma Pech was standing over my bed and saying something. She was repeating a sentence over and over that, at first, was completely indistinct, but then became more and more distinct. She said something, asked about something. It was almost half a century ago when I awoke for good, got dressed, traipsed into the kitchen. Nobody was there. I was tempted to run right over to Janek's place without breakfast, but my hunger was stronger, and in those days the preparation of scrambled eggs didn't drive me into such an abysmal depression as it does now. I got a frying pan covered with an eternal layer of grease from the pantry. I began to consider whether I would eat seven, or only five eggs. Grandma Pech was walking across the fieldstone-paved courtyard. Two steps behind her, Janek. Suddenly both of them—as if they were back in my dream—appeared in the kitchen.

"I wonder whatever could have happened to those binoculars?" Grandma asked in an amazingly cheerful tone.

"They fell into the river on us and got wrecked. Completely wrecked . . . It took us a long time to find them." Janek produced the binoculars we had found under the bridge from inside his jacket, and at first he made a motion as if he wished to place them on the table, but then, with sudden desperation, he handed his greatest treasure to Grandma. Everything fell into place. I had stolen out of love for him, he was giving up his treasure out of love for me. Everything fell into place. Everything except for Grandma Pech's reaction. She turned the old German ruin over in her fingers, and it was absolutely impossible that she would be taken in, that she would believe that this wreck, which had been lying in the water close to twenty years, had once belonged to Gustaw. This was completely out of the question, she was infallible in much more difficult matters, she infallibly recognized much more difficult objects, she couldn't be taken in by such crude frauds. And yet. And yet, without a single word, or perhaps even with an almost inaudible sigh of relief, she turned on her heels and moved off into the depths of the house, and after a moment there reverberated the sound of the doors to the back room being opened and closed.

VII

After we moved to Krakow, I lost contact with Janek, and the bits of news about him that reached us were most strange. Supposedly, he didn't study at all before his entrance exam to the blacksmiths' technical college. This, in itself, wasn't so strange. Janek generally knew everything even without studying, or he would catch up in a flash at the last minute—but this time he even let the "last minute" slide. The whole night before the exam, he sat in the attic and read old *Cross Sections*. It was incredibly stuffy; not even the night, not even the air over the gardens, which were going to seed, was cooler. In the morning, he went to take the exam, pale and as if in a fever, and—in short—he didn't pass. Janek Nikandy didn't get into the Blacksmiths' Technical College in Ustroń! A gigantic sensation, perhaps even cosmic, but, finally, transitory, justifiable on account of health problems, although—to be honest—even confined to his bed he ought to beat all the healthy ones hands down. But after all, there's luck in leisure. Everyone knew that he would pass the exam in a year, wherever he felt like it, and that he would make up for the year of delay whenever he felt like it. Except that in a year he didn't take the exam anywhere, and he didn't make up for any lost time, nor did he intend to make up for it. It was then I saw him for the last time in my life. We got off the Krakow train; there was a fantastic, rust-colored sunset, Janek stood on the platform. At first I thought he was waiting for someone, that perhaps by some miracle he had found out when I would be arriving with my folks, and that he had come out to the station. But he wasn't waiting for me, or for anyone. He stood on the platform, and he was looking at the train that was just about to set off further toward Głębce. What's new? Nothing. Playing soccer? No. Nothing—a russet sky over Czantoria Mountain.

Supposedly, a year later, maybe two, he began to study the Bible under the tutelage of one-eyed Mr. Nikandy, and it was announced that he would study theology and become a pastor in their Church. But before they managed to go into the details of the first three chapters of the Book of Genesis, Mrs. Nikandy, as beautiful as an Italian actress, fled the house with a certain wandering preacher, who was lacking any principles whatsoever, and both father and son lost, for some time, their zeal for studying the Bible. *Some time*—as it often happens—became time eternal. One-eyed Mr. Nikandy died of a heart attack less than a year later. After *some time*, Janek got a professional driver's license, and he became a driver in a quarry. He drank. He had an accident in which someone died. He landed in prison for a few years. When he got out he didn't really have any place to go; his sisters had found husbands, his brothers wives, and harboring a criminal under their roofs wasn't to their liking. He wandered a bit here and there. Then he disappeared. Supposedly he moved to Silesia, supposedly he found work there and married a woman who was much older. Supposedly as long as she was alive, things were OK. But when she died—a total decline. The last two years spent in rats' nests, under a sky of denatured spirits, over reptilian sewers. Basically, I don't even know whether he froze on the street that year, or the carbon monoxide in a makeshift mine shaft suffocated him. People say various things.

Breakneck Love

I GO TO BOOK SIGNINGS LESS AND LESS FREQUENTLY, BECAUSE I AM less and less able to tolerate nights spent in hotels. Not so much even the nights themselves, as the returns to the room in the evenings. Once a person has finally fallen asleep, it basically makes no difference where he is. But the empty evenings, during which, theoretically, anything might happen, but nothing ever does happen, are unbearable.

I don't know whether there exists a monograph entitled *Hotels and Suicide*, or even better: *A Baedeker for the Hotels of Suicides*. I don't know whether such books exist. Probably they do exist. All books already exist, so probably there is also a *Guide to Hotels in Which the Greatest Number of Suicides Were Committed*. But without even reading it, I know what is written there. The chapter about individual steps in the hallway. The chapter about the decrepit television. The chapter about the view from the window overlooking the wall of the neighboring building. The chapter about the light left on in the bathroom. The chapter about empty drawers. The chapter about the semi-darkness.

The chapter about the figure sitting motionless on the bed. I know those works by heart. I know those climates through and through. No one comes, no one knocks on the door, the telephone remains silent. You yourself don't feel like calling, besides there isn't really much of anyone to call. It is impossible to read; absolutely nothing is possible.

Every evening spent in a hotel is ghastly, but an *evening spent in a hotel* after *a book signing* is especially ghastly. In addition, there is the famous feeling of contrast—embarrassing in its superficiality, but for that reason all the more painful. An hour ago you were signing books, chatting with gusto, shining as never before. *Lyceum* students who secretly write poetry were asking for tips about writing, flushed female readers asked about the place of love in life with burning glances. Fifteen minutes ago, I was the incarnation of freedom and courage. Fifteen minutes ago, I was in the crowd, I was the soul of the crowd—now I sit here lonesome as the night is long. Basically, the more successful the event, the worse it is later.

None of the readers standing patiently in line for an autograph would ever come up with the daring idea of inviting the esteemed author for a vodka. It doesn't occur to them that this stranger from Warsaw, who practically drove off the intruders, is so afraid of returning to the hotel by himself that he would have had a drink with anyone. Never did a one of the ardently staring girls broaden the bravado of her gaze or make even a tender sign with an eyelid. Zero perceptiveness. Not a hint of the intuition that a person will desperately ponder from time to time whether to propose supper to the moderately alluring organizer, who is just then adding up the costs of the trip. In the end everybody scatters, and the moderately alluring organizers remain. Someone has to remain. Someone has to remain, so that someone doesn't kill himself.

I go to book signings less and less frequently, but when I get an invitation to make an appearance in my parts—on the whole—I don't refuse. Sentimentalism and Lutheran phantoms are stronger than the fear of spending the night in a hotel. When Lutherans from Cieszyn Silesia invite me, the phantom of duty engulfs me.

Last year, in the middle of November, I traveled to K. Everything took place as usual, or even worse still. In my parts, even moderately alluring organizers are out of the question. In my parts, the crossbar of piety is placed high. At meetings with my brethren, I deftly play the bard of the Cieszyn land, bound with the blessed fetters of Protestantism and well versed in the Bible. It goes without saying that I always have the insane temptation to blurt out some pieces of filth, which—especially in such situations—multiply in my head like mutant rabbits, but at least for the time being, Lutheran style is stronger than the deviltry.

In any case, in my parts even the most illusory illusions that some reader might propose a symbolic snack, or that some female Lutheran reader might wink at me wantonly, drop away to the nth degree and from the very beginning. To the nth degree squared, and from the beginning of beginnings. Of course, after the evening I will have to lend my features the expression of the weary pilgrim, take my leave of even the most alluring organizers, and, at a slow pace, and in a humble pose, cross the Market Square and sink into the abysses of the hotel *At the Sign of the Falcon*—leaving to the citizens of K., who watch me depart, at most the vague uncertainty whether I will spend the evening reading the works of Melanchthon, or those of Zwingli instead.

In the middle of November last year this was precisely how everything went, jot for jot, tittle for tittle. I took my leave, cut across the Market Square, got the key from the clearly already thoroughly potted receptionist; in the room I turned on the TV, took Zweig's *The World of Yesterday* from my bag, and sat motionless on the bed. Actually, it wasn't so bad. I could take a long shower, and then, once I had checked whether there was some detective show on television, I could begin to read. More than that. I could delay for an endlessly long time the taking of an endlessly long shower. I could check for an endlessly long time whether on the five foggy channels there definitely wasn't a detective show. Maybe there isn't one at the moment, but perhaps in fifteen minutes there will be. Fifteen times sixty equals nine hundred. If you count only a second per channel, that is enough to press each of the five buttons one hundred eighty times, but if you count two seconds, then it is enough to look at each of the five channels only ninety times, and if you allow three seconds per channel—which is just enough to get a sense of what they are offering on each channel—then it is enough to press each of the five buttons forty-five times. That's nothing. One, two, one, two, and the quarter of an hour is over. In addition to this, I could—which in the onslaught of sudden possibilities I had almost overlooked—prepare for an endlessly long time to read the book, which, it is not out of the question, I could read endlessly. Upon my word, quite a decent and peaceful evening was shaping up.

As it would turn out, this was not an empty omen. I don't know whether I had managed to push the button on the remote control even ten times when steps resounded in the hallway, and in a moment someone knocked on the door. A thousand hopes, a thousand disbeliefs, a thousand uncertainties, a thousand sweet visions flitted through my head. Flitted and vanished, just as soon as I had opened the door.

A tall, skinny old man with a neurotic face stood in the hallway. I had seen him less than an hour ago and remembered him well. He had been at the book signing; he sat in the second row and didn't ask a single question, although it was clear that he really wanted to. I had seen him ten minutes or so ago, perhaps thirty or so, but even if I had seen him a thousand years ago, I still would have remembered him: he had the sort of face you never forget. In his features and gaze, absolute madness was joined with the most elevated dignity—a combination that was common in the nineteenth, and even in the twentieth century; today it is completely rare. He was dressed in a light colored poplin overcoat, he held under his arm an ancient, massive pigskin briefcase, stuffed to the brim.

"I beg your pardon most humbly for disturbing your peace," he said with the strong and well-adjusted voice of someone who is used to the bold expression of his thoughts. "I beg your pardon most humbly for

disturbing your peace. I wanted to call from the lobby, but poor Emil
. . . is already in bad shape . . ."

"The receptionist?" My guess didn't require much perspicacity.
"Indeed, I also noticed that, in spite of the early hour, he is already
somewhat . . ."

"Early hour?" The old man smiled broadly. "Master . . . Can it be
that the master, contrary to appearances, has entirely broken with his
roots? Can you have forgotten at what hour the lights are turned out
at home, the curtains drawn? It isn't yet nine, but for Lutherans it is
the middle of the night, or in any case a very late hour, and Emil has
a sacred right to lay his weary head down on the counter. Well . . . but
I just, counting on a certain, so to say, relativism between our time
and the time of the rest of the world, I make bold at such a . . ." he
glanced at me questioningly, "basically, I don't know, whether it is an
hour that is at all acceptable . . ."

We were still standing in the doorway. I hadn't invited him into
the room, because I was counting on the business with which he had
come to me to be short; that he only wanted to ask for a belated
autograph, because at the book signing he hadn't had a copy of my
book; that he was bringing the scarf that I had left in the coat check;
that he wished only now, because he didn't have the courage before
other people, to offer me a volume of versified memoirs, which he
had published at his own expense; that—whatever he wanted from
me—he would vanish immediately.

It was as it always was. Just a minute ago I had been praying in the
depths of my soul that someone would appear, that something would
happen; but now I was absolutely certain that checking whether there
might be a detective show on one of the five foggy channels was the
one thing I desired to devote myself to—with passion and until late in
the night. Now the endlessly long postponement of the endlessly long
shower seemed to me an endangered pleasure that I needed to defend.
How many times was it like that? How many times had I prayed for
the presence of someone, and my prayers were heard, and God sent

someone's presence, and I, in the greatest panic, didn't even allow that person to cross the threshold?

"I forewarn you that my business is not quick or perfunctory." It didn't surprise me that he was reading my mind. "I want to tell you a story."

I wasn't keen on other people's stories. A least a year before, I had realized that there was no way, not even until the end of my life, that I would manage to write down what I myself remember. I wasn't curious about his story, but I also sensed more and more clearly that it was unavoidable.

"Please," I said with restrained cordiality, "come in, except that I don't have anything, I have absolutely nothing at all to offer you."

"I am invading your territory, but I don't come empty handed." With a sure step he entered the room, opened the briefcase, which was filled to the brim with various papers, extracted from it a gigantic bottle, its cap sealed with wax, and all of it wrapped in newspaper, as well as an equally gigantic thermos.

"They have glassware here, as far as I recall." On an absurd, utterly useless, typical hotel chest of drawers stood a bottle of Ustronianka mineral water and two glasses. "Please, if I may allow myself such an eccentricity. True, you are at home here, but in K., even *At the Sign of the Falcon*, I feel that I am the host. I have spent a good bit of my life in the bar downstairs, and besides, you know, I am familiar with every square inch here. That's right. I know the history, geography, and substance of every local square inch."

Only now did he take off his overcoat. He was wearing an archaic brown suit, perhaps from the fifties, or perhaps even from before the war.

"Help yourself, assuming, of course, you do drink. Because people say various things. But if people say various things, then that means that you do, in fact, drink."

"With you, I'll have a drink," I said with the resignation that I recall from old times, and which ritually signified, at the beginning, a few hours—and later, a few days—torn out of my life story.

"Perfect." With a tender gesture he grasped the bottle and skillfully rapped it on the edge of the table so that the wax seal split into two halves like a walnut. He removed the screw cap that had been underneath, and he poured into the glasses a proper measure of the cloudy drink for each of us. I caught the cold scent of October grass.

"Juniper berry vodka. Homemade, it goes without saying. It goes wonderfully with hot mint tea," he rapped a finger on the thermos.

"No thanks, for now," I shook my head.

"I understand perfectly. Old school. Without a chaser. Your health."

We each drank two rounds in silence. A warm sea current passed through us from head to foot. We took out cigarettes, lit them up; the smell of smoke was united with the smell of the juniper berry vodka, which was so intense that it seemed synthetic. "Are you reading Zweig?" He glanced at the book lying on the bed. "A forgotten author and somewhat, I would say, second-rate."

"I am reading him carefully," I responded. "I am reading him carefully and with delight. With absolute delight."

"Carefully and with delight? Aren't you exaggerating a bit? *Chess Story* is great, but the rest?"

"The rest too, God help me. Besides, you know, almost everyone would like to be a second Thomas Mann. But I wouldn't have anything against being a second Stefan Zweig. In youth, a person worships Mann, Dostoevsky, Faulkner, but slightly scorns Zweig, Chekhov, or Steinbeck. In old age, this changes, even turns the other way around completely."

"You know, there's no great gulf between Dostoevsky and Chekhov. As for the rest—I'd have to give it some thought. Your 'old age' is also rather debatable. Especially, so to say, in my context. But I hope you dream of being a second Stefan Zweig rather in quotation marks, and not with all the details?" He pronounced the name of the author of *Impatient Heart* with a grotesque German articulation and smiled.

"With all the details is an impossibility," I answered. "And besides, there isn't any sense in it."

"That's the point," he livened to the topic somehow dispropor-tionately. "That's the whole point, that if even one detail is lacking, it is impossible to repeat . . . I do not compare myself in the least degree with you, but I also dabble in writing, and it is precisely this problem . . . The problem of a certain lack . . . the lack of analogical detail is key for me. Yes, sir. I dabble in writing, and I have a few of my works with me." He pointed to the briefcase standing next to his chair, which still—as if nothing had been removed from it—gave the impression of being stuffed to bursting.

"I have them with me not because I brought them on purpose for a meeting with you, but because I never part with some of my works. Never. Yes, sir. I dabble in writing as an amateur, and perhaps not at all as an amateur. I have written, among other things, *A Natural History of the Cieszyn Land*. I do not carry around with me that one and only title that has appeared, up to this point, in print. That is, I do sometimes, but not always. It depends on my mood, as well as a whole series of other circumstances. Today I took with me three of my novels, which are of a documentary nature. One is about prewar times, the second about the war and the occupation, the third about Communist rule. That last one is a sort of Polish People's Republic family saga, and I am rather satisfied with the results. But I implore you! I implore you! Please have no fear. I do not intend to burden you with reading matter, to ask you for your judgment or some sort of support with the publishers. Granted, I have written quite a lot in my free moments, but I am in no hurry to get them published. No hurry at all."

I wondered how old he might be. In his manner of speaking, ges-tures, mannerisms, dress, he made the impression of an old man, my senior by a good half century, but, finally, let's not exaggerate here. I myself am over fifty, and even the most vigorous hundred-year-olds don't look as vigorous as he did. How old could he be? Eighty? Seventy-five? Was he young? Not much older than me, but stylized and made up to look like a venerable old man?

"Don't think about my age. I'm as old as everyone—to use the famous phrase of a certain Polish writer, who has been dead for quite a few years, and thereby is already, in the strict sense, as old as everyone. Eternity is endlessly short and always the same. But to return to my interests, I also have to my credit a book on March '68, a book about Martial Law (the least successful of them all), and a still unfinished piece that is completely contemporary. But—I repeat—I do not intend to present any of these works to you, not even fragments of them. I don't intend to summarize anything I've written. On the contrary, I wish to tell you a story that I haven't written down, and which I never *will* write down. I mention my passions only so that you might be able to figure out what sort of maniac you are dealing with.

"So, as you can quite easily see, I am the sort of maniac whose ambition it is to reflect with his pen the surrounding world and epochs in which he chanced to live. The reflection of one who is involved in the support of, and sympathizes with, the most noble of values. I am from an extinct tribe, one that thought that books must contain history, the nation, society, and patriotism. This was the spirit in which I have always given my lectures, and it was these convictions that I sought to produce in my pupils. Yes, sir! I am a teacher of many years' standing in the local *gymnasium*. A few times, in epochs of various thaws, I was even head of school. It never lasted long. Two years early in the Gomułka regime, one year early on under Gierek, and a few months during Solidarity the first time around. For years now, it goes without saying—retired. I belong to the tribe that was brought up on Stefan Żeromski. You would like to be Stefan Zweig, I would like to be Stefan Żeromski. Come to think of it, what an unusual couple of epigones! A second Zweig and a second Żeromski! A breathtaking stunt of the purest form. Let's drink to our grotesque-macabre duet! *Due Stefani—vedetti* of the evening! Let's also drink to the fact that we will never equal our masters. You in life, I in art. You will never commit suicide like Zweig, and I will never write like Żeromski. Incidentally, are you aware that a whole series of very interesting suicides has been committed here *At the Sign of the Falcon*? Yes, sir! Very interesting. But this is a topic for another time. How do I know that you won't commit suicide? I don't know. The thought often crosses your mind, that's clear. It crosses everyone's mind. It crossed the mind of the namesake of our deservedly weary receptionist, Emil Cioran. For all of his life, he was occupied with suicide. All his life, he wrote about suicide, and somehow or other he lived to be eighty. It seems that in your own family there was a figure who spent his entire life preparing to leave this one and yet, somehow or other, lived to a ripe old age. There are analogies. Besides, you know, you might simply not have time for suicide. You have to write your own suicide before the fact, and you have begun late. You simply might not have the time for it. And as Scripture says: To everything there is a season. Suicide also has its season. If a person doesn't manage to kill himself at the appropriate moment, he has to live thereafter for nothing. And many, endlessly many people live like that. They live only because it is too late even for suicide. Yes, sir! You don't have enough time to commit suicide, and I don't have enough time to become Żeromski. Let's hope! For, should it come to pass, *that* would be the tragedy. You, after your suicide, would at least have peace. But me? Suddenly blessed with the uncontrollable word-stream of the author of *The Coming Spring*? What would I do then? Please, in no way take this confession as fishing for compliments by claiming a lack of talent. On the contrary—I have talent. But I also have a certain lack. Precisely a lack. I lack the specific. I have a certain writerly lack that always seemed unimportant to me, but which, with time, has become a nagging one. Namely, I don't know how to write about women. And in my haughty, conceited opinion, it is only in this range that I'm not a Żeromski. Only in this one aspect. Because he knew how to write about women. Say what you want, he knew. I console myself, or rather I consoled myself, I consoled myself for a long time, that my pieces weren't any sort of romances but quasi-documents. I consoled myself that there exist outstanding works of literature—we need look no further than precisely the *Chess Story* of your master—in which there aren't any women or erotic love, but there is, nonetheless, a sharp image of the world. I comforted myself with a sort of unformulated moralizing program: that, supposedly, in an epoch of universal pornography, it is time for extreme puritanism. I comforted myself as best I could, but still, with time, the lack of an aspect which is not even so much romantic as sensual, became simply unbearable. Absolutely unbearable. You know, I don't know how to write about women, because I never think about women. I was once married, became a widower long ago; and the love affairs that came my way seem to me so remote today that I am almost certain that they didn't occur in my lifetime. I don't think about women, therefore I don't know how to write about them. So much is clear. It's impossible to record what doesn't take shape in your head. At this point, yet another troublesome plot twist comes into play, so troublesome, that in revealing it, I am bordering on exhibitionism . . .

"If you permit, another round for courage? To your health. To the health of the ladies. That's just it. It's easier after a drink. After a drink, it is a *lot* easier. After a drink, it is *much* easier to think about women. Much, *much* easier. The fact of the matter is, I don't think about women at all when I am sober. But once I have had a drink, I begin to think about them intensely, I begin to think about them fluently, and I begin to think about them copiously. Such is my—you must admit—rather boorish syndrome. After a drink, I get a hankering for the erotic. Not in any practical sense. After a drink, I get a hankering for sex—but in the intellectual sense. After a drink, I can compose romantic aphorisms; after a drink, I can think about the erotic in orderly fashion; after a drink (but a big one!), I am even able to sketch a bedroom scene. But only orally. Not in writing. If I knew how to write after a drink, I would be—if you please—Stefan Żeromski, in the strict sense; I would be Żeromski through and through; I would be more than Żeromski. You will forgive me, but if I knew how to write after a drink, I would be Żeromski to a significantly greater degree than you are Zweig when sober. Granted, better a sober Zweig than a drunk Żeromski, but the tragedy of Polish literature depends—among other things—on the fact that Żeromski didn't drink, and that Zweig wasn't present at all. Yes, sir. After a drink, I'd write totally unprecedented histories of sin, but after a drink I am unable to write a single letter. I can only narrate orally. Only oral transmission comes into play. The song of the Wajdelota. *Then*, I can tell a story. Yes, sir! That's when I can tell a story.

"When I found out that you were coming to K., I decided to have a drink with you and tell you the story that torments me. I decided that I would tell you a story that I am able to tell, but which I am unable to write down. It's a love story. It's easy to guess that I felt the lack of a sensual aspect in my works especially acutely when an emotional plot turn occurred in my own life.

"I fell in love. I fell in love with a student. I fell in love with a woman more than forty years my junior. With a woman, not a child. With a woman, not a girl. Anyway, her womanliness manifested itself rather occasionally and rather sporadically. The charm of changeability. Thanks to this charm, gray mice sometimes win the competition with out-and-out beauties. The out-and-out beauty is once-and-for-all and unchangeably out-and-out beautiful, and that's that. Zero changeability and zero surprises. But the gray mouse, for whom you wouldn't give five cents, all of a sudden—it sometimes happens—somehow magically rearranges her hair; the blouse on her flat chest opens mysteriously, although deceptively; her eye sparkles; a ray of light falls on her asymmetrical face—and there you see it: the mouse is transformed into the Miss! The potato-eater into the angel! Grayness becomes light!

"The virtues of my angel were basically exhausted with this sort of sporadic charm. To be perfectly clear: I sing the song of a very unremarkable person. This, in fact, was to be my doom. When an unremarkable person comes to be considered remarkable, it usually ends badly. Precisely this course of events occurred. First, she was a normal woman of unremarkable looks and average intelligence, but then—God knows who. Most certainly a fallen woman with a bird's brain and the looks of a whore. And even that isn't certain. In other words, it is even worse, because wandering about the cracks of existence is worse than whorishness. She's gone. It was the art of today, miserable and devoid of values, that destroyed her. It was aspiring to superiority, the appearance of which is given by the cultivation of art, that depraved her and cast her out of life. And it was the devil himself, who—having taken on the form of a film star who was known as a ladies man and had come to our parts—pushed her to this. He spent a night here. In the hotel *At the Sign of the Falcon*. I don't know whether it was precisely this room. Probably not. He didn't commit suicide. But he didn't live all that long afterward. No, I didn't kill him. I wished him nothing but the worst—death, too—but I didn't kill him. He died in an accident. You can't even speculate that I caused the accident through my obsessive thoughts. My thoughts were highly intense in their obsessiveness, but they didn't have any force, because they were mainly drunk. *What are you doing?—I think.*—He destroyed her life. He plunged her into the abyss of superiority. He seduced her with the mirages of alleged triumphs. He made her giddy, without even seducing her. Which is basically all the worse.

"Let's say her name was Wiktoria. It is only for the sake of appearances that I change her name, since the story is, to this day, discussed over and over and from every angle in K., and tomorrow morning, as soon as you exit the hotel, the first chance passerby will tell you who she was. Actually, you don't even have to go out. Emil will also be happy to reveal to you who the prototype for Wiktoria is. She was the daughter of the curator of the Lutheran church. Our parts—as you well know—abound in daughters of curators, daughters of pastors, daughters of presbyters, or daughters of organists. In spite of the indisputable sexiness of such descriptions, none of them ever came into question for me. Nor did Wiktoria—until a certain balmy September day—come into question. Never did any of my female students come into question. Absolutely not! Not even the hint of a thought. For an old teacher, who never thinks about women, thinking about female students as women was beyond all categories and didn't come into question a thousand times over. The dark side of the moon. The light of a star that would arrive on Earth in a million light years. Above all, my female students had no bodies. They were composed of navy blue skirts, white blouses, and sailor collars. Their heads contained, at best, superficial summaries of readings, badly memorized verses, and paltry essays. At best, because, on the whole, they didn't contain anything. And after the holidays, their skulls, light as dandelion fluff, had been absolutely swept clean of any sort of material. You could recognize this by their suntans and bovine bliss. On their faces, my dear sir, an even Balkan suntan, in their eyes, bovine bliss, and in their heads, a complete void. I know that I express myself like an old and grumpy pedant. Unfortunately, the continuation of this story will require much worse expressions. I will tell the beginning of the story in high pedant style. And the crux of the beginning, to which I am now passing, occurred right after the holidays.

"One fine September day, I called upon her to answer. O doom! O fate! O bloodied arrowhead! Yes, sir! One fine September day, a student, a third-year *lyceum* student, composed of a dark skirt, white blouse, and sailor collar, with the first name, let's say, Wiktoria, and the surname, let's say, Złotnica, stood at the blackboard and—not a peep. I ask about the greats—nothing. I ask about Mickiewicz—nothing. I ask about Gombrowicz—nothing. I ask about Sienkie-wicz—nothing. I ask about whatever—nothing. What did you read during your vaction? Nothing. Where were you during the vacation? In the mountains. What mountains? In our mountains. In Wisła. And you didn't read anything in that Wisła? Nothing during the entire vacation? Nothing. Well, yes—I say with the studied venom that my students, especially the boys, adore—you, Złotnica, ought not go to the mountains, but rather to the sea. That's what I'd advise you to do. At the seaside, at least there is iodine. In the mountains, even in our mountains, and maybe especially in our mountains, there is no iodine. And the lack of iodine, plus Lutheranism, produces—as it turns out—pitiful intellectual results. At least in your case—I enunci-ate clearly and slowly—at least in your case, Złotnica.

"The class, of course, howls with laughter. I cast my victorious glance over the laughing faces, I turn my face toward her in order to wrap up and conclude the matter with a final grimace full of pity, and suddenly I see a miracle taking place before my very eyes. Suddenly I am witness to a most genuine, biblical miracle. Suddenly I see how the word—forget the word!—suddenly I see how the lack of the word—for, after all, she wasn't able to stammer out a single word—and so, suddenly I see how the lack of the word becomes flesh! Suddenly I see how ignorance becomes flesh! First—from her head, through the collar, blouse, skirt, down to her very feet—there runs a most distinct shiver. It is as if a delicate lightning bolt had pierced her, and immediately thereafter the void was filled. Suddenly I see how a delicate neck, the most delicate in the world, just now created, emerges from a sailor collar. Suddenly there appears from under the sailor collar the outline of collarbones just a moment before shaped from clay. And the thin shoulders begin to support the white blouse, and the frail outline of a bust takes form before my eyes, and the daringly projected construction of hips becomes noticeable under the dark skirt, and even the shoes with flat heels are suddenly filled with feet, and all of this takes place quite literally before my very eyes.

"'Professor,' says the body created only the moment before, and shivers, as if it had experienced the cold of the earth's atmosphere for the first time, 'Professor, I did, indeed, read a few books, but none of these books was a book by Stefan Żeromski, so, in the professor's opinion, it is as if I didn't read a single book.'

"For the first time in my life, I look her right in the eyes, and so, it seems to me that her eyes, too, had only now been called into existence. For the first time in my life, I look a female student in the eyes, and, for the first time in my life, I see gray lightning bolts. In the classroom, it is as quiet as the grave. The quiet before the storm. But no one knows that it will be a storm full of gray lightning bolts, and that it will be a storm raging in my heart.

"'In other words, when I say that I didn't read a single book, from the professor's point of view I am telling the truth. But my admission is none of the professor's business, nor where I go for the holidays. I am a Lutheran, and I am certainly a better Lutheran than your Żeromski, who converted to Lutheranism only in order to get a divorce. But he is buried in the Protestant cemetery, and, if only for that reason, you ought to have respect for us, and not ridicule us for lacking iodine—in other words, for having a screw loose.'"

My collocutor, or rather, my narrator, interrupted his story; he poured some more into the glasses, and he drank it off, without raising a toast or even checking to see whether I would join him; and he poured again, and he drank again; he made a motion as if he wished to take off his jacket, but then shrugged it off, lit a cigarette, inhaled two times or so, and looked me in the eye.

"Yes sir!" Gray. She had eyes like mine, like my father's, like my brother's, and, funny thing, like those of my departed wife. Very funny, but also slightly terrifying. One of a thousand very funny, but also slightly terrifying, details. If I knew how to capture all of them, I could write a shocking love story. The very first scene, the very beginning of emotion—seemingly nothing: the boorish professor and the desperate snot-nosed kid, but what an avalanche, what a cataclysm, what an earthquake. In my absolute confusion, I was certain that she, in a sudden illumination, knows everything, that she saw my sudden infatuation as clearly as can be, and she came out with—God help us—the story of Żeromski's Lutheranism, which was, in fact, lined with a romantic plot turn, in order to finish me off with an ostentatious allusion.

"As a non-believer, I'm not crazy about either Catholics or Lutherans, and I'm especially not crazy about Lutherans. Why? Because I know you. I know you better than the Catholics. As the author of *The Natural History of the Cieszyn Land*, I have come to know, inside and out, all—as you would put it—the Lutheran phantoms. Lutherans are more convenient for caricature and derision. To make fun of Catholics in Poland is a shallow art. Lutheranism, through its exoticism, lends to an anecdote an additional—I would say—aesthetic force. Besides, in my agnostic opinion, in matters of faith and God, Lutherans are more right than Catholics. And whoever is more right is more comical. It's an old truth. The most ludicrous are those who are right a hundred percent of the time. May the Lord God defend us from those who own one-hundred-percent infallibility. My truth is as old as the world: there is no God. We are mayflies who have learned how to build Gothic churches, fly into the cosmos, and compose symphonies. We are mayflies who have written the Bible, painted *The Final Judgment*, and made films with Greta Garbo. We are mayflies who elect the pope, and we are mayflies who sometimes withdraw our allegiance from the pope. We are mayflies who turn to dust after death, and we are mayflies who are capable of composing a sentence about that turning to dust. And please do not protest and assert that mayflies who have constructed violins and are capable of composing string quartets are not mayflies. All the more are they mayflies. All the more tragically—mayflies. Sometimes, when great misfortune incapacitates us, it seems to us that there exists something more; it seems to us that we see or hear signs: a light over a house, a knocking at the window, the cry of a child in the garden . . . Perhaps you know that, in a certain piece of biblical apocrypha, one of Job's clones utters the sentence: 'Suffering incapacitates me like a crying child?' We are all clones of Job. Our appearance has been altered in the hands of the demon of fate. We are all mayflies. We are mayflies, who suffer from a lack of iodine.

"No. I never asked her to forgive me. Broad anti-Lutheran jokes were, in my classes, a daily affair. My joke about the connection between iodine and Lutheranism was nothing exceptional. The exception was the fact that she talked back. And of course it was exceptional, and even very exceptional, that—when she mouthed off—I fell in love with her. As far as that joke is concerned, to this day I believe that I am right. To this day, I believe that Lutheranism plus the lack of iodine is an intellectual tragedy. You can prove this, if only through negation. For you can turn the matter around and say legitimately that Lutheranism plus iodine is an intellectual, and not only intellectual, fulfillment. Just why is it that Protestantism enjoys all sorts of triumphs, for example, in Scandinavia? Well, it is precisely because those are maritime countries and full of iodine. Scandinavian Protestantism, my dear sir, is the height of democratic freedom, economic efficiency, and intellectual power. Unfortunately, you can't say the same about Beskid Mountain Protestantism.

"I interrupted the lesson and left the classroom. I told the head of school that I wasn't feeling well, and that wasn't a lie in the least. I didn't feel well. Not at all well. I shut myself up at home, having covered the windows tightly, and put on a CD with the sonatas of Franz Schubert, and I drank, in the course of the afternoon and night, three bottles of vodka, pure vodka, if you please. It went down like water. The best proof is this: in the morning, as if nothing had happened, I was off to school. Not that I was happy as a lark and in a perfect mood. Not at all! Ill treated, dejected, with a pierced heart, but still as if nothing had happened. Each subsequent day, it was as if nothing had happened. Life went on as if nothing had happened. I conducted my lessons and performed all my obligations according to routine. I limited the number of anti-Lutheran jokes during my lessons, but I didn't give them up entirely. I never returned to the aforementioned incident. I took great care not to betray my emotions, in other words not to be especially severe with her. It is well known that showing affection is most generally, and most ineptly, masked with brutality. I tried not to make that mistake, and I think I was successful. For a time, of course. In the evenings, I would get drunk, and then I would allow myself embarrassing scenes. I imagined that we were doing together all those things that make for a great love: we go to the movies, we eat suppers, we play chess, we watch detective programs on television. I staged in my mind our shocking conversations about what we needed to buy for the house, when we would finally decide to remodel the bathroom, and where we would go for vacation. With complete detachment from this world, I began to believe that we would be accepted, that our neighbors, and, in general, *all* the inhabitants of K., would respect the uniqueness and beauty of our story. Sometimes a drunken blubbering accompanied my amorous cantos, but everything was done behind closed doors, in isolation, as a conspiracy of one. And she? Nothing. To be honest, it isn't worth talking about her. If it weren't for the fact that I had fallen in love with her, there wouldn't be anything to talk about at all. You couldn't even say that my love had lent her a glow, or something like that. Rather, on the contrary. What hadn't been extinguished up to then, now went out. The eyes went out. I avoided the gray fire. I was to see how they burn only one more time. Only once. Altogether, two times. For a shocking love, this is not, you must admit, an excessively overwhelming result.

"She still didn't stand out in any way, she was still an unremarkable student, and still an unremarkable, even a *very* unremarkable beauty. She didn't depart from the pack. It goes without saying that I always knew where her slender back was in the hallway or the schoolyard. What direction she was running, whether she was approaching or withdrawing. Only *I* took note of the color of the hairband with which she tied up her pony tail, and when she changed that hairband. I knew by heart all her skirts, T-shirts, turtlenecks, blouses, shoes. I knew all her pairs of flip flops and all her tennis shoes. Every night I embraced her specter, and every morning I couldn't wait to see her. And every day I cursed her; I wanted her to get lost, to finally get to her senior year, pass her *matura*, and go to the devil—that is to say, to the Psychology Department in Krakow. She was planning to study psychology, which casts a characteristic (gray) shaft of light upon her dullness. Whoever doesn't know what he wants to study, what he wants to do in life in general, chooses psychology. After all, mass interest in psychology doesn't prove that Poles are a nation of born psychologists. Mass interest in psychology proves that Poles are a nation that doesn't know what to do with itself. In any case, the tragedy—if that's what you can call it—continued, but it was under control. Everything seemed to be heading toward a dull and bleak, but definite, end. The next vacation passed, the empty-headed young people, covered with a Balkan suntan, returned to school. Wiktoria

Złotnica was to take her *matura* in a few months. In a few months, my Gehenna was to end, or at least undergo a significant thinning out.

"Posters announcing the visit of the film star who was known as a ladies man appeared in our city in October. They were a vulgar yellow. That—as you know perfectly well—is the color of absolute doom. Let's drink. The film star who was known as a ladies man came to our town two weeks later. Let's drink, because it is time for a change in language. On the first weekend in November, he made an appearance in our theater, which sent the local intelligentsia into transports of delight. Since, in addition to the reputation of a ladies man, he also enjoyed the reputation of a fighter for liberty and independence, the delight he aroused was all the greater. During Martial Law, he had boycotted television, he had put on patriotic one-man plays in churches, all the while emphasizing that his cousin on his father's side had been murdered at Katyń. You must admit that this is an irresistible mixture. A Katyń skull sprinkled with *eau du Cologne*, the scent of which burst from him a mile away, plus a good voice, plus the jaded countenance of the aging heart-throb—this was a combination before which the thighs of the noblest of Mother-Poles parted. Black lace thongs *à la* November Uprising fell away smoothly. So the rumor had it, in any event. On the day of his performance, I ran into him on the Market Square. I bowed obsequiously, glanced into his lifeless eyes, and I knew right away: none of it was true. There was no reason to envy him. He had dreadful sorrow in his eyes, perhaps even death. Theoretically, he was at the absolute top, and yet it was obvious that, in fact, in the depths of his soul, he was completely finished. There wasn't anything to envy, and certainly not the women. He never had any women. And not because he was of a different orientation, which is common nowadays. He didn't participate in this commonplace. He never had any women because he was a prisoner of his own reputation. The evening after his memorable appearance—when I again sat down to drink in solitude, and when, once again, I gained fluency in the drawing of erotic deductions—I solved this paradox. Well, you see, acquiring the name of a well known ladies man is the greatest erotic disaster that can meet a man. Since all the women know that you will take everything, not a one of them will go with you. Do you understand? Not a one of them will go with you out of—it goes without saying—reasons dictated by ambition. Namely, she does not wish to join the masses allegedly possessed by you. She does not wish to vanish in the masses allegedly screwed by you. The universal conviction that you screw on a mass scale renders individual screwing impossible for you; *ergo*, it renders any screwing whatsoever impossible. The final result is that you don't screw anything. The greatest nonentity and erotic sad sack screws more than you do. Even endlessly more, because, compared with zero, any result is endless. You enjoy the reputation of a well known ladies man, but you don't screw anything. Something for something. Life is full of dark paradoxes. The film star who was known as a ladies man was in the snares of such a paradox. I understood this at once, and I calmed down. That evening, over a lonely glass, I deftly gave the thing a name, but I had already calmed down in the afternoon. I calmed down as soon as I caught sight of him on the Market Square. As soon as I sensed the black aura of dreadful sorrow emanating from him. The envy, irritation, and fear that all men feel when, in their circle, there appears a well known seducer, withdrew from my heart. Prematurely! A hundred times prematurely! He had seduced her! He'd seduced her after all! He seduced her in the worst, the most terrible, the most far-reaching manner. Let's drink to the perdition of all the seducers in the world. Let them be damned! Let them perish for all time!

"The evening came. The evening of Doomsday came. The performance was so-so. Dull and boring. That is, dull and boring to a certain moment. Formally, everything was OK, even more than OK. The hall of our county theater drowning in yellowish light. The cloudy crystals of prewar chandeliers and pillars of Stalinist dust over the bordeaux-colored seats. He, dressed in black from head to foot, and ostentatiously pale. Powdered. A storm of applause to greet him, a vibrant silence as he recites great Polish poetry, and enthusiastic animation as he tells anecdotes from theater scenes or film shots.

"At the end, he proposed a short course in acting, an improvised theatrical workshop in a pill. Perhaps in the auditorium there are some dormant outstanding talents—it's high time to wake them up. Can you guess what happened next? He—so he says—considers himself a searcher, acting no longer suffices for him, he has decided to try his hand at directing. He was preparing just then, at the Old Theater in Krakow, an adaptation of Fyodor Mikhailovich Dostoevsky's *Crime and Punishment*, and now we, through our common efforts, will do a makeshift staging of one of the scenes—namely the scene of Raskolnikov's conversation with the servant woman Nastasya. Could we have volunteers here on stage? We need a couple of young, courageous people. If you please, who is willing to act in *Crime and Punishment* under my supervision? Who is willing to square off against the immortal, but also dangerous, phrases of Fyodor Mikhailovich? He invites them to join the game, but not only the game, for he knows perfectly well that these sorts of exercises often give quite a lot. Often more than work with professional actors. So he invites them to join the game, but he also asks for collaboration. Can you guess who landed on the stage? To this day I have a feeling of unreality about this matter. Who has the courage? Who will be first? The first was a pastor's son. It was absolutely certain that, of the boys, the son of Pastor Morowy—famous for his daredevil lifestyle—would be the first to raise his hand. And it was just as absolutely certain that the slender arm of none of the girls would be waving above the heads. Too great the phantoms, too strong the atavisms. In these parts, we never lacked for little harlots, and what harlots they were! But to respond publicly to the summons of a film star who was known as a ladies man? To react to his encouragements? To succumb to his invitation? To go up on stage? To become an actress—even for a minute? It is not fitting, it is not fitting, a hundred times no! And those snot-nosed girls—among whom there wasn't a single virgin, especially after the last vacation—sat with sulking expressions, and, with their facial features, they made it clear that no: not them. I understand your self-restraint, I understand your stage fright—the star pontificated from the stage—those are traits that provide outstanding predictions of true artistry. Timid people—oh, the paradox!—become the greatest actors. In that case, he would help the shy neophytes of the theater and choose one of them arbitrarily. He doesn't allow himself the word "casting." The choice is difficult, and you can see with the naked eye, that, if not all of them, then the majority of the stars sitting in the audience would be up to the task, so he has to act somewhat randomly. And he looks around shamelessly, and the beet-red flush greedily burns the powder on his mug—maybe you, yes, the lady in the fourth row, in the jeans jacket, yes, please, right this way.

"Something lay dormant, after all, in that princess from mouse lands. Not only did her heart beat mousily. Her blood must have had a higher temperature than that of a mouse. Did he sense this? Did he sense what I did? Why had he chosen her? Had I sensed what he did? Is that where my love came from? Today a person is wiser. Seemingly wiser, because over time all speculations become irrefutable. In any case, what happens, happens: the curator's daughter goes up on the stage, and the acting assignment that is set before her—by not so much a real director, as a film star ostentatiously playing the role of a director—is the following: she is supposed to go into the little room, where Raskolnikov is sleeping, wake him up, and exchange a few lines with him. Do you recall that scene? Yes, sir! Before the murder of the pawnbroker. The star emphasized this aspect, and with pathos he suggested to the young Morowy, who was convulsed with dopey laughter, that he was supposed to play a man who isn't yet a murderer, but who the next day would be one. A brazen little shit. A bit of a brazen little shit. No matter. They were supposed to end the scene with the rather well known fragment: 'What are you doing?' she asks. 'Working,' he responds. 'What sort of work is it?' 'I think.' And then—as you recall—Nastasya bursts out laughing, 'she reeled with laughter.' Because Nastasya—the star explained—is a joker, and it is very important to make sure that it comes out credibly here. It is necessary not only to burst out laughing, but to burst out laughing in such a way that the spectator would know immediately that laughter is one of the modes of being of this character. But at the same time, remember, Wiktoria, that laughter is one of the actor's most difficult assignments. Only the greatest can truly manage this. But please, my dear child, give it a try, give it a try.

"I won't belittle her and say that she *tried*, and she managed so-so. No. She managed quite well. She completely eclipsed the buffoonery of her partner. She received thunderous applause. The star clapped the most fervently, then he kissed her hand obsequiously, then he pointed out the sign of her victory—the ovation of the audience. Then he raised her arm, like a victorious boxer. My beloved was experiencing the greatest triumph of her nineteen-year-old life, and at the same time her life had ended. You know, I clapped then like the rest of them. I was proud of her. I was surprised by her unexpected ability, but I also didn't have a shadow of a doubt that this was a one-time ability, and that it stemmed from limitation. It might seem that I was badmouthing her on account of disappointed love, but unfortunately it's true: my beloved was thoroughly limited. You know, one of those who sit when they sit, stand when they stand, walk when they walk. No quotation marks. And so, when she was supposed to enter Raskolnikov's little room, she entered thoroughly; when she was supposed to awaken him, she awakened him with all zeal; when she was supposed to laugh, she laughed with all her heart and all her snout. In a certain sense she had the predispositions for acting. She had the predispositions, which is to say, a certain lack of shame and a certain intellectual limitation. Unfortunately, not a red cent's worth of talent. But it was already too late. The wind had been sown.

"The news that Złotnica was dropping psychology and setting off for acting school had, at first—at least for me—a purely rhetorical form, but then it began, drowsily, to take on flesh. *People are saying that the daughter of the curator made such a good impression at workshops conducted by the famous star that, instead of going to study psychology in Krakow, she ought to go to acting school in Warsaw.* I was certain that such a purely theoretical compliment was circling in the air—nothing more. But I see that she is taking on some sort of, in her opinion, riveting artistic magic! She starts dressing with bohemian promiscuity! She puts the curator's tweed sports jackets directly over lace bras! Hair let down like the muse of all the arts blows in the wind! She answers questions not with her own, but with an allegedly actor's voice! She sits in the school bench like the worst whore! She makes ostentatious faces! She is an actress! Jesus Christ! She is already an actress! An actress! Actress!! Actress!!! *Our actress*, they call her. But no, my dear sir. I wasn't mistaken. Not a hint of talent. A complete clod! I was infatuated with her, I was bewitched, but, in spite of the amorous prism, I saw what I saw. In every pose, a false note. In every word, a lie. You sense such things. You don't have to be an expert. You could see with the naked eye that nothing would come of this. Not a chance. She wouldn't get into acting school. Even if the minimal requirement there was a 0 mark on the entrance exam, she wouldn't get in, because she was considerably below that level. She wouldn't get in on the first, or the second, or the hundredth try. Life goes into complete disarray. Of course, not our life, not my life with her. I allowed myself such visions only during my evening deliriums, and, in reality, I didn't take this into consideration at all. I took into consideration that she would choose—out of insecurity—to study psychology; finish, or not finish, a more or less accidental education; find a job in her field, or not in her field of study; get married, for love or out of necessity; return, or not return, to K.—but that she would truly live. Perhaps in poverty, perhaps without love, but in reality, not in an illusion. Not in a humiliating illusion, humiliating because it is marked by an aspiration to superiority. Who knows which is better? Is that what you say? That is not, my dear sir, an accurate doubt. Living an illusion is ghastly; and living an artistic illusion—which is also, by the nature of things, impossible to realize on account of a lack of talent—is a disaster.

"She was nineteen years old, she crossed the Market Square with the gait—as it seemed to her—of Julia Roberts. She smiled—in her own opinion—like Sharon Stone. There stretched before her the allegedly most renowned theatrical scenes in the world, the lights of the great film studios shined. But in fact, there stood before her the muddy path into the abyss. What is more, there was no way to stop this. Supposedly, the curator and his wife were inordinately proud that they had given the world a star. There wasn't any question of any sort of conversation with her. I didn't even take it into consideration. I wouldn't have managed.

"Above all, I was afraid. With time, the dread that someone might notice my affection for her became my first dread and pathological obsession. But now, when, in connection with her future career, which would assuredly be marked by famous romances, and in connection with the jackets worn over lace underwear, her—I would call it—mousy magnetism grew; now, if it should turn out *that Mr. Professor has also joined our star's fan club, which has arisen spontaneously*; now, at the very thought of being unmasked, I sank below the earth. On the other hand, I was afraid that I would become known as an envier, *ergo* public enemy number one. I was not so afraid of being known as an envier as I was of being known as an enamored admirer, but the discomfort of becoming a public enemy hung in the air completely realistically. Almost the entire city supported her, however; almost all, even the greatest skeptics, basically hoped that, come fall, Złotnica would set off for the acting school in Warsaw, and already by spring we would get to watch her create ever more important roles on television. I couldn't let on about my mean-spirited lack of faith in that success—not only to her, *but also to essentially our entire community*. It would look like the bitter old fart wishes her ill, selflessly envies her, doesn't appreciate her talent, and God knows what else. And so, I suppressed it in myself. And I let all this out during my solitary evening drinking bouts. Witkacy used to say that without alcohol and narcotics he would never have achieved certain solutions in painting. Although, on the whole, I consider him a psychopath, I could accept this particular idea of his three-times over. First: without juniper berry vodka—as I mentioned at the beginning—I would not have attained fluency in the spinning of universal erotic deductions. Second: without juniper berry vodka, I would not have been able to present certain troublesome *concreta* and shameful details—first to myself, and now to you—with the proper realism. And third: without juniper berry vodka, I would not have crossed certain boundaries, which, supposedly, I crossed. *Supposedly*—because I don't remember. For that reason, in the finale of my story I am condemned to a complete lack of details and to the speculative mood. Supposedly, I paid a nocturnal visit to the home of the curator, Mr. Złotnica, and, supposedly, I perpetrated disgraceful things there. Supposedly, an evening visit by Wiktoria at my home also took place. I imagined both events a thousand times. A thousand times I imagined my visit to Wiktoria's parents. A thousand times, in a delirium of absolutely watchmaker's precision, I conducted with them an inordinately important conversation. A thousand times I pronounced a thousand convincing and irrefutable arguments. A thousand times they yielded to my arguments. A thousand times I was there in my drunken dreams, and with one of my wakings it turned out that, indeed, I really *was* there! In a delirium, but also in reality. As always: it seemed to me that it just seemed to me, but I really had gotten dressed, set off, gotten there, and, supposedly, knocked on the door of the curator's house at two in the morning! It seemed to me that I was dressed, but I was in incomplete dress. Supposedly, very incomplete. It seemed to me that they were receiving me in their sitting room at a copiously stocked table, that I was sharing my doubts about their daughter's fate with eloquence and wit, whereas, supposedly, I lay down on a crate of winter apples in the hallway, and there—reeling as I lay—talked gibberish, saliva flowing from my lips; I fell asleep and woke up again, and finally, somehow, they dragged me to the car and got me back home.

"A thousand times I imagined that Wiktoria came to me; a thousand times I opened the door for her in my delusions; a thousand times I embraced her in greeting and farewell, and suddenly it turned out that one of those delusions wasn't a delusion. Which of her phantasmagorical visits took place in reality? Was it the time when she came in a black jacket and a scarf, light blue like the Roman sky? Or the time when it was well below zero, and she came in a balaclava helmet? Or the time when she stood quite a while in the doorway and smiled mysteriously? Or the time when she ran in, literally burst into the entryway, and, with the exclamation—I'm about to pee my pants!—fell like a bomb into the bathroom, and immediately a bestial sigh of relief resounded from in there? When was she here? The time when she stood over my corpse and cried? The time when my corpse sat in an armchair and spoke to her. I don't know. Everybody but me in K. knew—not me. Everybody knew all the details—not me. You understand that the consequences of such a stormy finale,—with my participation, but without the participation of my consciousness—was my retirement. Moving out of K. was beyond my means. I thought about suicide, but those were weak thoughts, deprived of expression. I took up literary work, which had always been on my mind, and for which I now had ideal conditions. I was completely isolated, no one came to see me, no one called. Even the postman, the kiosk keeper, or the saleswoman in the store communicated with me—I would say— rather perfunctorily. I was in ideal solitude, *ergo* I had ideal conditions for writing. And I did not waste that gift.

"I could—and maybe even I ought to—end my story here, but like the debutant who is uncertain of definitive meaning, I will add an epilogue. I add it because it happened. The curator's daughter got into drama school. Supposedly. Supposedly, with gigantic success. Supposedly, at the top of her class. Supposedly, the entrance commission, which was composed of nothing but actorly celebrities, was absolutely delighted. How those pieces of information came to me—I truly don't know. I don't recall any informer or any conversation that initiated me into new details. In K., for a long time, absolutely no one wanted to talk with me—and about Wiktoria, to this day no one will exchange a word with me. But I did find out. Apparently, in small towns pieces of news literally fly through the air. Further news appeared. The sparrows on the rooftops twittered triumphantly that the doom of my life was an unusually victorious student, that she was passing all the exams with bravado, that she was receiving exceptionally interesting and lucrative proposals. For the time being, however, she wasn't accepting any; first she wanted to complete her diploma course, then she would make a choice. It wasn't certain, however, whether the choice of the first serious role would be in the homeland or abroad.

"Do you understand? The curator and his wife, stupefied and hounded by the necessity of the success of their allegedly remarkable child, were close to bullshitting their neighbors that Hollywood was fighting over this complete loser! They continued without moderation in that fiction. The curator, whenever he set out for a meeting of the parish council—a glow radiated from him. The curator's wife, whenever she bought cheese in the market—she assumed the pose of the mother not so much of Sharon Stone or Julia Roberts, because those names said little to her, but rather the pose, let's say, of the mother of Gina Lollobrigida. She summoned up the pathos and the dignity, and her gestures were a bit hit or miss, but still she was called the "Mother of Gina Lollobrigida" in the more astute circles. In addition to this, there appeared the so-called highly eloquent detail. Very eloquent. So eloquent that it was much more than a detail. Namely, Wiktoria completely stopped showing up in K. She didn't come for holidays, not even for Christmas Eve. No triumphal visits of the future, or already almost fulfilled, star in the hometown. Didn't she have the strength for such shenanigans? Was she learning her parts, and since she was receiving nothing but Shakesperean roles, there was in fact no time for anything else? Was she slaving away—day in, day out, and nighttime, too? In my opinion—day in, day out, and nighttime, too—if there was anything Shakespearean about it, she was at best giving blow jobs in some Warsaw brothel. One way or another, I decided to get to the bottom of the matter. I decided to check on the course of her Shakesperean career with my own eyes and palpibly.

"After two years—when the storm around me had died down, when they had stopped following my every step, and when *The Natural History of the Cieszyn Land* had appeared in print, which had repaired my reputation a bit—I set off for Warsaw. In conspiratorial secrecy, it goes without saying, and skillfully laying a false trail. I confided in the kiosk keeper—who had become, with time, a bit quicker to chat with his customer—that I was heading to Krakow for a few days in order to do some digging in the archives of the Jagiellonian Library. In the course of a couple hours, or perhaps in the course of one hour, the entire city knew where I was going and why. The matters of the world are simple. I went to Krakow by PKS bus, from Krakow by the InterCity express train to Warsaw. I intended to stop in the Hotel Europejski, in which I had had the occasion to stay in the old days. Never mind in which years and under what circumstances.

"It was the beginning of April, and pathological heat waves prevailed. You know how, sometimes in early spring, when the snows have barely receded, there occur two, three scorching days. Sudden and deceptive surges of tropical temperatures. Blinding white air, sultry weather, women's bared necks, a narcotic and basically perverse aura. I walked from Central Station, tired, slightly tipsy, because, of course, I had been drinking the whole way, incessantly, but very prudently. I was delighted with the masses of yellowish air that were surrounding me, and I was absolutely certain that right away, on Aleje Ujazdowskie, on Nowy Świat, at the latest on Krakowskie Przedmieście, I would run into Wiktoria. At first it seemed to me that every fifth woman on the street looked like her; then every second one; then all of them. Do you understand? I saw her everywhere.

"Was I still in love with her? Had I loved her at all? Is the story I am telling definitely a love story? Granted, there can be love without a single touch, for in the end I never touched even her hand, not even accidently. Granted, there can be love which is accompanied by barely two glances, or even a glance and a half; for I saw her grey eyes the second time when she was at my place, when she was lamenting my corpse. So the second glance was not only blurry, it was also partial. There are also loves that are more platonic, and more reserved. But were my delusions love? Was my breakneck love a real love? If love is a delusion, then I loved her. If what goes on in a severed head can be called love, then I loved her. I loved her, and I longed for her. And sick with love and savage longing for her, I went to look for her in

Warsaw. That is to say, I went to meet her in Warsaw. I was absolutely certain that I needn't do a thing—not a gesture, no telephone call, no need to help fate along. That any moment, she herself would come out to meet me with her dance step. She didn't. This didn't shake my intution, and it strengthened my certainty of her downfall. In the hotel kiosk, I bought a newspaper with the obvious classifieds, and having settled into my room, freshened up, taken a shower, and opened the bottle planned for the afternoon, I began to look for her. It didn't take long. After a minute, I came upon the classified ad: "Slender student—privately," and right away, all the words and all the letters of that offer shined with the green light of hope and began to flicker at me like an emerald neon. I called. Her voice had changed. I, too, pretended to be someone else. I didn't want to frighten her off. Once she appears, it will be too late for flight. After half an hour, there reverberated a knock at the door. True, in the course of that half hour I had drunk a significant portion of the alcohol allotted for the entire afternoon, and yet, I was sober like never in my life. But even if I had been unconscious, I still would have known the taste of defeat. I still would have known the fiasco of my own intuition. It goes without saying: it wasn't her. A massively built, gloomy young lady from the suburbs entered the room and asked what I felt like. What I felt like? An immediate return home. Immediate flight, running like hell. Suddenly I saw, with crystal clarity, all my lunacies, all my childishness, suddenly I regained the fullness of my shaken cognitive powers. Suddenly I saw myself, a retired teacher in a brown suit, sitting in a hotel room in the company of a paid tart. Through the open window came the clatter of the hot city. You could hear the whirr of the jackhammers, the high creak of cranes, the murmur of cars driving by, foreigners were chatting in front of the hotel entryway, someone laughed, someone called somebody from far away. I was outside of all this. I was separated from everything by an impenetrable Chinese Wall. Suddenly I understood how horrendous and terrible my life was. Suddenly, in a deep and thoroughly existential sense, I sobered up, and in the flash of a second I understood that, as soon as I was alone, I would do myself in, I would hang myself on my belt or slit my wrists in the hotel bathtub, because I just didn't have the strength any more. I didn't have the strength to leave here, to return to the train station, to go to K. by the night train. I didn't have the strength to do anything. I wouldn't ever leave here. I would die here.

"Luckily, I'm a drunk, and we all know what a drunk does when he sobers up, especially when he sobers up in tragic fashion. Yes, sir: he starts drinking all over again. So I poured myself a drink then. The massively built, gloomy young lady from the suburbs didn't refuse the refreshment. We sat, and we chatted about life. We went on living. The nightmares didn't stay long. They came in through the window, they went out the door. It wasn't bad. It already wasn't bad. A pleasant chat with a Warsaw whore as a means for saving one's life, and perhaps even a means for living. It goes without saying that I didn't question her whether there wasn't perhaps among her colleagues a certain failed actress named Wiktoria. I didn't proceed to such shamelessness, but also—judging by her bored expression—there wasn't any great innovation in my questions. I asked her why she did what she did for a living, when she had decided to do it, how it was the first time, etc. Supposedly, all her clients posed the same questions. Oh, why should I have been original? I didn't worry in this case about my lack of originality. All the less did I worry about the fact that it was she who turned out to be the original. I would say, very original. 'Why do you do this?' 'For the money. I need the money. I need quite a lot.' 'Do you have some serious expenses? Debts?' 'Debts, no, but expenses, yes. I have to put on my daughter's First Communion in May. You need money for a good First Communion.' Yes. The story is reaching its end. As you can see, my new acquaintance was not only not Wiktoria—she wasn't even a Lutheran. In a sentimental reflex, I paid her a couple grosz more, and the next day I returned to K. From that time, which is to say, for the last two years, I haven't budged from the spot.

"In a fundamental sense, nothing has changed here. The latest local news says that Wiktoria completed her degree with distinction, that she has accepted a role in an unusually popular series, and soon all of K. will be sitting down before their television sets in order to marvel at the pearl that our land has produced. Sometimes I think that if this had been true, I would have the punchline of all punchlines. A punchline that is light, edifying, comic, and surprising. But this is not very likely. Back then, two years ago, on the next morning, I dropped by the acting school on Miodowa Street on my way out of town. Besides, this was not far at all from the Hotel Europejski. For Warsaw—very near by. A person named Wiktoria Złotnica had never studied there, nor had anyone by that name been accepted in the program. We have few, desperately few surprises in life. Time for bed. You especially deserve it. Please forgive the intrusion. In any case, we have spent a pleasant evening, a remarkably pleasant evening. And now—however this might sound—I vanish without a trace."

I awoke in quite good shape. I felt ill treated—it goes without saying—by the story I had listened to; with pathological clarity, I recalled my guest's every word and every gesture, but I was not threatened with any interruption in my life's story. I ate breakfast, packed, and turned in the key at the reception desk. Emil was also already moving about, barely, but still—he was moving. I didn't ask about anything. I knew perfectly well that if I were to ask about the retired teacher in a brown suit, who knew the history, geography, and substance of every local square inch inside and out, I would discover that he was either an absolute lunatic, or a complete drunk, or both.

A Corpse with
Folded Wings

I

GRANDMA PECH'S SPIRIT DOESN'T VISIT ME. NOR DO ANY OTHER
spirits. When I dream of the old house in the center of Wisła, it is
always empty and lit. I walk through the swept courtyard, through
the hallway, through the rooms. There isn't anyone anywhere, but I
hear someone's steps ahead of me. I enter the kitchen, and sometimes
someone is there. From time to time I see her. She sits at the enormous table covered with a sky blue oilcloth. On her head she has a
carefully tied scarf with a pattern of black roses, on her shoulders a
brown Silesian jacket. She sits at the table, but she is dressed as if she
were going somewhere right away. Somewhere far. Not to Wojnar's
to go shopping, not even to the market. Somewhere far, and at an
unusual time. In my dream, it is always a late hour. The majolica
clock over the door to the hallway says that it is almost ten, and
she is setting off somewhere. Someone is supposed to come for her.
The gate is wide open, you can hear the rattle of a britzka crossing

the bridge. The yellow light of the kitchen window makes a regular rectangle on the river stones of the courtyard.

Whenever we came late, and the gate was closed, we would look through the slits to see whether the light was on the stones. It usually was. It always was. We would knock on the window, or we would bang at the front. Grandpa Pech would come through the hallway and open the door. Suddenly the day, which was already over, gained extra hours. The evening, which was already almost night, became early evening. A fire burned anew under the cooled stove. Supper was long past, but we were just sitting down to supper. It was dark all over Wisła, but at our house the lights were on for a long time yet. I loved late arrivals and prolonged evenings—later on, it was never possible to outwit Time so easily.

For years now, the gate has been gone, as is the light on the river stones, the kitchen, the hearth, the table covered with the sky blue oilcloth. All are dead now, and their spirits do not come. They don't come when I'm awake. They come in my dreams—but that is vanity. The dead came to Grandma Pech, both when she was asleep and awake, both day and night. Now there is complete stagnation—no one comes. Not she herself, or Father, or Uncle Ableger, or Janek Nikandy. They won't come, although I focus like hell on them and on their other worlds. They don't come, although I pray that they come. I summon them with biblical demagogy, and I even blaspheme against their memory in the desperate hope that, if in no other way, they would at least drop by to give us a little scare. But nothing. Neither hide nor hair. Is Warsaw too far away for them? A deadly joke, but I don't cross people off the list for being dead.

Last evening the door bell rang. I was already certain that my old man had finally—exactly ten years after his death—made up his mind, and he was dropping by to pay a spectral visit. Nothing of the sort! The usual street fraud, claiming that supposedly her purse had been stolen and she didn't have enough money to get home. Even a rather nice looking babe. I gave her five złotys. Not so much out of desire, as anger that it was she, and not the spirit of an ancestor. They don't come. Although sooner or later someone will come. A destroyed city, an empty apartment, absolute twilight, complete solitude—ideal conditions for the dead. Eventually, they will come. At the worst, they will say of me that I went crazy.

Grandma Pech conversed with the dead. That's an understatement. Well before someone died she often started to receive signs from the heavens. When Mila from Wierchy died, a half year earlier God struck the kitchen oven so forcefully that the pots almost fell. I was there. They were sitting at the table, drinking tea with rum, and suddenly it sounded like a stone quarry in the stove. They looked at each other for a fraction of a second and right away began to find thousands of reasons: wet coal was crackling in the hearth; a cast iron rib had cracked; the metal plate on one side had become completely bent; the badly positioned stove damper had fallen off; we have to throw away the old tea pot, because it's going to pieces with a horrible bang; there's something in the courtyard; something at the Nikandys'; something in the heavens.

But for that fraction of a second, as they looked at each other, they managed to ask themselves silently: Which one? Which one of them would soon die? They both knew the secret alphabets of death. The lot fell to Mila. She was a large, stout woman, and she had always had heart troubles. In half a year she would begin to feel sick. Not so very sick—she wouldn't even lose consciousness—but still, sick enough that the ambulance would come, they would take her to the hospital, and basically no one knew what would come next. The kitchen was full of people, everyone was waiting for news, uncanny Pospiszil was calmly reckoning whether Mama—in my parts, to this day, men have the fatal habit of calling their wives "Mamas"—would return home for the holidays. Of course she would return, what do you mean for the holidays, what's the date today? The tenth of December! What do you mean for the holidays! Mama will return well before the holidays! And even if! Even if, God forbid, there were some complications, because a person has to be prepared for everything, even so, they will certainly discharge her just in time for the holidays! They

Jerzy Pilch

will discharge her for the holidays. They always discharge almost everybody for the holidays. How could this be: the holidays without Mama?

And here, for a good hour already, life without Mama had been going on. They couldn't get through on the telephone from the hospital, what was the hurry with this news after all. Finally, Grandma will take the telephone call, and right away—despair, sudden lament, the first steps of the funeral dance. Mama has died! Mama has died! She was with us even yesterday, and today she is gone! Grandma will run in from the hallway, where the telephone on the wall, fastened to a special pedestal made of black metal, was now like an altar of evil. She will glide with a quick but at the same time solemn step, she will rush to uncanny Pospiszil, grasp him by the head, embrace him, and shout like in the circus: Mama has died! Mama has died!

The sudden expressions of despair were the most difficult to understand. After all, she well knew at whom the shot under the kitchen stove had been aimed. So what shock are we talking about? What surprise? She knew that it was about Mila, not about her.

This didn't happen in my sleep. It was in the early morning of a certain winter day. All of Wisła was buried in snow up to the rooftops, and it must have been twenty below zero. Somebody was sitting then on the round stool at the sewing machine. She had recently gotten up, was walking about the room and braiding the plait that she never cut, and she wasn't afraid, and she wasn't ashamed, because she sensed that that someone could be a messanger—frozen, dusty, dead tired, but from over there. Perhaps even the same one who once had visited Abraham, or the one who had dissuaded Joseph from leaving Mary, or the one we sang about in the Christmas carol: "On earth are the earthly, in heaven, the angels." You couldn't see his wings, but it all fit. Can you see birds' wings when they sit on branches? Has anyone ever seen a sparrow sitting with its wings spread? Or a titmouse? Or a blackbird? Birds spread their wings in flight; it must be the same with angels. True, on the lithograph that was hanging over the bed you could see the spread wings growing out of the angel's back, but every time she looked at that picture, the thought came to her that the picture was painted nicely, but that the painter had probably never seen even a partridge in the grass, to say nothing of an angel. The one who was sitting on the round stool at the sewing machine must have had his wings folded. An angel with folded wings. A strange expression, but she liked it a lot. And he had just said—the stranger with the folded wings—that she would still, for many years, see signs and hear voices. It flitted through her mind to ask about Gustaw. Just how was he doing? Had his cracked skull grown back together? Did he remember her? But she let it go, since this might displease him. She has been with her second husband for a long time now, three children with him, grandchildren, and there she goes asking about the other one. God didn't take him so that she could long for him. She didn't ask.

Grandma Pech outwitted death by her eternal readiness for it. That was how she lived to be ninety. For as long as I could remember, she had been saying that it was time to leave this world, that she had just one desire, to fall asleep in the evening and not wake up in the morning, and she always wore black. Even when she wasn't entirely in black, she always wore something funereal, even if it was only a scarf with black roses. In other words, she was ready for death every day, she had the angel's assurance that she would live to see a thing or two, she had been forewarned about God's decisions. She was doubly, or perhaps even repeatedly, fortified; she had been expecting Mila's death for half a year. But in that case, what was the reason for her race from the hallway to the kitchen, feverish and stately, like an up-tempo cortège? Why, and for whom, that grabbing of uncanny Pospiszil by his gray mane? Why, and for whom, those theatrics?

For the Lord God. For half a year, day after day, Grandma Pech had awaited Mila's death with a heavy heart, but also for half a year she had been gearing up for her performance on the occasion of that death. She couldn't foresee all the circumstances, but it turned out almost ideally. Grandma Pech was the Lord God's dancer. She didn't have the slightest doubt that He never took His eye off her, and that

Jerzy Pilch

in important moments He scrutinized her carefully. Her faith was pure and steadfast, but it plunged her into an aesthetic of despair, because it seemed to her that the Lord God, the angels, and, in general, all the inhabitants of heaven were the audience before which she was performing. She did her best, but she didn't know the duplicitous art of solemn gestures. She couldn't even feign sorrow over someone's death very well. And when she thought about herself, she went numb with fear. Just how would that be? Through one's whole life, a person hadn't been anywhere, hadn't traveled, hadn't met anyone. A person hadn't even been to Warsaw, and now you have to exchange a few words with Lord Jesus, greet the archangels from up close. God! How will this be? My Grandma Zuzanna, *née* Trzmielowska, *primo voto* Branna, *secundo voto* Pech, wasn't afraid of death—she was afraid of leaving Wisła.

II

SHE DIED IN LONG DRAWN-OUT AGONIES. I SAW HER FOR THE LAST time two weeks before her death. For the previous nine years, ever since Grandpa Pech had died, she had lived alone. For the last year, she lay in bed in the small room. I sat on the round stool at the sewing machine. She told stories about the church fair, about gingerbread, and about the taste of freshly pickled cucumbers. I realized that she was talking about the taste of cucumbers from the year 1912. Twenty years later she fell in love with the young butcher Gustaw Branny. A dark, almost indecipherable photo from their wedding party was hanging over the little chess table. Today it is easy to say that clouds were gathering over the young couple. If you stare at the background, you can see more than clouds, and more than the black trunks of pine trees—you can see corpse-white lightning bolts slashing through the darkness.

To the left of the groom sits his sister Mila, with uncanny Pospiszil. Pospiszil's uncanniness, in my mind from back then, was based on three circumstances. First: he had a twin brother. Second: a year after my aunt's death, the devils carted him off to hell, and he cursed horribly, horribly. Third: he was an enthusiastic phillumenist.

He showed me his collection once. Oh, the varieties and origins of matchbox covers he had there! Egypt, The Congo, Bechuana, Tanganyika, Laos, Oran, Siam—God knows what else. Everything the same size, poor pictures, wretched paper, zero serration. In those days, I collected stamps, and Pospiszil's phillumenalia made a gloomy impression. It seemed to me that he, too, really wished to collect stamps, but, as some sort of punishment, he was only allowed this pathetic stuff. Or that those were stamps, but that the devil cut the edges at night and spilled acid on them, which made the colors fade, the paper get thin, and the glue come off the back. Pospiszil was amazingly proud of his collection. He presented it with the superiority of the magician initiated in who knows what sort of arcana. With the proficiency of the old pedant (before the war he had taught at the conservatory), he tested me to see whether I was reacting with the proper humility, and I felt ashamed of him with the terrible shame of the child who is ashamed of adults. To make matters worse, the Pospiszils' house in Wierchy was huge and unfurnished. All the rooms were painted yellow, and there was not even a stool in a single one. In the living room, there was a piano covered with a shiny violet dust sheet—and that was that. Maybe they lived on the second floor, maybe they were remodeling just then, painting, changing the stoves—the explanation wouldn't be complicated, but in my mind there remained the yellow light of the walls, the empty rooms, and Pospiszil showing me, with pomp and solemnity, the most pathetic little scraps of paper in the world.

When he died a year after Mila's death, his identical twin brother came to the funeral. I suppose they didn't get along, because I had never seen the twin before. Supposedly he lived in Gdynia. Or on some other moon. Actually, I don't have to elaborate on the images and circumstances. Just imagine the funeral of a twin, which is attended by the other twin. Maybe you have been at such a funeral?

Jerzy Pilch

It is obvious what sort of irresistible thoughts one has then. And what is more, I was seeing the other Pospiszil for the first time in my life, and I didn't really know that he was—perhaps didn't even really know what it was: twinness. My Aunt from Wąwóz had twins, but they weren't similar. And here you had the identical voice, the identical motions, height, gait, hair, even clothing—all identical. It couldn't be anything other than that the corpse had crawled out of the coffin and was standing over its own grave. Years later I feel like laughing, but then? Horror! And there were the amazing stories: that the deceased—if he was deceased, if the coffin wasn't empty—had died horribly, how he howled, cursed, blasphemed. Horror! Fear, genuine, piercing to the marrow like frost. Fear that somewhere here, over the cemetery on Gróniczek Hill, emissaries of hell were circulating, that, granted, Father Kalinowski conducted the right services, that we sing and pray, but that the devil already has everything in his care. Years later—when Father died and over his grave a black, July downpour broke out—I recalled a shadow of that fear.

III

ON THE PHOTO HANGING OVER THE LITTLE CHESS TABLE, BLACK clouds and the black branches of pine trees bend over the wedding guests. Black pine needles rain down upon my Grandma's bonnet, but she doesn't know about it. Leaning on the distinctive shoulder of the young butcher, she has before her yet a year of faith in love, a year of faith in the world's sense, a year of faith in God's goodness. In nine months, she would give birth to a son. In twelve months, on a sunny September afternoon, someone would drive up in front of the house on a motorcycle. Someone with dark folded wings? Most likely yes, although this isn't all that important. What is important is the motorcycle—a DKW Sport 500, the 1929 model. A black, shining spider, which could reach the unprecedented speed of seventy-five miles per hour.

As late as the fifties, when some stranger from Katowice left a Junak in the courtyard, the neighbors gathered, and the Nikandy boys, by some miracle (to tell the truth, by using a common nail), got it started and made laps, there was a great spectacle. And twenty years earlier? Before the war? Almost ten years before the arrival, with an infernal clatter, of motorized Wehrmacht troops through the Kubalonka Pass? In the year of Our Lord one thousand nine hundred and thirty-two? At that time, the good citizens of Wisła didn't gather out of curiosity at the sound of an approaching motorcycle. They locked themselves in their houses, maybe they even barricaded themselves. They definitely prayed.

O unhappy Gustaw Branny! Why didn't you hide in the back room? Why did you allow yourself to be tempted by the devil on the motorcycle? Why did you want to go for a ride? O master butcher, who obtained all those licenses from the Butchers' Association in Skoczów! Granted, if you had hidden and not set off on your last ride, I wouldn't be singing you this little song, because neither I nor my Mother would be in this world, but Grandma would be happy. Was that the reason almighty God, or the devil on a motorcycle, smashed your skull—so that my life might be possible? And it is possible only because I defend myself from its anguish by writing? Are those the sorts of pranks you have in Your head, Lord God?

For half her life, Grandma told the story of the scene of his departure. Gustaw sat on the motorcycle, they set off in the direction of *Oasis*, he turned back, waved, and that was that. I heard this sentence a thousand, a billion times. Nothing more. Gustaw sat on the motorcycle, they set off in the direction of *Oasis*, he turned back, waved, and that was that. Her story about the tragedy was a single sentence. Never a single word about who came running with the news. Never a single word about how she flew to that bend in the road. Never a single word about the stump that Gustaw's unhappy head hit. Never a single word about how he looked in the coffin. Never a single word about washing and dressing the corpse. Never a single word about the funeral. I hear her wailing in the ice-cold house of Wisła butchers, and she recalls the wailing that was the omen of his death. She was sure that it had been caterwauling. The windows of the back room look out on a garden full of wild apple trees, tomcats from the entire Principality of Cieszyn constantly prowl there, and often, in their amatory frenzies, bawl their heads off precisely like year-old infants. Six weeks before Gustaw was killed, you could hear the screaming cry of a child in the back room. She was certain that it was tomcats' laments, although something didn't fit. Only when she went in there on the evening after the wake did she recall her own anxiety.

In the back room stands a stove made of cornflower blue tiles, a gigantic armchair, a pear wood wardrobe, a double bed, a small table covered with a lace table cloth. On the wall hangs an image of a Guardian Angel and a Becker clock. You couldn't hear it ticking. It is quiet, dreadfully quiet. My twenty-five-year-old Grandma looks through the double window at the outline of Jarzębata Mountain. Never would she put it this way, but her skin is dead, her soul is in ruins, her heart is burnt to ashes. Not only is the Jarzębata beyond the double window. The entire world is beyond the double window. She herself is beyond the double window. Her legs, her arms, her head—they have been separated from her; she walks, sits, moves her arms, sees, and hears only because, with her last reserves of strength, she commands her legs and arms to move, her eyes to see, and her ears to hear. And now there is quiet over the entire field, now it is quiet like in Gustaw's coffin. Even the tomcats have fallen silent, they aren't in the garden, the child isn't crying.

Suddenly, it was as if a windowpane had shattered, as if the band at a fair had started to play. Suddenly she hears that cry, suddenly she hears the cry from six weeks before and recalls that it hadn't come from the garden, but as if from behind the armchair, and the armchair doesn't even stand under the window. And she recalls that her heart shuddered then, because that sound was not only unusually loud, it was also horribly distinct; it was full of syllables, as if a crying baby were saying something, shouting something, as if it wished to say, to shout out some word. And with all her strength, she recreates that meowing, that whimpering, which was not meowing and was not whimpering. God, it is good that You give me signs, but why are they so unclear? Grandma Zuzanna listens intently and with a sort of tension, as if she were praying for Gustaw's resurrection and had a chance at it. She listens and suddenly hears, suddenly she hears precisely and runs through the entire house, and just as she was standing there in her Silesian attire, which she hadn't yet changed after the funeral and after the wake, she runs to the stable, leads Fuks out, harnesses him to the britzka, which is standing by the shed, opens the gate, and off she goes! Giddy-up! Giddy up! Fuks! Giddy-up to Wierchy!

I'm not able to describe her life as I would wish. I don't know how to recreate it day by day, page by page. Isolated images flare up, and I approach them, but I, too, am helpless. The lonely ride of Grandma Zuzanna at dusk through a lifeless prewar Wisła is like a Handel aria. A few hours after the funeral of her beloved, a young woman stands on the rushing carriage, turns onto the bridge, drives into the dark valley, a gust ripped the scarf from her shoulders and unbraids her plait. Fuks gallops lightly, the wheels rattle, the river flows toward them, and above them, in the dark blue sky, an angel sings: *Lascia ch'io pianga mia cruda sorte, e che sospiri la libertà.*

At the Pospiszils', the lights are shining in the windows, Grandma walks through the yellow rooms, no one is surprised. It was almost as if Mila had been waiting for her. First they embrace, then they look at each other for a long time. They sit in the living room. There is no question of eating, but a sip of pepper vodka can't hurt. Mila's famous pepper vodka. Old Roth buys it all the time and does great business with it. He served it at the wake. After two rounds, the hubbub of voices was louder and louder. Lord Jesus, let me wake up. Lord God, wake me up. After the funeral, they asked to go to Roth's, because— where else? She didn't really know where she was. A year ago she hadn't believed that she was at her own wedding party. Now she is supposed to believe that she is at the wake after Gustaw's funeral? She drank about three glasses, but she didn't feel a thing, not even the fiery taste.

"Mrs. Professor, Mrs. Professor," old Roth bowed and scraped to Mila, "Mrs. Professor. When Mrs. Professor makes her *pepper vodka from Wierchy*, it is paradise mixed with hell! It is as if you were drinking fire mixed with sky. It is as if a cloud pierced by lightning had passed through your throat! Mr. Professor," he addressed Pospiszil. "Mr. Professor, you have a genuine Eden in your cellar!" "Eden in the cellar, hell on the ground floor," responded Pospiszil, who was well known for his splendid ripostes, and the laugh of the funeral-goers rose to the heavens.

Not only Mila's pepper vodka, not only the other liqueurs, but especially the preserves, jams, cucumbers, mushrooms, home-made wine were delicacies. When the summer or the ski seasons came, Roth made out like a bandit on those delicacies. With Mila's compotes alone he did better business than with the Brannys' mutton. Which does not mean that he lost money on the meat.

"I don't lose on anything," he used to say. "I don't lose on anything, because I like the Christian verse that says 'In the beginning was the Word.' In my tavern I, too, give the word at the beginning. Before the dill soup, I give the word dill soup; before the omelet, I give the word omelet; before the schnitzel, I give the word schnitzel; before the apple torte, I give the word apple torte—but *what words they are*! How they are written, and on what paper! How they are bound! Garnished with what additional words! Officers' soup! Omelet *á la Lisbon*! Emperor's schnitzel. Apple torte *cumulonimbus*!"

When, toward the end of the fifties, I found among some old papers a *Menu of the Restaurant and Confectionery of Maurycy Roth in Wisła*—covered with fossilized dust, but practically without damage—it seemed to me that I had discovered an illuminated Benedictine manuscript or a folio from a biblical papyrus. It was as if my delight was supposed to survive old Roth, murdered in Auschwitz.

Before the pepper vodka was the word pepper vodka, and after the pepper vodka was the word pepper vodka. People were still talking about Mila's pepper vodka long after the war. And now, as I record this story, *pepper vodka from Wierchy* is warming the blood of

Grandma Zuzanna. She didn't feel the icy wind during her ride, she was completely numb from the cold, and finally there was a tiny bit of warmth, minimally deeper breaths, a trace of relief. Mila raises the lid of the grand piano. Gustaw had visited them a few weeks before the accident. "'Sister,'" he said, "for that was how he always addressed me, with strange solemnity and tenderness. I loved him very much, and he loved me too. We were good siblings, even very good, but sometimes when he lost all moderation with that *sister* of his—*sister* this, *sister* that, *sister* the other thing, when he never said the shortest sentence to me without that *sister*—you know what I'm talking about, because you often heard it: 'Gustaw, what time is it?' 'Three, *sister*,' when he was often as if completely possessed by that *sister*, I would lose my temper. Was he making a joke or a mockery of me. But not then, on that occasion there wasn't time to feel offended, on that occasion there wasn't time for anything, because he was in a hurry. He said that he was *going to Ram Mountain for a sacrificial lamb*. He was always joking, not always in an appropriate manner. In any case, he was in a terrible hurry, and he dropped by as if for fire, or rather for water, because he called from the threshhold: 'Sister, I need to drink, sister, I'm horribly dry, *sister*, I will die of thirst before I return home, *sister*, save me!'" And she ran down to the cellar for a jar of gooseberry compote—gooseberry, when you need to drink, is the best, slightly tart, invigorating; when she makes it, she never overdoes it with the sugar—and she took the biggest jar she could find, and she returned quickly.

He stood by the grand piano, the lid had been raised, and he had a hand on the keys, and she was certain that he would immediately hammer out a few bars of "When the morning stars are rising . . ." that was all he could more or less play. But no, he didn't start to play, he turned around to her and smiled, and in his turn, and smile, there was something light—as if that turn were the beginning of flight. That became fixed in her mind. How wouldn't it become fixed. That's how she saw him the last time alive, and now it constantly seems to her that he is standing with his hand raised over the keyboard like some sort of composer, but the poor devil didn't have an ear worth a plugged nickel, just those disastrous notes of "When the morning . . ." desperately tapped out. He had probably learned while still in school. Not so much to play, as to find the right keys by memory, and whenever he found himself at the instrument, he immediately began to hammer away. All his life, that one and only melody, and barely at that. Even after death, he couldn't manage any better. Precisely an hour after his death, she heard someone playing, but, after all, there wasn't anyone at home; the grand piano was closed and covered with a cloth, but she clearly, very clearly—she wasn't imagining anything—she hears precisely the first bars pounded out by Gustaw's hard fingers. He had already been killed, he was already a corpse, he already lay, crushed by the accursed motorcycle, already his wings were folded, already blood was flowing from his head as if from a faucet; but he came once more, wanted to play once more, wanted to pound out the melody, as if he were thanking her for the gooseberry compote.

They embrace and cry, and it is a cry of despair, but also a cry of relief, for since both had heard, since both had received signs, there is no mistake, there is no doubt. Perhaps it was even for this reason that God had taken Gustaw, so that, through hearing, and sometimes later even seeing, He might let it be known that He is. He is. It could have been this way: until now, it had been up and down with their faith. They were too young, too fine looking, and too flighty. Zuza and Mila. It was up and down with them, and especially with their thoughts. But now God had poured His Spirit into them.

Grandma Zuzanna drinks off one more shot of pepper vodka and feels the surge of strength and hope. If the Lord God has given these sorts of signs, that means that there is a Paradise, there are angels, and there is eternal life. And Gustaw will be waiting for her there. Lord Jesus, this is all true! Everything she had learned in Sunday School, in religion, in confirmation classes—this is all the truest truth. She will live well—diligently and piously. She will bring up the little one so that Gustaw will be proud of both of them. And when she should, at some point, die, when she should finally die, what is she saying—finally?—right away, in a moment; life is like a spark, time flies ceaselessly, perhaps even when she falls asleep tonight, she won't wake up in the morning; it will be right away, it will be right away, as soon as she gets to Heaven, and Gustaw comes out to meet her, smiling so lightly, as Mila said, and they go to some corner where no one will bother them, and she will tell Gustaw everything, every little thing, week by week, day by day, how she raised the little one, how she lived. O Jesus, this is all true! O Jesus, how good that You had the baby start to cry in the back room! How good that on the way to Ram Mountain You sent thirst upon Gustaw and commanded him to drop by Wierchy for gooseberry compote.

And late, very late in the evening, Grandma Zuzanna will return home under heavens so star-strewn it was as if they were covered with snow. The cart goes calmly, the crowns of the trees almost bright, the clatter of the river and the great quiet over the mountains. Fuks pulls up to the gate by memory, a shadow rises from the bench standing before the front entry, runs up to the britzka, and offers her a firm hand, holds her a second longer, presses greedily, knows that he can. God is on his side.

IV

HONOR TO THE LORD ON HIGH AND THANKS BE TO HIS GRACE! No longer can the power and might of Evil bring us doom! Lord Jesus, this is all true! You are! He is! Everything that my Grandpa, Andrzej Pech, taught in Sunday School, religion, and confirmation class—it's true! God listens to prayers! His prayers were heard. After a year of imploring, his beloved was finally widowed. God has given a sign. No, God hasn't given a sign. God has given significantly more—God has killed her husband, God has left her with a small child, God has pushed her into his arms.

His arms were ready for the labor of life. They helped her get down from the britzka, then they skillfully unharnessed Fuks, guided him to the stable, and poured out some oats. He returned to the courtyard paved with river stones, but she was no longer there. A yellow light fell from the great window. He glanced up. The edge of the roof under which he was to spend the rest of his life was sharply silhouetted, the heavens were white with stars. He walked all around the house. In her room, which faced the garden, it was already dark. She hadn't turned on any of the lights, she had felt a surge of exhaustion so terrible, as if she were about to lose consciousness. She undressed in the dark, blindly threw her skirt, blouse, and corsette on Gustaw's bed. She fell asleep with a light heart. Only just before falling asleep did she recall the hand offered to her as she got down from the cart, and then the skillful unharnessing of Fuks. "Why does that postal clerk feel so much at home?" she thought and, fortunately, tumbled into the deep well of sleep. Fortunately, because if she had begun to search for divine signs in this question, she could have gone mad. There is no reason to exaggerate about the divine signs. They are everywhere. In any case, they were there in the question she asked before she fell asleep: "Why does that postal clerk feel so much at home?" He had helped her down from the cart, and a year later she married him.

V

THE PHOTO FROM THE SECOND WEDDING PARTY HANGS LOWER, IT is much clearer, and I look at it much more often. There are significantly fewer guests, not even twenty. Grandma Pech is again wearing Silesian dress, Mila again sits on her left with uncanny Pospiszil. They look exactly the same as in the first photo. The strangest of all is the fact that the elder Brannys also look exactly the same. At the wedding party of their son, they look exactly like they do at the wedding party of their widowed daughter-in-law. No change in facial expressions. Between the first and the second photograph, they had lost their first-born son. Now a woman, a stranger to them, who had been his wife, is marrying a postal official, to whom she would bear children under their roof, but you can't see any of this in their faces. Perhaps because they are just as gloomy at the first wedding party as at the second.

Heavenly musicians play and angelic choirs sing for the groom. He listens to them, dressed in a tailcoat with silk facing. He has crossed his legs in a worldly manner, his shoulder touches Zuzanna's shoulder, no further miracles are necessary. But in order to honor that miracle, he had Master Potulnik sew him a tailcoat. And he looks out of this world in it. There is no darkness in the background, nor are there evil signs. One dark window foretells how much misfortune is allotted to each.

The background is a white wall, behind which an ocean of objects reaches as high as my shoulders. Piles of prewar newspapers will be like lighthouses, decaying dresses and jackets like shifting sand dunes. Chowderhead the cat will go carefully along the treacherous bank, over which I will fish out from the depths occult novels and forbidden romances. In the middle, snatched up by a vortex, a golden trumpet—which came from who knows where the day after the festivities—circles in a pillar of sunlight. There I would find wooden heads from a puppet theater; there, one day, would come to the surface the skeleton of a leviathan completely plastered with fantastic account books; there I would come upon the menu from Roth's tavern.

Diving in there took courage, but once you got down below, once you passed the shoal of Austrian coins, the keys to long-forgotten doors, spare parts for all the mechanisms in the world, once you had gone through the darknesses, and finally through the thickest layers strewn with mothballs, as low as possible—then you could see the white outlines of a sunken city: the ruins of marble counter tops, a gigantic scale, an amazing tree stump, an incredible ax, hooks bared and incomplete like the fangs of a mammoth. Even today, it is with the greatest difficulty that I realize that my Atlantis was a prewar butcher shop. Business was still booming during the war. No one ever spoke about it, but supposedly things were going well, even very well. The Germans had taken Roth and his entire family. There was less competition.

The last clients were soldiers of the Red Army. They rode down into Wisła through the Kubalonka Pass, just like the Wehrmacht, except that they came on horses. Grandpa Pech used to say that they had been fortunate enough to get an exceptionally honorable unit. They wanted to pay for everything, but they didn't have any money. And you could see that they were hungry: at the very sight—at the very scent—of sausage they started shaking. No wonder—come war, come occupation, we always had sausage. One had a Turkmen kilim or a Kyrgyz carpet strapped to his saddle, or perhaps a Persian rug, in any case an amazing fabric in a pagan design. But it was out of the question, he wouldn't give it up. He jabbers something feverishly, you could guess that he wants to get to Berlin with it, but probably not in order to hoist a colorful banner on the Brandenburg Gate, rather in order to return from Berlin with this treasure to Alma Ata, or God knows where. It was out of the question, he wouldn't give it up, he wouldn't give it up for any sausage. He wouldn't give it up for anything. Not for anything in the world. Grandpa went off to his hiding place and returns with two quart bottles of moonshine. The moonshine has the same color as Mila's prewar pepper vodka. The comparison means nothing to the stubborn Bolshevik, and he continues to shake his head no, although no longer with the same conviction. But his buddies, unusually honorable Soviet *soldaty*, were in favor of the transaction. They attacked him furiously. It was as if the horses had caught the smell, they began to snort. Finally, the *kamandir* himself issued a *prikaz*: let there be a strengthening in Polish-Soviet trade relations. And so there was. They each got a ring of sausage all the same. They ate, they drank, and off they went. And the marble countertops, tree stump, scales, hooks, and gigantic ax slowly began to sink to the bottom.

VI

THE OLDER BRANNYS, ONE AFTER THE OTHER—IT WAS STILL DURING
the German occupation—died of distress, in other words, a natural death. "Mother supposedly heard that there was a knock, once,
twice. I didn't hear anything," Grandpa Pech's blood didn't yet boil
on account of the signs that were constantly coming to *Mother*, but
he was already jealous of them. In accepting the fact that one amazing miracle had occurred in his life, and not expecting any further
miracles, not even small ones, he had probably committed an error.
He didn't lose faith in God, but it is not so much faith as life itself—
if it is not strengthened by signs—that weakens. "I don't need any
divine rumblings. Mother hears all the rumbling of this world and
the next for me," he repeated with with a sneer, although in the word
"Mother" there was the least amount of sneering. Liberated from
the majority of the local customs, he was liberated from the dreadfully suicidal constant "*Mother*-ing" only by his intonation, but in my
Lutheran parts even that is quite a lot.

They had four children, one died. Depraved by her excessive
caresses, the boy from the first marriage had barely finished school
when he ran away from home and vanished like a stone in water.
Mother must think about him from time to time. She doesn't let
on, but she thinks. How is he faring? What is he doing? Is he even
alive? He must be, because if he had died, she would have heard a
sign. A knocking. Usually at the window. The deceased mainly knock
on the kitchen window. Old Lady Mary—three clear knocks on the
pane. Uncle Paweł—the same thing. Old Man Trzmielowski—six
strokes, precisely half a year before he died. Master Sztwiertnia—a
clatter in the hallway. Adam Czyż—a clatter in the attic. One-eyed
Mr. Nikandy—again on the pane. Pastor Morowy—a lightning bolt
over the cemetery. Bandmaster Jan Potulnik—a knock on the wall.
Sister Ewelina—on the ceiling. Ferdynand Pustówka—on the table.
Uncle Ableger—for a very long time on the window pane. Emma

Lunatyczka—lightly on the window sill. Wolfgang Kleist—a racket in the pantry.

Little by little there wouldn't be a single square inch in the house where some deceased person hadn't rapped. Thank God the Communists are in power, and there is peace and no turmoil, because if it were a time of war, pestilence, or earthquake, then all the dead people that Mother knew would have torn the house down with their knocking alone. Even the baby, who died a couple days old, managed to stop the clock after its death. Her other three children throve. One son became a lawyer, the other a fitter, the girl a doctor. But they made tragic marriages. One to a spineless sataness, the other to a woman with no mind, the son-in-law in Krakow joined the Party.

They all always gathered for the holidays, but the true time of joy, of rejoicing, would arise when they departed. Finally you could hear the ticking of the clocks. All five. One in the ice house, one in the back room, one in the entrance, one in the kitchen, and also the cuckoo clock in the hallway. An ambition, unclear at first, that all of them strike simultaneously gradually turned into a maniacal obsession. He would grab the round stool standing next to the sewing machine, holding it like a four-legged pike set upright, carry it before him, place it forcefully under one clock after the other, climb up to the high mechanisms—not without quiet curses—and work for hours on their coordination. It often seemed that Grandpa Pech, standing on the stool, had become paralyzed, his arms stretched out to each subsequent clock face, and that he would remain in that pose for the ages. And, in fact, he did spend whole ages minding the clock hands and listening to the ticking, and he would freeze in the hope that all the bells would ring out in unison at last, and he never managed it.

Sometimes, on a dark winter night, he would wake up and, numb with hope and fear, he would await the coming hour. When he heard five or six tolls it was all the worse, because it was time to get up right away. But when the eternally unsynchronized clocks rang two o'clock, or best of all midnight, he didn't fault them for their irregularity. Sometimes even a shiver of delight would come over him: so much more time for sleeping until morning.

The five regularly wound clocks were like the breathing of the house. The dreadful offspring with their dreadful spouses and their even more dreadful progeny would depart after the holidays. The house became deserted and deadened, but it recovered its circulation, the mechanical hearts began to beat, the ticking crickets hidden in the corners regained their vigor, and that was good.

Icy, black January arrived, after that an even icier and blacker February. He would get up with Mother in the darkness, light the fire under the kitchen stove, put on his postal clerk's jacket, tie the cornflower blue tie of the Postal Chief, eat breakfast, and walk slowly through the gray center of town to the office. He would return for lunch, Mother would serve a thick and almost brown chicken broth with noodles, he would eat, then lie down for a bit, close his eyes, listen to the absolutely undisturbed five-fold ticking. Today I think that he also kept watch over the clocks so that their brittle, earthly ticking might stand up to the unearthly rattlings.

March was brighter. Whenever they had to go anywhere a bit further away, Fuks would now be harnessed to the cart, not the sleigh. In April, they stopped heating the rooms, even the coldest air was lined with the scent of the grasses' stormy onset, larks began to appear over Partecznik. By the beginning of May, summer uniforms were the rule at the post office, the winter ones landed in storage. The underwater city was covered with successive layers of postal uniforms. In June, heat waves smelling of hay burst forth, the first female vacationers were sunbathing on the river bank. In July, carters brought coal for the winter, and wood was cut; then came the rains and the floods. In August, the air in the kitchen became as thick as quince syrup; Mila would come and help Mother with the compotes, pickles, and plum jams. In September, there were occasional blades of grass whitened by the first light frosts. In October, the smoke that backed up from the cold stoves filled the house like tear gas.

His birthday was on the twenty-seventh of November. The postal workers would take up their seats at the table. Mother served everything she had—chicken broth, cutlets, potato pancakes. A gallon jar of marinated mushrooms went from hand to hand and seemed to diminish like a rapidly melting, huge, red-brown candle. For his fiftieth they gave him a *tableau* beautifully executed by an artist from Ustroń. Gold letters proclaimed the glory of Mr. Chief, inserted among which, wrapped in gleaming ribbons, were the photos of all the female clerks and the postmen, then he himself in the middle, suitably enlarged. All of it in a cherry wood frame, which on the next day came to hang next to the likeness of the Guardian Angel in the back room.

How many Novembers have passed since that time? Ten? More than ten, because at his sixtieth he still saw very well, glaucoma wasn't yet blinding him, and Mother was also still in good form. Her legs hurt, and a sore under her knee just wouldn't heal, but she was still in good form. They didn't put on birthday parties any more, because they didn't have the energy for such things, and their pension wasn't enough for it, but they were still in good form. So more than ten Novembers have passed. Fourteen, maybe fifteen.

When December came, Mother would always turn the house upside down in preparation for the holidays, but this time she turned it upside down and back again, a hundred times over. She must have done it to spite him—after all, they were supposed to go to their daughter's for Christmas Eve. "Woman, verily I say unto thee: cease thy labor"—whenever he got boiling mad, the language of the Bible would take possession of him. The greater his fury, the more solemn the rhetoric. In the depth of his heart, Christmas Eve at their daughter's suited him even less than it suited Mother, but of what significance is the depth of one's heart? In the depth of his heart, even the son-in-law who had joined the Party was pious.

In the new house, which he had built at the foot of Jarzębata Mountain, there was enough room to put up eight Christmas Eve tables and eight Christmas trees. You could have Christmas Eve in the dining room, Christmas Eve in the hearth room, Christmas Eve in the salon downstairs, you could have Christmas Eve everywhere. And there was half—and maybe even an eighth—of the work with the cooking and the baking, because there were also eight burners and ovens in the kitchen, and maybe eighty-eight. And you don't have to wash the dishes, because there is a machine that washes them for you. They have amazing things there: all the furniture in the world, even a rocking chair.

"You two take a rest, have real holidays for once in your lives, I'll take care of everything," their daughter practically choked with joy at the prospect of *the first Christmas Eve in the new house*. Everything she said was indisputable, and yet you had the impression that she was talking nonsense—the nature of the world is unfathomable. Please yourself. Peace be to this house. You can have a chair that rocks, a machine that washes dishes, verily I say unto you: you can even have, brothers and sisters, a toilet that will wipe your rear for you. But they agreed, because how could they not agree. Before long, they would be sitting at the Christmas Eve table by themselves.

So Mother got down to *resting*. She began *to rest* with a vengeance. Every year it was a horror from morning to night: cleaning, sweeping, putting things in order, but now it seemed that she would jump out of her skin. She scrubbed the runners and the rugs on both sides. She totally emptied all the wardrobes, and she laundered every blouse, skirt, shirt. The same thing with the sideboard: she washed and polished sets of silver that hadn't been used since the war, she lined shelves with parchment paper, she brought every knife, every fork, every spoon to a jeweler's sheen. She wiped the hobs on the kitchen stove with an emery cloth. She went through the attic. She almost tackled the store, which is practically impossible to enter by now. She almost set out upon the impassable ocean of objects. Luckily, she gave up. But now she scrubbed every lamp—not just every lamp—she unscrewed and scrubbed every bulb from every lamp. She washed the walls, which were covered with oil paint. She dug out from under the benches old ugly shoes that no one would ever again put on a foot, and she gave them a good shine. It isn't worth talking about waxing the floors, washing the windows, laundering the drapes and the curtains, that was a constant—now, it goes without saying, the variants increased infinitely. His blood boiled, he did his best to restrain her, but she didn't respond. After one of the times, when, on the verge of apoplexy, he roared for the hundredth time—"Woman, verily I say unto thee: cease thy labor!"—she raised her head and said with a colorless, tired voice: "A person has lost everything in life, and now even the holidays are gone."

What was he supposed to do? He helped as much as he could, although by evening he was barely alive and could hardly see anything. And when, two days before Christmas Eve, he finally went in the late evening into the back room and began to prepare himself for bed, and he glanced at the wall, and he saw what he saw—he thought at first that this was finally the last straw and that his eyes had entirely given out from the stress. True, he hadn't gone completely blind, he wasn't plunged into eternal darkness, but from that time forth, he would see only apparitions. From today, only terrible visions would present themselves to him. The first of them was this: that, on the wall over the bed, in the place where, ever since his fiftieth birthday, the golden-silver *tableau* had been hanging, there now hangs the portrait of Gustaw Branny.

He remembered that portrait from before the war. For a while yet, after their wedding, that likeness of Mother's first fellow had been hanging in the icehouse. Whether it was there until the deaths of the old Brannys, he wasn't sure. But after their deaths, for certain after the war, it had been taken down and carried off to the store, and it had vanished for the ages in the avalanche of junk. Perhaps it had even gone up in flames one winter in the stove? But it is unlikely that Mother cast it into the fire, and he would most likely have remembered such a distinctive action as burning the portrait of his predecessor. And he thought that he was *not* now seeing the portrait of the Gustaw who was killed on the motorbike, but rather his prewar specter; that everything had gotten mixed up in his head and that, instead of the genuine one, the prewar wall was presenting itself to his half-blind eyes, and the wall from another room to boot. I won't believe it until I touch it. So he touched it. And still he didn't believe.

The dawn of the next day came nonetheless, and in the snowy bright it was impossible—either through tricks of sight or through losses in the field of vision—to avoid the painful truth: that Mother, in the fervor of her cleaning, had introduced a new order. No illusions. She had taken the little homemade birthday greeting down from the wall and hung Gustaw's portrait in its place. He had never been jealous of him. Never did he harbor in his heart even a hint of despicable male sorrow that he hadn't been the first. Perhaps even on the contrary. Perhaps he was so happy that the other one had gotten himself killed that he had understanding for him even in this? All the joy the guy experienced in his short life was during that year after his wedding. And what could his joy have been, when Death was circling around him the entire time? Perhaps he even knew that a sudden end had been allotted him? Perhaps he had heard or seen signs? What is there to envy in this? God protect us against everything that Gustaw Branny had in life.

Nor was he jealous of anyone later on. It was more likely Mother—a far sight more likely that it was Mother—who could have been jealous of various female postal clerks. And she *was* jealous. And she had reasons for it. And what reasons they were! Jesus Christ! I was nine years old, Grandpa Pech often took me along to the post office, and at least three girls in tight-fitting navy blue smocks awakened mad desires in me. I stared at them greedily, and I was absolutely certain that at least two of them were reciprocating my gazes. I was ready for everything, and they were ready for everything. In any case, at least one of them was most certainly ready.

Someone will try to explain to me now, with psychoanalytic erudition, that, in the postal pinafores that highlighted their shapes, they looked like thoroughly mature versions of my female classmates, and that is why they turned me on so much. That's right. That was precisely their appearance—thoroughly mature fourth-graders. And what of it? This doesn't change the tension they aroused in me, and I in them. And the tension *Grandpa* aroused in them? Mr. Chief? Who had passed his *matura* before the war? A romantic lover, the strength of whose feelings was so great that it blew his rival off a speeding motorcycle as if he were a feather? A man whose fervent prayers were answered for the return to him of a woman betrothed to another? The hero, for that reason, of local ballads and incredible love stories? A lieutenant from the September campaign? A well-built man in the prime of life? A believer, and yet intelligent? A drinker, and yet refined? Born here, but speaking like a Varsovian? A connoisseur of the Bible, and of chess? That's right: my Grandpa Andrzej Pech was a man of panache and eroticism. In my parts, to this day, these are exotic attributes. My parts are not the land of panache and eroticism. My parts are the land of divine signs, suppressed passions, and photographs of young boys in Wehrmacht uniforms hidden away in secret drawers.

No two ways about it. Grandma Pech, even if nothing ever happened, had countless reasons to be jealous. He didn't have any. But now, when the portrait of Gustaw had appeared over his bed, he realized that for several decades in his wife's life there had existed a stream about which he hadn't had a clue and about which he hadn't guessed in the least. A story long ago finished—it turns out—wasn't finished at all.

The thought never crossed his mind that Mother, who was in cahoots with dead people, had some sort of particular contact with her deceased husband. He hadn't connected the one with the other. In his jealousy over otherworldly signals, there wasn't a hint of jealousy over Gustaw. But now there appeared not the hint, but the jealousy itself, painful to boot, the sort of jealousy that is aroused not by trysts, but by letters written in a hidden and secret cipher. Were they engaged in some sort of spiritualistic correspondence? In some sort of occult communication? Was he speaking from the other world? Was he making some sort of signs? Maybe all that constant knocking of various dead people, or of those preparing for death, was a smoke screen covering uninterrupted signals and signs? Had the deceased Gustaw Branny been pounding on the kitchen window since before the war? Was he assuring her of a love that had outlasted death? Was he whispering to her, telling her what to do? Now, in the course of the holiday cleaning, had he tapped out the request to return his portrait to its place over the bed? Lord God, forgive the short temper, but this version of life beyond the grave, this version of repenting souls, or even this version of the resurrection of the body—*this* is out of the question. Entirely out of the question. In any case, *he* certainly didn't hear anything. He didn't hear anything, but he certainly sees the portrait over the bed. Until yesterday his birthday *tableau* had been hanging there, and now it was the portrait of the other one. Now it was over the other one that the Guardian Angel was keeping watch. At least Mother didn't clear the bed away. Verily, woman, I render you grateful obeisance that you didn't take my marriage bed from me! A marriage bed, moreover, that is not my marriage bed, but the bed of your first betrothed, from almost half a century ago! Jesus Christ! You have to stop thinking. Life has already passed, and there is no point in recreating it anew in one's thoughts. Especially if it was different than you thought. You have to stop thinking. You have to go to your daughter's for Christmas Eve.

VII

ACROSS THE BRIDGE, AROUND THE SPORTS CENTER, THEN RIGHT AND a little bit more toward Partecznik, and there you are. The whole time, a level, straight road, only later, just before the house, does it get steep, but also not for more than twenty yards. On Christmas Eve itself, it snowed the entire afternoon, but the ploughs were out driving like God knows what. It was probably because some Party mandarin in the little castle on Kubalonka was putting on a Christmas Eve fête, and the whole vicinity was on alert. They dressed up as was fitting, they strapped to the sled the net with the presents and the great pot of cabbage that Mother cooks every year for Christmas, and giddy-up! Giddy-up to Jarzębata Mountain! They went, and all the time it seemed to them that this wasn't Christmas Eve, because, after all, on Christmas Eve you don't budge from the house. Even in thirty-nine, in order to get home in time for Christmas Eve, Grandpa Pech had made a run for it from a German transport. And he got there on time. But now they are leaving home, and, wrapped in thick blankets up to their ears, like a couple of vagrants, they drag the sled with the bundles behind them.

They don't know the word unreality; on the contrary, everything they pass on the way—that was their world. The park, the Monument to the Silesian Woman, the bridge, the mill buried up to its roof, the completely frozen Mill Stream, the Stawarczyks' house and the Mitręgas' cottage, the prewar villa of Professor Gawlas, the footbridge over the stream, the turn toward Partecznik. The lights at the house of Janek from Wymowa were on, probably he is already sitting down to supper with Hela. Then another bit, as if through a gigantic corridor of snow; finally, the white wall of the forest and the dark silhouettes—ours are already waiting for us.

But no one runs out to meet them, they stand as if frozen, from close up they all also look strange and uncomfortable. What, in the name of God the Father, has happened on this Christmas Eve? Nothing has happened. Nothing big has happened. It was just that the snowplow hadn't removed the snow right up to the house, because it is too steep, and now it wasn't clear how Mama would make it up there. Grandpa would somehow manage, but Grandma—with those legs of hers? She can manage on level ground, even uphill, but not in snow like that. Somehow we'll manage. But how? Maybe we should take the bundles off the sled and come up with some way to slide her up there on the sled? Out of the question. She would sink and be suffocated, on Christmas Eve to boot. So how? No idea. We've got to come up with something, because everyone will freeze to death here; they were forecasting minus twenty-five degrees for that night. My Christmas Eve story is silence full of helpless shame. Grandma Pech's story about Gustaw's death was a single-sentence. In my Christmas Eve story there is no room for even one sentence.

Suddenly an absolute idea flashes in my head, suddenly I feel like the writer who, finally, after a long silence, has composed a phrase that is not only beautiful, but also thoroughly true, and who knows that after that phrase others would follow, equally beautiful and true. Suddenly, he feels the pride of the group leader, the ship captain, the troop chief, perhaps even the pride of the family father, who, with one gesture and one thought, finds the way out of a stalemate. And so I say, with hasty enthusiasm, that it would be best and safest for Grandma to force a safe passage through the snow on the wicker rocking chair, which is standing by the fireplace. We'll seat her comfortably and, as if on a throne with runners, as if on a royal sleigh, we'll haul her right up to the threshold. And I'm already half turned, at a half run, already as if on angel's wings, I fly to get the rocking chair, which will immediately become a novelistic vehicle, and I hear how Father and Mother suddenly begin spasmodically to shout each other down: Out of the question! The chair will be destroyed! Absolutely out of the question! The new piece of furniture will be destroyed! Out of the question. And I freeze, and everyone freezes, as if the whole frost forecast for that night, and even a frost two hundred degrees colder, had come falling down from the heavens at precisely that moment.

My aunt, the pious bigot, explains that perhaps there wouldn't be great damage, and perhaps none at all—after all, the snow was fresh, and as clean as a whistle to boot. But what are you talking about! You have to have air for brains to say such reckless things! Who wastes things that were acquired with the sweat of one's brow? Who? What is more, everything, every little thing was wangled through connections! Where are you going to find a chair like that now? Where? Nowhere! And everyone understands, and Grandma Pech understands, and Grandpa Pech understands, and he says: Peace be to this house! And with a firm motion he takes Grandma by the arm, and off they go.

Jerzy Pilch

They move decisively, and they walk quickly. The way now seems shorter, the sky full of stars, the snow crunches under their feet. It is as if Grandpa even sees a bit better, and her leg—miracle of miracles!—hurts less. She has a bit of a guilty conscience that she has made such a muddle, but she feels his hand, he feels her arm, and he knows that this is the arm of the woman of his life. The closer they get to home, the more sprightly their expressions, the more their moods improve. It is good to return home for Christmas Eve.

Right off, Grandma will warm up the rest of the cabbage, which she had left in the pantry for New Year's. They will sit down to the table, say a prayer, share the Host with each other, and sing: "The time of joy and cheer to this world has arisen! For a Savior, a Redeemer, to sinful man is given!" And then Grandpa, in a surge of euphoric spirits, which he hadn't felt for years, will grab the round stool and head off toward the clocks. He hadn't wound them for God knows how long. Already the year before—even after lugging a painter's ladder into the house and climbing up on it as high as he could—instead of clock faces he saw blurry white spots. Now, on Christmas Eve, he didn't regain his sight, but, so it seems, he counts on a more spectacular miracle.

He winds one after the other, he turns the key with youthful verve, he moves the hands by intuition, which is to say—blindly. The last clock in the last room hangs directly across from the portrait of Gustaw Branny. Granted, in his all-embracing euphoria, Grandpa does *not* come to the sudden conclusion that the old photograph fits in here quite nicely, that perhaps it is an even better decoration than the faded *tableau* from ages ago; the entire burden did *not* disappear from his heart, but he shrugs it off as a mere trifle: one has other truly important matters to deal with! He winds the last clock and, weary from his high-wire stunts, he returns to the kitchen and waits for the new hour. And the minutes drag on, as in sleepless nights, and finally it is nine, and at first, for a long time, for a very long time, nothing happens, and nothing but an even more dramatic ticking is to be heard. Then—as if someone were taking an endlessly deep breath, as if someone in the depths of the house were pushing on a door handle, as if a dropped ten-złoty coin were rolling endlessly long across the floor—the slowly gathering racket of the springs, finally one clock, with the greatest difficulty, tolls three times, another not at all, the third rasps and wheezes, like a patient attempting in vain to come around from general anesthesia, the fourth begins to toll feverishly and ceaselessly, as if it were announcing fire or war, the fifth is carried away with the volcanic cough of the dying consumptive. Grandma hides her head in her arms, she has a terrible desire to laugh, but she doesn't want to hurt Grandpa with her laughter; she leans over the table and doesn't see that he, too, more and more heartily, and more and more proudly, smiles to himself.

VIII

She died nine years after his death, and she behaved dreadfully at the time. Not as dreadfully as Pospiszil, but, nonetheless, as if she didn't believe in God at all. She didn't want the pastor. In the end, it was only after long persuasion and urging that, not even so much with reluctance as with hostility, she received communion. Then for three days she howled and shouted; we weren't certain whether it was in delirium. I don't want to die, I don't want to die, she repeated with a voice so hoarse it seemed absolutely not hers. From her leg flowed puss mixed with blood, as if from an open faucet. Before her very last breath, she livened up so much that it seemed that her strength had really returned, as if she had recovered and arisen from the dead. Then she collapsed somehow strangely into the depths of the damp sheets. It was clear that this was the end. The end, but not quite. Suddenly, with yet another strangely energetic motion, she reached her hand out in our direction, and with a bent finger she indicated that someone should follow her. She wanted to take someone with her. There's no point in trying to hide it: everyone had real shivers going up and down their spines. Father died a year later. Death never ends. As we were burying him, a black tropical storm passed over one half of the cemetery. Ten yards away there was still sun, but over his grave it poured so much that it seemed that any moment his coffin would float to the top.

The rocking chair is still like new. No one has sat in it for thirty years. Once it suddenly rocked in the void. As if a powerful draft had passed through the closed doors and windows. As if someone nearby had spread their wings darkened by the damp.

A Chapter about a
Figure Sitting Motionless

I

ANKA CHOW CHOW WAS CRAZY ABOUT GIRLS, AND THE PIPE DREAM
of the majority of men—to find themselves in an intimate situation
with two young women who have a thing for each other—was within
reach.

It took a few months, however, before I realized what sort of chance
was standing before me. I was approaching fifty at a dizzying pace,
and for two years I had become less and less successful at hiding an
unpleasant fact: namely, that I was becoming obtuse at an equally
galloping tempo. Above all, I wasn't able to hide it from *myself* under
any circumstances.

I didn't recall the family names of people I knew perfectly well. I
would forget the first names of my closest friends. I would ask someone a question, and a minute later I would repeat it, convinced that
I was asking it for the first time. Keys, glasses, IDs, watch, money,
telephone—everything was constantly vanishing without a trace.

Every morning I took fortifying vitamins and pills that are supposed to enhance the working of the brain, but by around noon I was never a hundred percent certain whether I had already taken the redemptive tablets, or not yet. Plans I had made to meet with people slipped my mind. Telephone numbers I had known by heart for years—as if drowned in my bodily fluids—blurred and couldn't be recreated. I had to check the day's date a hundred times. A few times, while filling out various forms, I had to really concentrate in order to recall my own address. Forget about family names. A year ago, maybe half a year, for a good quarter of an hour, I wasn't able to recall the first name of John Paul II.

In such a pitiful state, it wasn't so much that I didn't even understand Anka Chow Chow's hints for a long time—just as perverse as they were subtle—as that they completely escaped my attention. She was always the first to notice the super misses on the street. She subtly sketched breathtaking scenes, she tempted with the skill of the seasoned habitué, and I didn't have a clue about what was going on. It's quite another matter that a deception had taken place at the beginning, which excuses me a little, although it adds no finesse to the affair. In any event: at the dawning there was a deception, which lulled me to sleep.

Namely, when, on the first night, I poured a hailstorm of typical male questions upon Anka, she answered them all in the negative. Or, at best, hesitantly. No. Never. Don't know. Maybe. When? What do you mean when? When was your first time? Don't know. At the university? No. In the *lyceum*? No. Grade school? No. Well, when then? Never. You were never with a guy? No. The left hand doesn't know what the right hand is doing? No, it doesn't. If it wasn't with a guy, then maybe with a girl? No. Listen, I don't want to be indiscrete, but whom *were* you with finally? Nobody. Nobody? Nobody. He was a nobody? No. He turned out to be a nobody? He didn't exist at all. You don't want to talk about him? No. He was a nobody, because you don't know who it was? No. No one? Don't know. You don't know by what miracle it happened? Don't know. You suddenly found yourself at a risqué party? Maybe. You got drunk, and you don't remember anything? I've never been drunk in my life. If you weren't drunk, you have to remember. Don't have to. Have to. I'm the specialist on memory losses in this story. You have to remember. You can't remember something that didn't happen. I'm not sure we are understanding each other: I'm not asking how many times you went with whom, or whether you were engaged; I'm asking who it was you slept with. I didn't sleep with anyone. Are you sure? Yes.

Anka Chow Chow had never slept with anyone, and not so much that piece of news in itself, as the laborious road of questioning to get there, so exhausted my cognitive facilities that along the way I didn't notice how she shuddered and swallowed hard when the question came about the girlfriends. She denied it, but she shuddered and swallowed hard.

She was twenty-three years old, and she was a virgin. I didn't get excessively excited about this. In times of excesses, you come across excesses like this one, too. For instance, these days, among the thoroughly purebred aristocracy, the snobbism of the old-style wedding night is supposedly spreading. True, Anka didn't look like a purebred aristocrat—or any other sort of melancholic who isn't in a hurry to go to bed with you—but that was without significance. The reasons why she remained pure to such a ripe old age—whatever they were—were not sensational. Anka's virginity was not in and of itself sensational. What was sensational was the fact that, in spite of having slept with me, she desperately maintained that she remained intact.

Daybreak was approaching, and she was still intact! A bloody, icy sun was rising over the horizon, and she dug in her heels, insisting that nothing had changed! After a night spent in my arms, she was still intact! And that was after a night without sleep! After an active night! Exceptionally active! Without any miracles, because never, not even in my glory days, did I perform miracles, nor did I promise them, and now—it goes without saying—all the more so; or rather—all the less so. After all, I am growing weaker not only in the brain. Last week, for example, I did five deep knee bends on the balcony, the result of which was that I sustained a painful contusion of the calf muscle. And so, I repeat, without any miracles and without acrobatics. But what was supposed to happen, happened. But I was in you, wasn't I? Yes, you, were, but not entirely. I'm not completely typical.

In fact, her architecture *was* atypical, and although her long (five feet, eleven and a half inches) serpentine body performed remarkable contortions, it wasn't easy to slither into her. But for God's sake! I did it! And not just once that night! And not just superficially, but profoundly! I have gone dull-witted, perhaps I have hardening of the arteries, the beginnings of Alzheimer's or Parkinson's, but, after all, it isn't the case that half an hour ago I hadn't had a woman, and now I am dreaming that I slid into her to the full length. If it were the other way around—that I had had her half an hour ago, but now the fact had completely slipped my mind—I would be quicker to agree. But this? Although, on the whole? Who knows? There is no way to be sure. The sex maniac always overestimates his possibilities. And the sex maniac who is aging and showing signs of dementia? Forget about it. I decided to stick to the facts. I decided to recreate the events step by step, and even to record the facts.

II

HALF A YEAR AGO, I WAS ABANDONED BY THE LAST IN A SERIES OF women with whom I had intended to live in a house eternally buried in snow, watch films on HBO in the evenings, drink tea with raspberry juice, etc. I will answer the question whether that was the fledgling singer in a lizard-green dress with a warning: never get involved with fledgling artists. If they begin to develop—art will, perhaps, be a winner, but life (especially yours) will be the loser. And if they don't begin to develop—well, forget about it.

However this may be, feeling an ever more painful void and despair, I plunged once again into the whirlwind of casual comforts. Each time, the desperation of such doings was greater, and their effect—ever more pathetic. I tried to pick up waitresses in bars, saleswomen in stores, I sought out girls sitting alone in movie theaters. With lonely female swimmers on the brain, I began to go to the pool. In a search of rash manicurists, I became a regular client of beauty salons. Since it is much easier to find a vegetarian on her own than a carnivorous single, I forced myself to eat the grassy fodder, and I started frequenting vegan bars. I responded to even the riskiest of invitations, and I wandered around what were often completely hopeless vernissages, launchings, and premières. I went to shopping centers. It has long been well known that, in the heat of shopping, some young ladies grow weak and bare their souls in risqué fashion. Almost every day, I spent some time at Central Station, and, in the shoals of female travelers ceaselessly swimming through the underground passageways, I sought out those *who quite obviously were not in any special hurry.* By some miracle, I refrained from the street pick-up, but I considered completely seriously listing a matrimonial classified in the newspaper.

I placed great hopes in Empik bookstores and music shops. For a guy past fifty, who is afflicted with mental deconcentration, these were not bad spots. After all, I was unlikely to penetrate discotheques, cult bars, or enthusiastically engage in *clubbing.* And it wasn't a matter of my old gray head, which could arouse panic and embarrassment in such company. I could handle that with ease. I've gotten through much greater moments of shame in my life. For me, for motor reasons, there can be no question of any form whatsoever of late-evening, to say nothing of night life. In the evening—I'll say something shocking now—I'm often sleepy. After watching "The Facts" and the main broadcast of "The Evening News," my day is basically done. I'll look the newspaper over once again in the armchair, glance again at the book I've been reading for a week, but my head is getting heavy, my eyelids are drooping. In that sense, the bookstores or other newsstands that are open until 10 P.M. are night clubs as far as I am concerned, and at that late hour I didn't even go there.

I would drop by in the early afternoons and make a solemn inspection of the candidates. Only those who sat in the armchairs and read serious literature came into question, or who listened to classical music with cosmic headphones perched on their heads. Readers of magazines and those listening to rock I eliminated *a priori*—this is, by the nature of things, a shaky selection pool. I put my bets on connoisseurs of Beethoven and Tolstoy: communing with the classics usually guarantees quite decent perversions. Besides, it is clear that if they sit for a long time—reading carefully or listening at the store—they've got time. What is more, since they read and listen at the store, they quite clearly don't have a penny to their names. They clearly don't have enough cash to buy a book or a CD and take it home with them. Poverty is never especially required, but in this case it isn't bad. It is always easier to persuade, and to lure into harlotry, a poor one than a wealthy one. Finally, spying on what they are just then reading or listening to facilitates striking up the conversation remarkably.

But the matter is, I never did strike up a conversation. In practically none of the places mentioned did I once successfully strike up a conversation. I managed a few futile wheezings, but let's pull the curtains on all that. My agony was intense. I chased after them like a madman, and I set off like a lunatic, but I had no certainty, and the uncertainty weakened the beauty of the madness and the impertinence of the lunacy. Sensing that I didn't have a chance anyway with the conspicuous super babes, I placed my bets on the middling ones. But before I could approach the middling-gal I had singled out, I was seized by embarrassment over taking the easy way out, and I gave it up. Falling from one extreme into another, I now raised the bar to the maximum, and I desperately swore that from now on I would penetrate nothing but masterpieces. But whenever any miracle of nature appeared, I lacked reflexes and courage. As a result, the one and the other, and basically all of them, slipped by right under my nose. I would return home, and the mistakes I had made, the capitulations and the bad estimations, made my head burst. Suddenly, I became starkly aware what treasures had slipped through my fingers that afternoon. In my imagination, I replayed all the episodes one more time, corrected the mistakes, I was quick and decisive; now everything was a success, everything came true, the specter of the beauty seen an hour before took me by the arm, set her hair and her shoulder strap in order, and the pain was unbearable.

At the same time, I tried to keep a tight rein on myself. I didn't spend entire days searching for the next woman of my life. In the mornings, I worked as before, although somewhat more nervously. Toward evening, as usual, I would drop by *Yellow Dream* for a grapefruit juice. Every two or three weeks, I would make the trip to watch Cracovia matches. Somehow I got by. Somehow, with the greatest difficulty, I continued to breathe.

III

I don't rule out the possibility that I traveled to Cracovia matches in order to liberate myself, even briefly, from apparitions. While I was still on the express train to Krakow, I would check to see what sort of female travel companions were sitting in the adjoining compartments—but just as a matter of habit and reflex, without translation to reality. Whoever travels knows that there are always at least a few intriguing female travelers in every express train between Krakow and Warsaw. But the fact that I left them alone was not a question of choice. By getting on the train at Central Station, in a certain sense I was abandoning myself. I left my Warsaw solitude, which was unbearable and without which I couldn't live, and, together with that solitude, I left the despair of warding it off.

I hope this is clear. Although it is entirely clear only to those who wake up alone, turn on the radio, take a shower, and are not even in the worst of moods. Who knows? Maybe they will meet somebody today.

It is completely clear only for those who eat their dinner alone in an almost empty café and lose their sense of taste. Even when they daringly order the most expensive *frutti di mare*, their sense of taste is gone—the whole time, it seems to them that, besides them, no one eats alone. Besides them, no one ever eats alone—the entire city sees this, and everybody is staring at them. How many times can you look at your watch and let the audience know that you have dropped by just in order to have a bite as quickly as possible, since in a moment— thank you very much!—you have an incredible date, perhaps it will last until the crack of dawn. So how are you supposed to perform *the bite as quickly as possible*, when you feel like sitting a bit, even with a leaden heart; and everyone knows that it was only after leaving that the lead would become all consuming.

It is completely clear only for those who wake up in the night, and their throats go numb because they are alone; they have no one to embrace or to cover up, they have no one to bring a glass of juice from the kitchen, and in the morning they won't have anyone with whom to listen to the radio, read the paper, eat breakfast.

It is entirely completely clear to those who, one fine day, actually meet someone, eat dinner with someone, go with someone to the movies, go to bed with someone—perhaps even sleep with someone.

But it is absolutely completely clear to those who wake up in the middle of the night and are terrified by someone sleeping next to them, and by the thought that they won't be on their own for a few hours more, and then the whole morning, and it is awful, awful. And they count the seconds and minutes of the never ending nightmare, and somehow—with the greatest difficulty—they survive it; and then they are granted a beautiful, solitary day. They take a deep breath and suddenly feel how an overwhelming joy gives depth to their breath- ing. From the empty house, they gaze through the window at the city's rooftops rising before them. The long afternoon has the taste of overripe cherries and the scent of a stuffy garden. In the evening, the telephone rings persistently; with a strange smile they do not lift the receiver.

IV

I was so accustomed to solitude, I made of solitude such an endlessly thick basis for life, that the quotidian circumstances in which people feel lonely—a journey, a train, a night in a hotel—these were, for me, crowded meetings and mass entertainments. Obviously, I preferred that no one come into my compartment (first class, smoking, by the door), but once someone did come in—be my guest, we can even exchange a few words. But on the whole, no one did come in—I have an inhospitable facial expression. I was traveling to a Cracovia match, and I felt as if someone had taken a leaden overcoat from my shoulders. I had before me a day, or even two, during which I would desire nothing other than that my team win. I wouldn't be chasing after anyone. I wouldn't be experiencing future fiascos, I wouldn't spend the evenings making inquiries into what mistakes I had made and what God-sent opportunities I had wasted. Even if I should wake up bright and early in my hotel room, these wouldn't be any sort of black hours. I would put on a bathrobe, order a pot of strong coffee and a dozen or so pieces of letter paper from *room service*, and I would write down what I dreamed.

I made the trips to Cracovia matches as if going on holidays or vacations. My constantly overheated nerves would calm. I would sit in the stadium of my childhood. Over the Rudawa flowed the same clouds. Behind my back was the Gomułka-era apartment block from which I had once wanted to leap. Before me, the Commons, overgrown with Asiatic grasses—everything was still like my memories, and everything had already changed, as after death. Orchestras played the most beautiful marches in the world, torches made of newspapers burned, there were no darknesses over the stadium, the singing of the fans rose on high. For ninety minutes, plus the halftime, I had the feeling of complete harmony—there was no despair, no longings, the hunger for touch did not consume me, I didn't think about women, there weren't any women.

As you can easily surmise, I caught sight of Anka Chow Chow for the first time in my life at a Cracovia match. True, she claims that this was not the first but the second time—that, however, is an ambiguous claim.

She sat a few rows lower, and throughout the entire match (Cracovia-Górnik Łęczna) her unparalleled head didn't even budge. During the halftime, I went down and stood right beside her. She sat motionless. I attempted, purely rhetorically, to make eye contact. The warrior's repose is one thing, but an unparalleled head is quite another. Besides this, the situation itself, the image itself—a babe at a match (to speak precisely: such an unparalleled babe at such a miserable match)—was a complete innovation. I didn't tumble immediately into the abyss, I didn't fall into the routine ruts, I didn't jump into my old skin. The stadium didn't suddenly become the next place for the hunt. My peace was not disturbed, but my curiosity was mightily aroused. Her perfectly indifferent sight was firmly fixed on the middle of the field. I returned to my place.

I know what you are thinking. It seems to you that, since I had come upon a young miss at a soccer match, I ought immediately to have surmised that something wasn't quite right with her. The jigsaw puzzle is constructed from the very beginning as a logical whole, except that I didn't see it. Or I pretend not to see it. But after all, it is obvious: a young miss, a lone young miss to boot, goes to a match— something isn't right. I don't know. I don't know whether something isn't right with a young miss who goes to a match by herself. I haven't the faintest clue. But I do know that with Anka everything was right! Absolutely entirely right! As right as can be. She wasn't, not in the least, some sort of tomboy or possessed of a manly nature that had been imprisoned in a woman's body. More than that. Among the women known to me, she was in the absolute top tier of femininity. She was feminine in the deepest and thoroughly Heraclitean sense. In addition to which, she was terribly hot for girls, she liked girls, she liked chatting with girls, she was curious about girls, and she had nothing against far reaching adventures with girls. If you think that there is some sort of contradiction here—that's your business. I don't know the secret of her soul and body, and, to tell the truth, I never even tried to find out. I am writing down only what I experienced and what I saw. I experienced a lot, I saw "as if."

Nothing in her came from the masculine element, from masculine disguise, from a masculine interference. And even if it did—what of it? What does this explain? What sort of relief does such psychology bring? What sort of initiation and what sort of knowledge? There was—let's assume—some sort of excessive masculine element in Anka. So what is this supposed to prove? What is supposed to follow from this? Yet another proof of the Lord God's absent-mindedness, in that, when He was creating Anka, He measured out the proportions imprecisely? Yet another confirmation of nature's blindness? And so what of the fact that God is imprecise, and nature blind? May the Lord God protect us against our own precision. And may He never bestow nature with too sharp a vision.

After the match, I returned to my hotel, took a hot shower, and slept like a log. I awoke at six. I ordered coffee and paper. Fog was hovering over the city; from down below you could hear the clatter of horses' hooves. I wrote a few sentences about Janek Nikandy, but I still had the sense of the complete elusiveness of his life. Suddenly and feverishly I felt like returning to Warsaw. A sudden fear and a sudden longing. The fear that something would happen, that someone would imprison me here, and I would never return to Sienna Street. And a horrendous longing for my 430 square feet, which are like the deck of a lifeboat. All my life I had been swimming in deep water and in the darknesses, and finally, toward the end, I felt the hardwood floor under my feet, and a good light falls from behind the armchair. A sudden longing for Warsaw, as if I'd spent I don't know how many years in God knows what sort of emigrations. Supposedly the greatest nightmare of emigrants is the dream that they are back in the home country and can't leave. My greatest nightmare? Toward morning, J.P. appears and says I will never return home. As in life, he trembles from hatred. I curse him as in life. I curse his eternal torments. O God, cause it that he not suffer for all eternity; cause him to disappear once and for all.

My longing took on no desperate and caricatured incarnation. I went down to breakfast calmly, I ate—as is always the case in a hotel—significantly more than normal. I collected my few pieces of gear, and I set off for the train station on foot. Along the way, on Pijarska Street, I got a stock of newspapers for the road. The express trains from Krakow to Warsaw depart on the hour. I easily made it in time for the nine o'clock train.

In first class, the compartment for smokers was completely empty. I ensconced myself skillfully; I picturesquely strewed newspapers, bag, and jacket on the seats. No one could be in doubt that all those objects belonged to numerous travelers, who had just that moment stepped out for a second; every last one of them—it goes without saying—a smoker. In order to confirm this, I smoked for six, closed the door to the corridor, and drew the curtains. Musty train car air turned, in the blink of an eye, into molten stone. There was a minute until departure, I was already in a state of homeostasis, in other words equilibrium, when the door opened, the curtains parted, and into the compartment stepped—you guessed correctly—Anka Chow Chow.

My heart soared on high, my soul—so be it—sang out, but my defensive habits, plus my hardened arteries, did their bit. "This is a compartment for smokers," I snarled ferociously. "*For . . . for . . .*" I found myself tongue-tied. The more difficult word—*compartment*—I remembered; the banal one—*smoking*—completely slipped my mind, but I immediately remembered and snarled out the entire phrase, although at the end in a voice incomparably weaker than at the beginning. To tell the truth, at the beginning my voice was routinely hostile, but at the end—having overcome my habits and realized who the miraculous interloper was—it was inordinately ingratiating.

Here is compartment for smoking. As God is my witness, I couldn't help myself. Linguistic degradation consists not only in the fact that, with age, one's vocabulary shrinks. This isn't all that painful; in the end you can always find some synonym or periphrastic formula. What is painful, truly painful, is the persistence in one's head of a constant store of phrases, which—whether you want it or not, whether they fit the context or not—one pronounces automatically in a certain moment and with a dull satisfaction.

"I know that this compartment is for smokers," her voice was like shivering steel, "I'm looking for a compartment for smokers."

"During the match you didn't smoke. At least I didn't notice that you did."

"I didn't smoke during the match," she said very slowly. "During the match I didn't smoke," she repeated even more slowly and examined me carefully; or you would rather have to say that she struck me with a short, forceful gaze. "I didn't smoke at the match because I don't smoke any more. For a year—however this might sound—I haven't had a cigarette in my mouth."

Before I managed to express my eager and highest amazement, she pointed out a mighty impressive bag to me with her glance. With my last bits of strength and with the greatest difficulty, refraining from any commentaries concerning what must have made it weigh two tons, I placed the ghastly duffel on the rack.

"What were we talking about?" I was panting like a dog.

"We? I don't believe we were talking. For the moment, you were attempting not to let me into the compartment."

"Oh yes, of course," I shouted almost triumphantly. In any case, the life of the dementia sufferer is not the worst; true, it is full of black collapses, but once a person recalls something, it's like an orgasm. "Oh *yes*, of *course* . . ."

"I prefer the smell of cigarette smoke to the natural stench," she explained calmly. "Of the two evils, I prefer smoke. Don't feel hurt, but for the time being your only virtue is that you smoke Gauloises."

Jesus Christ, I quietly heaved a sigh, it's a good thing that this rabid she-cat doesn't have a tail. She would have destroyed the compartment with it.

V

Compared to Anka, I was lacking any sorts of lust whatsoever, a young virgin, innocent of the facts of life. My obsession with broads, compared to her obsession with broads, was nil. My debauchery, compared with her debauchery, was despicable. My thing for girls, compared with her thing for girls, wasn't a thing at all. My staring at women, compared with her staring at women, was clumsy, vulgar, and boorish.

I am not engaging in any sort of masochism, I'm not bowing and scraping before feminists, I'm not pouring the ashes of cremated instincts upon my male head. Granted, I can say that my staring at broads is bestial, but I can also say that it is metaphysical. I can repeat after Miłosz: "It's not that I desire these creatures precisely; I desire everything, and they are like a sign of ecstatic union." But I can also say: I stare at the them the way a dealer in live goods appraises the strongest female slaves. I stare all-embracingly.

Frankly speaking, I often leave the house only for that purpose. And if not only for that purpose, then *also* for that purpose. The constant thought that, on my way to work, shopping, the café, a meeting, or wherever, *I'd have a little look around* helps me live. That's how it always was. If not my whole life, then quite certainly well before the definitive departure of subsequent girlfriends.

If it weren't for the women I encounter on the street, I'd limit leaving the house to the absolute minimum. There are certain things I wouldn't do at all. Most certainly, I would drop by *Yellow Dream* for my afternoon grapefruit juice less frequently, and perhaps not at all. I would buy myself a juice maker, and it would come out cheaper. Nor would I take any walks around Warsaw. I've come to like this spectral city, but if I were supposed to take walks around it without encountering any girls—no thanks! I wouldn't spend time at Central Station, I wouldn't drop by department stores, I would even go less frequently to my dry cleaner on Hoża Street, where by some divine coincidence the best pieces of Warsaw ass have their super rags cleaned.

But there they are, and I circle among them. I circle, and I stare, sharply and importunately. Not that I have any sort of strategy for importunate staring. It is simply stronger, a thousand times stronger than me. I am incapable of not staring at décolletage. I stare ravenously, I salivate like a snot-nosed kid, my snout gapes like that of a village idiot, I stand there like the ninny at a wedding, I begin to sweat and to shake like a serial murderer. Whenever some super babe passes me by, there is no force on earth that can keep me from turning around to look. Quite often I don't just turn around to look, quite often—in order to lend stability to my backward gaze—I stop, and quite often the embarrassing thought of running after her does not seem embarrassing to me in the least. Whenever I see before me some noteworthy back, I lose consciousness.

I'm walking down the street, let's say it's Świętokrzyska, and my head is darting here and there like the president's bodyguard. I check out every passing woman, I am prepared for an assault from all sides, and I am ready to attack on all sides. I am unable to control this, even when I am with a woman.

When I was with the singer in the lizard-green dress, I moderated my staring, I tried not to stare, but often I couldn't manage it. I had more success in the company of Anka Chow Chow. I was scared to death of her, and because of that fear I didn't even have to pretend that I wasn't staring. I genuinely didn't stare. I didn't even cast any furtive glances. Until the moment when I realized that it was she who was staring for all she was worth. This didn't happen quickly, because she was a virtuoso. She took note of every detail of the make-up of every passing miss, but it looked like she hadn't even noticed that anyone had passed by. Even a normal, young, quick-witted fellow wouldn't have caught on right away, to say nothing of me. Besides, Anka's unyielding, still unyielding virginity was enough of a complication for me not to think about other complications.

"What do you like most in women?" she asked one day. "In what sense?" "In the sense of a part of the body. What turns you on the most? The bust? The rear? Legs?" "I don't know. It depends when," I answered. "It depends when. Depends who." "That's no answer." "It is impossible to parcel a woman out in body parts," I said loftily. "But of course it's possible. I begin with the back, and I advise you to do the same. The back is always interesting. The back is horribly important. A woman's back is an exceptional region." "Yes, yes," I said, "an exceptional region." I didn't remember anything. The back of Emma Lunatyczka, covered with icy sweat, like frost, and a complete void. I didn't focus on backs. I was an ordinary guy. Even a crazed sex maniac is, at his base—if I may so put it—an ordinary guy. And an ordinary guy checks, first of all, to see whether everything is in order. Whether or not, for instance, some sort of troublesome wart or a risky birthmark overgrown with a hard bristle sticks out. If it didn't stick out, things are OK. A back is a back. Just as long as there weren't any disturbances, especially of a textural sort, then things are OK. The back is nothing over which to go into transports of delight. Anka Chow Chow was higher by the length of that delight. She sang a hymn of praise and recited a great ode to the back. She told stories about the backs of Magda, Gocha, Bacha, Gracha, Ala, Ola, Viola, Jola, etc., etc. She told stories of the backs of the sleeping and the backs of the waking. About the backs of female masons, prisoners, and tennis players. About cold backs, warm backs, tired backs. About backs submerged in dusk. About the backs of Russian women, Irish women, and Bolivian women. Why precisely this combination—I don't know. Perhaps these were the acquaintances she happened to have, or perhaps it was a question of oceanic freckledness, Latin oliveness, and—for all I know—Siberian taste? Rocky backs, sandy backs, and backs as fluid as rivers. She devoted separate and—I'll say in all honesty—interminably boring strophes to a certain unparalleled back she had seen last summer on the beach in Kołobrzeg and which—she must have repeated a hundred times—she would never forget. "I could write a book about the female back," she said finally, and that probably wasn't an empty declaration. "The female back," she argued with passion, "is a neglected artistic field. Poets and novelists have rarely extolled the back, or not at all. In the *Song of Songs*—not a word about the Beloved's back. It is similar in innumerable romances and love poetry. It is much better with painting. Perhaps, in fact, you have to be a painter in order to feel and understand what an exceptional surface there is between the neck and the buttocks. Besides, just go and try to paint a back. It doesn't matter that you don't have any talent, those who do can't do it either. The bust, profile, shoulder, even the hand—*this* they more or less manage. But the back? Not even the most talented among them can capture the back. The back is the domain of the masters. Titian's backs. Rubens's backs. Forget about Rubens's busts. Take a good look at Rubens's backs. Examine how Rubens paints backs, and you will understand the meaning of sensuality. The first sensuality always concerns the back. Everybody blathers on in circles about the first kiss, but after all, it is always the case that, when you kiss her for the first time, your hand embraces her back. And without that embrace, without that hand on the back, there is no kiss. Just try to imagine the famous first kiss with your hands hanging loosely at the side of the body. Without touching the back there is no kiss, without touching the back there is no mutual inclination, without touching the back there is no sex, without touching the back there is no love."

Her fetishism confirmed an eloquent detail, which—it goes without saying—I noticed late. In general, it is good that I noticed it at all. The material for observation was abundant and near. She often brought girls along. To me. To my apartment. Like a complete sucker, I offered them permanent hospitality. Come on by, whenever you like, and with whom you like, the second room is free. Anka Chow Chow lived with her parents. This didn't bother her at all. Orgiastic inclinations are one thing, living with one's parents quite another. I understood this like Mozart understood music. Chasing after babes is one thing, waking up alone is quite another. My offer concerned the first part of that conjunction. Breakfast for three figured minimally in my considerations. But I imagined the role of host with juvenile generosity. Perhaps I didn't want to be the master of ceremonies, it wasn't quite *that* kitschy, but all the same I counted—no point in trying to hide it—I counted on the idea of being admitted one of these times.

She brought along girls who were wise and stupid, short and tall, with long hair and closely shorn, clothed indifferently and dressed to kill, fat and skinny, pretty and ugly, and when, finally, I began to suspect her of complete chaos in her tastes, I discovered the key. When, the next morning, I stumbled over the next backpack of the next girlfriend lying in the hallway, the puzzle arranged itself in a logical whole. Anka had a weakness for girls with backpacks. After the discovery of this shocking truth, I knew in advance the course of the subsequent evenings. If the girl who was accompanying Anka had a handbag, it ended with supper, and often only with tea. If the new conquest had a haversack or a shoulder bag, they would sit and chat for a long time, but always, even if it was in the middle of the night, the other one would go home. It was exclusively girls with backpacks who spent the night. On these occasions, supper would be intense, but short, they would quickly go to the other room, and the light was quickly turned off in there. Once, I couldn't stand it, I pretended that, half asleep, after a drink and in the dark, I had lost my way, and although I didn't see anything, to this day it seems to me that, in the white bank of tangled bedclothes, I saw Anka's hands on the duskiest and smoothest back in the world. (My delusions had not lost their panache.) I apologized, withdrew, and, pretending that I was reading a book, sat in the highest tension. It was just getting light when I finally heard steps. First Anka went to the bathroom, then looked in on me. "Why are you so upset?" she asked. "I hope you aren't jealous about a girl. Until you can remember where you saw me for the first time, nothing doing. To make it easier for you, I will add that it was not at the match. And if you remember, who knows—maybe?" She looked me in the eye, and it was clear that she knew my most shameful thoughts. She claimed that she was teasing me, but she inflicted torments upon me.

To force me to recall anything whatsoever—that was yanking my chain enough. To force me to recall something that I couldn't for the life of me recall—that was flagrant yanking. Just how much time had I spent in determining who looked like Tolstoy's son-in-law in a newspaper picture? And I was able to do that only because the matter concerned my childhood. Anka Chow Chow was most definitely not a character from my childhood. Of *that* I was one hundred percent certain.

Once, in my youth, a girl on a *Cross Section* cover enraptured me. There was something extraordinary in her facial features, in the arrangement of her shoulders (back?), in any case, I kept that issue for a long time, a very long time, I think it was still wandering about my papers until recently. Quite a few years later, I made the acquaintance of a fattish, but appetizing, retired model in her thirties. Among the yellowed photos from her glory days, which she eagerly showed me, was also that cover from *Cross Section*. The thought that the fattish retiree once had had an incarnation so intensely remembered by me gave unusual fuel to my fading desires. Now I instinctively repeated that path; I attempted to find among old photographs, images, street scenes, the one on which there appeared some sort of excavational image of Anka. Nothing of the sort came to the surface. I badgered her to give me at least some sort of trail, the trace of a trail. For a long time she dug in her heels, saying that she wouldn't.

Finally, seeing the total hopelessness of my dementia, she sighed and said: "OK, you could simply have seen me for the first time in *Yellow Dream*, since I, too, was a regular. The secret of our first meeting is not all that shocking. We simply saw each other in a café. As a consolation for that poverty, I'll tell you a certain story, or rather a scene, at which—in my opinion—you were present two or three years ago. That's right: you, too, were there indeed, drank the wine and the mead, but you didn't see a thing. Maybe you were staring in another direction, or maybe you were having a collapse. There isn't any sort of great plot to it, but hear me out, write it down, and print it; maybe the girl I will tell you about will read it, recognize the details, and report to us. I have been looking for her, and this story is like a letter in a bottle. I hope such a metaphor doesn't irritate you."

VI

AND SO, ONE DAY, LET'S SAY IT WAS ON FRIDAY, 2 SEPTEMBER, IN the year 2 . . . , a few minutes before 5 in the afternoon, Anka Chow Chow dropped by *Yellow Dream*, and, as she did every day, she ordered a double espresso. Her usual place by the window and at the same time right by the door—looking at it from within, on the righthand side—was occupied by a colorless and badly dressed girl feverishly tapping out SMSes.

"That spoiled my mood a bit, but only a bit. For the time being, it wasn't so bad that I would engage in a sclerotic battle for territory in a practically empty café. 'I beg your pardon most earnestly, but I always sit here. Would you care to . . . etc.'"

Nothing of the sort. She calmly sat down at that same panoramic window, except that she was four chairs to the right. Right in front of her, she had the little café garden, further, a view of Marszałkowska Street. She was in the very heart of Warsaw, and that still made an impression on her. Not that she was constantly staring at the Palace of Culture; for something like two years now, with the naturalness of the locals, she had ceased to notice that building, but she felt *not bad*—even *very* not bad—in its shadow.

She screened—if one may so put it—the house part and the garden part, and she didn't note anything worth noting. True, in the corner sat a rather ripe and rather spacious busty one with a daring décolletage in a brick-red dress, but her ripeness, spaciousness, bustiness, and even brick-redness could be located just as well on the plus side as the minus. Overall balance: zero. I do not need to add that in describing the *brick-red busty one*, Anka glanced at me unusually significantly. The phrase *brick-red busty one* made an impression on me, and I attempted to disinter her incarnation from countless layers of brain dust. Supposedly, I had stared at her so ravenously that I didn't see anything of the world beyond her. But neither her, nor the world beyond her, could I remember for all the tea in China.

The colorless girl finished tapping out SMSes, drank up what was left to drink, and left. Anka immediately moved and occupied her favorite position.

As a regular, I knew perfectly well the virtues of that spot. You sat on the invigorating border between the scorching day and the cold of the air conditioning; you saw everything, and simultaneously you remained in partial hiding. At any moment, you could set off on the chase for someone, and, at any moment, you could avoid unwanted company. At any moment, you could leave, or order something more, or—if a dire situation arose—you could dive into the depths and disappear in the toilet.

Anka took out a lighter and cigarettes. Before she lit up, that one wasn't yet there, but by the time she had lit up, she was already there. She must have arrived in the moment of concentration on the flame. In general, this didn't matter. It didn't matter in what fragment of a second and from what direction she arrived, whether she arrived from the left or from the right, whether from the Roundabout or from Wspólna Street. Nothing mattered. You could see with the naked eye that she was out of the question. And it is a matter of thorough indifference from what direction women who are out of the question arrive.

She was young, tall, and ravishing. But she was out of the question not because she was too young, too tall, and too ravishing. On that particular day, Anka had boundless enthusiasm and would have lunged at even that sort of beauty. But it was clear that this one had not dropped by for a solitary coffee. She had a date with someone.

"She looked around, searching for the lucky guy, whom I had already managed to hate with all my heart. She looked around, but he—most clearly—was not there yet. The ninny hadn't gotten there yet. Wait a minute, wait a minute. Let's not be reckless. He hasn't gotten there? Would he be late? Something didn't add up here." Anka Chow Chow pondered the situation, which was, on the one hand, seemingly entirely normal, on the other hand, entirely impossible. She pondered deeply and with a sort of quasi relief. She realized that her hatred was most likely premature.

It was more or less four after five, in other words the super babe had had a date for five o'clock, and since she came almost on time and was the first to get there, she had a date, almost a hundred percent for certain, with a female colleague, or some other cousin. If it had been a guy, no matter who he was—a Russian millionaire, a Hollywood star, a Milanese fashion designer—no matter who he was, he would have been waiting for her for at least a quarter hour. She was the sort of woman for whom you don't arrive late, or even merely on time. She was the sort of woman for whom you come well ahead of time, in order to have the illusion that the dates last longer.

She spotted a free table in the corner of the garden, at a maximal distance from Anka, but with ideal visibility.

"This offered me favorable conditions for observation. From the very beginning, I rejected all attempts at establishing contact with her. I drank coffee and contemplated her without painful emotion. The ritual thoughts that I would never have her, that I would never find out what her name is, and that, having seen her once in my life in *Yellow Dream*, I would most certainly never see her again, didn't trouble me in the least. She was a tall, slender, delicate, long-haired blonde. Tall, slender, and delicate blondes were, if I'm not mistaken, the absolute hit of your youth."

.

VII

So they were. She didn't have to *look at me questioningly.*
I knew perfectly well what she was talking about. Of course, they
were a hit. They were the ideal. They were the ideal not only of my
youth, they were the ideal in general. Until quite recently, tall, slender, and delicate blondes constituted the unrivaled model of beauty.
They became Miss Europe and Miss World. They were chosen as
the queens of *lyceum* balls and the Miss Congenialitys of university
villages. In stifling visions, they descended to us from the pages of
western journals, we saw them on the screens of movie theaters, we
read about them in novels, sometimes they passed us by on the street.
They took our breath away, but we didn't suffer; we were reconciled
to our fate. We rejoiced that they had been created; but we knew
that they were not created for us, and this caused us no pain. But
they—seemingly still worshipped and adored—began to show up less
and less frequently. There were fewer and fewer of them. They began
to disappear, imperceptibly but inexorably. The extinction approached
as quietly as a whisper. In the following years and decades, tall, slender, delicate, and long-haired blondes began to die out as a species.
I don't say that in the following years and decades there occurred a
holocaust of tall blondes, but something like an extermination took
place in all certainty. And this wasn't a symbolic or metaphoric extermination. No. The cataclysm began suddenly. Suddenly, there arose
the brutal storm of various retro- and afro-brunettes, multicolored
Iroquois women, wet Italian women, and punkers shaven as if for
delousing. Dusky pipsqueaks in combat boots, alleged Mullatoes, and
hothouse Latinas bred in solariums suddenly began to sting venomously. It never occurred to poor Witkacy, who prophesied extermination through the attack of Asiatic hordes, that hordes of female
Vietnamese vendors, Ukrainian cleaning women, and Russian whores
would bring this extermination on their rickety busts. In addition, a
propaganda campaign, prepared by who knows whom, was launched
to defile and slander blondes.

Thousands of jokes about blondes perfectly familiar to you, pasquinades about blondes, pamphlets against blondes got under the skin of the masses, who were always inclined to mount pogroms. The ideal of the blonde beauty has reached the pavement. The great extermination has come for the blondes.

How were the subtle and delicate, fearful and defenseless poor things supposed to defend themselves? What were they supposed to do? They did what all hounded tribes do in the face of extermination. They changed their confession and hair color, cut their hair short and colored it dark. They denied it over and over, and not for all the treasures in the world would they acknowledge their blonde roots. Those who had fallen the lowest, and those who were dyed the most, were first in line to attack their blonde former sisters. The most noble of them emigrated or went into the underground. And the tall, slender, delicate, and long-haired blondes definitively—so it would seem—disappeared from the face of the earth. Once in a while, we would see their shadows in archival films or on old photographs, but such traces only increased their absence.

I wanted to say that it is time to return tall, delicate, and long-haired blondes to grace; I wanted to deliver a daring and convincing defense of blondes; after the defense, I wanted to go on to a soaring encomium of blondes, but I gave it up. Anka's hair, thick as graphite, gleamed like Siberian anthracite.

VIII

THE GIRL WAS WEARING A DIRTY-RUSSET BLOUSE WITH SHOULDER straps and jeans. What sort of shoes she had on, Anka—strange to say—didn't know. In general, she didn't remember other details except for a wide pants belt with classical patterns. Was she aware that, sooner or later, the greater part of the image would irrevocably slip from her mind, and so—just like me in such situations—she concentrated on fundamental things? One way or another, God gave her a sign. The blonde's back was like a soaring flame. She had sat down, however, facing Anka. God had given her a sign, but He didn't allow her to contemplate it.

"What was I supposed to do? Get offended? Avert my glance? My cult of women's backs had not reached the point of such deviations, nor had I completely lost my marbles. Quite the contrary. What is more, the splendor of her collar bones rivaled the splendor of her shoulder blades. A rare case of complete harmony. I stared greedily. Not only at the collar bones. There is no point in hiding it. I was desperately and shamelessly fixed on the movements of her breasts under the dirty-russet blouse.

"Incidentally, the dirty-russet blouse was of an exclusive label, which one, I don't precisely know, but top of the line. That was quite certainly a piece of clothing purchased that summer in Rome or Barcelona." Anka emphasized this circumstance for my sake.

"For your generation, dirty-russet will be, until the end of your days, the color of People's Poland's train linemen. Granted, her blouse was dirty-russet, but this doesn't mean that it was a rag from a second-hand store or an air-dropped tatter from the times of Martial Law. But returning to her breasts, you have to say in all simplicity: they were fantastic. I don't know whether you are aware of this, but there exist certain types of fantastic busts that are not accepted by their owners, but even on account of that, on account of their—so to say—self-questioning, are all the more fantastic."

I wasn't aware of this. Anka, on the other hand, immediately knew perfectly well that the blonde beauty was not satisfied with her bust. It goes without saying that then, in *Yellow Dream*, that skepticism wasn't visible. It was quite easy to imagine, however, and even to behold clairvoyantly, how she stands day after day in front of the mirror and is in a bad mood, or, in the best case, has hefty doubts, because she thinks obsessively that they are too small, too delicate, too soft, too spindly, not spherical enough, etc. And what is more, those manias were justified in some sense. She did not—according to objective measurements—have an ideal figure. The geometrical profile of her body was not the full sinusoid in the desired places. Her bust was, in fact, too small, too delicate, too fidgety, and too spindly.

"Not that I would, you know, carp, but the rear that flashed at me a moment ago—regardless of its fieriness—is too flat. And yet, the overall sum: dazzling, captivating, and—as in some dreams—suffocating. The ideal of beauty is based on geometry, but the ideal of femininity is based on changeability. Forgive the erudite metaphors, but the ideal of femininity in its essence is not Euclidian—it is Heraclitean."

The blonde *belle* approached the counter, ordered tea (let's not get all excited about the informality of this choice), returned to the table, glanced at her watch. Anka wasn't especially curious about her tardy female colleague, nor was there even a hint of the rookie's speculations whether she, too, would be dazzling. That was even out of the question from the point of view of probability. There are few lasting and verifiable principles in the world, but the principle that, in a pair of girlfriends, one is the cow always comes true! Always! This is incontrovertible. "And so, I was curious, at the most, about the shape of the shadow that would approach her splendor any moment now."

And suddenly, there you have it! A complete change of situation! A sudden and unforeseen turn in a plot that had been foreseen to the last iota. Not one, but two shadows glide to her light! And those are not shadows in miniskirts or summer dresses! Those aren't shadows at all! Two flesh-and-blood guys approach her, greet her, make certain that they have come to the right person, take a seat, and immediately begin the conversation. Two guys of flesh and blood, and especially one of them. Although it is not easy to determine definitively which one of them was of flesh and blood, and which one less so. They seemed to be a couple: director and vice-director. Supervisor and the supervisor's deputy. Manager and the manager's assistant. Boss and his—for want of anything better—bodyguard. The boss, at first glance, gave the impression of being the guy of flesh and blood, everything in him was strong and distinctive: the solarium skin, the black shiny hair, the dark sports jacket, the gray slacks, the shirt with white and blue stripes, the appropriate tie, the impressive height, the beefy shoulders—in a word, a classic imitation of the Mediterranean lout. Whereas the other was grayish, slovenly, badly composed; it seemed that he was wearing a suit, but perhaps he didn't have a suit at all; his hair was somehow combed, or maybe not, maybe he was even bald; it was as if he held a stuffed briefcase tightly under his arm, but maybe that was an illusion. He was there, but perhaps he didn't exist at all. The first was distinctive in the extreme, the second extremely indistinct. Hence the doubt: which one was of flesh and blood?

The first spoke incessantly; as if persuasively and politely, but you had the feeling that this was the infamous "tone that does not tolerate objection." She listened, as if attentively and with interest, but you had the feeling that she was in an obedient, or even submissive pose.

The sudden presence of the bizarre—or stereotypical—couple didn't change Anka's situation in the least. The blonde remained beyond her reach and beyond her designs. She didn't even stop to ponder whether she had now become, more or less, attainable. She continued not to invest any hopes in this, but she became all the more attentive an observer. More and more attentive. More and more alert. More and more anxious. For something bizarre and morbid was beginning to happen in a corner of *Yellow Dream*. Some sort of deviltry was arising there, something viscous was flowing, something reptilian was slithering, an almost visible, yellowish and hideous aura began to engulf the entire trio.

"Do you understand? Have you ever had such situations? Seemingly nothing is happening, and yet an intangible filth is gathering? I'm not saying that it began to look like the boss of a brothel and his chief pimp were establishing conditions with a newly hired girl, but, to tell the truth, little was lacking for it. There was contempt in those guys, they were contemptuous in every gesture and inch of their bodies; even the fact that they didn't order anything was contemptuous, that they took care of business coldly and dryly, without even a mineral water. And no matter what sort of business this was: whether they were hiring her, or she them, whether she was borrowing money from them or they from her, whether, as a result of this conversation, she was to go to the bottom or they to jail, whether they were offering her a lucrative trip to the Canary Islands, whether she was their last chance, whether they were proposing a role in a TV series to her, whether she was recruiting them for a sect—no matter what the arrangement was: in them, there was contempt; in her, humility. Nothing more occurred. The fake Mediterranean lout finished his speech; she raised her head, asked about something; he answered, perfunctorily and while looking at his watch; she wanted to say something more, but they weren't listening, they were already getting up, already leaving."

IX

A HELICOPTER FLEW OVER THE CITY, THE CLOCK ON THE PALACE OF Culture showed a quarter past six. The light of dusk was as it was a thousand years ago, when, after a long trip, I got off the train, and I ran into Janek Nikandy at the station in Wisła. The black towers of the Palace soared into the rust-colored sky. The slender, long-haired blonde in the dirty-russet blouse opened up a copy of *Home and Interior* and read absorbedly. There wasn't any sign that the recent conversation had left a mark on her. She drank her tea slowly; all indications were that she would sit there who knows how much longer. I saw her precisely. Anka was right: I had been there. I, too, was there indeed, drank the wine and the mead. Suddenly the curtain disintegrated, and I saw everything: the badly dressed girl tapping out SMSes, the busty woman in the brick-red dress, the blonde in the dirty-russet blouse, the boss and his body guard, the throngs of passersby, the cars driving up Marszałkowska, the masses of scorching air. I saw, and I remembered, point for point, the entire July afternoon, all the intangible events and all the characters. All except for Anka Chow Chow. She wasn't there. She was right, but she wasn't there. Ever. I never met her at any match. Of course not. Columns of light over the stadium and suffocating downdrafts of ether on the Commons. The return to the hotel. The pot of coffee and letter paper. The station at dawn. The empty compartment for smokers. I don't remember. I don't remember a thing. I haven't left the house for a long time. I haven't left my room for who knows how long. For years I haven't ventured outside of my own skull. No one is here. It will soon be six. All of this is divine punishment for aversion to ambiguity. I tread very ambiguously. Step by step. Cautiously, and on the other side of Marszałkowska. Fluidly, as happens in the most fluid of dreams. As that time when we climbed up the railway embankment, and from the heights you could see everything as if it was on the palm of your hand: the cart crossing the bridge, Pastor Kalinowski leaving the parish house, the biplane over Jarzębata. I look from afar. From on high. The sky is ever darker. The coal-black light of your hair dies away. I am alone. I regain pain.

Snow for Two-Thirds
of a Day and Night

"Snow for two-thirds of a day and night,
and one-third in a dream?"
—Stanisław Barańczak

OLD MAN TRZMIELOWSKI WAS DYING IN THE NEXT ROOM; EMMA
the lunatic wandered about the entire house; old lady Mary prayed
in the kitchen; and Uncle Paweł, instead of keeping watch, snored
dreadfully. I wasn't afraid of anything. What is more, the gale was
such that—so it seemed—the frozen mountains would budge from
the spot. The gigantic wooden house rocked like Magellan's ship, the
roof creaked ever more loudly and distinctly; any moment its gibberish would become language; I think you could already hear individual
words. Objects glided from place to place, the shadows of the hands
that raised them were at times quite distinct—but I did nothing. I
calmly waited for the moment when, in the next room, the footsteps
of death would reverberate, when the old man would cease breathing,
when the old lady would cease praying, when Uncle would awaken
with a dreadful scream, when there would reverberate the crackle
of matches lighting the funeral candle, and when finally, worn out
by her lunatic wanderings, Emma, frenzied, pale like a corpse and

covered with icy sweat, would return to my bed. I was seven years old, and I had begun to sleep with her before I fell in love with her. Worse: I slept with the one, but I loved the other. Every night I stuck to Emma's cold sweat, and every day I played dominoes with Aria, Sister Ewelina's ward. Right after young Trzmielowski's wedding, it was still November, the snows of Greenland came tumbling down, we had a cold wave the likes of which the world has never seen, and for weeks on end it wasn't possible to budge from the spot. Illnesses, on the other hand, came with great ease and in single file: tonsillitis, flu, scarlet fever; I was suffocating and losing consciousness; Emma Lunatyczka's damp bedclothes weren't bad for that.

We travelled to the wedding party in britzkas; Pastor Kalinowski in a VW bug; wedding revelers who lived high up came down from the mountains on foot, and now you couldn't even get through on sleighs, now you couldn't even dig out the sleighs themselves. Quite another matter that the air, for November, was supposedly too mild. Old man Trzmielowski looked around anxiously and said that it didn't bode well. It ought to be fiery, but it is too warm. At that time he hadn't yet begun dying, he circulated, dressed in black, among the revelers, ate ravenously, drank aggressively, smiled sheepishly. All the local old men—whenever they encounter anything that does not have to do with carpentry, mowing, or some other sort of labor—smile sheepishly. He was such an expert on the air that predicts a harsh winter. But walls doubled to that extent?—beyond the walls of the house, walls of snow, walls of winter, load-bearing walls of ice, and the whole way through the yard to the can was like breaking through one wall after another. I felt their weight, their pressure, their red-hot plaster.

"Do you remember a winter like this? Was it ever like this? Maybe in the emperor's time? Maybe before with war with Japan?" Uncle Paweł awoke with the shakes, dug himself out from under pelts and sheepskins, and although he had something completely different in mind, led by some mysterious instinct of politeness, he engaged the dying great-great-great-, however many times great-grandfather in conversation. He didn't look in the direction of the dark bed, he didn't check to see whether the old man was sleeping or waking, but he showered him with words.

"You must remember such a winter, at least one. Because if you don't remember such a winter, this means that there has never been such a winter, that it is happening for the first time. And if this is for the first time, I will have to talk differently with Mother."

Uncle put on high boots, threw the sheepskin coat over his shoulders, which less than a quarter hour ago had covered him like a blanket, and disappeared out the door. After a moment, from the depths of the house, there reverberated raised voices; doubled steps went across the attic; someone cleared a way through the courtyard; horses snorted in the stable; some ancestor resting on a pile of cornflower blue pillows began in a whisper to tell some story from before the times of narration. The door opened, and Pastor Kalinowski—changed beyond recognition, in a flannel shirt, with a steaming mug of coffee in his hand—entered and pulled up a stool and sat at the head of the bed; at the spot where, any moment now, a six-foot black scythe would appear.

Sometimes, from the snowed-under center of town, you could hear bells. Had the sexton climbed the tower as usual? Did he see the tufts of smoke over the snowed-under environs? How did he manage with ropes that were frozen solid? Did shadows in hoods help him? My fever jumped, I wasn't seeing phantoms, phantoms were my fervent dream. Some sort of connections existed. Tunnels carved out by animals, perhaps on the surface, and in the other direction you had to drag yourself to the road to Polana. Sometimes Pastor Kalinowski would disappear for a day, two days; the little room over the stairs, in which he lived, was locked up tight. Maybe he broke his way through by some miracle and was conducting a funeral in the labyrinths at the cemetery or a service in the icy church? Not likely, but who knows?

From time to time, everybody kept getting lost. Most often it was Uncle Paweł, but at least with him the matter was clear; it was known to one and all what he was looking for. He had been drinking since the wedding, which is to say, for four months now, and he still had something to drink. He must have been distilling it from the snow. Besides, there could still be reserves frozen in the cellars for all time. The Trzmielowskis prepared for the wedding party as if they knew that it would last half a year. Seven bridesmaids alone, of whom three were identically pregnant. All of them in the eighth month, and all called Hanula. All had dresses, veils, and sulfuric acid prepared, in order to disfigure, as soon as she left the church, the most beautiful of them, the one whom the groom would choose. The four other Hanulas finally gave up, dressed in black, wound black scarfs around their heads, and sat in the same pew. Young Trzmielowski had spent a May night with each of them, but God hadn't been on their side. He didn't stop the blood. He didn't send them an appetite for herrings and pickles, and He didn't cause their bellies to grow. For what sins?—nobody really knows. Their lives are over. One of them will throw herself under a train in three years; the second will still be living today, if she lives, in black; the third will emigrate, and they will say of her that she became a popular waitress in a Roman café; about the fourth, absolutely no news would be heard. Four fewer, but two were still in play. Two, because the prettiest is already standing at the altar. But those others in unstarched dresses, with veils aslant, with pots, from which a yellowish-brown smoke belches forth, are somewhere in the vicinity. They descend from the mountains, they are already at the station, they walk around the ski jump, and perhaps they are already circling the church.

There are people everywhere, even in the balconies, but no one is capable of concentrating on the bride and groom standing at the altar. Even the masters of ceremonies are looking around apprehensively. Old lady Mary, the bravest of them all, stands up from the pew time and again, goes out, comes back. Nothing gets better. The organist plunks away, but no one knows wedding hymns. In the hymnal, there are three wedding hymns for every hundred funeral dirges. Three pathetic hymns to the matrimonial altar for a hundred fantastic ones to the coffin. At burials and in cemeteries, everyone sings in top form.

At weddings, no one can be bothered with pious ditties. And now? No point in wishing for better! The sulfur is about to flow, the terrible scream of the scalded bride is about to soar above the steeple. Finally, the organist plays *When the morning stars are rising* . . . but this causes an even greater muddle, because some are singing: "When the morning stars are rising/ Earth and sea Thy glories praising/ Join all nature's voice in singing/ Praise to Thee, Oh God, we're bringing," and the rest, from out of the blue, although to that same melody: "In the path of Christ the Lord/ Let us sing with one accord/ For Christ this way did bring/ After eating songs to sing." It was as if a swarm of buzzing hornets was flying under the church's ceiling—such tension, and then suddenly quiet, a calm as after a storm. As then, when I stand in the window and gaze at the steaming stones of the Wisła courtyard, at Chowderhead the cat, walking cautiously between the puddles. Peace and quiet, as if there were no God and all his ghosts. Brethren, silence your hearts. Supposedly the four black Hanulas got up and left, and that was a guarantee that nothing would happen. But as soon as they moved away from the altar, the organist—he must have been completely out of it by now—started in on: *For he's a jolly good fellow* . . . Only now did old lady Mary fly up the stairs to the organ like a jet plane; the sudden relief gave her more strength. But before she got there, he had started in on *He that dwelleth* . . . and it came out so well that people were sorry to leave the church steeple behind. The horses were washed, their manes plaited, to the britzkas, my damsels, to the britzkas. Through the ill-boding November air, around Czantoria, around Jarzębata and Kamienny, and up the serpentine road to Kubalonka, and to the station, and just a bit past the station. Seven barriers along the way. Dirty sheepskins on the left, ram's fur, coal on the faces. We get past a few Beelzebubs and a barrier! A barrier on all three bridges. A barrier at Jurzyków, a barrier in Jawornik, a barrier in Gościejów, and, just before the house, yet another barrier. Paper money and combustible schnapps. Bread and salt. The musicians walk out into the courtyard and sit down on stools, and at first it is quiet, as if the celebration were coming from far off, but then ever louder and ever stronger, as if we were closer and closer to the meadow on which the first couples are dancing, as if I saw more and more, as if—only then—I was everywhere and saw everything, and as if—only then—I could tell of everything.

It was God's doing that I sat at the table next to Emma Lunaty-czka; that was a miracle, because the wedding guests came in a horde, and there were probably twenty-five tables, through all the rooms, like a white path through a labyrinth. Emma Lunatyczka was wearing an incomplete Silesian costume, and this—fuck it—killed me. In two weeks I was going to come down with whooping cough, scarlet fever, an infection of the inner ear, flu, tonsillitis, everything. In two week, unconscious, with a 104-degree temperature, I was to find myself in her bed. But now, on the spot, I came down with a bad case of incomplete Silesian costume, and later on it would be a bad case of any incomplete costume in general. Incurably, and for the rest of my life. Emma was wearing a heavy velvet skirt with a navy blue edging at the bottom, but a blouse of quite a different sort. The incredible blouses of delicate linen, and with the open shoulders and the small mandarin collar—the young girls would be wearing them half a century later. Christ the Lord! What a combination this was! A carnival bottom and white linen top. She looked as if, not yet ready, while searching for a sash or a bonnet, she had gotten mixed up with the wedding revelers, or like a mad procession of dancers had barged into her dressing room and swept her up just as she was standing there. The young girls, who were blind to her charms, comforted her in the corners: Don't worry, we'll find the whole costume for you for the next wedding! For sure! Emma thanked them humbly, but her gray and sparkling eyes betrayed her—she knew that she was the queen.

I wandered around the whole house: in the first room, those who were playing on combs prepared for their performance; in the second, those who were playing on bottles; in the third, miners from an American gold mine were changing into full regalia. The hallway was high, dark, and cold, like in a knight's castle, all the doors black and tall, behind the fifth were reserve food supplies, behind the sixth a fire burned in the stove, around which sat the four black Hanulas. I was sure that they were crying; they had cried the whole time in the church, and it looked like they would go on crying until the ends of the lives—but no way! Heated, flushed, with black scarfs already undone, though not yet removed from their heads, they were as happy as clams, as if the decision had been for them after all.

"Join us, little girl," said the one seated farthest away.

"I'm not a little girl," I answered hundreds of times with a well-tested, maximally cold voice.

"But you look like a little girl. And if you look like a little girl, then you are a little girl, at least a bit. And if someone is a bit of a little girl, that means that he is in general a little girl," the leader of the quartet of black Hanulas glanced at the three remaining ones and added significantly, "it is impossible to be slightly a little girl. It's just that we had bad luck."

And they began to laugh horribly, they roared with laughter, to this day I haven't heard such laughter, nor have I seen such wallowing in laughter. All of a sudden, out of the blue, they stopped, and, as if they had practiced it a thousand times, with one melodious motion they slipped the undone scarfs from their heads.

"For now, we are undressing for you, a bit little boy, a bit little girl," the whole time one of them did the talking, the others nodded their heads in agreement and looked at her with affectionate admiration and gratitude for expressing herself so beautifully in their names. "For now, we are undressing for you, but we don't know what will come next. We prefer not to know. We prefer to pretend that we don't know."

The second and third Hanulas were blondes; the fourth was the most beautiful brunette in the world, and when she stood up and opened the little door to the stove and began, in the glow falling upon her, to add wood to the fire, she became so inhumanly beautiful that I got the shivers.

"Why are you so feverish, little girl?" the leader of the Hanulas came closer; she was the ugliest of them, and it wasn't clear whether

her plait, red in the light of the fire, was really red. "Why are you so feverish? You take care of yourself! Feverish little girls have to take special care of themselves. Don't dance immoderately."

The music came from all sides. Both the comb trio and the bottle quartet walked through all the halls and stairways. They walked in the direction of the courtyard and played like the possessed. The Potulnik brothers and Master Sztwiertnia were still having another shot, they were still puffing on their cigarettes, but they, too, began to look around for their instruments, for stools. Janek the tailor, on trumpet, the most talented of them all, was already climbing the podium, following him Władek the carpenter, on trombone, then Jurek the roofer, on clarinet, then Józef the bricklayer, on second trumpet, then Andrzej the stove-fitter, on accordion, then Master Sztwiertnia, on percussion, finally, old man Potulnik, on bass. The bottles and combs against the wall on the other side were already providing the melody, setting the tone; the Potulnik brothers and Master Sztwiertnia were gazing at them attentively and listening closely; with the greatest attention, they prepared to enter upon the appropriate chord. Everything I have learned about the seriousness of art I owe to the musicians of Wisła. The Potulnik brothers with their instruments, with sheet music and music stands, dressed in white shirts and black vests were like members of the Philharmonic (all, except for Janek the tailor, on trumpet, had taken off their sports jackets to play). And those who were playing on bottles and combs were street musicians without elegant tailcoats and instruments, because, finally, what sort of instrument is that: a piece of parchment applied to a comb or to a bottle with the bottom broken off. But the music was one, the perfect pitch was the same, and the same the respect for the craft. And a faithful memory—for the Potulnik brothers and Master Sztwiertnia had perfect memories of weddings from times gone by, festivities at which *they* had accompanied on bottles and combs the orchestra of old Nogowczyk, all of which has long turned to dust; and those members of the Philharmonic leaned down over their droning just the same way from the heights of the podium and played with them just the same. That's right: they played with them. The music came from all sides. Master Sztwiertnia, the brothers Potulnik, all the Wisła musicians with the talents of Mozart: we can hear you. We hear your music. The grass rises on Gróniczek Cemetery Hill, and the heavens part over Czantoria.

About a month ago, I bought a CD: *Mozart, Prague, Les dernières vendanges*. A group called "Le Trio di Bassetto et ses invités" plays little pieces of Mozart and little pieces of little known or entirely unknown Czech composers of his era. My God! It isn't any "Trio di Bassetto," it's the Potulnik brothers and Master Sztwiertnia who are playing! The spirits of the brothers Potulnik have been incarnated in that "Trio di Bassetto!" Even more! One of the "invités"—the percussionist—that isn't the spirit of Master Sztwiertnia! That is Master Sztwiertnia, flesh and blood! I recognize him without the shadow of a doubt! *Only he* had that incomprehensibly rhythmic and at the same time thoroughly free, delicate, and exceptionally strong beat on the drum.

There are thirty-one seconds of music on that CD composed by an anonymous contemporary of Mozart's, and those thirty-one seconds are my life, my childhood, my literature, and my music. My eternity lasts thirty-one seconds. Play that over my grave, but four times. Let me be granted a fourfold eternity. Let me be granted a whole one hundred and twenty-four seconds. I'll have clay in my ears, but I will hear. That is the music that the Potulnik brothers and Master Sztwiertnia played at young Trzmielowski's wedding. This is music that was recorded then and there. God already had the suitable equipment in the fifties of the twentieth century. That is the music to the accompaniment of which funerals walked and wedding parties drove through the streets of Wisła; this is the music to which floods, snows, and heat waves descended upon us. Our sky brightened and darkened to this music. Andrzej Wantuła would visit us to this music, to this music we would sit down to the Christmas Eve table, this music was playing when Grandpa would light the fire in the hearth at dawn, and when anyone entered our gigantic kitchen. This music was there when, one fine day, an angel with folded wings stood in the middle of our courtyard that was paved with river stones.

The brothers Potulnik and Master Sztwiertnia played their hearts out, time after time and with variations, *langsam und trübe*. The four black Hanulas suddenly began to crowd before the mirror. I again looked into all the rooms, but they were all empty. There weren't even the miners from the American gold mine dressed up in uniforms. "Aria! Aria!" I called as if in my sleep, "Aria, where are you?" She was the first and the greatest love of my life. God sent me many fantastic women. I have been with completely dazzling women; I loved them, and they loved me, but however often I think of Aria in a gray skirt sewn from an old coat turned inside out, whenever I think of that little girl, older than me by three or maybe four years, I am always certain that she was meant for me. She would have kept watch over me, at her side I would have had a good life, we would have set up house together in an old house, eternally covered with snow. Every Sunday we would have gone to the main church service, in the evenings we would have played dominoes and drunk tea with chokeberry syrup. Sometimes, when she would have gone on some larger shopping errand to Cieszyn, and if the couple hours without her were unbearable, I would have taken a thick notebook with green covers and attempted to continue the story about chess or about my first love, which I had begun long ago. But always, before I could compose even one sentence, I would hear her opening the gate and walking across the yard, and I would leave my writing and go out to meet her and relieve her of the heaviest bag with the books, wine, and bread, and we would sit in the kitchen, and she would tell me the news. This would have been a thousand times better than the fulfillment that is granted to me now: when, after constructing the hundredth, or even the thousandth sentence, no one opens the gate, no one goes through the yard, and no one tells me the news. I have what I wanted: I can compose sentences to the bitter end.

Aria! Aria! Aria! Aria in my dreams. Emma Lunatyczka in reality. My hands passed along the icy skin, raised the nightshirt stiff from the cold; touch took me once and for all into its animal possession. Touch and betrayal. In the very middle of the darkness, I would get out of bed. Somewhere under its frame stood the chamber pot, against which I had a psychological block, unlike, incidentally, Emma, who—no matter whether conscious or unconscious, in a lunatic march or with entirely deliberate shamelessness—if she felt the need, would sit down and fire away with a sharp, and at the same time delicate, stream. I couldn't do it. I had to pull on my shoes, put on a shirt, sweater, whatever was handy, and fight my way through the ever colder circles to the can in the courtyard. I never had yellow fever or malaria, but from those times I knew what malarial or yellow-fever shivers meant. At times the courtyard looked like a golden meadow. The curtains of the next frosts hovered above, and on the snow were impressed countless stamps of constellations. I ran over them with the lightness of a ballet dancer. The can was always the beginning of the abyss. The devil is caked with shit. Death smells of the rust that has settled on the scythe. The four black Hanulas danced until they dropped; they ought to dance to the last black thread; they ought—almost naked, emaciated, dead tired—to freeze in their dance, as soon as the first Sunday of Advent comes. But the smell of rust came earlier.

Two days before the death of old man Trzmielowski, Uncle Paweł got up, lay down, walked, flew like a madman. One impulse after another. One spasm after another. Not a moment of rest, violent and anxious sleep, his face blackened, dried froth in the corners of his mouth. It wasn't so much that the bottle was always at hand, as that it was always *in* his hand. The last one, and almost empty. An absolutely full moon hangs over the courtyard and gilds the path to the can. I returned to an empty bed. Emma—whenever it took hold of her especially forcefully would scoop up the featherbed. She would carry it before her in her errorless wanderings, and she slept on it as if on a cloud. Everything makes sense. Death would arrive any minute.

Uncle Paweł would catch sight of it two days earlier. He would come to, and he would see, from the depths of the hallway, Death riding on a cloud. It keeps on riding, but instead of making the turn, it bypasses the door behind which the old man was waiting for it. It rides further. Rides further, rides straight on. It is closer and closer. It's right around the corner. The smell of rust already fills nostrils fossilized from hooch. "Wrong address! Wrong address! Reverse! Back!" Uncle's shout rises to the heavens, although he himself isn't certain that he is saying any words. "Wrong address! Reverse gear! Back up! Back and to the left! Wrong address!" He shouted so loudly that the cloud that was preceding Death retreated and completely melted away. The wrestling of the delirious with the lunatic was like the wrestling of Jacob with the Angel. The brownish sweat of the alcoholic against the icy sweat of the lunatic. Real death came two days later. You couldn't hear its footsteps, no one saw the scythe resting on the headboard. Although the mistake had been definitively explained, Uncle Paweł still didn't really believe in miraculous survivals. All the less did he believe that there was nothing left to drink. For the time being, since there would be this and that at the wake, and they would need quite a lot of it. But no way would he wait for the wake. When would the smugglers come down the mountains? When would the little church bells of their Czech half-quart bottles ring in the backpacks? When? The old man lay belly up, the old lady was wiping his aquiline and yellow profile with pure spirits. With each wipe the old man's profile took on aquilinity, yellowness, aquilinity, yellowness. The bottle stood on the stool, more than half was left. Snow was piling up on the roof, someone shouted in the depths of the house, Emma laughed bizarrely in the kitchen, something fluttered in the attic, something struck—like a lightning bolt, but a weak one. The old lady left the old man, who was now almost completely ready for the coffin, flew through the hallway, through the courtyard, and back again. How long was she gone? Five minutes? Not even five minutes! And there wasn't a drop of the spirits left! The bottle was empty! It looked like the deceased had come to for a moment, looked around, found it, took a goodly chug, and fallen asleep for all time. "It was stronger than me," old lady Mary would say later on, "it was stronger than me. For a fraction of a second, a terrible suspicion crept into my heart: he arouse from the dead, drank it off, and died for good."

The history of the evaporation of the spirits for wiping the skin of the deceased has no explanation, nor even a continuation. The gods of understanding and elegance celebrate. They clink glasses, who cares for what. Uncle Paweł tells the story to the end of his life—about how Death got the wrong address. I look around, where is that little black whore heading! Where? Heading for me! Precisely for me! You've got the wrong address, you little black whore! Reverse and turn left! But she stumbles onto me like an avalanche from beyond the grave! This is the end, so I think! And so it has come now! But never, no, not ever, we will never surrender! With what is left of my strength I part the black dunes, and I look, and the beast has Emma's head, Emma's nightshirt, Emma's ass, and Emma's tits! And if it has the head, nightshirt, ass, and tits of Emma, then it is Emma. I'm alive, I haven't died.

After the old man's funeral, the Christmas holidays came at a gallop, after the holidays—hog slaughtering time. Hogs possessed by demons and dripping blood ran through the courtyard, fell into the snow, hid themselves in the drifts, fought and squealed, as if their further life were important. Drifts and specters. Half-naked butchers surrounded them in an ever tighter circle. Tables continued to pass through the rooms, the fat flowed through them. Ice blocks as large as the pyramids, cut out under the bridge, glided by on carts. After the hog-slaughtering, Aria departed forever. I don't know whether she is still alive. If she is, then she will be pushing sixty. Wedding, funeral, holidays, hog-slaughtering. Flu, scarlet fever, whooping cough, pneumonia. One hundred and twenty-four seconds of eternity. During the Christmas Eve supper, Sister Ewelina impulsively sneezed, and the candle on the table went out. The impulsiveness spoke clearly: of all of those gathered here, you will die first, Sister Ewelina. There was no help now. The sleigh was already setting off to dig the hole. By sleigh to the hospital in Cieszyn. The feverish head on the massive thighs of Emma Lunatyczka. Aria! Aria! Aria! Where is our life?

Jerzy Pilch is one of Poland's most important contemporary writers and journalists. In addition to his long-running satirical newspaper column, Pilch has published several novels, and has been nominated for Poland's prestigious NIKE Literary Award four times; he won the Award in 2001 for *The Mighty Angel*. His books have been translated into numerous languages, and his novels *A Thousand Peaceful Cities*—chosen as a *Kirkus Reviews* Best of 2010 book—and *The Mighty Angel* are also available in English translation from Open Letter.

David Frick is a Professor in the Department of Slavic Languages and Literatures at the University of California, Berkeley. He won a Northern California Book Award for his translation of Pilch's *A Thousand Peaceful Cities*.

Open Letter—the University of Rochester's nonprofit, literary translation press—is one of only a handful of publishing houses dedicated to increasing access to world literature for English readers. Publishing ten titles in translation each year, Open Letter searches for works that are extraordinary and influential, works that we hope will become the classics of tomorrow.

Making world literature available in English is crucial to opening our cultural borders, and its availability plays a vital role in maintaining a healthy and vibrant book culture. Open Letter strives to cultivate an audience for these works by helping readers discover imaginative, stunning works of fiction and by creating a constellation of international writing that is engaging, stimulating, and enduring.

Current and forthcoming titles from Open Letter include works from Argentina, Bulgaria, Catalonia, China, Germany, Iceland, Poland, and many other countries.

www.openletterbooks.org